the
dark
king

the
dark
king

GINA L.

MAXWELL

Entangled Publishing, LLC
644 Shrewsbury Commons Ave., STE 181
Shrewsbury, PA 17361
rights@entangledpublishing.com

Amara is an imprint of Entangled Publishing, LLC.

Visit our website at www.entangledpublishing.com.

Edited by Liz Pelletier
Cover design by Elizabeth Turner Stokes
Cover images by Paitoon Pornsuksomboon/Shutterstock
ThereIsNoNe/Shutterstock
Interior design by Toni Kerr

ISBN 978-1-64937-327-4
Ebook ISBN 978-1-64937-328-1

Manufactured in the United States of America

First Edition September 2022

10 9 8 7 6 5 4 3 2 1

AMARA
an imprint of Entangled Publishing LLC

ALSO BY GINA L MAXWELL

FIGHTING FOR LOVE

Seducing Cinderella
Rules of Entanglement
Fighting for Irish
Sweet Victory

PLAYBOYS IN LOVE

Shameless
Ruthless
Merciless

STAND-ALONE ROMANCES

Hot For the Fireman

For everyone who has discovered their true selves and the greatness they are capable of.
And to those who feel stuck or too scared to take that first step: Be brave, my darlings.
Turn that page and start a new chapter. Remember that you are the author of your own story, and you deserve a damn good one.

At Entangled, we want our readers to be well-informed. If you would like to know if this book contains any elements that might be of concern for you, please check the back of the book for details.

CHAPTER ONE

CAIDEN

Sex sells.

It's a commonly used phrase because it's true. For as long as dicks have been getting hard, men have emptied their pockets when presented with their ultimate fantasies. Big or small, obtainable or not, it never matters. When the blood rushes south, the wallets open up.

And here in Sin City—where deviance and debauchery reign—we sell every fantasy known to man and then some. It's what we do, and we're fucking *good* at it.

Standing at the two-way mirror from the office that looks out over the main floor of Deviant Desires, I watch as men of all ages and backgrounds throw their hard-earned money at the busty brunette dancing on the stage wearing nothing but body glitter and a smile. They cheer and shout while making lewd gestures and rubbing the hard-ons through their pants. Because every time she makes eye contact, she's selling them the fantasy that she can be theirs for the right amount of money.

And the right amount is always *more*.

Business is good—it always is—but it'd be a whole lot better if my manager wasn't skimming the profits and smacking the girls around when they don't suck his cock for the promise of better shifts.

Narrowing my gaze on one of the girls giving lap dances on the floor, I use my preternatural vision to see what lies beneath the caked-on makeup. She's hiding a bruise on one cheek and marks in the shape of fingerprints on her arm.

It's solid enough proof that the information my men gave me earlier isn't just hearsay, and it sets my fucking teeth on edge.

The girl isn't one of my subjects—she's human, after all— but she *is* my employee, which puts her under my protection. I don't believe in abusing the innocent, and I'm not in the habit of mistreating my employees. This asshole is doing both.

It's rare that I make personal appearances at any of the several dozen businesses I own all over this city—I have people for that—but today, I'm making an exception.

"I've just received word he's entered the club, sire. Madoc has him."

Turning, I give Seamus Woulfe a droll look.

My senior adviser is sitting in one of the chairs in front of the desk, his black suit pristine, silver hair and full beard perfectly styled. To look at him, you wouldn't know he's almost four hundred and fifty years old, although in the last decade, the lines around his eyes have become more pronounced and he's slower getting around.

Facts that my younger brothers, Tiernan and Finnian, tease him about mercilessly. As our father's lifelong best friend, Seamus is like an uncle to us, and in an official capacity, he's my most trusted adviser and near-constant shadow.

Only the members of the Night Watch—my team of personal guards—are with me more often.

"Enough with the sire crap already," I grumble as I take a seat behind the desk. "It sounds ridiculous coming from you."

He simply shrugs. "You've deigned to leave your tower for once. There, you're Caiden Verran, my pseudo-nephew and all-around pain in my ass. Out here, you're my king, and I'll address you as such. Don't like it, leave me back at the tower."

I roll my eyes. There are two places I spend my time—Midnight Manor, the estate of the Night Court's royal family where I reside, and Nightfall, my hotel and casino on the Vegas Strip—neither of which is a tower, but Seamus amuses himself by likening me to a self-imposed Rapunzel who locks himself away from the rest of the world.

But I don't have the luxury of a carefree life like my brothers.

Though the media has dubbed the three of us the Verran Kings of Vegas since our father passed seventeen years ago, I've been the only one with an *actual* empire to run as king of our people.

I scoff at his suggestion. "Like you'd listen if I told you to stay back."

His golden eyes twinkle with a smile big enough to flash his fangs. "No, Your Majesty, I would not. But you're welcome to try anyway."

Our familial banter is cut short when Madoc, one of my Night Watchers, opens the door and shoves the manager in my direction, causing him to tumble onto the floor. My lip curls in disgust. He looks like he just came from getting sucked off in his car. His charcoal suit is wrinkled, tie loosened with top buttons undone, and his shirttails are sticking halfway out, like he was hastily tucking them back in before Madoc got ahold of him.

It's far from the professional appearance I demand of my managers, and I know for a fact he didn't look like this when we hired him. He's let himself go and gotten sloppy. Considering everything else I know, I'd bet my crown he started partying too hard. I don't mind if my managers want to let loose with the occasional party favor—a little nose candy now and again isn't enough to get in the way of their jobs—but when the only things you care about are doing lines of blow and getting blow jobs, it becomes a problem.

A *big* one.

Nodding to Madoc, I let him know that I can take things from here.

Once the door is closed, Seamus gets up to lock it and stays on that side of the room, wisely keeping out of the line of fire.

"Ralph, so nice to see you," I say, the tone of my voice making my sarcasm clear.

He struggles to his feet, then does a piss-poor job of pulling himself together, tugging on his jacket and swiping his greasy hair back with a meaty palm. Already, beads of sweat are dotting his forehead, and I can smell the stench of his dampening armpits.

There are certain preternatural abilities my kind all share: superior strength, healing quickly, and heightened senses. It's times like this when I wish I didn't have the benefit of that last one.

"Mr. Verran, hey there," he says, his gaze shifting to where Seamus guards the door, then back at me. "To what do I owe the pleasure? Comin' down to inspect the goods?"

"I think you've been doing enough *inspecting* for the both of us. Sit," I command. And like a cowering dog, he does.

Steepling my fingers in front of me, I get straight to the point. "How long have you been stealing from me, Ralph? And before you attempt to lie, I suggest you don't."

Ralph gulps audibly and shifts in his seat. "About three—" I arch a brow. "Okay, six. About six months. But come on, man, it's not like you need it. You fuckin' *own* this town. You probably got more money than Oprah! I just gave myself a little raise, that's all. I mean, *I earned it*. Deviant's the number one strip joint for miles around. Everyone knows we got the best whores in Vegas."

The fact that he's justifying his actions like a spoiled child is enough to fuel my rage. But referring to my employees as "whores" offends me on a personal level. My city is, and always has been, sex-worker positive, and his lack of respect for the women who have more balls to do what they do than he'll ever have hanging between his legs only serves to enrage me further.

I rise and slowly walk around to stand in front of him, then ease onto the front of the desk in a casual stance, my hands gripping the edge on either side to hide the way my fingernails have sharpened into points. Staring down at him, I bring up the second—and more important—reason I'm here.

"And did you also *earn* the right to demand sexual favors from them, then put your hands on them when they said no?"

"That what you heard?" Ralph scoffs like the accusation is ludicrous, his eyes darting around the room and landing everywhere but on me. "They wish. Like I'd want any of their used-up puss—"

I strike, cobra-quick and just as deadly, gripping him by the throat. His Adam's apple bobs against my palm, and I scent the blood trickling from where my nails pierce his fat neck. I jerk him up and lift him to meet my six-foot-five eye level, leaving his feet to dangle in the air.

Satisfaction flows through me as I watch his face turn darker shades of red and his eyeballs begin to bulge out of their sockets.

Before he has a chance to pass out, I easily launch him across the room. Seamus steps aside just in time, avoiding being the meat in a Ralph-wall sandwich.

I wait to speak until I'm certain I have Ralph's attention, then usher my warning with a deadly calm. "Insult those women again, and I'll cut out your tongue and eat it while you watch."

I wouldn't want to, of course—not the eating part, anyway—

but my reputation in this town as a volatile wild card when offended is well-known, and sometimes examples need to be made.

Ralph is wise to fear me and what I might do.

Except when he pushes unsteadily to his feet, the look on his face isn't one of fear. It's pure, unadulterated malice. *Interesting.*

Tilting my head, I study him like a lab rat choosing to go left when it should have gone right. I would normally just end this and get on with my day, but he's piqued my curiosity.

"Fuck you, Verran," he hisses. "I've had enough of you threatenin' me and stickin' your nose where it don't belong. Now, I suggest you walk outta here, and when the books are a little light, you look the other way. Or I'll tell the whole goddamn world what you people *really* are."

Seamus and I share a brief glance and arch of our brows. Crossing my arms over my chest, I give Ralph my undivided attention, even more curious now. "Which is…?"

Confidence curls his upper lip into a sneer. "You're a fuckin' *faerie*."

Surprise lances through me, but I'm careful to keep my bored expression firmly in place. "That's a shame, Ralph. Had I known you were such a bigot, I never would've hired you to begin with."

His sudden confusion is almost enough to make me smile. Almost.

"What? No, that's not—" He growls, clearly frustrated. "I mean a *real* goddamn faerie, with the wings and magic powers and shit."

"Ah, I see now. Seamus," I say conversationally, "am I sporting wings I wasn't aware of?"

My adviser clears his throat to hide his amusement. "No, sir, no wings," he says, switching to the more common "sir" that my people use in the company of humans.

It's true—it has to be, because lying is the *one thing* our kind can't do—I don't have wings. All members of the Night Court—along with the equally culpable Day Court—were stripped of their wings, and the royal blood lines of both courts were robbed of our magic to manipulate shadows and light, respectively. Two of several consequences heaped upon us at the time of our exile some four hundred years ago.

Since I was born after the banishment, I only feel an objective sense of loss, in that I know I *should* have them. But for Seamus and the others who hail from Tír na nÓg, I imagine it feels the same as a human after a limb is amputated.

Devastating at first, but after a couple of years—or centuries—you grow accustomed to the loss.

Snapping out of my thoughts, I continue. "And, Seamus, have you ever known me to wield magical powers of any kind? Beyond my reputation with the women for having a magical dick, I mean."

This time, Seamus isn't as successful at cutting off his chuff of laughter. I'm not particularly humorous. I'm more of a sharp wit and dry sarcasm kind of guy, leaving the jokes to my brothers, who don't have the burden of ruling on their shoulders. So, no doubt my magical dick comment took Seamus by surprise, for the humor and the fact that since I took the throne, lunar eclipses occur more often than my dick sees any action.

Sadly, with a kingdom to rule, I don't have the time to indulge in all of life's simple joys like my brothers do.

Regaining his composure, Seamus answers. "No magic powers that I'm aware of, sir."

"Nor I of you, old friend." I look back to Ralph, whose face is now a bright tomato red. "Guess that settles it, then. No wings and no magic." Both true statements, if a little misleading.

"You motherfucker," he mumbles, fishing a small container

out of his pocket and unscrewing the cap. "I've been waiting for the chance to do this. You're gonna be sorry when you're on your knees and helpless as I beat the shit out of you and leave you for dead. And then? Then I'm gonna do whatever the hell I want with every bitch in this place, and there won't be a damn thing you can do about it!"

With that, a severely unhinged Ralph cackles with glee as he dumps the contents of the container onto the floor.

Well, well…

Someone's been doing a little too much googling.

I don't move, simply arch a brow and wait.

Suddenly, Ralph's elation dies a quick death as he realizes neither of us has dropped to our knees, compelled to count every grain of salt in the pile at his feet. "I—I don't understand," he sputters, panic blooming in his beady eyes as he tries to figure out where he went wrong. "Why didn't that work? You're fairies—*I know you are.* It said pure iron or salt… You're supposed to be down there counting the fucking salt!"

I should probably care what led him down this path—why he thinks I'm something most humans write off as fictional—but I don't. It's already been a long day, and he's been tapping out an Irish Riverdance on my last fucking nerve since I learned what he's been up to.

"Poor Ralphy. Didn't anyone ever tell you not to believe everything you read on the internet?" I *tsk* and give him a pitying look. "For what it's worth, your whole approach was a horrible idea. If you ever suspect you're in the presence of the fae, the very *last* thing you want to do is act like an asshole. Word is they offend easily and have tendencies to retaliate in brutal and creative fashion."

A switchblade suddenly appears in Ralph's hand, the knife flicking into position with a metallic *snick*. "Fuck you, Verran. We'll do this the old-fashioned way."

And now I'm done playing around.

Dropping the ruse like an anvil, a malevolent grin slides onto my face as I abandon my glamour and let Ralph get his first look at the real me: pointed ears, golden eyes so bright they almost glow, and deadly sharp canines.

He gasps, and I revel in the spicy scent of his fear.

"You should've gone with iron, Ralph."

"F-f-faerie!"

Loosing a ferocious growl, I cross the distance faster than he can track and pin him against the wall. "It's *fae*, you sniveling piece of shit. And I'm the motherfucking *king*."

With that, I use my bare fists and brute strength to unleash the day's frustrations on Ralph, punishing him for all his transgressions against me, my business, the workers under my protection, both human and fae alike. The whole thing lasts less than a minute but probably feels like an eternity to the man lying battered and bloody on the floor, whimpering in pain the same way I'm sure the women did after he assaulted them.

Seamus walks over and offers me the handkerchief from his pocket. "What do you want to do with him?"

"Tell the assistant manager he's been promoted. Then have Madoc take him out to Joshua Tree and send him through the veil. If he's lucky, he'll get to dance and drink himself into a stupor with the other assholes at the Spring Court. If *I'm* lucky, he'll be captured by the Winter Court and tortured for fun."

Honestly, it doesn't matter whether it's the Summer, Winter, Spring, or Fall Court that finds him once he's in Faerie, the world my ancestors hail from—a place in Ireland that exists in what humans call a parallel universe—or how they treat him while he's there. They'll get bored of him after a few days and spit him back through the veil.

Unfortunately for Ralph, a few days in Faerie could be a

hundred years or more over here. A punishment that amuses me more than the swift finality of his death would, since a human mind cannot travel back from Faerie and survive fully intact.

Seamus dips his head in acknowledgment and leaves to follow my orders. Wiping the blood from my hands, I exhale slowly, regaining my legendary control and applying my glamour once more.

This wasn't how I saw this meeting going, but that's on Ralph. During his Google search, he should've paid less attention to the myth about counting grains of salt and more to the myriad warnings against insulting members of the fae. Especially the ruler of the Dark Fae.

Tossing the blood-stained handkerchief onto Ralph's chest, I stride out of the manager's office, where Seamus is waiting for me. "Let's get out of here."

"To the tower it is, sire."

"Keep it up, wiseass, and see if I don't make you walk back to Nightfall."

He gasps dramatically. "That would be uncommonly cruel, Your Majesty. You know how slow I am these days."

"Slow, my ass," I say, cutting him a dubious look. "I saw you dodge that Ralph bullet like you were two hundred years old."

He opens the rear passenger door of the Bentley for me. "Well, don't tell the princes. It would take all their fun away."

He winks, making me grin and shake my head as I slide into the car. Once the door is closed, I exhale slowly and let the adrenaline of the past hour drain out through my feet into the floorboards. Despite the neon chaos going full bore outside my window, a quiet stillness wraps itself around me, and I feel like myself again.

Seamus gets in behind the wheel and asks the same question he always does, whether he knows the answer or not. "Where to?"

"To Nightfall, old friend."

Soon I'll be back in my own office where I can relax in my usual fashion—pouring myself an expensive drink while the humans pour their money into my city.

It's fucking good to be king.

CHAPTER TWO

BRYN

Stepping out of the cab, I tip my head back and stare up at Las Vegas's most popular hotel and casino, Nightfall.

I can't help but gawk in appreciation at how the black glass and clean lines appear to merge seamlessly with the night sky. The hotel is magnificent, and this is only the front. I'm not a Vegas expert, but I know from the website that Nightfall is taller and larger than every other hotel on the Strip and sits at the far end as though arrogantly lording its power over all the others.

It's weird to say about a building, but it's damn sexy.

The cab driver gets my attention and rolls my carry-on to where I'm standing on the curb. I tip him generously, then take a minute to be present in the moment instead of rushing ahead to the next one. I've always been what my mom called "a real go-getter," so it's hard for me to get my brain to stop spinning like a hamster wheel twenty-four-seven, but I'm trying.

Tucking my long blond hair behind my ears to keep the desert breeze from blowing it in my face, I close my eyes and take a deep breath...then slowly release it as I allow myself to experience the cacophony around me.

The traffic, the people, even the neon lights—they all mesh together, creating the sound of *excitement*. It feels like a humming in my bones, a vibration in my blood, and standing still while everything around me is urging me to *GO* is more than this Zen novice can handle.

Giving in, I grab the handle of my carry-on and pull it behind me as I finally stride through the automatic doors of my destination. A welcome blast of air-conditioning breaks over my body when I enter the lobby that's just another version of the hustle-and-bustle outside. Once I make my way to the back of the check-in line, I look around to take everything in, even more impressed than I was with the exterior.

The design of what I can see in the lobby is the embodiment of nighttime opulence—all sleek and contemporary in swaths of black and midnight blue, accented with gold and silver. The lighting above isn't large fixtures but rather thousands upon thousands of tiny gold lights hanging by invisible strings, giving the appearance of stars shining up in the sky.

It's incredible.

The line moves forward a few steps. I move with it, then take out the folded letter from my back jeans pocket—the letter I've been reading over and over to make sure I didn't miss any fine print. Biting my lip, I carefully comb through the information one last time and breathe a sigh of relief. The words haven't magically changed or anything, so I think I'm good.

I damn well better be.

Forty-eight hours ago, I booked a flight for this sponta-neous trip to Vegas from a random offer I received in the mail. I'd just been fired—sorry, *let go due to organizational changes*—from my job as a public relations specialist, so I should be more concerned about saving money right now instead of blowing it. But I'm a firm believer that the universe sends us signs that lead us toward our destiny, and I always follow the signs, hence why I'm standing in Nightfall's lobby right now.

To be honest, though, I also needed this.

Just a quick weekend getaway to shake off all the negativity and enjoy life, even if I am currently unemployed. It's only for the weekend, so it's not like I'm being hugely irresponsible. Only mildly. Then I'll fly home to Wisconsin and hit the ground running with my job hunt first thing Monday morning. I'll be back in the saddle in no time.

The woman in front of me looks to be in her early thirties with a cute brown bob that frames her heart-shaped face. Like everyone else in the immediate vicinity, she continues to look around while we wait. Our gazes catch, and being the natural extrovert I am, I give her my most welcoming Midwestern smile that says, *Hi there, I'm open to having conversations with strangers.*

Her eyes instantly light up, and she takes my cue.

"Oh my freaking Gawd, can you believe this place? It's so gorgeous, I feel like royalty or something," she gushes in a southern accent that reminds me of warm apple pie and sweet tea. "Hi, I'm Mandy."

Her excitement is contagious, and my smile grows. "Hey, I'm Bryn. And I know, right? It feels otherworldly in here. The pictures on the internet don't do it justice."

"You've got that right. I've stayed in five other hotels on the Strip while waiting to get into this one. There's simply no comparison, and I haven't even gotten out of the lobby yet," she says with a chuckle. "Don't get me wrong, the others were great and all, but when a place is booked out three years in advance, you know it has to be something special."

Wait, what? Record scratch, time out, hold the damn phone. "I'm sorry, it sounded like you said you made these reservations *three* years ago."

"That's what I said all right. This trip is three very long years in the making. I feel like Cinderella, finally getting invited to the ball," she says, laughing. We move forward in the line, and when we get to our new spots, she asks, "Why, how long did you have to wait to get in?"

"Um…two."

"Only two years? Damn, girl, you got lucky."

I wince and flush with guilt. "No, not two years. Two days."

If Mandy's jaw wasn't firmly attached to her face, it'd be on the floor right now. "*Two day—*" She cuts herself off, and I swear a light bulb must go on over her head that I can't see. "Oh my Gawd, you're like a movie star or something, aren't you? Girl, I *knew* you were too beautiful to be a real person, I just *knew* it. I don't keep up with celebrity news, though—"

Okay, so her light bulb might be screwed into the wrong socket. I have a gap between my front teeth that I've tried to hide in every picture taken of me since the seventh grade, and there's not an exercise that exists that's managed to rid me of my "hippy" figure and perpetual bubble butt. I'm not Hollywood Hot. If anything, I'm more Next-Door-Neighbor Cute.

"No, I'm not famous, that's not it. Here, wait…"

I dig the letter with the promotional offer out of my pocket again and hand it to her. As she reads, her expression changes in gradient shades of emotions, from confusion to surprise to wonder. It's probably how I looked when I read it the first time, too.

Finally, Mandy folds up the letter and hands it back with a bemused shake of her head. "Wow, Bryn, you *are* super lucky. As my daddy would say, it sounds like you got yourself a horseshoe up your ass. If I were you, I'd be marching that horseshoe down to the tables tonight."

"I suppose I should," I say with a smile. "When in Rome, right?"

"Girl, this ain't Rome. It's *Vegas*, baby. A magical place where a single roll of the dice can change your life forever."

As I'm contemplating all the possibilities of that statement like it's a choose-your-own-adventure novel, there's some kind of commotion behind us near the entrance. A crowd is moving en masse across the lobby with a person of extreme interest somewhere in the middle.

I can't see who it is, but I nudge Mandy and nod. "Looks like you might get your celebrity sighting after all."

We start to chuckle, but when two gigantic bodyguards push the crowd back enough for us to finally catch a glimpse of who all the fuss is about, our humor is knocked flat on its ass, replaced by slack-jawed, in-danger-of-drooling-in-public *awe*.

Seriously. I've never seen a more beautiful person—man or woman—in all my life.

Hair black as pitch, aristocratic nose, cheekbones even Cher would kill for, and a sharp jawline accented with the perfect amount of sexy stubble that I bet feels amazing on a woman's inner thighs. Wearing black from head to toe with shirtsleeves rolled up strong forearms, he carries his suit jacket thrown over his left shoulder with the crook of a finger.

He looks like your typical wealthy businessman except for one incongruous detail: a wide, black leather cuff on his left wrist. It's like a warning disguised as an accessory, letting everyone know in his own subtle way that he's not what he seems, and they'd do well to remember it.

It's the sexiest thing I've ever seen.

Everything about him *screams* "ultimate fantasy," like he was designed by the gods themselves for the sole purpose of making panties wet the world over. I don't know if that's true, but I can attest to at least one pair in this very room.

"Who...is *that*?" I'm not even sure if I ask the question out loud until Mandy answers.

"Caiden Verran," she says, fanning her face with a hand. "He's the owner of Nightfall and like a billion other places in this city. They call him and his brothers the Verran Kings of Vegas. Either way, I'd be more than happy to serve him for the rest of my days, amen."

We giggle—*giggle*, for chrissake—right as he passes us, not more than twenty feet away. It's not possible for him to hear us over the guests and photographers shouting to get his attention. And yet, right at that moment, his head turns to where we're standing near the front desk, and his eyes lock onto mine.

My God, his *eyes*. They're a warm golden amber color, yet no real warmth emanates from them. I'm completely entranced, unable to move or breathe, while he continues to walk in the direction of the elevators. Unaffected, expression unchanging. But his gaze burns into me until he's forced to look away.

"Whoa," Mandy says on a laugh. "Pardon my French, but Mr. Sin City himself just eye-fucked you like his name is already branded on your ass."

"What? No, that's not what that was. Not unless it was a hate fuck. He looked like he wanted to murder me."

"Yeah, with his *dick*."

Laughing, we turn back to see two spots open at the front desk and we're the next in line. "Listen, Bryn, my girlfriends and I will be bouncing between the casino and the dance club tonight. Come find us, and we'll show you how to party *Vegas*-style."

"Thanks, Mandy, I just might take you up on that."

She gives me a wink, then we both step up to the two waiting hotel staff members at either end of the counter.

"Hi there, and welcome to Nightfall," the woman says in

greeting. She's gorgeous with radiant dark-brown skin and burgundy corkscrew curls that reach her shoulders.

"Hi," I say, returning her smile as I place my purse on the counter. "My name is Bryn Meara. I have a reservation for two nights."

"Wonderful, let's get you checked in." Her fingers fly over the keyboard, eyes glued to the screen. After about a minute, her brows knit together, and my stomach drops. "I'm so sorry, Ms. Meara, but I don't see a reservation for you."

I swallow the lump forming in my throat. "Are you sure? Because I got this letter in the mail—" I start to retrieve it for the third time when a man interrupts.

"Thank you, Anya, but I can take it from here." I glance up to find a manager of some kind stepping in behind the computer, offering an apologetic smile. "I'm so sorry, Ms. Meara. We had a glitch in our system, and it double-booked your room. Unfortunately, the other couple has already arrived, so the room is no longer available."

"Oh, I see." I don't want him to feel bad, but I can't keep the dejection from my voice or hide my crestfallen expression. For all my worrying that something would go wrong, I didn't think it would actually happen. I truly thought I was meant to be here this weekend.

Now reality is throwing punches, and I don't have the energy to bob and weave. Maybe there's a motel with a vacancy on the outskirts of town somewhere.

"However," he continues in an overly chipper tone, "I do have a VIP suite available from a last-minute cancelation, so I'm going to upgrade you at no charge and ensure you receive all the VIP perks during your visit to apologize for the inconvenience."

My eyes open wide. "Wow, really? That's amazing, thank you!"

I catch Mandy staring at me. She mouths the word

"horseshoe," then points to her butt.

I laugh and roll my eyes at her, but she might have a point. That did feel like more luck than fate, so maybe I have both going for me right now. Guess now the only thing left to do is ride this Luck Dragon for all she's worth and see how far she takes me.

Look out, Vegas, here I come.

CHAPTER THREE

CAIDEN

"Mr. Verran, over here!"

"Caiden, Caiden! Can I get a selfie? *Pleeeeeease?*"

"I love you, Caiden Verran! *Have my babies!*"

"I said back the fuck up. *Now*," Connor Woulfe growls. He uses his massive body and outstretched arms to hold the crowd at bay while his twin brother, Conall, ushers me onto my private elevator and enters the security code. As the doors begin to close, Connor joins us, and then all the shouts and flashes are blessedly sealed off.

I don't love the out-of-control attention that comes with owning this city. To humans, money and power equal celebrity, and celebrity breeds *fans*. My upper lip curls just thinking of the word. It's part of the gig, I know this, but it doesn't mean I have to pander to it.

Tiernan says being a goddamn recluse (his words) only serves to make it worse, but I think it'd be like this regardless. You don't see people leaving Ryan Seacrest alone, and that asshole's everywhere.

Thankfully, I don't have to worry about that kind of nonsense with my subjects. There are thousands of Dark Fae in Vegas and the surrounding area, but they don't scream for selfies or beg for my sperm. I have immense love for my subjects. Humans…not so much.

Which is why being in the business of exploiting their vices is so ideal.

Speaking of humans, my mind slips to the woman from the lobby. Since fae can sense others of our kind, I know for certain she's human. *I wonder what her vices are… Maybe she doesn't even know what they are yet…*

But because she *is* human, I shut that thought down before my dick gets any bright ideas.

Her beauty was stunning, there's no denying that. Even travel disheveled in a hip-hugging pair of faded jeans and ridiculous T-shirt that said "Drink Wisconsibly" on it. Even with the slight gap between her front teeth that somehow enhances her looks instead of distracting from them. I don't know what made me look over at her or why it was so hard to tear my gaze away, but it doesn't matter. On the rare occasions I make time for pleasure, I don't do it with humans. Not anymore, not since becoming king.

Fucking them is too much of a security risk for a number of reasons. Plus, my sexual tastes run darker than most of them can handle anyway. They all wanted the Fifty Shades experience until they were bound by my rope and under my command.

That doesn't stop them from pursuing me, though. Doesn't matter how much of a surly asshole I am. They can't help themselves. Fae are extraordinarily beautiful. If you ever hear someone described as having "a certain glow" about them, they're most likely fae. Humans are drawn to us without quite knowing why. Sometimes it's a blessing, other times it's a curse.

For me, it's usually the latter.

A throat clears, snapping me back to the present. The guys have taken a relaxed stance against either wall, arms folded across their tree-trunk chests and regarding me with identical amused smirks.

"What?" I snap.

Connor arches a brow. "See something you like, sire?"

"Fuck off." That was for using my title. The Woulfe brothers are co-leaders of the Night Watch, my security team of personal bodyguards. They're also Seamus's sons, so we've been friends since birth. They're the last two people, besides my brothers, who need to use formalities, but they like getting under my skin as much as their father does.

"What?" Connor asks with fake innocence. "I'm just saying, if you want us to fetch something for you, we could do that."

"I don't know what you're talking about, but I wish you'd shut the hell up. Your voice is grating to my ears."

Conall's deep laughter shakes his shoulders, moving the ends of his wavy reddish-brown hair. "Finally, someone else said it. I've been telling him that our whole lives." Connor flips his brother off, and just when I think I've successfully switched the topic, Conall switches it right back. "Come on, CV, you can't fool us. We know what you look like when you see something you want."

"And you want that human something *fierce*," Connor finishes with his shit-eating grin.

"What I *want* is a drink and some peace and fucking quiet." Thankfully, the elevator dings to signal our arrival before they can share any more of their ridiculous speculations. I step out first, then turn to block their path. "Take the rest of the night off."

Their hands shoot out to prevent the doors from closing, their expressions suddenly all business. Connor narrows his eyes at me. "You know damn well we don't go anywhere until you're back at Midnight Manor."

I give them an admonishing look. "I also know it's been too long since you've been on a run, and if you put it off any longer, you'll be no good to me at all. And don't tell me you're fine because I can see that you're not."

Connor swears under his breath while Conall drags a hand over his face in frustration.

Beyond our usual preternatural abilities, some fae are blessed with rare special powers unique to their bloodline. Things like the gift of foresight, healing others, manipulating nature's energies, sensing approaching danger, and more.

The members of the Woulfe bloodline are shapeshifters. More specifically—and not surprisingly—wolf shifters. They can communicate telepathically with wolves out in the wild and shift their forms at will. The animal is as much a part of them as being fae, and if they ignore it for too long, it takes its toll physically.

I noticed it this morning when we left the manor. Their muscles are bunched with tension and their golden eyes—the color all Dark Fae possess—have grown dull.

"All right," Connor says, relenting. "I'll call in for replacements."

I shake my head. "Not necessary. I'll be working late, so I'm just going to crash in the penthouse."

The brothers do that annoying twin thing where they share a conversation with each other using only a look. It's Conall who voices it aloud. "Working late again, CV? You might want to consider fetching that pretty admirer of yours and going on a *run* of your own." He waggles his eyebrows suggestively like I need help catching on to his juvenile euphemism.

"Yeah, you're crabbier than usual lately," Connor adds unhelpfully.

"Duly noted and now dismissed. Just like the both of you are." When they don't make a move to leave, I arch a brow and deadpan, "Seriously, I've had more than enough of your ugly mugs for one day, so kindly fuck off before I lose what's left of my sunny disposition."

They snort at that, but it gets them to finally lower their arms from the sides of the elevator. Aiming identical dimpled smiles at me, Connor offers a sarcastic, "Have a good night, Your Majesty." Then Conall gives me a double-middle finger salute just before the doors close.

"Assholes." My mouth tips into an amused half grin as I cross the empty reception area.

I can already taste my favorite Irish whiskey and feel the knots in my shoulders loosening. I quickly punch in the code to my office and enter the quiet—

"There he is!" Tiernan's shouted greeting hits me from where he and our baby brother—if you can consider someone a baby at 116—are arm wrestling on the coffee table in my sitting area furnished with a leather armchair and couch.

So much for peace and fucking quiet. I release a heavy breath and shut the door, resigned to the fact that I won't be decompressing as originally planned anytime soon.

My brothers rarely drop by unannounced, which means they're here for a reason.

Might as well join them until they spit it out.

But first, a drink.

I bypass the large desk and ignore my laptop with the inbox of nagging emails, heading for the bar on the far side of the room.

Finnian greets me with his wide grin and smiling amber eyes that say he's happy to see me. It's one of the few things in this world that tugs at my black heart. Sometimes it's hard for me to see him as a grown male instead of the baby-faced youngster who stuck to me more than my own shadow.

He's wearing his usual uniform of T-shirt and jogger pants with athletic shoes, and his dark hair is mussed on top like he just rolled out of bed even though I know he didn't. The only one of us who isn't a night owl, Finn wakes at dawn and clocks several hours in the gym. Then he spends the

afternoons training in various fighting styles with the Night
Watch. He doesn't have a head for business like me or have
Tiernan's effortless charm that works on our business partners
as much as it does his lovers. But like Tier says, if the zombie
apocalypse ever happens, Finnian will be the one to lead an
army against the undead and save us all.

Finn must be done messing with our brother because
Tiernan's grin is quickly devolving into an ugly grimace. As
I pass behind where he's sitting on the couch, I give him a
smack to his head. "You look constipated."

"Yeah, well, *you* look—" The sound of fists slamming onto
the table signals the end of the match. I don't even have to ask
who won. "Damn it! Caiden distracted me. That one doesn't
count."

Finn laughs. "I suppose the other several hundred wins
don't count, either."

I'm about to side with Finn when I notice the designer case
for The Devil's Keep—one of the most expensive single malt
Irish whiskeys in the world—sitting open on top of the bar.
"Are you fucking kidding me?" Turning back, I see the bottle
on one of the side tables. Half empty. "Hey, assholes, that's
a twelve-thousand-dollar bottle of whiskey you're drinking
like it's water over there."

They keep straight faces, but mischief dances in their eyes.
"Ah," Finn says to Tiernan, "now we know why it tastes so
good."

"I believe you're right, little brother. Another?"

"Don't mind if I do, big brother." Finn chuckles and holds
his glass out for Tier to refill.

Deciding I'll plot their untimely deaths later, I grab my
own glass and stalk over to them. I swipe the bottle out of
Tier's hand and sit on the other side of the couch from him
before pouring myself three fingers and setting it where they
can't reach it. I take a generous sip of the liquid gold and revel

in the smooth fire as it slides down my throat.

Fuck, this is good. I'm glad I have another bottle stashed away at the manor.

Finn relaxes his huge frame into the chair and aims a playful smirk at Tiernan. "I'm impressed, T. Have you been working out more? You almost had me there for a second."

Tiernan's eyebrows shoot toward his hairline. "I did?"

"Fuck no, not even close." Finn chuckles, then blocks the couch pillow Tier chucks at his face.

"One of these days, I'm gonna beat your smug ass."

"You know what the definition of insanity is, right, Tier?" I let a slight grin tug on one corner of my mouth. "Might want to keep that in mind the next time Finni issues you a challenge."

Finnian might be a lot younger than Tier and me, who are both in our one-sixties, but the kid is a natural beast. At six foot seven and gods only know what on the scale, he's the biggest of the three of us.

"Get bent, big bro." He gives me a crooked grin. "Where the hell have you been, anyway? We thought for sure you never left your tower, and then we come to say hi and you're suddenly MIA."

Great. Seamus must have said something, and now I'll be lucky if they don't start calling me Rapunzel. "I had something to take care of down at Deviant. There was a problem with the manager."

"And?"

"Now there's not." I don't have to say anything else about his fate. My lack of explanation *is* the explanation.

Finnian's expression sobers, growing contemplative as he so often does. "It ever bother you guys that the humans we punish get to go to our home but we don't?"

Tiernan and I share a look. Then we regard the only male in this world or any other we love more than ourselves. Long grown by the time Finnian came along, we helped our parents raise him; we taught him how to play, how to lead, and how to fight. There's nothing we wouldn't do to make him happy.

Unfortunately, sometimes I think what would make him the happiest is if our banishment was lifted and we could finally live in Tír na nÓg in the Faerie realm.

We don't fully understand why he's always felt the loss of a place we've never even seen, but then, for as gigantic as Finnian is, he's the most sensitive Verran brother. Like a big teddy bear with muscles. And since I'm about as sensitive as sandpaper, Tiernan takes point. "*This* is our home, Finni. Vegas. It's all we've ever known."

"But it's not our *real* home, T. It's not where we belong," he says, irritation lacing his words.

That raises Tiernan's hackles. He sits forward on the edge of the couch and rips off the kid gloves. "Like hell we don't. We might not hail from this world, but we've made it our own. We helped our father build this city out of nothing but desert sand and turn it into one of the greatest places on earth. We are the Dark Fae of the Night Court of Faerie. Whether we're allowed to live in that realm or forced to live in this one, it will never change who we are, brother."

Finn drops his gaze to the floor, carefully weighing Tiernan's words against his own thoughts. He feels too much at times, and I hate seeing him struggle because of our grandfather's sins. We were born long after Domnall Verran died, but it was his actions, along with those of the Day Court king, that caused our courts' exile.

The fae are a proud and fickle people. As I told Ralph earlier, we don't like being insulted.

And when you insult Aine, the One True Queen, she's bound to fuck with you in a *very* big way. Like eternally banishing you and every member of your court to the uninhabited deserts of the human world and heaping on a few curses for good measure.

Tiernan gives me a look that says, *Your turn.*

"Finnian," I say firmly and wait for his gaze to meet mine. "Tier's right. We have more here than we ever would back in Tír na nÓg. As the eldest of the Dark Court's royal bloodline, the position of ruler fell to me after Father died. But as the owners of Nightfall, and everything else worth a damn in this godsforsaken desert, we are *all* kings. All three of us. We are the Verran brothers of Vegas, and *this* is our fucking kingdom."

Finnian squares his shoulders and sets his jaw, seemingly appeased by my speech. I arch a brow, asking him if he's good. He gives me a firm nod. "You're right, Caiden. I'll remember what you both said," he says. "Promise."

"Fucking cheers to that." Tiernan raises his glass and drains the rest of his drink. The corners of Finn's mouth lift slightly, and I can see his good mood returning.

"Excellent. Now, why don't you two tell me why you're really here, so I don't have to drag it out of you?" They exchange a conspiratorial look like they're each claiming *not it*. Holding back a sigh, I choose for them as I refill my glass. "Tiernan. Speak."

"It's nothing, really. We were just wondering if you'd put any thought into bringing anyone to the Double E."

"The Early Equinox ball?" My brows knit together. Why would either of my brothers care if I— *Oh, hell.* "Mom put you up to this."

It's a statement, not a question.

This isn't the first time she's broached the topic, but using my siblings as messenger boys is a new angle. Apparently, approaching your one-hundred-and-seventieth year means your mother starts harping on you about settling down and popping out "wee bairns to ensure an heir."

Though, I'd wager she wants little cherub grandbabies to bounce on her knee a lot more than she gives a fig about continuing the bloodline.

Tiernan frowns dramatically. "Honestly, Caiden, I don't know why you'd want to think the worst of our mother. Can't we just be curious about—"

Not in the mood for a "fae truth"—not a lie but also not an answer—I cut a glare over to Finn. He winces, and the real truth tumbles out. "She threatened to smash our PS5s if we didn't try convincing you to bring a prospective consort as your date."

"Hey, traitor, what the hell?" Tier narrows his gaze on Finn. "He barely even looked at you, and you just rolled over and showed him your belly."

Finn shrugs one big shoulder. "It was a really scary look."

Tiernan's eyes widen, and he throws his arms out. "You're *bigger* than him!"

From experience, I know that once they start bickering, it's better to just let it run its course. Plus, I don't have the energy to play referee tonight.

Standing, I cross to the wall that holds half a dozen screens showing live security footage of different high-traffic areas throughout Nightfall. There's a security room with all the latest high-tech monitoring systems manned by the best security team money can buy, but I like checking on things myself.

You might say I have control issues.

What Finn said Mom expects of me soon tumbles around in my mind, leaving a residue behind that will tarnish my mood for the rest of the night.

A prospective consort. Not a prospective bride or wife or queen. *Consort.*

One of the curses paired with our exile is related to royal marriages. If either king of the Day or Night Court takes a true queen of fae blood, they will start to weaken and eventually die if their mate is ever "more than a stone's throw" away from them. An appropriate punishment, considering it was an illicit affair between the Day king and Night queen—my grandmother—that caused the feud between the courts, resulting in our exile.

The curse was supposed to prevent something like that from happening again—it's hard to have an affair if your mate is always around—but an indirect side effect is that it makes the kings extremely vulnerable. To kill the king, simply separate him from his queen and let the curse run its course.

So, infidelity aside, getting married is literally hazardous to a king's health, and why it's necessary to choose a fae female as consort to carry on the royal line.

Obviously, my mother was a consort. We weren't a family in the true sense of the word; it was closer to growing up with divorced parents. She had separate living quarters and we went back and forth between there and the royal manor. Their relationship was more transactional than anything, presumably so neither would get too attached and long for something they couldn't have.

Either way, I hated seeing the wistful look in her eyes when he was around, only to be treated with the kind of mild affection people have for their neighbor.

In my opinion, the role of consort is demeaning, and I don't look forward to the day when I'll be forced to become my father and bear children with a female I won't be able to offer more than a platonic relationship based on co-parenting.

Sliding one hand into my pocket, I lift my glass with the other and take another long pull of whiskey. I shove the irritating thoughts to the back of my mind and study the monitors for a distraction. I can switch the feeds from my computer if I want, but usually I keep them on the same ones. Everything appears normal. Business as usual, as expected.

But then I see *her*. The woman from the lobby.

If I thought she was beautiful before, I don't have the word for how she looks now. Tight black cocktail dress that hugs her slight curves, long hair flowing down her back in loose waves, and mile-long legs meant to wrap around a male's waist.

"Damn, who is *that*?" Lusty appreciation coats Finn's tone from where he stands next to me. I was so wrapped up in watching her walk through the casino, stopping to check out different tables, I didn't even notice my brothers had quit their bitching to join me.

"I don't know," I answer honestly. "I saw her in the lobby not even thirty minutes ago."

Tiernan chuckles. "Must have been eager to get her night started. I like eagerness in a woman."

I almost growl that she's off-limits, but I catch myself in time. She's not off-limits to them or anyone else because she's nothing to me. Just some human dropping money into my pocket, like all the others.

Finn elbows me in the side. "You should take *her* to Early Equinox."

"She's human."

"So?"

"So, if I took *any* female—which I'm not, but if I did—it would only be to appease our mother, who wants me to bring a prospective consort, meaning *fae*, not human."

Tiernan pipes in. "We're in a very progressive age right now. Why not two consorts? One to carry on the royal line and the other to carry out every filthy fantasy in that big head of yours."

"You're a dumbass. Get out, both of you. I have work to do."

They do their fair share of protesting and griping, but finally I'm rid of them, along with what was left of my finest whiskey. I sit at my desk with every intention of working, but my eyes keep wandering back to the screens and clicking through the different feeds to follow her.

I don't know why I'm so drawn to her. That mystery is grating enough on its own—never mind the underlying desire

I feel tugging at my balls—and has me grabbing my suit jacket to stalk toward the hall before I even know I'm moving.

If I want to exorcise this woman from my mind, I need to prove to myself that she's no one special.

CHAPTER FOUR

CAIDEN

By the time I get downstairs, she's exchanging money for colored chips at the roulette table. I planned on posting up across the casino and simply observing first to see what I could learn about her, but as soon as we were in the same room again, I felt this strange *pull*. Like I need to be next to her.

And that's how I find myself striding across the gaming floor, using a glamour that will mask my presence to humans aside from another body to move around. It's a trick I almost never use, as it would be viewed as weak for a fae king to want to avoid attention. But in this instance, I don't want anything interrupting my investigation of this woman, least of all another mob of admirers.

The only one I want admiring me is her.

Taking the spot next to her at the table, I'm hit with her sweet scent of vanilla with a hint of oranges. She smells like a damned Dreamsicle, and my mouth is already watering.

"You know," I say to her, "roulette has the worst odds of all the games you could play in a casino. The house has a greater advantage."

She smiles, then turns her head to respond. Recognition

flashes across her face, and her smile drops into a parted gasp of surprise. "It's you."

"Caiden Verran, at your service." I raise my right hand between us and turn my palm up like we're meeting each other in my royal court instead of a loud casino floor.

Her almond-shaped eyes are hazel, I realize. A beautiful mix of greens and golds swirling within her irises as though battling for dominance, and I get the distinct feeling that this woman has more things battling for dominance within her than just her eye color.

"Bryn Meara," she says with a shy smile, and once again the small gap in her otherwise perfectly straight teeth bewitches me.

She hesitates at first, then slips her hand into mine. My fingers close around hers eagerly as I bring them up to my lips, holding her gaze. She flushes pink when I press a kiss to the back of her hand, holding it longer than strictly necessary.

I actually have to force myself to release her or risk things going from romantic to creepy.

Since when the hell are you romantic, anyway?

Since never is the answer.

I admit something about this woman makes me want to charm her, though. To make her smile and hear her laugh. To see if that pretty flush covers her whole body when I make her come from devouring her sweet pussy.

"Players, place your bets," the dealer says, breaking up our staring contest and drawing our focus to the table. He's fae, and when we make eye contact, he gives me a reverent nod and smiles wide enough that his inhumanly sharp canines peek out.

Not that the humans at the table notice. We use glamours so they never notice our fangs, our ears, or the preternatural brightness of our eyes unless we want them to. Like with Ralph.

Bryn glances up at me thoughtfully, then slides all her

chips—a sum worth three hundred dollars—onto the black rectangle for a single outside bet, giving her a fifty-fifty chance of doubling her money. The dealer waves his hand over the table and states no more bets can be placed, then drops the silver ball into the wheel.

It spins around several times before finally dropping into a pocket.

"Black seventeen," the dealer announces.

"I won!" Bryn laughs and claps in excitement.

"Beginner's luck," I tease, grinning down at her. Even with her heels on, I tower over her.

"Not luck. Just reading the signs," she says with a cheeky smile.

I chuckle. "What signs?"

"We're in Nightfall, a hotel with a very clear theme and color palette made almost entirely out of black and blues so dark, they're practically black. You, the owner of said establishment who is standing next to me, has black hair, a black suit, and a black leather cuff, if you're still wearing it." I raise my arm and pull my sleeve up enough to show her she's right, amused she noticed such a detail earlier and remembered it. "She couldn't have made her signs any more obvious. All I had to do was follow them."

"She?"

"The universe. The path she's leading me down right now has a definite dark horse theme. Maybe that's what you are, my dark horse. And betting on you just paid off."

I can't help it. I laugh. Not the soft huffs or muted chuckles as are my habit. It's a full-out laugh coming from deep in my belly. "Does that mean we have a long night of gambling ahead of us?"

Her eyes widen, and she shakes her head. "Definitely not. I planned on playing with a set amount of money and no more, win or lose. I did that, so now I'm done. It was nice chatting with you, Mr. Verran."

"Call me Caiden."

"All right. It was nice chatting with you, *Caiden*," she says with a smile. Then she collects her winnings from the dealer, scoops the chips into her purse, and walks away from the table, essentially dismissing me.

I follow as though tethered to her by an invisible thread, compelled to go where she goes, and I don't even question it.

When she leaves the casino and crosses into the atrium near Darkness, Nightfall's dance club, my curiosity gets the better of me. "Why didn't you place smaller bets? Why chance losing it all in one shot like that?"

Bryn stops and turns around, a brief look of surprise flashing across her face to find me still with her. Recovering, she considers her answer for a moment before speaking. "I don't really do anything by half measures. I'm an all-or-nothing kind of girl, so it was either not play or lean into the risk. And what's life without taking a few risks now and again, am I right?"

"Some might say it's not worth the potential fallout." I step in closer, leaving only a handful of aching inches from my chest to hers. "That it's better to be safe than sorry."

Hazel eyes framed by thick lashes bounce between my gold ones. The air around us feels charged with electricity, like if I reach out and touch her, we'll blow every fucking breaker in this place. Finally, she answers, her voice soft and breathy. "I'd rather be sorry for taking a thousand risks than be safe for never taking any."

I can't decide if that's truly the most amazing thing I've ever heard or I'm just drunk on this woman's refreshing authenticity and think everything she says is a revelation. Either way, I can't bring myself to care. I want to hear more. I want to know who she is and what she likes. What her dreams and aspirations are.

Or not. We could sit and talk about the weather, and I'd be fine with that, too. As long as I can spend time with her, I'll be happy.

Happy. Not usually an adjective I use to describe myself. Serious, hardworking, loyal, content, even surly or grouchy if you ask those closest to me. But happy? No.

It sounds foreign even in my own thoughts. But why should I question it? If I'm feeling happy, then that's what I am.

Although, something deep in the back of my mind is telling me maybe I *should* question it. Except if I do that, then I'm choosing the safe route, and I like Bryn's philosophy for taking risks. That maybe pursuing whatever this is could be worth that risk.

Even if it means I'm sorry for it later.

"Do you like dancing?"

* * *

"Uh-oh, you're empty. That won't do." Bryn gestures to the bartender, holding up my glass. When he stops in front of us, she offers him an apologetic grin. "Hi, Brandon. Sorry, can we get him another one, please?"

The first thing Bryn did when we took our seats at the bar was ask Brandon his name. Every interaction with him since, she's made it a point to address him with it. That, combined with her habit of apologizing every time she asks the man to do his job, tells me she isn't comfortable treating people as though they're beneath her.

I bet if she didn't think it would cause a scene, she'd prefer to go behind the bar and get her own drink in favor of bothering Brandon. And she'd probably still leave him a tip.

"Of course, I'd be happy to," he says with a megawatt smile, stopping just short of adding a wink.

A handsome kid in his mid-twenties, Brandon obviously knows how to turn up the charm to eleven, as all good bartenders do. But sensing I'd have a problem otherwise, he's keeping it at a max of nine with Bryn, sparing him from my infamous deadly glower and getting demoted to barback.

Smart kid.

He continues talking as he grabs the bottle of Redbreast from the back wall and pours three fingers of the single-malt Irish whiskey. "How about you, Ms. Meara? Can I get you another dirty martini with extra olives?"

She waves him off. "Oh, no thank you, I'm still nursing this one."

He places the rocks glass atop a fresh black cocktail napkin with the Nightfall logo in silver. "Here you are, Mr. Verran."

Before I even get a chance, Bryn is saying, "Thanks, Brandon, you're the best."

Then I watch in amusement as she repeats a routine I've seen her do twice before this. Earlier when we sat down, she cashed in two twenties for singles, then arranged them in a neat stack in front of her. Every time Brandon serves us, she takes a few dollars from her stash and slides them across the bar to the inside rail.

Just as she's doing now.

The kid cuts a questioning glance in my direction, and I give him a discreet nod. There's no reason for her to be tipping him, because the drinks are going on my tab, but I have a feeling not doing so would break some Wisconsinite law, so I'm not fighting her on it.

Brandon relaxes and accepts the money graciously, then says he'll be back to check on us soon.

She's so adorably Midwestern in everything she says and does. I've spent no more than thirty minutes with Bryn Meara, and I've cataloged a dozen things that set her apart from anyone I've ever met.

When she suggested we get a drink before heading to the dance floor, she tacked on "my treat" at the end. I didn't know whether to laugh or check her for signs of fever. I'm a known billionaire in the human world and ruler of an empire in mine; I've never had a female, human or fae, offer to pick up the tab.

I objected, of course, but she insisted, joking it was the least she could do after taking a whopping three hundred dollars from my casino. I laughed but finally relented on the condition that after our first drinks, everything went on my tab. She agreed but continues to tip Brandon regardless.

It's cute as hell.

She catches me looking at her and blushes. "What?"

"Nothing." With two fingers, I try to rub the smile from my lips, but the best I can do is hide it because the damn thing's been stuck on my face from the moment she called me her dark horse—a description that hits a lot closer to home than she realizes.

She narrows her hazel eyes at me. "It's something."

Nodding to her pile, I decide to tease her. Just a little. "Do all Wisconsinites leave their money out as a dare for less upstanding citizens? Or is this another of those risks you so enjoy taking?"

Glancing around, she realizes no one else has any money out on the bar and chuckles, shaking her head in a self-deprecating manner. "I knew it was only a matter of time until I showed my country mouse roots. Back home in the townie bars, it's common practice to throw your cash down in front of you. Most of the time, the bartender just pulls what they need every time you order a drink, and then you slide money over for a tip each round. You can even leave your spot at the bar to play the jukebox or go to the bathroom and no one messes with your stuff."

"Impressive. But this is a far cry from a townie bar. I guarantee if we turn our backs even for a second, it'll be gone just as fast."

She wrinkles her nose and reaches for the stack. "Guess I should put it away, then."

I stop her with my hand over hers, both of us frozen as we hold each other's gaze for an eternal moment. Her hand is soft and fine-boned with long, graceful fingers and French-manicured nails. "Don't worry, Beauty," I say, my voice husky as the endearment rolls off my tongue before I can think better of it. "I'll keep an eye on it for you."

My gaze is drawn to her mouth as she lightly bites her lower lip. Not out of coyness or calculated seduction, but maybe a habit she does whenever she's turning thoughts around in that gorgeous brain of hers.

When she feels the weight of my stare, she releases it, clearly flustered by my attention and causing my dick to stir in my pants.

I stroke my thumb across the back of her hand, and I swear I feel her skin heat beneath mine. A deep hunger urges me to kiss every fingertip, every knuckle, then continue exploring until I've devoured every inch of her delectable body.

I probably would have, too, if she didn't finally pull her hand back, breaking the spell.

She busies herself with healthy sips from her martini, and I follow suit by tossing back the contents of my drink like it's a rail shot and not an expensive sipping whiskey. By the time I place my empty glass on the bar, my lascivious thoughts are once again under control, and the flash of lust in her expression has been replaced with a wry smile.

I arch a brow. "What's that look for?"

"I was just wondering, how exactly does one become the *king* of Vegas?"

Be vague and pivot, that's the name of the game when talking with curious humans. "By buying anything that's for sale and other boring business stuff. I'd rather talk about you.

What's a saint doing in Sin City?"

That earns me an eye roll, but she appeases me anyway and starts talking. I manage to keep the conversation focused on her over the course of another martini for her and two more glasses of Redbreast for me. When she notices I'm empty again, she signals for Brandon, and less than a minute later, I have a fresh drink in front of me.

We clink our glasses together and take a drink. "You know you don't have to get me drunk in order to take advantage of me, right?" Smirking, I set my glass down and wink. Because apparently I'm just as charming as my bartender around this woman.

"Oh, I know. That's not why I'm trying to get you drunk." Her green-and-gold eyes dance with mischief as she adds, "I was hoping that before I *do* take advantage of you, I could get you to dress up like that gentleman over there."

She nods in the direction of the dance floor, and when I follow her line of sight, my poker face nearly shatters. A man, probably in his sixties, is dancing like he's John Travolta from *Saturday Night Fever* and wearing an ensemble that would give *Tiger King*'s Joe Exotic wardrobe envy.

His bright purple metallic shirt with gold tiger stripes is unbuttoned to his navel, revealing a heavy gold chain resting on a thick mat of silver chest hair. The white pants clinging to him like a second skin leave absolutely nothing to the imagination, tragically so, and his platform shoes look like an invitation for twisted ankles.

But the man is tearing it up better than the humans a third of his age, so good for him.

Turning my attention back to Bryn, I take a sip from my fresh drink. "Sorry to disappoint, Beauty, but you'd never get me drunk enough to wear something like that."

"Because the fancy-schmancy king of Vegas would never be caught dead wearing something outrageous and fun?"

I lock my serious gaze on her and answer her with a straight face. "Because my ass would never look that good in those pants."

It takes her a few beats to process the quip, then she bursts like a balloon being popped. Her laughter is genuine and uninhibited, and I think she even snorts in the middle of it.

Her joy is infectious, and I have to wonder if this emotional high is what Tiernan feels every time someone laughs at his jokes. Even if it is and I somehow turned into a regular comedian like my middle brother, I doubt it would feel anywhere close to as good as getting this reaction from Bryn.

After only a single hit, I'm hopelessly addicted. I want more.

More of her laughter, more of her smiles…just *more*. And if there's anything I'm damn good at, it's getting something I want.

CHAPTER FIVE

BRYN

'm starting to think Mandy was right and I really *do* have a horseshoe lodged in my butt. Because universe guidance aside, how do you explain a free trip to Vegas, VIP suite upgrade with tons of perks, doubling my money on a single bet, *and* somehow catching the attention of a real-life Prince freaking Charming? *Luck*, that's how.

And since I've never been one to look a Luck Horse in the mouth, I've decided to throw caution to the wind and just go with the flow.

A flow that—thank you, sweet baby Jesus—happens to include the tall, dark, and handsome-as-hell Caiden Verran.

When I left the roulette table, the last thing I expected was for him to follow me. Hell, I was shocked he'd even approached me in the first place. But as the owner, making the rounds and talking with people is probably a nightly routine for him. After all, building a rapport with your guests and making them feel special is the best way to get them to return. It's PR 101.

So I was fully prepared to take my winnings and the memory of him kissing my hand with me to my room—the former padding my regular bank and the latter padding my spank bank. A girl can always use fresh fantasy fodder.

But thanks to that metaphorical horseshoe, instead of heading upstairs for a lonely night with myself and my memories, I'm sitting next to him at the bar of the night club, turned toward each other on our stools, and having a blast.

For the past hour, we've been mostly people watching, which may or may not include making up funny stories about why they're in Vegas. I never would have guessed this intense man would be this hilarious. I'm pretty sure my sides are going to feel like I did ab crunches all night. Laughing until I cry isn't my favorite reason for being sore the morning after, but it's a close second.

And who knows? The night is still young. If my luck holds out, maybe I'll be sore in more places than just my sides. Stranger things have happened, right?

"That's a beautiful necklace," he says after our last bout of laughter dies down. "Does it have special meaning? You keep touching it like you're reassuring yourself it's still there."

I glance down to see that I'm indeed fingering the pendant nestled in the center of my chest. When I was in my room getting ready earlier, a hotel attendant arrived with a selection of expensive necklaces I could choose from to borrow for the evening, compliments of the manager to again try to make up for my lost reservation. All five pieces were gorgeous, featuring black obsidian pendants that tie in with the overall theme of the hotel.

Nightfall's branding is on point, that's for sure.

I chose the one with a teardrop shape outlined in tiny diamonds dangling from a delicate silver chain, but I'm wondering if I shouldn't have politely declined instead. I'm wearing a borrowed necklace that would cost me God only knows what to replace if anything happened to it, which apparently makes me subconsciously fondle the thing. So, yes, in hindsight I should've said no, but it's too late now.

Either way, I'm not telling Caiden where it came from. The staff have been so accommodating, and I don't want the manager to get in trouble for double-booking my reservation.

"No special meaning," I say, dropping my hand to my lap. "Nervous habit, I guess."

He arches a dark brow, a playful smirk flirting with his lips. "Am I making you nervous, Beauty?"

Well, when you look at me like that...

He's taken to calling me Beauty, which does things to me no man has ever managed with the utterance of a simple endearment. Normally if a guy I just met started calling me by a pet name—especially something so over-the-top complimentary—I'd laugh and walk away, leaving him to hurl his sorry flattery attempts at someone else.

But with Caiden, it sounds as though he's wrapped the word in truth before letting it leave his lips. I think it's the way he looks at me, like he's merely commenting on what he's seeing. I believe that in his eyes I truly am beautiful, and I swoon a little every time he says it.

I'm not sure what this is between us exactly, but I like it. He swings us effortlessly like a pendulum between playfulness on one side and wickedness on the other. It's such a cliché to even think it, but I've honestly never felt this way about a man before.

Tucking my hair behind my ear, I scoff dramatically to distract him from noticing the flush I feel heating my cheeks right now, then mutter an unconvincing, "You wish."

His laugh is a deep rumble emanating from his chest that rolls through me like thunder. It's hard to not continually stare at him, but there's not a woman on earth who would blame me. The man wears sex appeal like a tailored Armani suit, for chrissake. He must be six and a half feet tall if he's an inch, his broad shoulders and large hands making a girl imagine holding on to either or both, and my fingers are dying to run through his longish, wavy black hair that hints at an unruly desire to fall out of place.

What captivates me the most, though, are his eyes. They're the color of molten amber and dark promises, and every time he looks at me, it's like I can feel him reaching deep inside me to stake his claim on my soul.

Which is ridiculous, Bryn, because you only just met the man. If anything, his eyes are telling you he wants to bang your brains out, and let's be honest here, you'd be more than okay with that.

"I'd be *very* okay with that."

"Okay with what?"

My eyes fly wide as I realize my internal monologue escaped through my alcohol-weakened filter. And now my inability to hide my reaction to that fact—*thanks a lot, martini number three*—has *him* realizing what I did, causing an amused grin to slide onto his too-sexy-for-my-own-good face.

"No, it's—it's nothing." I wave it off.

"Didn't sound like nothing."

"Then you'll have to take my word for it, because it was very much nothing." I try to hide my smile behind the rim of my glass, but if his laughter is any indication, it's not working.

Why did I insist we have drinks before dancing, again? Oh, right. Because I wanted something to take the edge off. Except I'm pretty sure the edge was hacked off two dirty martinis ago, and we just keep drinking. Caiden's been ordering three fingers of whiskey like it's water, and by my count, he's had at least five hands' worth already. I'm sure it's obvious to anyone watching that we're feeling no pain over here.

Then again, when I scan the busy bar around us, no one *is* watching.

"Hey, how have we been left alone this whole time? It's almost like you're a regular guy or something."

He tilts his head. "I am a regular guy, Bryn. Made of flesh and bone with the same wants and needs as any other."

The tone of his voice lowers meaningfully on that last part. It warms my insides and sends a blush to my cheeks that has nothing to do with alcohol. Although, I'm sure it's not helping. So, on that note, I set my glass on the bar and signal to the bartender that I'm done.

Turning my attention back to Caiden, I say, "You know what I mean. I saw what happened today in the lobby. You don't even have security with you, so how are you not surrounded by all your—"

"Annoying, overzealous fans?"

I gasp and lightly smack him on the shoulder. "Hush your mouth, mister," I admonish through a chuckle. "What a terrible thing to say about your *adoring* fans."

He glances down at his shoulder—as if I could've done any damage even if I'd punched him as hard as I could—then arches a brow at me. "Did you really just tell me to *hush*?"

I match him eyebrow for eyebrow. "To hush your mouth, yes, I did. Don't tell me you're unfamiliar with the phrase."

"I'm unfamiliar with anyone being ballsy enough to scold me like a child."

"Oh, please, I'm from Wisconsin. Whether we were raised on a farm or not, we all have basic knowledge of how to castrate a bull. If I were you, it wouldn't be *my* balls I was worrying about. So be nice."

His eyes grow big as he stares at me for several seconds, then finally breaks into a hearty laugh with a disbelieving shake of his head. "I don't know how you do it. You threaten to make me a eunuch and scold me—*twice*, I might add—and I'm more turned on now than I have been all night."

That makes me laugh more exuberantly than it would

have an hour ago when I wasn't quite so buzzy, but I stopped censoring myself a while ago. "I don't know, but if I can figure out a way to make that sound like a skill, I'm going to add it to my résumé for my job search next week."

"We can workshop it tomorrow over breakfast, how's that sound?"

Heat creeps into my cheeks as desire pools between my legs. "We'll still be together in the morning?"

Caiden's nostrils flare slightly as his gaze drops to where I'm squeezing my thighs together for the tiniest bit of relief, and my breath catches in my throat. When his eyes raise to meet mine, he gives me a playful wink. "If I have anything to say about it, we will be."

And just like that, the mood feels lighter again. I love his humor and how easygoing he is. He's not at all how I thought he'd be from the glimpse I saw of him in the lobby, and I couldn't be happier about that.

"Seriously, though," I repeat, honestly curious. "What's your secret?"

Something I can't quite read flashes in his eyes. Then he simply lifts one large shoulder and nods to the people in the club. "Everyone here is wrapped up in their own experiences. At night, I'm able to blend in easier because they're not expecting or looking for me. They're busy enjoying themselves and everything Nightfall has to offer."

I nod. "That makes sense. Lucky me, then, because it means I get you all to myself."

"It's me who's lucky tonight, Bryn."

Staring into my eyes, Caiden takes my hand and holds it against his scruffy jaw, then brands the inside of my wrist with a searing kiss. My entire body shudders with an aching need. His gaze bores into mine, making me feel transparent. My secret urges and hidden desires, everything is laid bare for him to study, to learn. *To exploit.*

Caiden rises from his bar stool to stand in front of me, then uses a finger to guide my chin up as he slowly leans down. My eyes flutter closed. I feel his warmth and smell the whiskey on his breath as his lips ghost over mine. Air is caged in my lungs as I wait for his kiss.

But it never comes. Instead, his mouth moves to the side and caresses the shell of my right ear as he whispers, "I'm doing my best impression of a gentleman, Beauty, but I can't go another minute without feeling you against me. Come dance."

I nod absently, and seconds later, we're in the middle of the dance floor. We're surrounded by people, and yet, as he pulls me against him and our bodies move with the erotic beat of the music, it's as though we're the only ones in the club. For a high-powered businessman, Caiden dances like Channing Tatum. He takes over and leads, using his hands and body to direct mine until our movements are seamless, like we've done this together a hundred times.

The way he holds me against him makes me feel desired and safe at the same time. It allows me to unplug my brain and give up complete control to him in a way I've never done before.

And it's fucking *euphoric*.

I'm not thinking about bills or job hunting. I'm not worried about having to manage a whole new team that I'll have to retrain and give orders to, day in and day out at an entirely new job.

In this moment, I'm just...*his*.

It's not until now that I realize I've always held leadership roles in my life. Even in school, I was the captain of my debate team and president of the student council. I'm always the one making decisions, executing plans, and telling others what I expect from them or what I want.

Even in the bedroom.

I've never had a man use intuition or read my body language in order to bring me pleasure. Not that there's anything wrong with expressing what you want in the bedroom, but *damn*. It'd be great if I didn't have to for a change.

If I had a man who would simply take control.

I bet Caiden would take control and then some.

That's when I decide, right here and now, that if given the opportunity, I'm going to have mind-blowing sex with the king of Vegas.

Caiden's eyes darken to a rich honey. My thoughts must be written all over my face. His hands splay possessively on my back and pull me closer as he guides a muscular thigh between my legs, giving me the tantalizing friction I crave. The vodka swims faster in my veins, melting the rest of my inhibitions, then setting them on fire for good measure.

I wind my hands around his neck and push my fingers up into his thick hair before curling them into fists. His eyes lower to half-mast and stare intently at my mouth. I drag my bottom lip through my teeth and twist my hips with the music, adding extra pressure when I graze the impressive erection straining between us.

It's too loud in the club to hear it, but I can *feel* his growl as he descends to finally claim my mouth. I open for him immediately, welcoming his tongue to swirl and dominate my own, and Jesus-fuck does he dominate. He kisses me like how I imagine he has sex, with slow and forceful thrusts. It's not hurried or frantic, but there's nothing weak or passive about it, either. It's a controlled power.

One that says, *Lie back and relax and I'll give you more pleasure than you've ever known.*

He's so damn perfect. If I ever decide to settle down and get married, I'd want it to be with a man just like Caiden Verran. Hell, if he proposed right now, I'd say yes.

When we eventually come up for air, chests heaving as we

try to catch our breath, he looks down at me with something like a sense of wonder. And then he smiles.

"I know what we should do next."

I return his smile, butterflies erupting in my belly all over again. "Lead the way."

CHAPTER SIX

BRYN

A distant knocking manages to interrupt my dream of a handsome, dark-haired prince with the body of a god making slow, sensual love to me. I try to ignore the pull of my conscious mind and fall back into the dream, but once I realize someone's at the door of my suite, it's no use.

"Room service," a muffled voice announces.

Groaning, I fight through the thick cotton in my brain and reluctantly roll out of the luxurious king-size bed. I take the sheet with me, since I have no idea where my clothes are, nor do I care in the slightest about that or anything else right now. My head is pounding like I replaced all my blood with vodka, and the sun streaming in through the parted drapes feels like a letter opener is stabbing me in the temples.

Fuck me sideways. I haven't felt this hungover since my Gamma Phi Beta days.

More knocking makes me pick up my pace as I shuffle across the huge room with the black sheet wrapped tightly under my arms. I unlock the door and yank it open to find a young man in a hotel uniform holding a tray of items.

"Room service," he says with a bright smile.

I can only imagine what I must look like. My eyes are squinty because they refuse to let me pry them open any farther, I probably have streaks of makeup in all the wrong places, and I'm afraid to even imagine the tangled state of my hair.

I start to speak, but I sound like Oscar the Grouch, so I clear my throat and try again. "I'm sorry, but I didn't order room service."

"No, ma'am, you didn't *call* for room service. You filled out the request form and hung it outside your door last night." He lifts the tray higher and smiles again. "Coffee and croissants."

My mouth instantly waters. *Thank you, Past Bryn, you fucking gem, you.*

Playing the part, I roll my eyes and feign a recollection I don't have. Because *coffee.* "Oh, that's right! Can't believe I forgot. You can put it right over there, thanks."

He steps into the room and sets the tray on the low table in the small sitting area. After I sign for it and add a generous tip, I hand him the leather folio and walk him back to the entryway. I hold the door open for him, and when he crosses the threshold, he turns to give me a friendly wave. "Please let us know if there's anything else we can do for you. Have a good morning, Mrs. Verran."

I bark out a laugh, then clap a hand over my mouth when he looks at me like I've lost my mind. "I'm sorry, it's just that you called me Mrs. Verran and not Ms. Meara."

Understanding dawns on his face, followed by yet another smile. This guy is *way* too chipper for this hour. Whatever hour that is. "It's okay," he says reassuringly. "You're not the first newlywed to be surprised when she hears her married name for the first time, or even the fifth. I'm sure you'll be used to it soon enough. Bye now."

And then Mr. Chipper walks down the hall, leaving me standing in a sheet in my open doorway, frozen in dread.

No, that's impossible. He's mistaken. Someone saw us together last night, and they made a strange assumption that...

My gaze lands on my left hand where it's braced on the wall, and my squinted eyes finally fly wide open. I release the door and snatch my hand off the wall like it's a hot stove, then slowly—so slowly—move it closer to my face. I mean, I must be seeing things, right? It must be a weird trick of the light or some kind of strange indoor mirage.

I just need to take a closer look, and then I'll find that my hand is exactly the same as it was when I left my room last night.

Except that's not what I find at all.

Because there, at the base of my third finger, is a classically understated platinum band that looks an awful lot like a wedding ring.

"Oh my God," I whisper at my finger. "Bryn Emily Meara, *what did you do*?"

"I'd like to know the same fucking thing."

I jump almost clear out of the sheet at the sudden interruption of a snarling masculine voice. I spin around to a very pissed-off—*very naked*—Caiden Verran. Slapping a hand over my eyes, I squeak in protest. "Jesus, put some clothes on!"

"There're three condom wrappers on the floor. Something tells me we're way past concern for propriety."

Now that I'm fully awake thanks to the adrenaline I just mainlined, I'm noticing details I didn't when my zombie ass rolled out of bed. Like the fact that my body feels sore in places it hasn't since I had a few unremarkable nights with a guy I was dating about a year ago. Which means we definitely had sex last night.

Three times, if the condom wrappers can be believed.

Then I freeze, realizing two things. The first is that I'm not the only one who doesn't remember parts of last night, and I don't know if that's a good or bad thing.

The second is that I'm probably missing at least two condoms from my suitcase—I can't imagine wallets can fit more than one comfortably—which means Caiden knows I traveled to Vegas with an entire box of Trojans, like I was planning some sort of sexcapade during my two-day trip. Awesome. That's not embarrassing at all.

Jesus, I can't believe I had sex multiple times with a man I can only assume is a legendary sex god, and I can't remember even a single minute of it. Shakespeare never wrote anything so tragic!

At least we used the condoms. That alleviates a whole array of other potential tragedies. Hooray for silver linings.

Snapping myself back to the present, I keep my eyes shielded and skirt around him in search of something I can put on.

"You say that, but I think it's the whole tree-in-the-forest thing," I say, "so I'd appreciate you covering up."

That's not technically true. I'd actually appreciate him standing on the coffee table and letting me ogle his perfect naked form until it's time for me to leave for the airport, but my parents raised a good girl. Mostly.

"What tree in the forest?" he asks, clearly frustrated. "What the hell are you talking about?"

"You know, if a tree falls in the forest but no one's around to hear it, does it actually make a sound, that thing." *Jackpot.* The black fluffy bathrobe provided by the hotel is still lying on the chair where I left it, so I quickly pull it on and cinch it tight before dropping the sheet. "In our case, if we can't remember seeing each other naked, are you really past the concerns for propriety?"

His answer is a snarl. "I'm glad you think this is all a joke."

I hear the jingling of his belt as he pulls his suit pants on, and I start to breathe a little easier. Sighing, I turn to face him. "Look, Caiden, I don't know—"

Sweet baby Jesus. So much for breathing easier.

He's still gloriously shirtless, standing there with his feet braced apart and his arms crossed over his muscular chest like some kind of half-dressed white-collar warrior. Dark hair forms a happy trail from his sternum, beneath his arms, down through the valley of his chiseled abs, and below his navel to disappear behind the unbuttoned waist of his pants barely hanging onto his hips.

When I manage to drag my gaze back up to his face, his amber eyes are slicing into me with accusations like daggers. And *that* is what finally knocks some sense into me.

Narrowing my eyes at him in return, I throw my arms out wide. "What the hell is your problem? Why are you looking at me like I stole your dick and fed it to my dog?"

He raises a brow. "Colorful."

"I'm Irish," I snap. "We're a colorful people."

Holding his left hand up, he shows me the same platinum band as mine, only wider, on his finger. "Why am I wearing a ring, Bryn?"

I release a heavy breath, already tired of this conversation, and make my way to the couch where I have hot coffee and flaky croissants waiting to give me a dose of comfort. "Well, either we had such a good time together that we got matching best-friend rings, or..." I pause to pop a buttery piece of heaven into my mouth. "Or we got married."

Caiden growls, snatching his dress shirt off the floor. He glares at me as he stabs his arms into the sleeves. "Obviously we got married. My question is *how*. Did you drug me? Is this some kind of marriage scheme to get money out of me? Because if so, I can guarantee you won't get a fucking dime."

I almost choke. Pressing the back of my hand against my lips to keep from spitting my food onto the table, I stare at him like he just grew a second head. Or third, depending on how you look at it.

"You think I *roofied* you?" I can't decide if I'm more outraged or amused. When all he does is arch an arrogant brow, I decide I'm both and let out a mirthless laugh. "Listen, as funny as that is, I don't remember anything after the nightclub. Which isn't surprising, since I'm pretty sure I drank enough Grey Goose to pickle my liver. But if you'll recall, Mr. Morning-After Asshole, *you* were the one who approached me at the roulette table. *You* were the one who pursued me and asked me to have drinks and go dancing. Ring a bell? I didn't instigate anything with you.

"So if I stashed Rohypnol in my purse on the off chance that the extremely wealthy owner of my hotel would take an interest in me long enough for me to enact some outlandish marriage scheme for tons of money, then honestly? I deserve the Con Woman of the Year Award."

"Fuck." Scrubbing his hands over his face, Caiden sighs heavily and drops onto the oversize chair adjacent to the couch. And because I'm *not* a morning-after asshole, I pour him a mug of coffee and hold it out to him.

He accepts it with a curt nod, which is apparently his version of a thank-you.

He sits back and spins the ring on his finger. "I just don't get it. I've never drank so much that I can't remember what I did."

Thinking back to some of the wilder frat parties in college, I wince. "Wish I could say the same. Though it's been more than five years. Damn martinis," I mutter.

He scoffs, then glances at his watch and swears. "I have to go." He drains the mug of coffee, even though it has to be scalding hot still, then gets up and starts buttoning his shirt with deft fingers.

Suddenly a stream of images flash behind my eyes…

Long fingers trailing light circles on my belly, warm lips pressing kisses on my heated flesh, my body writhing with need, whispered promises, a hot tongue swiping through my arousal…

"Bryn, did you hear me?"

"Huh?" I blink several times and hope my face doesn't look as flushed as it feels. "Sorry, what was that?"

He studies me for several seconds. "Did you remember something?"

You mean you worshipping my body like I have the power to grant you eternal life? Like that kind of something? "Nope," I say, shaking my head. "Not a thing."

Caiden jolts back into action, grabbing his wallet and phone from the nightstand. "My lawyers will start the annulment process. I'll also have them send over an NDA for you to sign, as well as any staff members who had a role in our little mishap. I can't have this getting out and causing a media frenzy."

I can't help but stare at the man with cold eyes and rigid posture and wonder where the man I met last night went. This Caiden Verran isn't anything like the Caiden who called me Beauty, who made me laugh, who looked at me with tenderness and made any excuse to touch me, even a simple brush of our fingers as he handed me a drink.

And if those flashes I got a minute ago were bits of my missing memory, he'd been a gentle and thorough lover, too. Romantic, even. Where did *that* man go?

"Don't worry about me," I say coolly. "I don't make a habit of bragging about things I regret."

His jaw muscles pop, and I notice him absently spinning the ring with his thumb again. Then he opens the door and gives me one last parting remark. "My people will be in touch. Enjoy the remainder of your stay, Bryn."

Giving him a saccharine smile, I don't bother hiding the snark in my tone. "Enjoy your hangover, Caiden."

CHAPTER SEVEN

CAIDEN

"Wheels up in ten, Your Majesty."

"Thanks, Duncan." I nod, dismissing my pilot to go do his thing. I have a meeting this afternoon in Manhattan about opening a Nightfall Hotel (sans casino) in New York, and I'm praying this hangover will be gone by the time we touch down at JFK.

Slipping my sunglasses on to block out as much light as possible, I settle back in the leather chair and close my eyes. What an absolute clusterfuck today has turned out to be. And it's not even noon.

How I went from having an amazing time last night to waking up in a world of hurt and married to a woman I knew for less than twelve hours, I have no fucking clue.

I thought my question about her drugging me was valid—I don't ever let myself get blackout drunk—but as she pointed out, I was the one who pursued her, not the other way around. That's not the only thing that doesn't make sense, though. Even if I was drunk off my ass, I can't see me agreeing to marry anyone, much less a human. The repercussions of something like that are not small.

I'm the fucking king; I don't get to make frivolous, drunken mistakes.

Besides that, it's completely out of character for me. Hell, the whole *night* was out of character for me. I've never taken interest in anyone enough to approach them like I did Bryn, and I can't even begin to explain all the flirting and laughing and *dancing*.

I actually danced in a crowded nightclub like some ordinary fuck-boy. Thank gods I'd had enough sense to use a glamour or there'd be pictures splashed all over TMZ right now.

After the club, it's a complete blank. I don't remember getting married or even which of us suggested it. I don't remember going to her suite or anything that happened to result in three condom wrappers—which had to be hers because I haven't needed to carry one in forever—or the fingernail marks on the backs of my shoulders.

Okay, that's not entirely true.

When she turned to face me with the silk sheet clinging to her breasts, her hair tousled and cheeks flushed, I did remember something.

Hands fisting my hair, soft moans and whispered pleas, raining kisses all over her naked body, sucking the tight bud of a pink nipple deep in my mouth, sliding my cock into the wettest, hottest pussy I've ever felt, pumping in slow, steady thrusts...

The memory wasn't much, but that small glimpse was enough to make my dick react. From *vanilla* sex. I don't do vanilla anything. If that was the entirety of our experiences together, I'm shocked I even got off at all.

None of it makes any damn sense.

The seat next to me creaks with the weight of a large body settling into it. "Damn, CV, you don't look too hot." Conall. He's the only one who uses my initials as a nickname. "Here, drink some water, you could probably use the hydration."

Cracking my eyes open, I see him holding out a cold bottle of water. I take it gratefully and drink the entire contents in one go. Refreshing, but not helpful.

When the rumbling of the jet engines whir to life and the plane starts taxiing toward the runway, I force words through the tightness in my chest. "Where are the other two?"

"In the back. Connor's racked out on a couch and Dad's doing one of his crosswords at the table." I nod. "So, spill. Why do you look like a big pile of shit?"

"Anyone ever tell you you're a real charmer?"

"All the time." He drops the humor and studies me with a keen eye. "Seriously, bro, what's going on?"

"I have a bit of a problem." I release a heavy exhale. "I met up with that woman from the lobby last night. Bryn Meara. A lot of drinks were involved and we…"

Conall lets out a deep chuckle. "You dirty dog. Banging human chicks again with the rest of us peasants, eh? Thought those days were behind you."

"No, we didn't—I mean, we *did*—but that's not the problem."

"I should fucking hope not. Wait, then what *is* the problem?"

The front of the jet lifts as we take off, and my stomach cramps. The change in air pressure as we ascend feels like the oxygen in the cabin is getting sucked out through the vents. I've never had issues flying, never had motion sickness or air sickness or even seasickness. This isn't a hangover. It's like some kind of virus, and it's getting worse with each passing minute. The only problem with that theory is that fae don't get human viruses.

So what the fuck is wrong with me?

I push my sunglasses up and pinch the bridge of my nose, trying to breathe through the feeling of my organs being squeezed in a juicer. A cold sweat breaks out all over my body, and I'm getting light-headed.

"Caiden, you need to cancel the meeting right fucking now."

The concern in Conall's voice jolts me into action. I stand and move past him. "No, I'm fine. I just need to splash some cold water on my face and—"

Someone turns the world on its side, and I go down in the aisle.

"Connor! Dad!"

I try to lift my head off the floor, but it takes too much effort. Through partially open eyes, I can see all three men hovering over me.

Seamus lays a hand on my forehead. "What's wrong with him? How long has he been like this?"

"I don't know, not long. He went from looking hungover to looking like death in a matter of minutes. One second he was telling me about a woman he was with last night and then this."

Seamus's head snaps up. "What woman? Were you with him?"

Connor swears a blue streak. "He dismissed us so we could run. He said he was working late and staying in the penthouse."

"Careless pups," Seamus growls. "I'll deal with you later. Right now, we need to figure out what's wrong with him. Connor, search his phone. See if there's anything in there to give us an idea of what he did last night and who he was with."

My tongue is thick in my mouth, but I manage to eke out a word on a pained groan. "Bryn..."

"Bryn Meara. That's what he said her name was. They had drinks and then spent the night together."

Seamus's eyes lock onto something at the base of my throat that causes his thick brows to knit in confusion, or maybe concern. Without warning, he rips my shirt open, and all three Woulfes let out a chorus of curses.

I lower my gaze to where they're staring and manage a hoarse "fuck" of my own.

Just beneath my skin is a web of thin black lines emanating

from the center of my chest. They look like poisoned veins growing in length and stretching in all directions. Conall notices the silver chain around my neck and pulls it out from underneath me and over my head. Letting it hang from his hand, the platinum ring swinging at the bottom is like a pendulum of doom.

Don't ask me why I put the wedding band on a chain around my neck instead of in a junk drawer somewhere. I can only plead temporary insanity.

"Caiden, that problem you mentioned," Conall says, "did it have anything to do with this?"

I manage to nod once. The fact that I can't just tell Seamus everything myself is frustrating as hell. Clenching my teeth, I force one last detail past my lips. "Married...her..."

Seamus's eyes widen. "Is she Dark Fae?"

"No, Connor and I both saw her. She's human."

"Well, it wasn't a human wedding," Connor says, holding out my phone to show a picture on the screen. "That's Gilda, the High Priestess, performing the Dark marriage ritual."

"Dear gods," Seamus whispers. Then he barks his orders. "Tell Duncan we need to get back to Vegas as quickly as possible. If Caiden gets much farther away, his body will start shutting down. And call Tiernan and Finnian. Tell them to get the girl and all her belongings and hold her at the manor. She won't be leaving until we can figure out who she is and what she wants."

Gravity finally prevails over my weakening body, and I go completely limp. I'm vaguely aware of being moved to the bedroom and cool cloths swabbing over my forehead and chest, but nothing helps to cool the fire consuming me from the inside out.

The pain is excruciating, and I start wishing for the one thing I've never wished for in my life: death.

CHAPTER EIGHT

BRYN

Well, this trip turned out vastly different than I anticipated. Not that I had a whole lot of expectations for a spur-of-the-moment weekend vacation by myself to a place I've never been. But I certainly didn't plan on meeting and marrying a multimillionaire within the first twenty-four hours.

Lying out by the pool, I soak up the desert sun in the royal-blue bikini I bought in the gift shop and people watch while playing with the ring on my finger. It's a nice damn ring, so I don't see why I should take it off before I have to. Plus, it's keeping the single guys trolling for easy targets at bay, which is a nice bonus.

A trio of women passes in front of me, laughing together as they make their way back from the bar with fresh drinks, and a sudden pang of loneliness pierces my chest.

It didn't bother me to travel here alone. As an only child, I learned how to entertain myself. And though I'm on friendly terms with everyone I meet, I've never had any ride-or-die girlfriends, so I've been pretty much a solo act my whole life.

I never minded, though, because I was extremely close

with my parents. Jack and Emily Meara were young when they started our little family, so they didn't have a hard time relating to me like a lot of older parents did. We had fun together, the three of us. I was never lonely because I always had them.

Until the car accident three years ago. Since that day, I've learned what it feels like to be truly alone. Admittedly, I'm good at using my work as a distraction, which is why I want to find another job as soon as possible once I get home.

Most days, I'm fine. But a day like today, it would be nice to have a girlfriend or even a mother figure to talk to. Anyone to listen to my wild story, then validate my feelings that Caiden Verran has a giant dick. I mean, *is* a giant dick.

Groaning, I drop my face into my hands and try to scrub the image of his glorious body—including the part that describes his true personality—from my mind.

The word of the day is: FORGET. *Forget* that a mega-hottie Prince Charming picked me up in the casino last night. *Forget* that he had me falling for him inside of an hour. *Forget* that I drank my weight in vodka and somehow ended up married to said mega-hottie and then had what I can only assume was a marathon of mind-blowing sex. And definitely *forget* that the Prince Charming turned into a hideous frog the following morning.

Yep, that's what I'm going to do. Forget the last twenty-four hours and focus on making the rest of my stay here awesome. Just me, the sun, a good book, and—

"Excuse me, are you Bryn Meara?"

I stare up to see who's blocked my sun, and my mouth drops open.

Two men are standing next to my chaise, but these aren't any ordinary men. Each of them is strikingly handsome, though in different ways. The one who spoke is wearing a white polo and pressed khaki pants over an obviously very fit and toned body. His hair is more of a dark brown but could look black in the right lighting, and his strong jaw is clean-shaven, showing off a sexy dimple in his chin. He's also smiling down at me.

The other one is *not*.

I think the one giving me the stink eye is even more gorgeous than the charmer. He's *huge*. Like, the size of a mountain huge. Maybe he's a professional football player? He certainly has the build and muscles for it, and it fits with his look, which is black athletic pants and a red sleeveless T-shirt that's stretched tightly across his chest and showcases the best arm porn I've seen in real life. He has swarthy dark features: black hair shaved close on the sides and longer on top, flawless tanned skin, and a neatly trimmed shadow beard surrounding full lips.

I'd bet my wedding ring that these are Caiden's brothers.

He told me stories about the three of them together when they were younger. Maybe they know about the wedding and are here to warn me off their brother.

Done and done, my guys.

"My name is Tiernan and this is Finn. We're Caiden's brothers."

I smile politely but decide not to verify one way or another I know what they're talking about. "Can I help you?"

The grouchy one—Finn—bites out a reply. "You can if your name is Bryn Meara."

Smiley shoots Grouchy a look, then turns back to me. "What my ill-mannered brother is trying to say is that Caiden is back at our manor and your presence has been requested. We're here to escort you."

"Ah, I see." I actually don't see at all. Caiden made it perfectly clear I'd be dealing with his attorney and wouldn't see him for the remainder of my trip, so I don't get why he suddenly wants me at his house. "Well, you can tell your *other* ill-mannered brother that I'm more than happy with my accommodations at his lovely hotel. His request has been declined."

I rest my head back and close my eyes, but they don't take the hint. I'm getting aggravated now. All I want is to relax and soak up some vitamin D. That's what I came out here for. And it's being ruined by one Verran brother after another.

"Bryn, I know Caiden can be a boorish ass." The apology in Tiernan's voice has me curious enough to open my eyes again as he lowers himself to sit on his haunches. "And those are usually his good days, so I can only imagine how he acted when he woke up to realize he was married with no memory of it."

"*Boorish ass* is putting it mildly."

Tiernan chuffs a laugh. "I'm not surprised. But that's not who he is at heart. Underneath all the gruffness, Caiden's a really decent guy. Once he was able to get some...*distance* from the situation, it pained him greatly. Now, he very much wants you to come to the manor to rectify the situation."

I narrow my eyes. "If he wants me to come so much, then why did he send you two like a couple of errand boys? Why not come himself?"

"Unfortunately, he's currently indisposed. He had an important meeting scheduled with some big New York investors this afternoon. Plus, between you and me and the giant behind me, I think he's probably afraid you won't want to come. Our brother is tough on the outside, but his ego is more fragile than a butterfly wing."

Finn snorts. "I'm so telling him you said that."

I grin wickedly. "Not if I tell him first."

Tiernan arches a surprised brow while a half grin transforms Finn into a boyish Adonis. Then he says the first semi-nice thing since arriving. "Okay, I kinda like her."

"Well, you won't get a chance to tell him anything unless you come with us," Tiernan continues. "So, what do you say,

Bryn? Will you put Caiden out of his misery and come to the manor?"

I chew on my lip while I think. "He really and truly feels bad?"

Both of their expressions turn sober. Tiernan holds my gaze for a few seconds before saying, "I can honestly say that he's never felt worse in his whole life."

While I think he's waxing hyperbolic, it's a testament to how close they all are that they're this bothered by Caiden feeling badly for acting like an ass. It makes me want to go just so I can help ease their worry for their brother. But if I'm being honest, there's a part of me that wants to see Caiden again. Especially if I'm getting an apology.

Maybe we can even put everything behind us and remain friends. And one day we'll look back and laugh about the night a Vegas king met a Vegas virgin and they did the most stereotypical Vegas thing ever.

Sighing, I sit up and swing my legs over the side of the chaise. "Okay, I'll go. Let me grab my things real quick."

Tiernan stands and takes my hand to help me rise. "That's not necessary. We'll have one of our staff members collect your belongings and deliver them to the manor." When I just stare at him, he adds, "We're on a bit of a time crunch. I need to get back for a meeting with our security team, and I'm sure Finn's overdue to get his muscles oiled."

Finn grimaces and flips the smiling Tiernan off, making me laugh.

I like the dynamic they have and think it would be fun to watch them interact, especially with Caiden. Would he be the guy I met last night, this morning, or a mix of the two?

There's only one way to find out.

Wrapping my sheer white sarong around my hips, I step into my sandals and give a nod. "Okay, let's go. We don't want Finn's muscles getting dry."

This time, Tiernan laughs, and Finn slits his gaze at me. "I take back what I said earlier."

They escort me back through Nightfall and out the main entrance, where a midnight-blue Range Rover is waiting.

Finn drives while Tiernan takes the passenger seat, and I slide into the back. Finn turns the radio up to a level that makes talking awkward, so I sit quietly and enjoy the view as we drive away from the main strip.

The farther we go, the more affluent the neighborhoods become. I expected that, considering I'm going to the residence of the man who owns most of Vegas. But I couldn't have dreamed up the kind of luxury presented in such massive scale as the houses we're approaching now.

My eyes are wide and mouth agape as I take in the rear view of one situated on a short cliff of desert rock. It has a very modern style with multiple swooping arcs for a roof, large square pillars around the outside living areas, and clean lines throughout. An infinity pool spills over a wall of shiny black tiles.

If that wasn't impressive enough, four streams of water shoot up from the ground in front of the infinity wall to land in the pool, and five more stream down from an overhang on the other side from the second level. Walls of glass make up the entire back of the house.

It reminds me of a dollhouse when you open it up and can see inside every room. Only the dolls who live there are apparently richer than God.

"Damn," I say in awe. "I wonder who lives there."

I didn't notice that the radio was turned down until Tiernan answers me. "We do."

When I get over my shock, I say wryly, "What, no helipad?"

"Don't need one." He looks back at me over his shoulder and smirks. "We have a private jet."

I roll my eyes. "Of course you do."

Finn parks in a garage so clean, you could eat off the floor. There are three other vehicles I don't know the names of but can guess at their ridiculous costs based on looks alone. The guys usher me through a door and into the house. We walk down a short hall that leads to the main living space, which is an underwhelming term for what it is. There are hundreds of details to take in, but I don't get to appreciate any of them.

"This way," Finn says, taking me by the arm and guiding me up a flight of stairs.

Wide, thin stairs that are lit up from the inside with blue lights like something out of the future. I get the impression that nothing in this place is normal or plain. But again, I'm not getting the chance to find out.

"Where are we going?" I peer behind me where Tiernan is trailing after us, looking to him for answers, since he seems to be the more reasonable brother.

He gives me a tight smile. "We're taking you to the room where you'll be staying. You can relax in there until Caiden's ready for you."

We reach the second floor, and I have a few seconds to appreciate the pale marble floors, glass railings surrounding the two-story entry with enormous chandelier, and the phenomenal view of the Strip from the wall of windows I saw as we drove up. But Finn is walking me around the chandelier toward the front of the house, where he opens a door to a bedroom and deposits me on the king bed.

My brows knit together. "Why can't I wait for Caiden by the pool?"

Finn stares at me for a moment with what appears to be regret in his eyes. Then he turns abruptly and walks out the door. Tiernan points to things around the room like he's a real-estate agent trying to make a sale.

"There's a gas fireplace and TV with every streaming channel you can think of, plus a hard drive with thousands of movies. Some books on the shelves you might enjoy, as well. Over here is a stocked mini fridge, and we filled that cabinet there with pantry items and paper products like plates and napkins, that sort of thing. There's an en suite bathroom with standing shower and Japanese soaking tub, which you absolutely must try, it's amazing. And I'll have Madoc run your suitcase up to you when he arrives. As you can see, you'll be plenty comfortable here during your stay."

I push to my feet and fist my hands at my sides. "Tiernan, what the hell? Why does it sound like you're leaving me in here indefinitely?"

He moves to the doorway, one hand on the knob as he offers me a sad smile. "Not indefinitely, Bryn. Only until Caiden's health returns and we figure out a way to reverse the damaging effects from your wedding. For what it's worth, I am sorry for the inconvenience."

"What? What do you mean his health? And what damaging effects?"

Stepping out into the hallway, Tiernan shuts the door. Then I hear the sound of a dead bolt being thrown. *From the outside.*

I race over and try the handle, but it's completely ineffectual. I bang on the door with my fists and shout for someone to help me, but no one answers.

The large window is a single pane of glass that looks like it moves on a track electronically. Even if I attempted to break it, I'm too high up to escape without breaking both my legs or more.

I'm officially trapped.

The prisoner of three extremely wealthy and unbelievably sexy brothers. Somewhere, there's a romance reader swooning at the very idea. But I'm no romance heroine, and I have no idea what the hell is going on.

This dream trip just turned into a nightmare real fucking quick.

CHAPTER NINE

CAIDEN

It's not quite seven in the morning on the day Bryn is due to fly home. But she won't be leaving Vegas today. She won't even be leaving my house. Not until I figure out how to sever this tie to her that almost killed me when I was thirty thousand feet in the air.

The minute Tiernan and Finn arrived with her, I *felt* it.

The steel band squeezing my chest and crushing my ribs began to loosen. Breathing became easier, and my heart started a slow descent into a normal range. It took all night for my body to completely repair the damage, but it worked.

Thanks to Seamus's realization of what was happening and quick actions, I survived.

Sitting in her room, I study her as she sleeps and toy with the ring I'm still wearing around my neck for only gods know why. I realize watching her sleep is a bit stalkerish, but I can't help myself. Something about her draws me to her.

As soon as I woke up this morning, I showered, threw on a pair of jeans and a black Henley, and sought her out. The top item on today's to-do list is getting to the bottom of this entire situation, and I had every intention of waking her ass up to do just that.

Then I walked into the room and saw her.

Everything inside me shifted. Like it was creating space for her to stake her claim, to plant roots so deep, I'll be unable to dig her out even if I wanted to. The bitch of it is, I *don't* want to. I don't understand what this hold is that she has over me.

It's disconcerting at best. Fucking terrifying at worst. I should be running in the other goddamned direction from this woman.

Figuratively speaking, of course, because physically I can't be much farther than the twelve thousand square feet the manor allows us. But I already know that staying away from her will feel…unnatural. Wrong.

I use my fae senses, searching for something about Bryn that reads as *other*. But her scent, her energy, her appearance, everything says she's human. Seamus, whose senses are vastly stronger due to his age, said the same thing. He doesn't detect anything odd or off about her.

So how in Rhiannon's name did the marriage curse get activated? It only happens with a true mating of Dark Fae to Dark Fae, and it's the same for the Light. There shouldn't be any magical consequences or repercussions if a king marries a human.

She's an anomaly, my Bryn Meara.

She's not yours, Verran. She's a temporary problem that needs solving. End of story.

Setting an elbow on the arm of the chair, I rest my head in the cradle of my thumb and forefinger and study her, still absently toying with the ring in my other hand. She's lying on top of the covers, wearing the blue bikini and sheer sarong my brothers said she arrived in. I have to wonder if she fell asleep like that by accident or if she refused to indulge in the comfort of the bed as part of her silent protest.

There's nothing in here or the bathroom that indicates

she's had anything to eat or drink. Knowing she's denied herself basic needs churns like acid in my gut. I want to punish her for not taking care of herself. To put her over my knee and spank her tight, round ass until it's cherry red. That's the last time she'll get away with it, even if I have to feed her myself.

Bryn stirs in her sleep, rolling onto her back. If I thought the view of her ass was amazing, the one of her full breasts cupped by the triangular scraps of material is breathtaking. Long blond hair fans over the pillow like it was waving in the wind when time froze. Sable-brown eyelashes rest on her high cheekbones, and her pink lips part slightly with her deep and even breaths.

My heated gaze travels lower. Over her breasts and down the flat expanse of her smooth belly. She has a silver bar in her navel with a clear cubic zirconia stud in the shape of a sun on top and dangling crescent moon outlined in CZs on the bottom.

It's fucking sexy as hell, and it makes me want to dip my tongue into her belly button and tug on the piercing with my teeth.

Just as I'm about to go down a very dirty path in my mind that will cause my jeans to get extremely uncomfortable, I notice her left hand resting on her lower stomach, and all thoughts grind to a halt.

She's still wearing the wedding band.

A mix of emotions flows through me. Pride, relief, shock, frustration. I clench my fist around my own ring, feeling the smooth edge of the metal bite into the meat of my palm.

I don't know how to reconcile any of my feelings, and it only serves to put me in a pissy mood.

Tucking the chain and ring under my shirt, I extend a leg and use my foot to jostle the mattress. "Rise and shine, Sleeping Beauty. It's time we have a chat."

Bryn does that morning-stretch thing where she reaches her

arms above her head and arches her back. Her bikini top shifts and one of her breasts threatens to spill out. Forcing myself to look away, I get up and face the window that looks out onto the circular driveway and front of the property. The award-winning views are on the other side of the manor, but those rooms all have a wall of solid glass that opens electronically onto the outdoor living spaces. My brothers were worried she might start throwing chairs around in an attempt to break out, so they thought it was safer to put her over here.

"Well, look who it is. My kidnapper," she says, her voice husky from sleep.

I turn to face her and stop cold. Even rumpled and furious, she takes my breath away. She's like the sun with her pale hair and golden skin.

I keep expecting her shine to wear off. But every time I see her, I'm stunned all over again.

Hiding my thoughts behind a droll look, I cross my arms over my chest and meet her glare for glare. "I'm hardly a kidnapper."

"Oh, right, you couldn't be bothered to do the dirty work. You're my kidnappers' boss."

"Bryn," I say in warning.

"Prison warden? Sorry, I'm not sure which kind of asshole you identify as, but I'm fairly progressive, so just let me know and I'll be sure to use the proper term."

"Let's start with you telling me who you are and why you came to Vegas."

She crosses one long leg over the other, then folds her arms defiantly under her breasts. Damn it, why is she still wearing that fucking swimsuit?

"Why didn't you change into normal clothes or pajamas for fuck's sake?" I ask.

Fire shoots from her hazel eyes. "Gee, that would've been nice. If only someone had brought my things as promised."

I look around and sigh. The Night Watchers are phenomenal guards, but they're shit butlers. "I'll send your things up as soon as we're done talking."

"You can get them now because I'm not talking to you. I want my things and an Uber to the airport. Then I hope to never hear from or see you again."

"Not happening, I'm afraid. You'll be my guest for the foreseeable future until I can figure out our problem."

Her frustration visibly mounts, her volume rising with every sentence she bites out. "*What* problem? So we had a drunken quickie wedding in Vegas, big fucking deal. We just get it annulled like everyone else and move on with our lives."

"I'm afraid it's not that simple with us. Something... happened after we got married."

"I believe we established that with the physical evidence we left on the floor. I still don't see how that translates to me being held prisoner in your house."

I clench my jaw and exhale slowly through my nose, trying to keep my temper from getting the best of me. This is an impossible fucking situation. Seamus warned me against telling her the truth because she could use that information with malice. That doesn't worry me, though. Even if she did manage to escape, she wouldn't make it far before Connor and Conall tracked her down. Any harm done to me would be minimal before she was dragged back to the manor.

I'm more worried about her knowing too much about us. About letting her into the inner circle of our world when we go to great lengths to keep our secrets, or at least ensure they're considered fiction. A human with so much fae knowledge who's released back into the wild, for lack of a better term, is a danger to my people and our way of life.

If I can find a conjurer, they'd be able to spell her memories and wipe out anything involving fae once this is over. But fae who can conjure are extremely rare, and they almost never advertise their abilities, so they're even harder to find. *Fuck*.

"Bryn, I need you to answer my questions. Who are you and why did you come to Vegas?"

"I already told you all this the night we were talking at the bar."

"Humor me."

Huffing out a breath, she pushes to her feet and begins pacing the room. "My name is Bryn Meara. I'm a PR specialist, but I'm between jobs right now, so I thought it was the perfect time for a quick weekend getaway to decompress before starting my job hunt next week. I planned on lying by the pool, eating great food, and exploring the hotels. That's it!"

"That *can't* be it, Bryn." My own frustration is starting to leak through the cracks in my control. "Why is it that I'm drawn to you like metal to a goddamn magnet? What is it about you that makes me act out of character, turning me into some kind of charming, romantic robot?"

She stops pacing and arches a brow at me. "Is that what I'm doing to you right now? Then your definitions of 'charming' and 'romantic' are a far cry from mine."

Taking a deep breath, I let it out slowly. "Not now. *Then*. The night we were together. I was acting...differently...than normal."

Throwing her hands up, she coats her words in thick sarcasm. "Ah, now it all makes sense! You were a nice guy for *one goddamn night*, so naturally, it must be *my* fault. Like I put some sort of hex on you that made you act like a decent human being. Wow, I hope you hear how ridiculous you sound. Congratulations, because you take gaslighting to a *whole new level*."

Grunting in aggravation, I rake a hand through my hair and turn to look out the window, trying to keep my shit together. This is getting us nowhere. Either she honestly has no idea what the hell she did, or she's a phenomenal fucking actress.

"Goddamn it, Verran, look at me when I'm talking to you!"

She throws her sandal at me, barely missing my head as it smacks against the window, and it snaps the thin tether on my control. Growling, I spin to face her and drop the glamour that masks my fae qualities, allowing her to see me as I truly am, fangs and all, for the first time. "Do something like that again and I'll spank your ass until it's numb."

Bryn gasps and scrambles backward onto the bed until she hits the headboard, but I don't give her time to acclimate to the shock.

"You want the truth so badly, Bryn? Here it is. I'm not a 'decent human being' because I'm *not human*. I am King of the Dark Fae of the Faerie Night Court. Something happened when you and I married two nights ago. Something that tied us together, not only as husband and wife but as *true mates*. Incidentally, there's only one way that can happen, and that's if the female I marry is also of Dark Fae blood. So, *again*, I have to ask. Who. Are. You?"

I stand firm at the foot of the bed, hands fisted at my sides and chest heaving with the indignation rolling through me. She stares at me, eyes wide as her mind works so hard, I can practically see the wheels spinning, trying to make logic of the illogical.

Then she does the unexpected.

She laughs.

"Oh my God, you almost had me." Her hand slaps over her heart as though forcing it back from where it tried leaping through her rib cage a few seconds ago. "I get it now. You're in a LARPing troupe, your faction or whatever is that Night Court you mentioned, and this is like a side quest or something. Right?" She laughs again, her relief as irritating as it is endearing. "Wow, you guys really take this stuff seriously, but I can respect that. Besides the part where you scared the shit out of me anyway. Are those contacts and custom caps?

They look really—"

She squeals when I grab her ankles and yank her down to the end of the bed where I loom over her, my hands on either side of her head. I lean in until her back is flush on the mattress with our faces mere inches apart. "Do these look like contacts and caps to you?"

I recognize the moment she realizes there's no telltale ring for lenses in my eyes. Then she drops her gaze to my mouth. Knowing she's studying my fangs makes them ache with the desire to be put to use.

Trailing a finger down the length of her neck, I say, "If you need proof of their authenticity, I'd be happy to oblige." The quiet, sharp inhale makes my cock jerk behind my zipper. "Would you like me to bite you, Beauty? Would that excite you?"

"No," she rasps.

The pulse in her neck flutters under my touch, and her pupils are dilating. I flick my eyes down to see her nipples furled and poking against her bikini top, and more than that, I scent the arousal between her legs.

Smiling wickedly, I press my cheek to hers and whisper into her ear. "Liar."

Abruptly, I push up and step away from the bed, changing the tone of our interaction to keep her off-balance. I don't want her getting too comfortable with me. I need to maintain distance between us while Seamus and I figure out how to fix this fucking mess, and we need to do it before word gets out.

She sits up again and is back to glaring at me. Good. I prefer the anger. Though I can still see an underlying sense of trepidation. She's not as confident as she wants to appear.

And now I have the irrational need to wrap her in my arms and offer her comfort. *Damn it.*

"I don't care how authentic you look—there's no way what you're telling me is true. That you're a faerie king and we somehow mated or bonded or whatever? And you know this based on what exactly? Because I sure as hell don't feel any different. If anything, *you* are the liar here."

I chuckle mirthlessly. "Ironically enough, lying is the one thing I *can't* do. Fae can't outright lie, no matter how much we want to. It's physically impossible."

I know I probably shouldn't have told her that, but fuck it. I need this woman to believe me if it's the fastest route to getting her to accept her situation here. I won't mention our use of wording loopholes and fae truths.

It's best she knows as few of our secrets as we can manage.

"Okay, good. Not that I believe you—or any of this—but let's test it out, shall we? Why did you come to me in the casino that night?"

"I told you, I don't know. I've never pursued a guest at Nightfall before, and I haven't slept with a human in seventeen years."

Her mouth drops open. "You didn't have sex for— How is that possible? You're not old enough to have had a seventeen-year dry spell. Unless you're telling me you were a vir—"

"Bryn, before you insult me with that statement, I said I hadn't slept with a *human* in that long, which is when I became king. And for the record, I'm a lot older than you think."

"How old?"

"It's irrelevant."

"Ha! You just lied."

"No, I said the answer is irrelevant, and it is. You don't need to know my age." Crossing my arms, I say, "You get one more question for now."

Bryn glares at me, like she's daring me to do or not do something with her eyes. "Why do I have to stay here, at your house, or even in Vegas? Why can't I fly home while you figure out all this mate bond stuff and let me know how it turns out?"

My jaw muscles work as I clench my teeth. I'm damned if I

do and damned if I don't on this one. I wish I could be honest with her. In the end, I have to choose what's best for my role as king. "I can't give you specifics. Only that I need you here until we can figure out how to undo what's been done."

She scoffs. "How convenient for you. And just how long is that going to be?"

If this truly is the marriage curse, then we're fucked. Since the day of our exile, both courts have searched for a way to break the curses Aine cast on us with no success. Even if we're the lucky ones to figure it out, it could take decades. "I honestly don't know. Could be weeks or months. Maybe longer."

"*Longer?* You intend to keep me here, with *you*, for possibly *years*? No fucking way, not happening. Not on your life, buddy."

That's exactly what it's on.

Ire bubbles over inside me and spills out from every pore, every cell. I don't like it when things are out of my control, and everything I try to grab hold of right now is slipping through my fingers.

Deep down, I know her behavior is normal—she *should* be fighting me on this—but on top of all the other shit I have on my plate, her provocation is the match to my fuse.

"Allow me to recap the situation for you so you'll fully understand. When we got married, we were somehow mated as only fae can be, yet you appear to be human. I still think I was drugged that night, and I haven't ruled you out as a suspect. You're to stay here on my property as my guest—"

"*Prisoner.*"

"Until such time as I know how to undo whatever the fuck you did. Don't bother trying to escape—there are guards surrounding the property twenty-four-seven because, as I may have mentioned, I'm a goddamn king."

She gives me a sarcastic smile that clearly says she'd like to knee me right in my kingly jewels. Damn but her brazenness makes me want to pin her to the bed and earn her submission with every moan I coax from her smart mouth. I bet she begs like a wet dream.

Keep it in your fucking pants, Verran.

Ignoring the ache in my balls, I press on. "You'll have free run of the house soon, but I need to do some things first. Fiona is my housekeeper. She'll be up to get you additional clothes for your wardrobe until we can arrange for a boutique to bring a selection here to you. She'll also make sure you're fed. No more of this starving-in-protest bullshit. You're not falling ill on my watch, so don't test me. Any questions?"

She scoffs and folds her arms under her chest. "About a million, but I'd rather eat glass than talk to you anymore, so you're free to go."

I smirk as I step in close, towering above her slight frame. "I don't take orders from anyone, Bryn. I told you: I'm the king. I give the orders, and everyone obeys. Including you."

Tilting her head up, she holds my gaze, defiance shining in her green-and-gold eyes. "I wouldn't hold your breath waiting for me to get in line, *Your Majesty*. It'll be a cold day in hell before I fall on my knees before you."

And now I don't think I've ever wanted anything fucking more. Bryn kneeling at my command. The need is like iron burning a hole through the center of my chest. But I'll be damned if I give in to it. "Don't worry, I won't ever ask that of you."

She lifts her chin confidently. "Because you know it would never happen."

"Because I know how you like your lovers. Gentle, tender. *Safe*. I'm none of those things. You couldn't handle kneeling for me, Bryn. It's as simple as that." Then, before I can think better of it, I press a soft kiss to her forehead, as though proving to her—and *myself*—that I'll never give in to my baser desires for her, regardless of what either of us wants. "Fiona will be by soon to help you settle in."

Without waiting for her response, I stride out of the room, pull the door shut behind me, and lock it from the outside again. I hear her growl right before there's a loud thud of something hitting the door.

At least it wasn't fragile. I don't want to have to worry about her cutting herself on broken glass.

Walking away from her shouted complaints and creative threats to my manhood, I make a mental list of things to give to Seamus in preparation for her extended stay.

But first, I need a cold fucking shower.

CHAPTER TEN

BRYN

After Caiden left my room, I decided a hot shower would help to relieve the tension in my muscles and, if I was really lucky, calm the frantic thoughts buzzing around in my head like an angry swarm of hornets.

Easier said than done when I've just learned that a magical race exists, and I managed to accidentally marry—or bond or mate or whatever the hell he said—their king. I don't even want to think about what that makes *me*.

Swiping my hand across the steam-fogged mirror, I have serious words with the woman staring back at me. *It doesn't make you anything because he doesn't want anything to do with you.*

Ouch. I don't know why knowing that stings so badly.

Holding up my left hand, I take in the simple wedding band adorning my finger. I should return it; it's the right thing to do. But it's my only proof that our one great night together wasn't a dream, and the thought of giving it up turns my stomach.

Slipping it off, I decide to put it in a safe place where it could eventually be found after I get out of here. Until then, it'll still be close to me.

I lift the lid on a small porcelain bowl sitting on the bathroom counter to find a supply of cotton balls. I set the ring on the pillowy bed and replace the lid, ignoring the pang in my chest when I can no longer see it.

I shake my head on a sigh. *Don't be so dramatic, Bryn.*

It's not like I want to be married to a man I barely know. A single good night isn't a qualified basis for a long-term relationship, much less a lifelong one. And if whatever he needs to figure out about our situation takes as long as he expects, that's exactly what it might be if I don't find a way out of here.

Which I *will.*

It might not be today or tomorrow or even next week, but eventually an opportunity will present itself, and I won't hesitate to grab onto it with both fucking hands. I just have to keep my eyes and ears open and bide my time.

Until then, my prison could be a lot worse. The shower has twelve different jets that hit my body from every angle and a control panel that allowed me to change the pressure, spray type, and even the lighting.

All in all, it didn't suck.

Wrapped in a robe I found hanging in the bathroom, I towel-dry my hair as I walk back into the bedroom. My eyes land on my suitcase and purse sitting on the bed that must have been brought in while I was in the locked bathroom.

Rushing over, I unzip my suitcase and flip it open. I never thought I'd be so excited to see my own clothes and toiletries.

My hands dig through the articles and different pockets, taking inventory, then do the same with my purse. It's all there, including the silver Celtic knot cuff link that Mom gave to Dad for their anniversary. He was wearing them the night of the accident, but only one was ever found and returned to me. I never go anywhere without it.

There is one item missing, but I'm not surprised. It would

be pretty careless of them if they hadn't confiscated my cell phone. Although I don't know what good it would've done me. I don't have anyone to call for help except the police, and something tells me the Verrans have enough money—or magical faerie dust, hell if I know—to make them look the other way.

I'm glad I locked the bathroom door now that I know someone was in here. I wonder who dropped my stuff off. My gaze travels from my belongings to the door.

There's no chance they were careless enough to leave it unlocked, right? The odds of that are probably zilch.

Then again, maybe I still have some of that horseshoe luck left over.

Unable to wait to find out, I pad quietly across the room and try twisting the handle…and *it works*.

My heart starts to pound as it turns all the way and I'm able to ease it open the tiniest crack. I stop and listen for any sounds that indicate someone's standing guard.

Nothing but silence.

Telling myself not to get too excited, I decide I'll do a quick peek into the hall to get my bearings and make sure the coast is clear. Then I'll come back in, throw on some clothes, and make a very stealthy break for it. Fingers crossed Caiden was either bluffing about all the guards posted on the property or they haven't had time to beef up their numbers yet.

Come to think of it, I didn't see a single one when we drove here, so I bet he's full of shit.

More confident in my plan now, I pull the door open and— "Oh my God!"

A wolf with rust-red fur jumps to his feet from where he was lounging in the hallway outside my room. Bright golden eyes freeze me in place. He growls low in his throat, lips peeled back from deadly sharp teeth.

What. The actual. Fuck. This can't be a normal wolf; he's

huge. As in, his massive head comes up to my *waist* kind of huge.

"Niiiiiiice wolfy. Please don't eat me." I hold my hands up and start to retreat with painfully slow steps. If I can make it to the bathroom, I can lock myself in until someone comes, but at this rate it'll take me a week to even get there.

"Connor, you mangy mutt, knock it off." A pretty girl about my age with long, flowing red hair comes around the corner and uses a hand to shove at the wolf's muzzle. I think my heart might stop as I wait for him to lunge for her throat, but he just glares at her. Fisting her hands on her hips, she says, "Don't give me that look. If you scare her to death, he'll make you into a new fur blanket for his bed."

The wolf chuffs—and I might be out of my mind at this point, but it sounds like a legit laugh—then rubs the top of his head on her hip for a quick scratch behind the ear.

"All right, all right. Go do a perimeter check or whatever it is you do. I've got things from here."

As he pads off down the hall, the girl enters my room and closes the door. Willing my heart to stop racing like a jackrabbit, I push my hands through my damp hair and take a few calming breaths.

Studying me, she frowns. "I'm sorry he scared you. He's really a big marshmallow once you get to know him. And despite the aggro display just now, he would never hurt you. He knows the consequences could be fatal."

Fatal for whom, exactly? Me because I might not survive? The wolf because he attacked Caiden's "guest"?

I suppose I'll just add it to my ever-growing list of unanswered WTF questions.

Before I can attempt to decipher that cryptic tidbit, she adds, "My name is Fiona, by the way. I'm the housekeeper here at Midnight Manor."

Fiona. So this is who Caiden sent to "help" me.

Wearing black leggings and an oversize T-shirt that hangs off one shoulder, she has that natural, fresh-faced beauty you see in commercials for facial cleansers. When he mentioned that Fiona was his housekeeper, I didn't know what to expect, being that this is the home of a fae king and likely everyone in it is something other than human.

At this point I wouldn't have been surprised if she turned out to be a grandmotherly teapot with a British accent and penchant for randomly breaking into song.

Her warm smile makes her golden eyes twinkle, and the tips of fangs peek out from between her lips. "It's great to finally meet you, Ms. Meara. You've been the talk of the manor this weekend."

She holds out a hand in welcome. I give it a discreet once-over, checking for I don't even know what—scales, claws, a joke buzzer tucked into her palm—but it appears no different than mine. And maybe I'm too tired to be wary of her or logic is telling me that if I'm not afraid of Caiden, there's no reason to be afraid of his housekeeper, but Fiona seems pretty harmless as far as co-captors go.

"Thanks, I think." I shake her hand, then blow out a heavy breath as I sit on the edge of the bed. "And you can call me Bryn."

"Bryn it is," she says, clearly pleased to drop the formalities. "I stopped in to make sure you're settled and see if there's anything you need."

"A way out of here would be great."

Her expression softens with an unspoken apology. "Anything but that, I'm afraid."

"Figured as much," I mutter. "Then I guess my second choice would be some company."

"Now *that* I can do."

Crossing the room, Fiona takes a seat in the chair I found Caiden in this morning and gets comfortable as though we're simply besties hanging out on a lazy Sunday afternoon. I suppose it's not that hard to pretend for my sanity's sake. Her whole aura radiates warmth and kindness, putting me at ease. Or maybe she's working some kind of faerie calming magic.

Honestly, at this point I don't even care. It's just nice to be in the presence of someone other than the three overbearing men I've dealt with recently. Not to mention the giant, furry sentry I met a few minutes ago.

"You know," I start, "I've heard of rich people keeping guard dogs, but a roided-out wolf seems a tad excessive. And illegal."

Fiona laughs, the sound light and airy, like a petal floating on the breeze. "Connor's not the kind of wolf you're referring to. He and his twin brother, Conall, are wolf shifters, a rare bloodline among the fae. They're also the king's personal guard, so if you saw him in public anywhere, they were the two brutes holding back the screaming fans."

I think back to when I saw Caiden in the lobby at Nightfall. His bodyguards were huge, and when I search my mind for more details other than Caiden's eyes on mine, I realize that the two men did look alike with the exception of their hairstyles. One wore his shoulder-length hair down and the other sported a man bun.

Still, it's hard to imagine either of them turning into wolves.

"Wolf shifter bodyguards. Because why not," I muse wryly. I wonder if I'll ever get to see a transformation. That seems like it should be a bucket list item. As long as I'm forced to be here, I might as well take advantage of experiencing the impossible.

That is, if this isn't some elaborate lucid dream or bad trip I'm having, which would honestly make more sense than the present alternative.

Observing Fiona more closely, I take note that her fangs are shorter, almost daintier, and I wonder if that's a trait specific to the girls or if it's different for every faerie. Fae. Whatever. "And what do you shift into?"

"I *wish*. I don't have any cool powers, unfortunately. Just a plain old fae."

She shrugs with a tight smile that doesn't quite reach her eyes. It's obvious she feels some kind of way about her abilities or lack thereof. Trying to lighten the mood, I narrow my eyes and pretend to look her over. "I suppose you seem okay as far as babysitters go."

Fiona grins for real this time and pulls her knees up to her chest, making herself comfortable. "Saw through that, did you?"

I roll my eyes. "It's not hard when I've been informed my freedom only extends to the property lines of this house for the foreseeable future. One minute I'm having drinks with a sexy, charming Dr. Jekyll, the next I wake up to an annoyingly-still-sexy Mr. Hyde, only to then be kidnapped by his equally attractive but no less annoying brothers."

She bursts into laughter. "I'm sorry, I'm not laughing at your situation, I promise. But if you thought King Caiden was charming, you were already well and truly intoxicated. The rest of your descriptions are incredibly accurate, though. Especially the Mr. Hyde one."

I turn that bit of info over in my brain, then decide not to tell her that I'd only had a diet soda before the grumpy regent started flirting with me like he had a PhD from charm school. I might really like Fiona so far, but I can't forget the precarious situation I'm in. It's better if I gather and hoard information rather than divulge it.

"So he really is a king, then. It's not just the self-purported title of a megalomaniac?"

She chuckles, then nods, her expression turning reverent. "I know it's hard to believe; he doesn't look nearly old enough. Technically he's the youngest to ever be crowned in fae history, which is why I think people tend to underestimate him. And Mr. Hyde personality aside, he's a great king, just like his father before him."

A king. I still can't quite wrap my mind around it. As an American, the whole concept is...well, *foreign.* "This is a lot to take in. I feel like Alice after tumbling down the rabbit hole. I'm still holding out hope that I slipped and hit my head at the pool, and this is all one giant hallucination."

Fiona nods thoughtfully and chews on her lip, like she's trying to decide what to say. "I can only imagine what it must be like for you to learn a world you never knew existed is living right alongside your own. If you have general questions about the house or your stay, I'm happy to answer them."

"That's it, though, right? No getting a complete history of the fae and a book of all your secrets?"

Smiling apologetically, she says, "I'm afraid not. Not from me, anyway. What the king chooses to share with you is his decision. I know you're not here by choice, Bryn, but I can't tell you how excited I am to have another female at the manor."

My eyebrows raise. "We're the only women here?"

Fiona holds up a finger. "Quick side note—and I know this is okay to mention—'women' and 'men' only refer to humans. We use 'female,' 'male,' or simply 'fae' for those who identify as other, neither, or somewhere in between."

"I'll do my best to remember that. I don't want to offend anyone, regardless of who they are, so I appreciate you telling me." Returning to her earlier statement, I ask, "So everyone else besides us here is male?"

"The cook and a few part-time staff members are female. Otherwise it's a giant sausage fest. And not in the fun *Thunder from Down Under* kind of way."

That makes me laugh. I really do like Fiona, and if I am stuck in this house—which apparently, I very much am for the time being—then it'll be nice to have a friendly face around.

Even though she's on the side of the "enemy" and I won't be able to completely let my guard down around her, she could still be a good ally. And if anyone has their ear to the ground and probably knows way more than anyone expects, it's a live-in employee.

"If you can't talk about fae stuff, can you at least tell me more about their king? Nothing serious, just a couple of girls talking about a boy."

My brain snorts at referring to Caiden as a boy. He's 100 percent man—no, *male*—and that's my damn problem. It would be so easy to let myself fall under the spell of that intense golden gaze and forget I'm his *prisoner*.

I need to find a way out of here before I get sucked into willingly sticking around. If that means pumping his sweet housekeeper for any information that might help me escape or know how to deal with my charming-turned-jackass husband, so be it.

All is fair in marriage and war.

Fiona's golden eyes light up, and I know I've got her. "I don't see the harm in that. Let's go to my bedroom so you can borrow some of my clothes until we can get you your own. We'll talk there." She rises from the chair and adds in a low voice, "It's farther from you know who's room."

"Perfect," I say with a smile.

She leads me through the manor, pointing out different areas like the kitchen, pool, home gym, and movie theater. When we finally get to her room, she tells me to take a seat on her bed and opens her closet doors.

As she starts pushing hangers back and forth, she pauses to glance at me with a mischievous grin. "So, what do you want to know?"

"For starters, what's his Prince-Charming-to-Beast ratio?"

"What do you mean? Here, this is a good one for wearing around the house." She pulls out a fitted green V-neck tee and thrusts it in my direction, so I dutifully grab it.

"I mean we've already established that he can be a bit of a grumpy jackass just like the Beast, right?"

"Oh! You mean like the 'Stay out of the west wing, it's forbidden' kind of Beast." Fiona laughs and I join in, because now I'm imagining Caiden with a huge mane of fur around his head. She takes out five more hangers with cute tops and lays them on the bed, telling me to pick whatever I want. "Yes, he's definitely that at times."

"Okay, but when I met him, he was the epitome of Prince— or I guess *King*—Charming. He was incredibly flirtatious with the smiling and the winking and the hand kissing."

Fiona's gaze snaps up from the drawer of shorts she was riffling through. "Hand kissing?"

"Hand kissing," I confirm with a raise of my eyebrows for emphasis. "Not to mention he was funny, and chivalrous, and kind. We had a lot of fun together. At least during the portion I can remember clearly. But I have snippets of memories from later that night, and he was great then, too. Super romantic and *very attentive*, if you catch my drift."

Abandoning her search, she joins me on the bed and draws her knees up. "Oh, I'm catching it. I'm just not sure I'm believing it. Not that I can speak from personal experience on the latter, but the king's reputation in that arena is the world's worst-kept secret, and nothing you've said of how he was with you that night sounds like him."

"As in he doesn't act like that in public?"

Fiona raises a perfectly shaped brow. "As in he doesn't act like that *ever*. The Verran brother you're describing is Tiernan. Finnian is a bit more reserved, but I'd even believe that coming from him. But the king? Maybe if he was high out of his mind." She giggles, then stops and stares wide-eyed at me. "Oh my gods, were you guys *high*?"

"What? No! All we had were a few...ish...drinks." She

winces like maybe that's the answer for why I'm thinking the way I am. Sighing, I say, "Listen, I work in public relations. It's literally my job to schmooze the unschmoozable, to charm people into buying the PR story I'm selling them even if it's a lie. So I know when someone is spinning me a web of bullshit, and I'm telling you Caiden was acting genuine."

To back up my own argument, I replay my time with Caiden in my mind, searching for signs that I might be wrong, but I don't find any. I stand by what I said—it wasn't an act.

"The only thing I don't know," I continue, "is *why* he acted that way with me when he's supposedly the Beast all the time."

She shakes her head. "He's not like that *all* the time. Well, okay, he kind of is, but in varying degrees. He's always very serious and businesslike, even here at home. That's his baseline, and with his high level of self-control, he rarely deviates from that. But when he does…"

Fiona makes a "yikes" face and lets me draw my own conclusions, which isn't hard. I've felt the brunt of what I assume was a watered-down version of Caiden's wrath, and that wasn't exactly a picnic.

I can only imagine the kind of carnage he would leave behind if provoked.

Yet, I can't stop thinking about the Caiden who swept me off my feet less than two days ago. Regardless of our alcohol levels and impaired judgment, the fact remains we got married. Which means one of us came up with the idea and the other thought it was brilliant.

Why? Because we were *extremely* into each other. Hell, we had so much chemistry, I'm shocked there wasn't visible electrical currents arcing between our bodies at the bar.

"I know this is a little far-fetched," she prefaces, "but what if you're supposed to be here? What if it's fate?"

"Yeah, no, it's not that." I shake my head for good measure. "I'm on very good terms with the universe. She wouldn't gift me my dream guy, give me both a wedding and thrice-amazing post-marital sex that I can't even remember, then tie it all up with a side of kidnapping. No, this has nothing to do with fate."

"When you put it like that, it does sound unlikely. Whatever the reason, I'm sure everything will work out for the best. Until then, just treat this like an extended vacation."

I scoff. "Yeah right. Like a vacation at the *Hotel California*."

Fiona offers me an empathic squeeze on my shoulder. "I'm sorry, Bryn. For what it's worth, I'm going to do everything I can to make sure you feel at home here."

"Thank you, Fiona," I say genuinely. "I appreciate that."

"Okay, what do you say we finish up here and then order in and stuff ourselves while watching movies in the theater room?"

"I'd say that sounds like a fabulous plan. I'm starving."

With that settled, she encourages me to browse for anything else I'd like from her closet while she calls a boutique where the Verrans have a line of credit open.

While I half listen to her arrange for a selection of items to be brought over tomorrow, I flip through the hangers on autopilot, my mind spinning with thoughts of Caiden. I know he felt something for me. I'm not saying it was the kind of something people typically get married over—even though we apparently did—but it was enough that if it was within his power, I think he would've granted my every wish that night.

My hands freeze on a yellow sundress as it suddenly dawns on me. *I know how I get home.*

Not by trying to *escape* Caiden but by convincing him that he wants to *let me go.* I nearly laugh with giddiness. Not only is this plan going to be more enjoyable to execute, but it's also 100 percent more likely to succeed than me trying to Houdini my way out of here.

My mom always said you catch more flies with honey, and it's a practice I've mastered and lived by my whole life. If I want to convince Caiden to let me go home, all I have to do is spend lots of time with him and bring that spark we had back to life. Since we live under the same roof, it won't be hard to find him.

Then I'll hit him with my winning personality and mix in a healthy dose of flirting for good measure. Before long, we'll be having a great time again, and he'll be way more open to suggestion.

I might even try and get another night of great sex out of him—one we'll both remember. Then, as we lay in post-coital bliss, I'll convince him there's no harm in letting me go home while he solves the issue with us being bonded. Easy. I can practically taste my victory already.

And for my next trick, ladies and gentlemen, I'm going to charm this Beast back into a prince...

CHAPTER ELEVEN

CAIDEN

After a day of Zoom meetings to replace the in-person ones I canceled in New York—because weekends don't exist for rich assholes like us plotting real-estate world domination—plus strategy meetings with Seamus and security meetings with all of the Night Watch, I needed some serious destressing time.

I spent a couple of hours in my home gym, speakers blasting music with bass so heavy I felt the vibrations in my teeth. As I pushed myself with the weights, I imagined purging all the obscene thoughts of a blond beauty with every drip of sweat that poured off my body.

When I reached the point where I'd collapse if I did one more rep, I rinsed off in the outdoor shower, poured myself a glass of Devil's Keep—because it's been a twelve-thousand-dollar-whiskey kind of day—and waded into the pool to relax and decompress.

Sitting on the submerged ledge on the far end, I've got my back tucked into the corner with my arms stretched along the tiled edge, whiskey glass in one hand. Of everything I incorporated into Midnight Manor's design, the pool area is one of my favorites. At night, the water is lit up from blue

LED lights recessed into the bottom, and a fire feature runs the length of the pool just beyond the edge of the infinity wall that makes it look like six-inch-high flames are dancing on top of the water. I like sitting here or even in one of the cushioned lounge chairs and take in my view of the Vegas Strip lit up in the distance like a neon rainbow of sin.

I love this fucking city.

I love what it does to support my people, that it's proof we know how to not only survive but *thrive* in a world that's not our own. More than that, though, I love its energy. The vibe it gives off when the sun goes down. It makes you feel almost invincible; just pull the right lever, flip the right cards, roll the right dice, or tuck enough into their G-string and anything's possible.

The phrase "What happens in Vegas, stays in Vegas" is the most genius marketing we ever came up with.

From the moment humans set foot in our city, they have a sense that the normal rules of propriety no longer apply. It's the ultimate free pass in their minds.

They can do whatever they want, whenever they want, and with whomever they want until it's time for them to go home. And we encourage the fuck out of that mindset.

Vegas is a place of perpetual night.

You won't find any clocks or windows letting natural light into our casinos, skewing your perception of time. We designed it that way intentionally. Not only because it represents the time when we as the Night Court are at our strongest and most vibrant. But also because those carnal desires you crave—the ones you refuse to acknowledge in the garish light of day—feel a lot less wrong in the dark of night.

Which is why as I sit here with minimal light to push against the shadows, I'm finding it damn difficult to remember why I can't sink my cock between Bryn's legs. It's not like we haven't already crossed that line. Though the fact that neither of us has clear memories of it fucking eats at me. Not for egotistical reasons but for ones of consent. In over a hundred and fifty years, I've never fucked anyone who wasn't completely cognizant of their actions—hell, I've never not been cognizant of *my own* actions—and the fact that I did that night makes no goddamned sense.

On some level, I must have known she was able to make her own decisions and just didn't give a shit that I wasn't thinking clearly.

From the moment I left my office to pursue her, I knew I was acting out of character. I just didn't care. Whatever I was feeling felt *good*. Good enough that I chose to ignore the part of my brain that had to have been sending up warning flares left and right.

And *that* is why I'm positive I had to have been drugged somehow.

But when? And by whom if not Bryn?

The only thing I had to eat or drink between dealing with Ralph and pursuing Bryn was the Devil's Keep my brothers and I shared. But they didn't have any unusual reactions, and they drank half the damn bottle before I even got there.

Nothing about this shitstorm makes any sense.

Between that and the desire still plaguing me to fuck my problems away with Bryn's sexy body, I'll have to drown myself in whiskey just to get any sleep.

I don't realize I've reached for my ring until my fingers graze the center of my chest and come up empty, and I remember that I took it off before my workout. Touching it has become an unconscious habit in the mere thirty-six hours since I woke with it on my hand. My pride insists it's only because I'm not used to it being there. Not because it's a subconscious need to somehow feel connected to Bryn.

As though my thoughts conjured her presence, she comes around the corner from the outdoor dining area wearing a black silk coverup that hits her at mid-thigh. Since the LEDs don't reach the far corners of the pool, I'm cast in enough shadow that she doesn't notice my presence.

I don't alert her to it, either.

I like being able to study her freely, like this morning while she slept. For as much as we talked Friday—the last thing I can remember us doing that night—there's still so much I don't know about her.

And I'm not one to leave a mystery unsolved.

She unties the belt from her waist and shrugs the thin robe off to reveal a black bikini that has my dick instantly saluting. I've never seen anything so sexy. A black string loops through a large silver ring at the top of her bikini bottoms, then stretches up to loop through the silver ring between her breasts and continues on to tie at the back of her neck.

All together, it looks like a normal strapless two-piece with the halter tie forming a skinny V down the center of her body that attaches to the bottom ring and pulls it up enough to frame her belly button piercing.

But on Bryn, that's not a swimsuit. It's a goddamn invitation to sin.

She walks gingerly down the stairs on the other end of the pool. Once the water is up to her thighs, she does a shallow dive and breaks the surface in the center. She smooths her hair back, then readjusts the cups of her top even though they didn't need it.

I watch in silence as she moves to where one of the streams of water arcs over the infinity wall to land in the pool.

She places her hand out to catch the stream in her palm, making it spray in every direction. Her face lights up with a wide smile of simple joy. It tugs at something inside me, the same as her laughter did the night we spent together.

I liked her laugh. It wasn't a controlled giggle muffled behind her hand. Hers was genuine, throaty and unapologetically loud.

Sometimes, she'd lean forward and brace a hand on my leg to help her straighten up again. Other times, she'd throw her head back and lay that same hand on her belly like she needed to hold herself together. It was infectious.

I think I laughed more in those few hours with Bryn than I have in the last decade combined.

When she turns and walks closer to the wall topped with flames, I finally break my silence. "It's real fire, Bryn. No reason to risk singeing your eyebrows off getting any closer to see for yourself."

Her head turns first, finding me easily enough in the shadows from the direction of my voice.

Then, with a devilish grin, she rotates her shoulders and starts toward me.

As she passes over the LEDs lit from the bottom, flashes of blue flood her body before being stripped away again. It's like a peekaboo show made of my own design, and it's not helping the situation in my shorts. Not that I've ever been one for modesty, but letting her know she affects me gives her an edge I'd rather she not have. Things are difficult enough as they are.

Reaching the side a few feet away from me, she folds her arms on the tiled ledge and rests her cheek on top with her head turned toward me as she bats her eyelashes. "Were you spying on me, Your Majesty?"

Fuck me. I know she's saying it to be a snarky brat, but my brain changes her words into a breathy plea and now my balls are beginning to ache along with my dick. "How can I be spying on you when I was here first?"

She arches a slim brow. "By not telling me you were here to begin with."

She's got me there. "I chose not to disturb you. Until you decided to get up close and personal with open flames. Do you do reckless things like that a lot? If so, I'll need to put a bodyguard on you for your own safety."

And mine.

Bryn snorts. "I'm good, thanks. I already have a babysitter."

I take a drink of my whiskey. "Fiona's hardly a babysitter. I asked her to help you with some extra clothes and make sure you were fed."

She lets her legs float up to the surface behind her, causing the globes of her ass to bob above the water. A seemingly innocent move, but it might as well be sexual warfare as far as my cock is concerned.

"Oh, she did. We're the same size, so she lent me some of her clothes. Then we raided the kitchen and brought every snack we could find into your gigantic theater room and watched the first three movies in the Fast and Furious franchise. She's been very helpful."

I scowl. "I'm not paying her to be your playmate, Bryn."

"Oh, I know." Lifting one hand, she studies her nails. "I'm just saying you should probably hire an additional housekeeper because Fiona and I are new BFFs, and we're going to be spending a lot of time together."

Meeting my gaze again, she beams a calculating smile at me and bats her eyelashes again. *Bratty girl.*

This is a new side of Bryn I'm seeing, and I find it rather amusing. Much in the way a cat amuses himself by watching the mouse play before he attacks.

Canting my head, I narrow my eyes. "Careful with that tone of yours, Bryn. I believe I've already threatened to spank you once. I'll give you a fair three strikes, but that was your second, and my spanking sessions aren't anything your sweet Midwestern mind can imagine. Tread carefully."

As I take a sip of whiskey, she studies me while chewing on her lower lip in thought.

I assume I've effectively put her inner brat in time-out when she ups the ante in our little mental game. "So, I may or may not have heard that's another reason they call you the Dark King. Because of your...spanking sessions and the like. Is that true?"

I'm not surprised my reputation came up. With how naturally inquisitive Bryn is, she probably grilled Fiona for every detail she was allowed to give. And it's not like anything (other than us being fae to the humans) about the Verran kings is a secret. Everyone in this city knows we're devious in the boardroom and deviants in the bedroom. We don't bother hiding who we are because we don't have to. We're fucking royalty.

I arch a brow. "Gossiping with your new BFF already?"

Bryn schools her features and says with a straight face, "Sorry, but I never reveal my sources."

That almost makes me chuckle in spite of my determination to not have a repeat of how I acted around her the other night. "In that case, I'm afraid I cannot confirm or deny your intel, Miss Meara."

"Mrs. Verran."

My heart skips a beat. "What?"

"Aren't I Mrs. Verran now? Technically, I mean."

"No. You're not, technically." Getting to my feet, I make my way to the stairs and out of the pool. I can feel her eyes following me as I grab the bottle of Devil's Keep I left on the outdoor bar and pour myself another three fingers.

"I don't understand," she says, her voice calling after me. "Something tells me you're not the kind of guy to insist a girl keeps her own last name."

Fuck it. Better make it four.

I toss back the first two and tell myself that it's the reminder of the blood curse that's suddenly got me in a shitty mood. Not because I liked the way it sounded when she referred to herself with my name. A name she cannot lawfully claim, now or ever.

On any given day, my mood usually ranges from normal

to mildly aggravated, with the rare—justifiable—outburst like I had with Ralph the other day. That's it. My control over my emotions is unflappable.

But in the forty-eight hours since meeting one Bryn Meara, my emotions have jumped around more than the needle on a guilty man's polygraph. At this rate, I'll have to invest in more bottles of Keep just to hold on to my sanity.

Bringing the bottle with me, I settle onto a cushioned lounge chair that faces the pool and the view before answering gruffly. "We saw the rings and assumed we had a normal wedding. We didn't. It was a fae marriage ceremony, which is what forms the true mate bond. Which means, among other things, your name is still very much your own."

"Oh, I see."

It's probably just my imagination that I hear disappointment in her words when I know better than that. Bryn is every bit the unwilling participant in this as I am, I'm beginning to believe—even more so, since I'm refusing to let her leave the manor until gods know when.

I'm proven right when she turns it into a joke. "Well, that's good. Saves me a trip to the seventh circle of hell, also known as the DMV."

As she emerges from the pool, she wrings the water out of her long hair, then fluffs and separates the strands so they fall in damp pieces around her shoulders. My eyes stay pinned to her as she walks to me and takes a seat on the next lounge chair over.

She stays facing me but leans back on her hands and extends her long legs into the space between us. It's not done in an overtly seductive way—her demeanor is casual, like it's simply a comfortable position for her to be in—but it makes me want to devour her from her pink-painted toes to her pretty pink mouth.

Looking back out over the pool, I say, "You should wear

swimsuits with a little more suit to them."

"I packed two for a two-day trip, and if you'll remember, I was forced to wear the other one as pajamas. I'll admit I bought this as more of a dare to myself and didn't really plan on wearing it, but beggars, choosers, yada-yada." She glances down at herself, then raises her gaze again to aim an impish grin in my direction that I feel more than see. "Why, don't you like it? This can't possibly offend someone with a nickname like the *Dark King*."

"It's not about offense; it's about walking around here looking like a fucking gazelle to a pride of lions."

"Lions?" Gasping, she sits up straight. "That would make you the *Lion* King."

I turn my head and glare. Not hard enough, apparently, because Bryn throws her head back in one of those sexy laughs. My mouth waters at the sight of her throat bared to me. An invitation for my lips, my tongue. *My fangs.*

Fuck. Me.

When she calms down again, she sits forward and folds her arms across her thighs, regarding me. "So I was thinking, since I'm your prisoner—"

"Guest."

"Hostage—"

"Roommate."

She sighs. "Your *whatever* for the foreseeable future, I think we should try to make the best out of our situation."

I regard her over the glass as I take another drink, primal satisfaction hitting me when she squirms the slightest bit under the weight of my gaze. "How do you propose we do that?"

"I think if we're going to remain...*roommates*...it should come with certain benefits, don't you?"

"Speak plainly, Bryn."

Her pretty hazel eyes roll. "Sex, Caiden. I'm saying we might as well have some fun by having—"

"No."

"No?"

"Yes, *no*."

"No. Just like that." When I don't elaborate, she pushes for more. "Why the hell not? You're obviously not opposed to no-strings flings, as evidenced by the other night, so what's the big deal?"

"I told you earlier. The male who was with you two nights ago was not the real me. The kind of vanilla sex we had the other night isn't my style and I can assure you, you're not ready for the kind of things I would do to that body."

Bryn captures her lower lip, and her brows draw together over the slender bridge of her nose. Goose bumps appear on her arms, snagging the attention of my preternatural sight that chases them as they climb the creamy skin of her neck.

I swear to Rhiannon, I can literally see her weighing this as one of her "risks worth taking," and I could fucking kick myself for teeing it up like that.

Maybe it'll be fine, though. Maybe she won't—

"You don't know that. Let's try it your way and find out."

Fuck. "Let's not. You might be curious about the darker side of sex, but I promise you won't like what I need to get off."

She visibly bristles, her back straightening and hazel eyes shooting daggers at me. "Don't tell me what I do and don't want, Caiden. Just because we tied the knot and had barely memorable sex a few times doesn't mean you know me."

"I remember enough to know what gets you off, and it isn't anything close to the kind of games the Dark Fae like to play in the bedroom. And I'm their fucking *king*."

"Just because I've never experienced something doesn't mean that I won't enjoy it."

Drawing on my control, I keep my tone even and firm. "The answer is no, Bryn. Drop it."

"Fine," she snaps out. "You don't want me hanging out with

Fiona and you've made it clear I won't be spending any time with you, so I guess I'll just be bored to death."

Turning away, she stretches out on the chaise like a sulking teenager, making my palm itch to correct her attitude with a few sharp slaps on her ass.

Just as I'm considering heading to my room to avoid temptation, she changes the subject. "I met one of your wolf friends today. Is he into the same stuff you are? I bet he is; friends usually share things like that in common. Or your brothers—maybe they'd be willing to spend time with me."

I grind my teeth together, thinking of my friends, brothers, or any other male "spending time" with her, but shove my violent jealousy down deep and hold fast to my control. Setting my glass down on the small table between us, I pick up my phone and shoot off a quick text in the Night Watch thread.

No one in the back of the manor for the next 15 min.

The guys will no doubt bitch to me about it later, but I know they won't go against my order. The entire perimeter has multiple security measures in place; they can rely on those for now. I lock the screen, turn it on silent, and put it back on the table.

"Come here," I command.

She turns her head to me, eyebrows raised. "Why should I?"

I pop my jaw. She needs to be taught a lesson before her bratty nature pushes us both too far. "Go grab your coverup, then come back here."

"Why?" she asks, her brat now on full display. "So you can show me what happens when I piss off the *Lion King*?"

"Strike three, Beauty." One side of my mouth pulls up in an evil smirk. "That ass is mine."

CHAPTER TWELVE

CAIDEN

"I won't tell you again, Bryn. You want to take a walk on the dark side? This is your last chance."

She hops to obey me this time, and if I wasn't so fucking keyed up, I might find it amusing. After retrieving the coverup, she returns to me in record time. I remove the silk belt, then drop the thin robe off to the side. She won't be needing it.

This isn't about making her feel comfortable. Just the opposite. I want her to feel exposed and vulnerable. Not that she will be—my text made sure of that—because regardless of what our status is or isn't, no one else is allowed to have any part of her body, even from a distance.

But *she* doesn't know that. Not yet.

I nod to my lap. "Sit."

She hesitates, her expression telling me she's not certain what I mean. At least this time she's not pretending.

"Straddle me, facing the pool."

Planting a knee on the cushion, she swings her other leg over, then gingerly lowers herself onto my upper thighs.

"Now is not the time for you to be shy."

I grip her hips with both hands and yank her back to set

her directly over my hardened cock. She gasps, and I'm glad she can't see the strain on my face from holding back my own groans of pleasure. She hasn't even moved or provided any kind of friction and already I can feel my control slipping.

"Should I—"

I cut her off with a hand covering her mouth and growl into her ear. "You've said quite enough for one night. There will be no more talking from you. If I ask you a direct question, you're permitted to respond with a simple 'Yes, Your Majesty' or 'No, Your Majesty' and that is all. Do you understand?" She starts to nod, but I release her and command, "Answer."

She swallows, and I can tell we're on a precipice.

The logical part of me silently begs her to say no, to end this game and go back to her room. But a bigger part, the part her ass is currently pressed against, craves for her to obey.

"Yes, Your Majesty." Her words are breathless and laced with desire, just as I imagined them.

Since becoming king, I've been addressed with that phrase thousands upon thousands of times. But hearing it from Bryn while she's under my control is like a high-concentrated dose of ambrosia pushed straight into my veins.

"Well done, Beauty. Arms behind your back." She doesn't hesitate, and I arrange her forearms one on top of the other, then use the silk belt to tie them in place, ensuring her circulation isn't cut off or her skin pinched. "Lean forward, face turned and resting on the chair between my legs."

I guide her with one hand on her shoulder and the other between her shoulder blades until she's at a downward angle, giving me a view to rival the award-winning one in the distance. I hook fingers in the material riding along her cheeks and gather it together in the center, exposing the full canvas of her ass save for the most wicked of spots. One I crave to play with but refuse to allow myself to start something I have no intention of finishing.

Ignoring the disappointment about that, I let my hands roam over her smooth skin, allowing her to get used to my touch and lulling her into a false sense of sensuality.

Normally, my sexual partners would get a safe word, but the whole point of this exercise is to get her to call it off and not want a repeat performance. For the first time ever, my goal is to *not* get a female to orgasm. And the only release I get will be by my own hand afterward in the shower. Again.

Besides, with the true mate bond in place, and with a human, I have no idea if a physical relationship would continue to strengthen that bond. Beyond that, everything about Bryn feels different, more intense. I never get attached to the occasional females I bed, but I have enough self-awareness that I'm already walking a razor's edge when it comes to this woman. My brain and my body can't decide whether it's latent effects of the drug from the other night or I'm feeling a genuine connection with her.

I've turned all this over in my head a hundred different ways, and the result is always the same: I can't risk sating the carnal hunger I have for Bryn.

But while my intention with this demonstration is to get her to admit—at least to herself if not to me—that she prefers her tried-and-true vanilla flavor of sex, I would never put her in any real danger.

Since the bond makes me sensitive to her energy, I won't need a safe word to know whether I'm pushing her too far. If she becomes afraid or anxious, I'll feel it.

She pulls my focus back to her when she rocks her hips, trying to create friction on her needy little clit. So I begin.

Lifting my right hand, I bring it down hard enough to smart properly. Her entire body tenses, and she sucks in a sharp breath but doesn't yet protest like I want. I resume rubbing and massaging her flesh, my thumbs teasing along the barrier of her bunched bikini, getting as close as I dare without succumbing to the temptation to skirt beneath the material.

As soon as she relaxes under my touch, I swat her on the left cheek and get the same reaction, but this time I don't let her get comfortable. I begin raining my hand down on both sides of her ass in an erratic rhythm so she can't anticipate when the next one will come. All while keeping my senses open for signs of distress and hoping like hell she'll command me to stop regardless.

She gives me neither.

Instead, she gives me soft moans and tiny pumps of her hips that rub her pussy on my aching dick.

As the one in the driver's seat, I shouldn't allow the movements, but my cock is a greedy motherfucker, and he's making a play for the wheel.

Getting nowhere with the spanking, I take a moment to admire my handiwork. *Fuck, her ass cheeks look good in blush red.*

Moment over, I pull her up and recline her so that the backs of her shoulders are against my chest, with her arms pinned between us. "Your spanking for the insolent attitude is over, but you should know two things. First, that spanking session was for beginners. I went easy on you, so don't make the mistake of thinking it would be as pleasurable if you earn yourself another one."

Then I unceremoniously tug the cups of her bikini top up, baring her breasts to the night sky and, as far as she knows, to anyone with a clear view of us. "Second, just because the spanking is over," I say, kneading them roughly, "doesn't mean your punishment *is*."

She whimpers and arches her back, offering me more. Offering me everything.

It's the last thing I need but it's the very thing I *want*.

Pinching her dusky nipples, I roll them between my fingers and revel in her soft moans as they wrap around my body. My chest is tight with an insatiable hunger for what I cannot have.

But every sound she makes, every roll of her hips, every shuddering breath from her lips makes me forget why indulging just this once would be so bad.

Such a naughty little temptress.

"Gods, look how perfect these tits are." I push the supple mounds together, making the perfect channel for my cock to slide through if we were in a different position. "Your nipples would look exquisite in my clamps. With a delicate chain going from one to the other for me to tug on and make you scream for me."

She gasps as I pinch a little harder and hold, giving her a sample of what she'd feel with my clamps squeezing her tight buds. When I finally release them to let the blood rush back in, a shiver rips through her body so intensely, it reverberates in my own.

"Well, well, this is a surprise," I muse more to myself than to her. "You like the bite of pain with your pleasure, don't you, Beauty?"

Her brows furrow, and she traps her lip as though trying to process a new revelation about herself. "Y-yes, Your Majesty."

"Do you also like that you're on display for anyone who happens to look our way?"

She stiffens and cages her breath. Encouraged by the change—hoping this will be her line drawn in the sand and my torture will come to an end—I think of how to build on the illusion of exhibitionism while avoiding any outright lies.

"I told you I have security who patrol the property. What do you suppose the odds are that we're being watched right now?" *None, if they value their lives.*

Her breaths are coming faster now. Other than the scent of her arousal that's making my mouth water, her energy reads neutral with it leaning a bit one way and then the other. Like it's teetering on a fence and hasn't decided which direction it wants to fall on.

Raising the stakes, I pull her legs out and drape them across my thighs to hang over the sides. She's spread wide now, with nothing to keep her modesty intact but a thin strip of soaked black material. I push her breasts together and pinch both of her nipples with the fingers of my left hand. Then I snake the other down her body and cup her pussy. *Hard*. Like I own every wet inch of it.

"Want to know what I think?" My thumb starts rubbing circles around her clit through her suit. She writhes in my lap, her ass rubbing on my throbbing dick and driving me to the brink of madness. I lightly score the tender flesh of her neck with my fangs on my way up to lick the shell of her ear. "I think you want to be seen. For them to see what a beautiful little slut you are for me, letting me take you however I please. Isn't that right?"

"God, yes," she moans.

A spike of arousal clashes with white-hot jealousy. In the past, I've played with partners who got off on being watched, and while it's not at the top of my list of things that turn me on, I enjoyed putting on a show in the interest of my lover's pleasure. But Bryn confuses everything about me I've ever known.

She's my own Helen of Troy, causing the different parts of me to war against each other in her name.

My brain wants to hold her at bay, knowing how dangerous she is to our life and our crown. My body wants to put her on display to be worshipped while I ruin her in all the best, darkest ways imaginable. And my soul, tethered to hers by the bond, wants to publicly stake its claim so everyone knows that slighting my queen will bring a swift death to their door.

My heart, though. My heart remains silent.

It watches the chaos with interest from afar but knows better than to venture out of the shadows for a female, regardless of any bond.

I jerk my left hand away, snapping my fingers off her nipples in a single sharp movement. She cries out, body bowed in a lovely arch with her head tipped back on my shoulder as the endorphins and blood rushing into her swollen tips flood her system.

Gods, she's stunning.

I grasp her jaw as I growl against her temple. "That is not the proper way to address *your king*, Beauty. Try again."

"Yes, Your..." She pauses, and just when I'm about to berate her, she whispers, "Yes, my king." I'm so stunned, my grip relaxes, and she's able to turn and peer up at me with those fathomless hazel pools. "I like that one better. Can I use that instead?"

Another iron nail is driven into my coffin.

Hearing her refer to me as *her* anything makes me want to lay the world at her feet.

My resolve continues to weaken with the intense connection I feel with this woman. But I can't fucking trust it. I can't trust *her.*

Swallowing past the gravel in my throat, I let my eyes bounce between hers as I weigh my answer carefully, then answer gruffly. "You may."

Because fuck it.

I like how she says it, and what she calls me doesn't change a damn thing.

Before my subconscious can call me out on my bullshit, I refocus on the task at hand, though I'm no longer sure of my end goal. I never intended to bring her to orgasm and now it's all I can think about. I need to know how her body writhes, see the ecstasy painted on her face. Will she moan as she comes or will she scream in silence?

Grabbing her face roughly in my hand, I ask, "Would you like me to continue touching you, Beauty? To make you come right here, where anyone can watch?"

"Yes, my king."

"Beg for it." She hesitates, and the part of me that is still sane jumps at the chance to shut this down. "Then we're done."

I start to push her away, but she counters it by leaning into me with all her (meager) weight. "*Wait*. Please touch me. Make me come. Please, my king, I'm begging you. Don't leave me like this."

"Let's test how much of a wanton little slut you are." Releasing her face, I yank the crotch of her bottoms to the side, exposing her pussy to our imaginary audience. I caress her swollen lips, rubbing and spreading her juices all over until she's completely painted in her own arousal. I growl with approval. "So fucking needy."

Bryn pants next to my ear and tries to move her hips to chase my touch. Unacceptable. I slap her wet pussy in punishment. She yelps and nearly jumps off my lap, but I'm holding her firmly around the waist, so she gets nowhere. "Hold still. You'll get the pleasure I give you and nothing more. Do you understand?"

She whimpers but answers properly. "Yes, my king."

"Do you want my fingers inside you? Filling and fucking you to completion?"

On a moan, she says, "God, yes, my king. Please give me your fingers."

"No," I say with as much cruelty as I can inject into the word. "You haven't earned them." I let my fingers massage the outside of her puffy lips. Then I set to work to make her do exactly what she's not supposed to, because I'm a sadistic bastard like that.

I drag her arousal up to her clit and start rubbing frenetic circles around the swollen bundle of nerves. "You'll come like this or not at all. And, Beauty, you'd better not come before I tell you."

"Oh, fuck," she squeaks out.

My other hand moves between her tits, grabbing and squeezing each large mound, then torturing her nipples with twists and tugs. All while keeping my fingertips focused on her clit. Her body begins to writhe ever so slightly, a slave to the waves of rapture rippling through it.

"Don't you fucking move," I growl next to her ear. She immediately stiffens, doing her best to obey, which pleases me more than it has the right to. "We need to make sure our audience has a good view of this dripping pussy."

"Oh, God, please."

"Wrong lord to be begging. Do I need to impose orgasm denial to teach you a lesson?"

"No! I'm sorry. Please, my king, I'm begging you. Please may I come?"

"No, you may not. Hold it."

Her frustrated moan is pushed through clenched teeth, and I know exactly how she feels because my balls have probably turned five shades of blue in the last five minutes. I've never wanted to fuck someone so badly. All it would take is a quick shove of my shorts and I could sink my thick cock root-deep inside her tight little cunt.

Bryn is mumbling nonsensical things between the most erotic sounds I've ever heard. Her limbs are trembling with the force of keeping her climax at bay. Sweat drips over my forehead with the strain of holding on to my control. If I don't let her come soon, I'll be blowing my load in my shorts like a fucking virgin.

She turns her face up to me, hazel eyes engulfed by the black of her pupils, and begs me to let her come, her words slurring together in one long, unbroken plea. "Please let me come please please my king please please please…"

Staring into those deep pools, I swear I can see the fire of her soul as a mirror image of mine. But then I blink and it's gone, leaving only my own intense desires and needs reflecting back at me.

Steeling myself for the onslaught of sensations, I finally give the command.

"Come."

This time I don't prevent her movements. I revel in the way she arches, twists, and writhes. I study the way her face reveals the ecstasy coursing through her, memorize the moans and near-screams. I keep my fingers moving on her clit to draw out every last ounce of pleasure before letting up a little at a time, helping her to ride the waves as they ebb and flow, until at last there are only tiny aftershocks elicited by the graze of my fingertip on her hypersensitive nub.

The last thing I want to do is stop touching her.

The next to last thing I want to do is get up and leave.

Ignoring my instincts, I quickly untie the belt and release her arms, helping her ease them forward and giving them a brief rub to ensure they're not too stiff. Her breaths are still coming fast as she continues to come down from the climax.

Everything in me is screaming to lean back and hold her to me as she levels out, like a compulsion.

Which is exactly why I force myself to untangle from her and get up.

She moves into the spot I vacated, lying back and looking up at me like I just opened a whole new world for her. If we were in any situation other than the one we're in, I would eagerly lead her through it and show her the kind of pleasure she's only dreamed of. But as we're in this fucking mess—and my plan to turn her off with kink has backfired spectacularly—that's the very last thing I'll be doing.

I grab the coverup and offer it to her. She accepts it and drapes it over herself like a blanket, tucking it under her chin as she stares up at me with the lazy grin of a woman sated and sleepy. And why the fuck do I suddenly want to see that expression on her face all the goddamn time, whether sex is involved or not?

"For the record, no one saw us. You might be okay with others watching you get fucked, but that's not something I'd be interested in."

Translation: I would cut out the eyes of anyone who saw what is mine.

"Well, that's good, because for the record, I'm not interested in being watched."

I scoff, caveman-speak for *yeah right*.

"I knew no one was out there, Caiden. You seemed to want me to think that there was, and I thought it was hot, so I played along."

"What makes you think there wasn't?"

Bryn glares up at me. "You know, it's really annoying how you keep underestimating my ability to read situations."

"Enlighten me, then."

"Fine," she says with a haughty raise of her brows. "The situation is that even though you might not be happy with the one we're currently in, it doesn't change the fact that you don't like sharing your things. And right now—whether either of us wants me to be or not—I'm sitting pretty underneath that big umbrella of yours that says MINE in big, bold, shouty caps.

"Plus, even if I didn't know you well enough to at least know *that* much about you, I could easily make the assumption based on you being raised as a spoiled, rich prince who then grew up to be a spoiled, bazillionaire king, and therefore making it fairly easy to assume you might act like a possessive asshole."

Crossing my arms over my chest, I narrow my eyes at her. "You got all that from 'reading' the situation?"

"One hundred percent," she says confidently. Then adds, "Also I saw your text."

I scrub a hand over my mouth to wipe away the unexpected amusement before it can show on my face. I don't have to worry, though, because it dies quickly when I remember that the one downside I was holding on to—that she wanted something sexually I wasn't willing to give her—has been ripped out from under me.

Frustration rides me along with the ache in my balls and the stiffness in my dick that refuses to abate until I get matters into my own hands. Quite fucking literally.

"I hope you enjoyed your lesson. That's the only one you're getting. Like I said before, I went easy on you. That was tame compared to what I'd do if I showed you the extent of my tastes. Do us both a favor and forget about making this into some kind of hostage-with-benefits thing."

Her eyes sparkle with mirth. "So you finally admit I'm a hostage?"

No sense in twisting the truth anymore. Maybe if she feels less at ease, she'll stop trying to turn this into something it isn't. "Yes, you are. You're a hostage with a certain amount of freedom. But the thing about freedom is that it can always be taken away. Remember that, Bryn."

She dips her head in feigned deference while a smirk plays at her lips. "Yes, my king."

And so the insolent brat returns so soon. It should piss me the hell off, but it doesn't. That it *doesn't* is what truly pisses me off, further adding to this emotional clusterfuck I find myself in around her.

Ignoring her bait, I palm my phone from the table and turn to leave. "I trust you can find your own way back to your room."

She lets me get as far as the entry to the house before calling after me. "At the risk of stating the obvious, it didn't work."

I don't turn around. I also don't go inside.

Taking that as permission, Bryn continues. "Your plan. Instead of making me believe you're not the kind of man who could ever satisfy me, you made me realize you might be the only one who can."

Closing my eyes, I force a deep breath through my lungs to reinforce my self-control before I toss all sense out the window and prove to us both just how fucking right she is.

"Goodnight, Miss Meara." Then I walk away like a coward retreating from a battle he knows he cannot win.

Because that's exactly what I am.

CHAPTER THIRTEEN

BRYN

"What am I supposed to do while you're taking all these meetings?"

"I told you to bring a book; you didn't listen," Caiden says, his eyes never leaving his phone.

"I've already read the books that interest me, and your library is small. Size matters, you know." I scowl. He doesn't even take the "size matters" bait.

"We have magazines in the reception area. Read those."

"Sounds riveting," I mutter as I turn to stare out at the scenery through the car window. Am I a grown woman pouting in the back of a chauffeured luxury vehicle like a petulant child? Yes. But does he *deserve* my "bratty attitude" with dozens of resort-like amenities at my disposal and how well I've been cared for by his staff?

Also yes! Because I'm pissed at him.

That night by the pool, he gave me the best sexual experience of my life, awakening urges in me I never knew I had.

Not until I met Caiden.

As I lay in bed that night, unable to sleep from the aching

need between my legs, I realized there had always been an underlying hum in my veins every time he was near. When our gazes locked together in the lobby, it was like something clicked into place, and suddenly these darker desires whispered through my mind.

But like wisps of smoke, when I tried to reach for them, they dissipated into nothing, as though I'd only imagined them.

Turns out they were just waiting for their master to coax them from the shadows. Which is exactly what he did when he restrained me with a silk belt and pushed me down on that chaise. Then he brought his hand down on my ass like he was striking the match to light those desires on fire.

Every growled command in my ear, every verbal surrender I uttered, every drop of pleasure-pain he inflicted was like tossing an accelerant. The flames grew higher, burned hotter. Until everything in me exploded, consuming the woman I'd been before I knew Caiden's touch, and from her ashes rose a woman plagued by curiosity and an insatiable need for *more*.

You'd think he would've been all too happy when I didn't run from his little demonstration. It should've given him the green light to do it again, take things further, explore each other until we've memorized every freckle and scar on our bodies.

Which—beyond the bonus of having great fucking sex— would've been perfect for my plan.

Sure, the timeline of me going home may have gotten pushed back while we banged like bunnies for a few weeks, but it wouldn't be much longer than that. Fiona confirmed that Caiden isn't the settling-down type.

So once we got each other out of our systems, he'd no doubt be eager to send me back to Wisconsin and just update me about this whole mate bond thing as needed.

Afterward, we'd remain casual friends who text each other on holidays and birthdays while remembering our time together fondly.

At least that's how it all played out in my head.

Instead, it drove him into hiding.

It's been *two damn weeks*, and the few times we've seen each other was only in passing. I've been left to my own devices to try and work off my sexual frustration, but nothing I do is good enough to take this edge off.

I used to joke (to myself, obviously) that I was the best I'd ever had. I know what I like, I don't have performance anxiety, and I sure as hell know where my clit is. But since that night, everything just feels…meh. Caiden Verran freaking broke me, and he's keeping the one tool that can fix me—*his* tool—far out of reach.

According to Fiona—the only one I don't consider part of the enemy camp—Caiden's been spending all his time either working in his home office or working out in his gym. I took up a workout regimen of my own, hoping he'd "catch me" in my skimpy exercise gear working up a sweat, but he never did. Taking dips in the pool every night to try and recreate the original encounter didn't produce any results, either.

Which means he's keeping track of my whereabouts for the express purpose of avoiding me.

I just think the whole thing is rude, and if there's one thing I can't stand, it's rudeness. He's a shitty host, that's all I'm saying. Have I told him that yet? I should.

"You're a really shitty host, you know that?"

"According to you, you're not a guest, which means I'm not any kind of host, shitty or otherwise."

"Well, even a prison warden checks on the inmates from time to time. So you're a shitty one of those, too."

His eyes are still glued to his phone, his thumb tapping the screen every so often. It's sporting a fancy new privacy protector, so he could be watching porn for all I know.

When he doesn't engage, I circle back to an earlier

argument. "I don't understand why I couldn't have just stayed at the manor."

"Because I said so, that's why."

I snort. "Oh, that's mature."

Suddenly, his head snaps up, and his golden gaze slams into me with ferocious intent. "If you're going to act like a brat, then I'm going to treat you like one. Continue pushing me, Beauty, and I'll have you over my knee and your bottom so red, your silk panties will feel like sandpaper."

Heat curls in my belly and sinks between my legs. Fighting against the need to squeeze my thighs together, I part them just a little. Juuuuust enough for... There. I watch with satisfaction as Caiden's nostrils flare and a muscle tics in his jaw.

I bite my lower lip and tilt my head as I regard him, my blond hair slipping off my shoulder to fall forward, drawing his eyes to my breasts for the briefest of moments before he corrects himself.

"That threat didn't quite give you the result you intended, did it?" I say.

Tension hangs so thick in the air between us, it's practically suffocating, and yet I welcome it. This is so much better than his apathy, than his avoidance.

I hate feeling like I'm the only one burning alive without his touch and his commands.

His jaw continues to work. I've noticed it's a sign his emotions are skating on the negative side of the spectrum— anger, frustration, aggravation. Sexual deprivation.

Unless he's *not* sexually deprived. My stomach churns at the thought that maybe he's been leaving at night to see someone else. He could even have a whole cavalcade of women visiting the manor for all I know. The place is gigantic, with at least half a dozen entry points, including a garage with a gigantic lift that takes his car straight up to a private entrance to his bedroom, of all things! Like he's fucking Batman or something.

The thought of him getting his rocks off with anyone else turns into a simmering rage. Seething, I throw eye daggers at him from the other side of the bench seat. "Are you still seeing other women?"

Caiden finally puts his phone away in his pocket, then calmly presses the button to erect the privacy screen between us and Seamus, who's driving us to wherever it is we're going. As soon as it makes it to the top, he turns to look at me, irritation sparking in his eyes like exposed electrical wires. "You were, and still are, the only woman I have been with since my coronation."

Yes, he told me that, and if he in fact can't lie, then it's obviously the truth. And I know it's incorrect to refer to fae as women, but I couldn't give a shit about etymology technicalities right now. "You know what I mean, Caiden."

"I don't think that I do, Bryn, so why don't you spell it out for me. And be very careful what you accuse me of," he says in a low voice, his tone a blatant warning all its own.

It's a warning I don't heed. Because the more my brain spins, the more I'm positive he's going behind my back to dole out pleasure to others that should be rightfully mine. If not for our supposed bond, then at the very least as compensation for keeping me in Vegas for reasons he *still* has yet to fully explain.

I.

Am.

Livid.

"Don't you threaten me, asshole. I don't care if you're the king of the world or the devil himself. I'll be damned if you get to do whatever the hell you please while holding me hostage *and* pretending I don't exist. You don't get to have it both ways."

Faster than I register his movements, Caiden grabs me by the waist and hauls me sideways into his lap with my back against the door. I wedge my hands between us and try to shove away from him. Not because I want to be anywhere other than right where I am. But because I *don't*, and I hate myself for it.

His powerful arm bands around my back to crush us together as his other hand grips my jaw firmly so I have no choice but to meet his burning gaze. "Listen to me very carefully, Bryn, because I will not repeat myself. I might not have entered this bond willingly, but until I find a way to sever it and free us both, neither of us will be sating our sexual appetites with anyone else. Human or fae. *No one*. Do you understand?"

My chest heaves with the quick breaths sawing in and out of my lungs, but as I stare into his eyes, I see the truth plain as day, and my pulse begins to slow. The cloud of anger wreathing my head lifts more with every second that passes, and finally, clarity returns.

Biting my lip, I fight back the hot pricks of tears and swallow past the lump in my throat.

"Fuck, I...I'm so sorry, Caiden," I say, vacillating between embarrassment and confusion. "I don't know what came over me, why I said all that. I've never been a jealous person, even the times when I had reason to be, and this is not one of those times."

He visibly calms, and though he doesn't release me, his grip on my jaw relaxes. "It's the bond. It can turn even the most easygoing of people into a green-eyed monster."

Thinking back to when he got pissy at the mention of me getting lessons from the Woulfe twins or his brothers, I add, "Or a possessive asshole?"

"Or a possessive asshole." The corners of his mouth quirk up the tiniest bit.

Other than our first night together, any amount of humor is so rare on him that it feels like a huge victory. He drops both of his arms to rest his hands on the seat but doesn't make me move, so I don't.

"I apologize for making myself scarce these past weeks," he says. "I thought if I stayed out of your way, maybe you wouldn't be reminded as much as to why you've been uprooted from your life."

"Yeah, fat chance of that," I mumble. Though his explanation is plausible, it also sounds like a cop-out. "Is that the only reason you've been avoiding me?"

He eyes me thoughtfully for several long seconds, then answers definitively. "No."

"You're not going to elaborate, are you?"

"No."

"Didn't think so."

I sigh, still reeling from my outburst that came out of nowhere. If the bond can cause such visceral reactions like that, is it even wise to be across the country from him? And if I'm being honest, with each passing day I've felt less concerned with getting back home.

It's not like I have anything to go home to anyway. No family, no true friends, no job. I don't even have a cat waiting for me to feed him. Besides, I really have gotten close with Fiona, and it's not like I'm living in a shack.

"I realize I haven't made this easy on you. What can I do to make your stay more enjoyable?" I instantly perk up and open my mouth to answer. "Besides that, Bryn. This is complicated enough without adding sex into the mix."

My body cries with disappointment, but I know he's right. Doesn't mean I have to like it, though. Thinking about his question, I answer him honestly. "Just don't shut me out. I don't want to feel like we can't be friendly with each other. If you're going to insist—aka force—me to be a part of your world, then let me *be* a part of it."

After a minute, Caiden nods. "All right, I can do that."

"And let me sit in on your meetings tonight."

"Absolutely not—"

"Come on, I'll be as quiet as a church mouse—you won't even know I'm there."

"And what am I supposed to say is the reason a human is sitting in on fae business?"

"You're the king. You get to make up the rules. Come on, you can't tell me there are *no* humans in your inner circle who you trust." The look on his face and the fact that he's not denying it means I'm right. "Exactly! So tell them I'm there to take notes, and I'll sit quietly and scribble everything down for you so it's not a lie, and you can fire me afterward."

He's right at the edge of agreeing, I can tell, but he's so damn stubborn.

"Caiden, please, all I want is for a chance to get to know you better. Seeing you in your element would go a long way in doing that."

"Just sitting there and listening, that's all?"

I nod emphatically. "That's all I want, promise."

"Okay, I'll have Seamus inform the appropriate parties."

I squeal in delight and do a quick hand-clap of happiness, then decide I might as well push my luck while I've got it. "And I want an e-reader with an unlimited book budget."

His mouth twists as he chews on the inside of his cheek to prevent the smile I can see fighting to get through. "You drive a hard bargain, but I think that can be arranged."

"Then we have a deal?" I hold my right hand up between us, the first sparks of happiness I've felt in days lighting me up inside. Gripping my hand for a single shake, he lets his micro-smirk come through, melting me in ways I can't afford, but I no longer care.

"We have a deal."

CHAPTER FOURTEEN

CAIDEN

With our destination only a few minutes away and Bryn back on her side of the car, I do my best to shake off the adrenaline from our fight. I don't know why I didn't anticipate it happening. We had two weeks' worth of combined sexual tension stuffed into this back seat, turning it into a fucking powder keg with a short fuse.

All it took to light it was a single spark of jealousy, and we both saw red.

It took everything I had to keep the raging storm within me contained. Primal instinct rode me hard, wanting me to mark her as proof of my claim on her and only her, regardless of if it can never be true.

The possessive streak between true mates is a serious one. I know it was the eventual catalyst that led to our exile here in the first place, but I never understood why, why the kings and queens back then didn't just stay the fuck away from each other instead of inciting a war.

Now that I've experienced the bond for myself, I get it. And what we have is mild in comparison to what it would be if she were fae. A fact that makes me both grateful and irrationally pissed off, which I refuse to analyze.

I have to assume her being human is why she also has some traits of the bond and not others. As far as I know, she can't read my energy like I can hers. Or maybe it's that she doesn't know how to harness the power to even try.

It would be interesting to try and teach her, but the less she learns, the better. The end goal still is, and always will be, to break the curse or sever the bond, wipe her memories, then return her to her old life.

"I know I shouldn't get greedy, but I've never been good at quitting while I'm ahead," she starts with a mischievous grin. I arch my brow and wait for her to continue, curious at where she'll take us next. "Will you answer some of my questions about the fae?"

"Bryn—"

"I know, 'secret race so secrets must be kept.' Fiona has told me a dozen times when I've asked. But I'm not asking for your nuclear launch codes or whatever. I'm talking very basic things. *Tiny* things." She clasps her hands together and gives me a pitiful look. "Pleeeeease, Caiden?"

I sigh, resigned in accepting my weakness with this woman. It's a damn good thing fae *don't* have nuclear launch codes or Bryn might be able to convince me to let her hold them for safekeeping. She already knows that the Dark and Light Fae are in the human world due to Aine exiling us for transgressions by our ancestors. I allowed Connor to give her that much. But she doesn't know about our curses or anything that would reveal our weaknesses. That would be plain foolish.

"Tell me what you want to know, and I'll answer as much as I can."

The delight that beams from her warms me like the Vegas sun just before it sets. "Why don't you have wings? Is that one of the myths about fae?"

A harmless enough question I'm happy to answer. "No, it's

not a myth. The fae back in Faerie all have wings, but both exiled courts were stripped of our wings, those at that time and all future-born, as part of our consequences."

"Well that hardly seems nice," she says, her nose wrinkled. "That One True Queen chick sounds like a real b—"

I stop her with a hand over her mouth and shake my head. "You never know who or what is listening." She nods and I lower my arm. "I assume you have more than just the one question."

"The fangs. I thought that was a blood-drinking-vampire thing, although yours are shorter." Her eyes grow wide. "Wait, are vampires real, too?"

I ignore that last question. It's an unwritten rule not to out other races. "Fangs were used to drink blood, but that hasn't been done for a millennium."

What she doesn't need to know is that it used to be a war tactic. Since fae powers come from their bloodlines, by drinking the blood of another fae, you're able to siphon some of their magic temporarily, depending on how much is taken.

Aine banned the practice to prevent any one fae with desires of taking her throne from becoming too powerful. Though it is possible to drink from another without siphoning their magic, and it's common for mated fae to do so during lovemaking. Or so I hear.

"Really? Why— Whoa." Bryn's line of questioning is cut off with an awed whisper. "What is *that*?"

I follow her gaze out the window to where the pantheon has become visible now that we've passed through the cloaking glamour hiding it in plain sight from humans. The massive structure was built with bricks made of black sand that gleam in the moonlight and towering spires on every corner that stretch into the night sky as though trying to touch Rhiannon herself.

I begin to relax as tranquility trickles into my veins like

life-giving water finding its way into the cracks of the desert. I've come to this place at least twice every lunar cycle since my birth—close to five thousand times—and yet it always feels just as awe-inspiring as my first memory of it.

"That," I say with great pride, "is the Temple of Rhiannon, the oldest Night Court structure this side of the veil. It was the first thing my father built for our people when they chose to settle in the Mojave Desert. According to the elders, he designed the architecture to exactly match the Temple we had back in Tír na nÓg."

She tears her eyes from the window to look at me with a frown. "Teerna-what?"

"Tír na nÓg. It's where the Dark Fae hailed from in Faerie. Think of it like a country or continent. Faerie is the world and Tír na nÓg is the region."

"Fascinating." Her attention returns to study the Temple as though drawn to it, an expression of awe on her face.

Seamus pulls around to the back, near the private entrance used by the royal family and parks. Connor and Conall pull the Range Rover in next to us and get out to secure the area. Once they're in position by the entrance, Seamus opens my car door. I exit the Bentley and extend my hand for Bryn.

As soon as our palms touch, her energy zings up my arm and down through the center of my body, settling heavily in my balls, where it kickstarts my cock into action. I've learned being around Bryn is a constant exercise in bringing my libido to heel. I feel like I'm seventy all over again, with no control over my own dick.

"Copy that," Conall says into an earpiece, then addresses me. "Madoc says the ToR is clear. We're good to go."

I nod and place a hand at the small of her back to guide her across the distance.

"What's the tore?"

"T-O-R, the acronym for Temple of Rhiannon. Something

Connor came up with for the Night Watch to use in commu-
nications. It became a nickname of sorts."

She smiles at the Woulfe boys as we approach them. "It
has a nice ring to it. I like it."

"That's what I thought, too. Good evening, Bryn." Connor
beams one of his panty-melting grins at her—because
apparently, he has a death wish—and holds the door open to
usher her inside with a sweep of his hand. "Welcome to the
ToR."

"Thank you, Connor, and it's nice to see you. You too,
Conall."

"Same here, Bryn." He gives her a smirk with a wink.

I glare at both of them as I pass, making them even more
amused that they rankled me. *Assholes.*

As I guide her down the long hall, I discreetly watch Bryn
from the corner of my eye. "I'm going to pretend I didn't notice
how familiar and casual you are with my personal guards."

"Perhaps if you hadn't ignored me the past two weeks, we
wouldn't have had the chance to become so familiar." Then
she turns a saccharine grin on me and bats her eyelashes, her
tell that her bratty side is about to make an appearance. "Be
thankful it's only in a *familiar* sense and not a *biblical* one."

My stride doesn't break as I lean in with a low warning.
"Strike one, Beauty."

I keep my eyes forward but hear her soft gasp and feel her
surprise burning a hole into the side of my face as we turn
a corner. Irritation at my lack of control pricks the back of
my neck.

If anyone else had tried a stunt like that to make me
jealous, I wouldn't have reacted on principle. But Bryn has
the ability to push my buttons in just the right way that I react
before I even know what the hell I'm doing.

I shouldn't have given her a strike; it implies a possible
repeat performance of that night by the pool or more—*gods,*

I want to do so much more to that delectable fucking body of hers—and Bryn's liable to earn the last two strikes on purpose.

Thankfully, she has enough self-preservation to change the subject instead of goading me further. For now.

"So, Rhiannon. Is she your version of God?"

"We have many gods and goddesses. Rhiannon's name means 'Night Queen,' and in the Faerie Faith, she's the Moon Goddess."

Bryn nods, genuine interest showing on her face. "And because you're the Night Court, she's the same as a patron saint in Catholicism—the goddess you pray to specifically."

"Correct."

"But you said tonight is about business. What kind of business happens at night in the middle of the desert in a church? Is this like Vegas gangster stuff?"

"Temple. And no, there will be no gangster stuff. Not tonight, anyway."

Her eyes widen on a quiet gasp until she realizes—or hopes—I'm not being serious.

My lips twist in amusement.

I like teasing her. I should do it more often, maybe.

Don't get any ideas, asshole. This is not a friendship, a hookup, or a relationship. At most, it's a respectful coexistence. Keep it that way, for her sake and yours.

I clear my throat. "Every month, on the evening of the New Moon, there's an assemblage for dealing with Night Court interests."

Her ears perk up at that. "What kind? Does it have to do with that other court in Phoenix Connor told me about? Ooh, are we planning to dethrone the Lannisters? What's our exit strategy if 'The Rains of Castamere' starts playing?" I silently scold her with the arch of a brow, causing her to grin sheepishly. "Sorry, big *Game of Thrones* fan."

"Of course you are."

It seems like everyone and their brother watched *Game of Thrones*, but I never cared to hop on that bandwagon. The war between us and the Day Court might have been before my time, but I'm only one generation removed, and my father had plenty of horror stories he used as lessons to his sons to illustrate why peace with an enemy, no matter how precarious, is always the better option.

It was because of his strong belief that a treaty was proposed and signed by both courts, giving both sides a chance at rebuilding after exile.

We approach a room where Madoc is standing guard outside. He nods in greeting, then holds the door open for me and Bryn to enter while my small entourage goes through the final preparations before we begin.

The conference room is no different than one you'd find in a board room of a Fortune 500 company. A large table takes up most of the space with five plush leather chairs situated on each side and one at each end, a minibar in the corner, and a wall of windows providing a distracting view of the desert beyond.

Sitting to my left, she says playfully, "Hmm, no territory maps on the table. So then we're *not* making a play for the Iron Throne down in Phoenix."

My upper lip curls in disgust. "If such a thing existed, I would absolutely not be 'making a play' for it. Sitting on it would either kill me or burn the flesh from my bones, neither of which I find appealing."

Bryn covers her mouth with a hand, then drops it and winces. "Iron allergy, I forgot. Sorry, bad joke. Then what *are* we doing?"

Her insatiable curiosity—about all things, not just fae—is one of the qualities I find so attractive about her. I'm the same way, and an image of us lounging in front of a fireplace while reading and learning about new things together makes me want to grab her and take her home to do just that.

Instead, I concentrate on adjusting the shirt cuffs beneath my suit jacket to give my hands something *not that* to do.

I hear a barely audible gasp from her direction and glance over to find her watching the actions intently. "Something the matter?"

"Hmm?" she says, her gaze snapping back up to mine, and whatever thoughts she'd been lost in are now gone. "No, sorry. You were saying?"

I'm more than a little curious about what she's not telling me, but Bryn is fairly transparent. She'll tell me in her own time. Until then, I'm trying not to be an overbearing prick who demands to know her every thought. "We're here so that I can meet with any Dark Fae who wish to speak with their king."

"Oh," she says, her hazel eyes lighting up with understanding. "Like when the wrinkly old king sits on his throne, and he passes down judgment when the peasants have disputes with their neighbors over who owns which tract of land or when someone reneges on the arranged marriage for their daughter and doesn't give the other guy the two goats he was promised."

"Bryn, you watch entirely too much TV."

She scrunches up her nose in the most annoyingly cute way. "Probably."

"You're partially right; the concept is the same," I concede reluctantly. "Except I meet with them in this conference room, and my subjects aren't peasants, nor are they worried about tracts of land and/or goats." After a brief pause, I feel obligated to tack on, "And I'm sure as hell not wrinkly."

Laughing, she gives me a once-over. "Maybe not yet, but with all the desert sun you get, I bet you look like a shar-pei by the time you're in your sixties."

"Considering I passed sixties a long time ago, I'd take that bet."

She stares at me quizzically, like she's afraid to ask. "How long is long?"

"About a hundred years."

Her jaw practically falls into her lap. "You're *one hundred and sixty years old*?"

"One hundred and sixty-nine. Don't worry, it's not like you accidentally married—and fucked—a male with one foot in the grave. My age is the equivalent to your thirties."

"Well, thank God for that, because there's age kink and then there's just disturbing. But if you're in your version of thirties, that would mean your average life expectancy iiiiiiis…?"

She trails off to let me fill in the blank. "In Faerie, we're immortal. Here? Around five hundred, give or take half a century." *One more thing to lay at our curse's feet.*

She shakes her head, eyes big. "Wow, I can't even wrap my head around that. Not that I want to give you any ideas, but why are you even trying to break this bond? You could just wait for me to kick the bucket and still have another three hundred years to live up the bachelor life."

Suddenly needing a drink, I stand and make my way to the console table with a small selection of liquor, wine, and bottles of water. "In theory, yes," I answer as I pour a few fingers of whiskey from the crystal decanter. "However, there's a very real chance that if you die—*when* you die—so will I."

"What?" Her voice is low, and I swear I can hear her swallow.

I toss back the amber liquid, and by the time I'm pouring a refill, Bryn is by my side and looking up at me with concern swimming in her golden-green eyes. "You mean eventually, right? *Eventually* you'll die, when you're five hundred and something?"

My expression softens. "No, Beauty." Unable to stop myself, I stroke a thumb along the line of her jaw. "The bond for a member of the royal bloodline is…" *Cursed.* "Complicated.

Plus, the X-factor of you being human makes it even more so. To be honest, we're not sure what the rules are for our situation."

Disillusionment falls over her face like a heavy veil. "That's why you won't let me leave, then. You need to keep an eye on me to make sure I don't inadvertently murder you just by falling down a flight of stairs."

She's guessed wrong, but again, I can't risk correcting her. I also can't lie, so I go with evasion and a bad attempt to lighten the mood. "I don't think that would be considered murder. Manslaughter at the most, probably."

Maybe I'm getting better at this humor thing, because her lips twist into a reluctant grin. "So I shouldn't play in traffic or anything, huh?"

I reply with a half grin of my own just as Seamus enters the room. "I'd appreciate it if you didn't."

"Okay, then, I won't." Grabbing a bottle of water, she turns to Seamus and says, "Let's help some fae with their goats, shall we?"

He laughs at her joke, having softened toward her in only a matter of days. The old wolf holds out his elbow for her to slip her arm through and then guides her back to where she was sitting at the table.

As soon as she steps away from me, it's as if all the warmth in the air left with her.

I wish I could be certain what's causing me to feel the things I do for Bryn. Part of me still thinks I'm experiencing residual effects of whatever was in my system the night we met. Most of me blames the fucking bond for screwing with my head.

But I can't ignore the speck of something that's only recently made itself known. And it's telling me that maybe— just *maybe*—this connection I feel between us is real.

CHAPTER FIFTEEN

BRYN

Releasing a long sigh, I sink lower into the Japanese soaking tub in my room, letting the vanilla-sugar-scented water melt the knots in my shoulders from sitting hunched over the dining room table all day. I don't mind, though, because I was finally getting a chance to be productive and helpful by using my PR job skills.

Besides, it gave me something to focus on instead of whether or not Caiden would be exacting his punishment tonight or not.

Sitting in on last night's meetings between Caiden and his subjects was fascinating. Some of the issues brought before him were minor and others a bit more involved. And some only wanted to speak with him personally, either to compliment him or give him news about the birth of their new grandchild.

But in every encounter, Caiden was treated with great respect and reverence.

It was obvious how beloved he is by his people, and even though he's not one for wearing his emotions plainly, I could tell how much he cares for them as well. I saw a completely different side of Caiden last night, and it endeared him to me all the more.

Then, of course, there was *the sign*.

Caiden was wearing silver Celtic knot cuff links. Identical to my dad's.

Just when I'd started getting used to the idea that I had no choice but to play the part of the kidnapped faerie bride, the universe stepped in to let me know that none of this is by accident. That I'm meant to be here with Caiden, even if I don't know exactly why yet.

The reason for my new project was the last meeting of the evening.

The Tallons are a sweet older couple who have owned a custom jewelry and crystals shop in the old part of Vegas since those early days when the city was just a couple of hotels.

They told Caiden that for several years, their sales had been drastically declining, and they were at a point where they could no longer feasibly keep it open, so they asked if he would buy it from them. They'd brought binders of their accounting books from the past ten years along with photo albums of their entire inventory in hopes Caiden would find it to be a good investment.

But it was clear that having to sell their business was painful for them.

Caiden told the Tallons he didn't need to see their books or inventory, that he would be happy to buy their business for well over market price to ensure they were more than financially secure without their usual revenue stream.

That's when I broke my promise to stay quiet and opened my big mouth.

"Excuse me, Mr. and Mrs. Tallon, but may I see your inventory album?" After getting over their shock that I dared interrupt the king—if they only knew how I spoke to him 90 percent of the time, they'd probably have fallen off their chairs—they happily passed it over. It didn't take me long to realize that their product wasn't the problem. Likely, it was an advertising issue.

I started asking questions about how they promote their business, how often they run sales, and where they advertised, the whole nine yards. I took notes from what they told me (admittedly they were the first things I'd written down all night—I was a sucky assistant), and when I had all the information I needed, I made them an offer of my own.

"Obviously, you're more than welcome to accept Cai—uh, His Majesty's offer," I said, "but if you'd prefer to keep your shop, I can help you do that. No offense, but your methods of advertising are old-school. You need to be where your customers are, and that's social media and the internet. I can help you rebrand and build a strong online presence that will get your product in front of millions of eyes, and if they happen to be in town and want to visit the shop in person, great. But if they like what they see and they're in Hong Kong, they'll be able to purchase online, and all you'll have to do is send it off with the daily delivery guy. What do you say?"

The Tallons were ecstatic. Caiden…was wary. "Those are excellent ideas, and if the Tallons are interested, I'd be happy to set them up with someone from my marketing department."

I gave him a tight smile. "That's not necessary, sire; it would be my pleasure to head this up."

"I'm sure it would, and I appreciate what you're offering, Miss Meara, but I'm not sure right now is a good time for you to be taking on such an involved endeavor."

"Well, I think it's the perfect time, Your Majesty. If you recall, you don't have much need for me, so I have plenty of free time." Then, smiling sweetly, I added, "Of course, if you'd rather give the project to someone else, I suppose I could always put my efforts into assisting your heads of security with whatever might be useful to them."

He stared me down and ran his tongue over the front of

his teeth before affecting a smile for his guests.

Grabbing my pen and notebook from me, he scribbled something as he told them that he'd make sure I was at their disposal. When he pushed the notebook back to me, it read *Strikes 2 & 3, Beauty.*

As the Tallons talked excitedly between themselves, I wrote my own note for him and pushed it back: *Worth it.*

I didn't waste any time, starting first thing today and working until my shoulders were screaming at me, hence the soak in this glorious tub. Feeling much better, I get out and wrap a towel around myself. As I pad into the bedroom, I mull over my options for how to spend my evening but find it may have already been decided for me.

On the bed is a short, white satin robe and a black envelope. Faerie wings erupt in my belly as I slide my finger under the seal and pull out the black notecard. In silver pen, instructions are scrawled in Caiden's handwriting.

Wear only this & enter my room to find your next set of instructions.

I quickly finish towel-drying my hair, don the robe, and make my way across the second floor to his room. I've never been inside, so I'm incredibly curious what the private space of a king looks like. Taking a deep breath, I let myself in, then close and lock the door behind me.

The room is *massive*. It takes up the entire half of the manor on this level. Walking in, my eyes drink in the extravagance of the black and silver decor with chrome fixtures and the back wall made entirely of movable glass panels.

His bed is larger than king-size and faces the glass wall that provides the stunning view of the Vegas Strip in the distance.

The balcony on the other side of the glass is impressive in both spaciousness and as an outdoor living area with furniture and big-screen TV and outdoor fireplace.

The only color in the whole room is an old wingback chair

with a dark wood frame and bloodred damask upholstery. It's angled in the far front corner that would allow him to see every inch of the room, like his own private throne over his personal domain.

I start in that direction, wanting to run my hand over the material where Caiden must have sat hundreds of times, but my foot crunches on something.

Peering down, I see another black envelope on the dark-gray carpeting and remember what I'm supposed to be doing.

Biting my lip in anticipation, I collect the envelope and remove the matching note card.

Kneel with legs spread, hands on thighs, and wait.

A shiver of excitement runs along my skin.

Lowering to the floor, I follow his instructions, setting the card off to the side. On the other side of the room—the same side as the chair—is an open entryway that must lead to the bathroom. The faint sound of a shower running reaches my ears, and my imagination runs wild.

Caiden standing naked in a huge enclosure with a dozen or more fixtures spraying him with water. His hands roaming over the hills and valleys of his cut muscles, reaching down to grasp his thick cock, slick with soap, and give it a few slow strokes...

I exhale a deep, shuddering breath and try to clear my mind. If I continue fantasizing, my hands will be doing their own touching, and I don't want to disobey him.

It's a strange thought—one I doubt I would've ever considered having before him—and yet I'm completely at ease with it. Submitting to him sexually brings me a sense of peace and rightness I've never had with another man, so I don't plan on questioning it or caring if others might think I deserve to have my feminist card revoked. I only care that Caiden promises what I've always craved...complete and utter surrender.

Eager to submit or not, though, waiting and patience are not in my top-five strengths.

It's taking all my self-control not to move from this position. The damp ends of my hair in front of my shoulders are soaking through the thin satin, making sections transparent, including my chest. My sensitive nipples already ache, the robe causing delicious tingles in my breasts as they grow heavy with need. Air caresses the wet flesh between my legs. And, oh God, I can feel my pulse throbbing in my clit, begging me to give it just one quick stroke with the pad of my finger...

The water turns off, and I hold my breath. Then he emerges, completely naked except for the leather wrist cuff and a silver chain around his neck with some kind of charm hanging between his taut pecs. Loose curls heavy with moisture hang over his forehead and around the pointed tips of his ears. His tanned skin is dewy from the steam, and as he moves, random droplets of water cut paths through the lines of his muscles.

Golden eyes hold me captive as he prowls toward me and stops a mere foot away. That's when I realize what's hanging from the chain. His wedding ring.

A feeling of possessiveness rises up inside me to see him wearing something that symbolizes our union despite how much he wants it to end. I almost make a comment but think better of it, knowing he wouldn't appreciate me speaking out of turn right now.

He won't be so lucky later.

I can't see it with my head tipped this far back, but I know his cock is within sucking distance. I can practically feel its looming presence, and the temptation to simply lean forward and take him in my mouth is almost overwhelming. He must see the longing on my face because he strokes an approving hand over my hair, then brings it around to cup my chin.

"You've done well, Beauty." His tone is gruff and commanding, sending a shiver down my spine. "You'll be rewarded for following my instructions. But don't forget that I owe you a punishment as well."

Biting my lip, I say, "Looking forward to it, my king."

He arches a brow. "Starting off bratty, are we? Bold choice." I can almost see him file my insolence away to take out later, and a tiny thrill races through me. "Before we go any further, I want you to know that you can stop what's about to happen between us at any moment with the use of a safe word. Then we'll end this here and now, no hard feelings. Nod if you understand."

I nod.

"Good," he says, watching his thumb rub across my bottom lip before releasing me. "Choose your safe word, something you'll easily remember."

I think about my first encounter with Caiden, how I played the riskiest game in his casino and came out on top. Playing like this with him feels just as risky, and yet I've never been more sure this is the right bet to make. "Roulette."

His eyes darken to molten toffee, igniting the fire in my belly.

"'Roulette,' it is. Let's begin."

He turns and walks away, and the way his ass looks as he moves should be illegal, all firm and round, with those sexy side indents I'd like to sink my nails into as he thrusts between my thighs.

Lowering his tall frame onto the red chair, he leans back and spreads his legs, offering me the perfect view of exactly what I want. He drapes his right arm over the side while his left hand begins lazily stroking his cock. My mouth waters at the sight.

"Strip." The command echoes through the room and disrupts the butterflies in my stomach. Hoping the slight trembling of my hands isn't noticeable, I reach up to slide the satin from my shoulders. "Fold it neatly and place it out of the way."

I quickly fold the robe and set it aside. When the air hits my damp nipples, they furl into tight buds and draw Caiden's gaze. His lips part enough that I can see the tips of his fangs. God, those are such huge turn-ons. The things I've fantasized involving the sharp tips of his canines would make me blush if I had to say them out loud, but it doesn't make me want them any less.

"I can't help but notice the way you're staring at my cock." His hand strokes from root to tip, then he twists his palm over the head before moving it down again. "Do you want my cock, Beauty?"

"Yes, my king."

"Then keep your eyes on me...and crawl to it."

I don't even hesitate. I get on all fours and crawl to him, hyperaware of every new sensation. The plush carpet gives way under my hands and knees with every step. Nearly dry sections of hair run down my back and blanket my upper arms. My breasts, heavy with arousal, hang and sway gently with my movement, and cool air kisses my swollen pussy lips that barely peek out from between my thighs.

When I reach him, I resume my original position of sitting back on my heels and wait for further instructions.

"Go ahead," he says. "Look at it."

Grateful for the permission, I lower my gaze and get my first up-close look at what Caiden's been keeping from me since our wedding night, and *Jesus Christ*. Molds of his dick should be made to create the perfect dildo and mass-produced for the whole world to enjoy. It's porn-star-long and impossibly thick, with a fat head and deep ridge that will add an extra pop of pleasure every time he pulls out. His hand stops to squeeze just under the crown, and I watch as a clear drop of pre-cum beads at the tip.

A mewl of hunger escapes the back of my throat as I bite

my lip in barely contained restraint.

"You want it?" He releases his heavy shaft and it drops to point straight at me.

I lick my lips, then flick my eyes up to his. "Badly, my king."

"Earn it."

"How?" I ask earnestly.

"By pleasing me, which you do by obeying me. And as there's the little matter of your punishment, we'll see how well you take it." He holds his hand out. "Up and over my knee, brat. It's time for your spanking. A *real* one."

Again, I don't hesitate. This is my darkest fantasy—the one that remained hidden until this enigmatic male sparked it to life—and I'm ready to own it. I *want* to give up control like this in the bedroom. And what's more, I want to give it up to *him*.

I let him help me to my feet, then guide me over his left knee and arm of the chair with his cock trapped under my belly. One of his hands caresses my back while the other roams over the globes of my ass. From what little I experienced with him out by the pool, I recognize this as the calm before the storm. The part where he lulls me into a false sense of—

Smack!

I hear the slap a full second before I feel the sting. *"Shit."*

"Silence." *Smack.* "You're allowed to make as much noise as you want, but no words unless I give you a direct order or ask you a question." *Smack.* "This is your punishment, and you'll take it without complaint." *Smack.* "Is that understood? Answer." *Smack, smack.*

I suck in a breath through my teeth as the flames lick the surface of my flesh, then mewl as he caresses the area, encouraging the warmth to sink between my legs and make me wet. "Yes, my king, I understand."

His fingers trace the cleft of my ass and follow it down until they're able to probe my pussy lips to find my entrance. "Already dripping. It makes me wonder if you defied me just to feel the sting of my hand again."

I open my mouth but stop myself from speaking. I'm not sure what the right answer is.

SMACK.

"Ahh!" That one was harder than others, yet again the pain melts into pleasure that causes a new rush of arousal. Caiden tests my reaction, sliding two long fingers deep into my sex, slowly pumping in and out of my tight channel.

"We'll see how brazen you are once I introduce you to the next part." Pulling his fingers out, he drags my wetness up to rub it around my asshole. Nerves I didn't even know existed suddenly light up with a zing, and he has me squirming on his lap in seconds. "Mmm," he says, the sound a low rumble in his chest. "So eager."

When he stops touching me there, I barely have time to register my disappointment before he rains down more slaps to my ass cheeks. He keeps the pacing and placement varied so I can't predict when or where his hand will land next. My body jerks with every sharp contact, but with his other arm holding me down, I'm unable to move very far.

Not that I want to get away, it's just that my actions are no longer driven by conscious thought. I'm operating on autopilot, not fully aware of my movements unless I concentrate on them, but even then it's like watching myself through the hazy veil of a dream.

Fire, warmth, wetness… Fire, warmth, wetness…

So good, so good.

How does something this painful feel this fucking good?

The pattern rolls through me again and again, sometimes overlapping and other times giving me a short reprieve depending on the cadence of his hand.

I'm both overwhelmed by the cacophony of sensations and hyper-focused on every detail. I can feel my arousal trailing down my inner thigh and the graze of his cock head on my belly. I hear the echo of each slap and the pounding of my heartbeat. I smell the soap on his skin and his unique scent in the air.

I focus on the carpet below me down to the individual threads until his hand holds a silver object in front of my face. It's bulb-shaped, with a pointed tip and a stem on the opposite side with a ruby-red gem the size of a quarter on the end.

"Do you know what this is?" he asks.

I blink a few times and try to answer, but the feel of his palm caressing the tender skin of my ass is distracting. Licking my lips, I finally manage to put words together. "It's a butt plug."

"That's correct," he says. "I bought it just for you." He turns it and shows off the engraving in beautiful script that says *Beauty* on the smooth metal surface. "Do you like it?"

I reply tentatively. "I think it's very pretty, my king, especially the engraving, but…"

"Go on."

I swallow and feel my face flush. "But I'm not sure if I'll like it *in* me."

"You will," he says, then his hand disappears from my view. A second later, I jump when a stream of cold gel hits the seam of my ass. Fingertips massage it around my asshole as he speaks. "What gives you pleasure is for me to decide. Do you understand?"

Never in my life has a man spoken to me with such disregard, and yet I've never been more turned on than I am in this moment. *Make it make sense. Or don't, actually.* I honestly don't care. Because with that one statement, Caiden has given me permission to not think, to just feel.

He's in charge of my pleasure, and it makes me shiver with anticipation. "I understand, my king."

"Good," he says with a wicked undertone that makes a fresh wave of arousal flood my pussy. Then his voice softens with his next statement—not much, but enough that I hear the Caiden from that first night come through the role he's playing now. "However, I'll remind you that you always have the option of using your safe word to stop anything at any time. Tell me you'll remember that."

"I'll remember."

"Good girl." A large hand smooths over my hair, then trails down my back to join the other one still massaging between my cheeks. "Now, let's get you decorated like a pretty little slut."

Butterflies erupt in my belly, their wings on fire from the sweet degradation of his words.

I *want* to be his slut, his whore, his dirty little every-fucking-thing. Because I know deep down he's not insulting me with these titles—he's *revering* me.

And that makes all the difference in the world.

Wedging the cool metal tip of the plug against my puckered hole, he works it in farther with a slow and steady push, keeping it moving forward to get past the ring of muscle that wants to clamp down to prevent the intrusion. "Relax for me, Beauty...that's it. Good."

My asshole stretches to accommodate the plug as it widens. It burns a bit and my brain is shouting that it's an exit only when Caiden reaches under me with his free hand and rubs my aching clit.

"Ohhh..." I moan that one syllable until I'm out of breath and the end of the plug finally slips in, allowing my hole to close around the stem.

"Fuck, that looks nice. Cherry-red ass with a gem to match." He taps on the jewel several times, causing the plug to move inside me. I whimper as intense pleasure vibrates through my entire body. "What do you think about the plug in your ass now, my little slut?"

"I love it, my king."

He lets out an evil chuckle. "Of course you do. Back on

your knees now, come on."

Caiden helps me off his lap and sets me carefully into my original position kneeling between his legs. When my butt hits my heels, I hiss and pop back up. He gives me a wicked grin, and his hard cock still jutting from his body twitches.

It turns him on to witness my discomfort by his hand, which turns me on in kind. Because at some point during my spanking, my arousal became directly linked to his.

"Now that your punishment is over, it's time for your reward."

It feels like a year has passed since that conversation, so I don't immediately remember what he's talking about. Then he gives himself a couple of slow strokes, drawing my gaze down to his mouthwatering member.

"What are you waiting for, Beauty? Show your king how you worship his fucking cock."

CHAPTER SIXTEEN

CAIDEN

On the outside, I appear seemingly unaffected, bored even, as I wait for Bryn to follow my command.

But inside, my pulse is jackhammering its way through my veins, and I have to consciously keep my breaths slow and deep or I'd be hyperventilating from the anticipation of finally feeling her mouth on me.

She licks her lips, leaving a sheen of moisture behind I want to taste as I suck and bite at her mouth.

Soon, you'll have her soon.

The thought has my balls drawing up tight and my cock twitching as she inches closer between my splayed legs.

She grasps my shaft in one hand and blinks in surprise when she realizes her fingertips are still an inch away from her thumb.

Peering up at me through her lashes, she licks the crown with the flat of her candy-pink tongue. I clench my jaw to keep my reactions at bay, my only tell the flare of my nostrils as a jolt of electricity travels down the length of my dick.

Watching her lap at the drop of pre-cum leaking from the slit is the most phenomenal thing I've ever witnessed.

My lids lower to half-mast when she swirls that wicked tongue around the head a few times. Then she sucks my cock into her hot mouth as far as it will go, and I lose my grip on my control entirely.

A growl rumbles low in my chest as my fingers tangle in her hair, and I begin to guide her movements. She can get my length about halfway down her hot throat and uses her hand to pump and twist on the half she can't.

Bryn sucks my cock like she's one step away from porn-star level. The intense suction and way she swirls her tongue around the shaft at the same time, ending with a flick against the sensitive spot below the crown, is incredible.

Staring into her hazel doe eyes, I groan. "Fuck yes, that's it. I'll have to teach you how to take my cock all the way to the back of your throat like a good little—"

Instead of finishing her upstroke, she reverses her direction as she moves her hand away and continues past the midpoint. I can't even disguise my shock when the head of my dick pushes past the opening of her throat and slides in until her lips are stretched around the root of my cock. She holds the position as she looks up at me, her eyes watering from the effort, but there's no sense of discomfort or panic in her energy.

"Fuck." If I let her deep-throat me any longer, I'm in serious danger of coming right the hell now. I've never pulled a female off me before, but I'm starting to think I'm going to have a lot of firsts with Bryn, which is a wild concept for someone who's been fucking for well over a century.

Guiding her with my hands, I push her gently back until my cock springs from her moist lips and lean forward to pin her with a hard glare. "What the fuck was that, Beauty?"

I meant to sound curious, but at the thought of her porn-star-blowing for some other guy, it came out as more of an accusation.

She smiles wide, clearly proud of herself. "I'm part of the

25 percent of the female population with no gag reflex. I've only done it with a dildo before, though."

Then she actually blushes with a shy giggle. It's so unlike her, and that glimpse of rare vulnerability from her is all too endearing.

This woman is dangerous in more ways than I can count.

I should be running in the opposite direction. Instead, I find all I want to do is draw nearer despite the myriad of warning signs surrounding her.

So I do.

With an animalistic growl, I pull her face to mine and devour her like prey. Lips smashed together, teeth clashing and biting, tongues thrusting.

It's not sensual or romantic. Not even sexy or erotic.

It's predatory and hedonistic, carnal and uncensored.

This isn't kissing. It's depraved, filthy mouth-fucking.

I grab her up and carry her to the foot of my bed where I reluctantly sever our connection to drop her onto the mattress. She squeaks when her tender ass stuffed with the plug makes contact with the comforter but recovers quickly.

Assuming I want her in the center of the bed, she starts to move toward the headboard. My hands latch on to her ankles, though, and yank her back to me.

She hisses in a breath from the friction on her sensitive skin that I beat until I was sure she'd be reminded of me every time she sits for at least a week.

"If I wanted you up there, I would've thrown you up there. If I want you to change positions or move, I'll tell you what to do or pose you myself."

Reaching under the bed, I retrieve the black duffel I stashed there before my shower. It's a small sampling of essentials I put together, not knowing what I might be in the mood for.

But I know now.

I take out a simple system of four leather cuffs and start by buckling the two larger ones to fit snuggly around her thighs. Then I do the same with the smaller set on her ankles. Finally, I position her arms straight out with her forearms together. Taking out a length of black rope from the bag, I wrap it around her wrists and begin working my way up.

When I reach her elbows, I finish off the wrap with a few well-placed knots and check my work to make sure her circulation hasn't been compromised.

Satisfied that everything is as it should be, I flip the switch on the tone and grab her by the throat with one hand and roughly pinch a nipple with the other. Then I loom over her until my face eclipses her vision, taking over her whole world.

"Before we continue, and because you're new to this, I'm going to reiterate this very important rule. Nod if you're paying attention." She nods. "Do not presume to know what I want or act of your own accord. It is not your role to think or make decisions in this space. You are mine to do with as I please, my dirty little slut. Understand? Answer."

Staring up at me with lust-glazed eyes, she whispers, "I understand, my king."

She might accept it. But can she admit it? "What are you?"

"Your dirty little slut."

Hearing her repeat my degrading words with the ghost of a smile on her face floods me with satisfaction and pride.

I'm not surprised she gets off on it, though. She hadn't balked at the small taste of degradation I gave her that night by the pool, and through the bond I can feel her excitement spike every time.

Besides, from previous conversations, I know a big part of her identity is that she pleases others by being the best at things or by being helpful and a positive influence. But that kind of constant pressure is exhausting.

I should know, because I'm the same as her in that respect.

Though for me, it's more out of a sense of responsibility and living up to expectations. But the point is, in a scene like this, we can both let go of our roles as being inherently *good* and embrace the versions of ourselves that thrive on being *bad*.

Kink allows you to embrace the part of yourself that isn't given free rein in your everyday life. And I want nothing more than to be the one to give Bryn that freedom.

"Fucking right you are." I reward her with a plundering kiss, invading her with a quick thrust of my tongue before biting her lower lip and tugging on it until it pulls free. "Now, turn over so I can see that pretty plug and my marks on your ass."

She rolls to her stomach, and I lift her hips up to get her knees and bound arms underneath her. Then I bend her legs and attach the clips on the ankle cuffs to the metal rings on the thigh cuffs. The way she's bound with the rope and cuffs, she won't be able to move, keeping her on display for me and in the perfect position for how I want to fuck her.

"Mmm, now that view is a thing of beauty." I grab the jeweled end of the plug and move it around in circles as I run a finger up and down her soaked slit, making her whimper.

Normally, I'd draw this out, maybe edge her for a while, deny her the orgasm she craves. But I won't survive it, not this first time.

I'm just as desperate to be inside her as she is to feel me. So I'm going to put us both out of our misery and save the sadism for another day.

She can't alter her position, but she's still able to move her hips, as proved by the way she's humping the air right now. "Such a needy little slut, trying to fuck my finger. Something you want, baby?"

"Yes," she moans.

I slap her already red ass. She hisses in a breath. "Yes *what*? Then tell me what it is."

"Yes, my king. I want your cock. Please, can I have it?

Please, my king, I want it so badly."

Leaning over her, I palm the front of her throat and pull her head back while I line myself up. "Since you begged so nicely. I hope you're ready to get the life fucked out of you." Then I slam my hips forward, skewering her on my cock.

She cries out and my vision winks away for a split second at the way her hot pussy spasms around me like a tight fist.

But I don't waste time letting either of us enjoy the moment. I start pistoning my hips, thrusting deeper and harder, again and again, bottoming out with each powerful stroke to chase the ultimate high.

Now that I've decided to give in to my baser needs for this woman, I can do all the things I've been fantasizing about whenever the mood strikes. But there's no controlling myself this time, so I won't even try.

Standing up straight again, I grip her ass cheeks and spread them apart to get the best view of her pretty cunt swallowing my cock over and over. The moans and nonsensical mumblings tripping off her lips make up my new favorite sex soundtrack.

Her energy is projecting so strongly, the air is vibrating with her pleasure, increasing mine a hundredfold.

"Oh fuck yes," she says, her channel getting impossibly tighter around me. "I need to come. Please, my king, may I come? *Please, please, please…*"

There's no way I can deny her, because I won't be far behind. Pressure is building at the base of my spine and in my balls. My orgasm is barreling down on me and no amount of mental gymnastics reciting boring facts will be able to stop it. Which means I need to justify my permission and put us both out of our misery.

Leaning over, I fist her hair and pull it back to speak in her ear again. "Since you begged like such a good little whore without needing to be reminded, yes." Then I allow myself a real moment amid the kinky chaos and whisper, "Come for me, Beauty."

And she shatters.

Her mouth drops open on a silent scream, her legs shaking as her pussy clenches and spasms around my cock. I continue to pound into her, going faster and harder. Her entire body begins to tremble, and I can feel a second climax overtake her, even more powerful than the first one.

And I can't hold off any longer.

The pressure crests and becomes too much to contain. I roar and slam into her one final time as spurts of my seed lash her pulsing walls, causing her to moan and rub her ass against me. I don't even know if she's aware of what she's doing, but if she keeps it up, I'll be tempted to go for another round.

I press a kiss to her damp temple. "Good girl, Beauty. Hold still. I'm going to remove the plug and get you out of the restraints, okay?"

She nods, then rests her forehead on her fists as she tries to catch her breath. I work quickly and efficiently, careful to pull the plug out slowly and set it off to the side to take care of later. Then I unbuckle and remove the cuffs before helping her onto her side.

As I undo the knots and start unwinding the rope from her arms, I do cursory checks on how she's doing, looking for any signs of distress and reading her energy to make sure I'm not missing anything.

Thankfully, she's properly blissed out in subspace, but she'll be dropping now that the scene is over, and it's my job to provide the aftercare that will allow her to come down slowly and help her with any complicated emotions that can sometimes arise.

The indents on her forearms left behind by the rope are beautiful—another example of leaving my mark on her body that speaks to that primal part of me.

Dropping the rope into the bag, I grab the small jar of

balm. "Almost done. This will help the healing process."

I carefully rub the ointment onto her ass cheeks until I'm sure I've covered everything that's red, then toss it in the bag and set it all on the floor.

"Come on, Beauty, up you go." I gather her against my chest and walk around the side of the bed. I get her under the covers, then join her against my better judgment.

I've never had a female in my room before, much less my bed. But thinking of sending her back to her room at any point tonight grates on me. I tell myself it's not a big deal, since we slept in the same bed the first night we met, then I put it out of my mind and set my focus where it needs to be.

Gathering Bryn in my arms, I stroke her hair back from her face and run a hand up and down her back under the covers. "How are you feeling, Beauty?"

"Mmmm..." She snuggles in closer, throwing a leg over mine and nuzzling her face in the crook of my neck. "I feel kind of floaty, like I'm in a really lucid dream."

"That's normal." I sense a ripple of something in her energy, but it's not strong enough to separate out from her general state of a pleasure hangover. "Is there anything you want to talk about, Bryn?"

"Nope. Time for bed." Her speech is slow with exhaustion, but I want to make sure there's nothing I need to address before I let her nod off for the night.

Keeping my tone light and teasing, I say, "Don't lie to me, Beauty. You can't afford to earn strikes so soon after your spanking."

She snorts a laugh but doesn't immediately capitulate, so I continue to caress her soft skin and force myself to wait her out.

Finally, she gives a half shrug, almost like she's giving in to an argument with her own brain. "I was just thinking that for a man who doesn't want to be married, you sure have an interesting choice in necklaces."

My movements pause long enough to signal my surprise. *Busted.*

I've only had it for a little over two weeks, but the chain with my ring already feels as much a permanent part of my wardrobe as my wrist cuff that I didn't think about Bryn seeing it.

"You're right, it's time for bed."

Her quiet chuckle vibrates against my chest. "That's what I thought."

Unable to stop the grin, I do my best to keep my voice stern. "Go to sleep, brat."

Sighing like a contented kitten, she whispers, "Yes, my king."

And as I listen to her breaths grow deep and even and feel her heart beating near mine, I lose another little piece of myself to my mate.

CHAPTER SEVENTEEN

CAIDEN

A huge part of doing business is schmoozing your prospective partners or investors. It's a fact everyone at my level takes advantage of, including myself. I've been flown all over the world to dine with foreign dignitaries, real-estate moguls, and hotel royalty under the guise of "doing business."

It's complete bullshit and a waste of time.

Contracts don't require beluga caviar, Wagyu steak, and bottles of Cristal to sign on the dotted line. But it's all part of the dance, and if you want to play to win, you have to follow certain rules.

Tonight, it's my turn to play the part of the gracious host to my new East Coast business associates who are working with me to build a Nightfall in New York City. I flew them out to Vegas on my G6, gave them each ten-thousand-dollar markers to blow in my casino this afternoon, and now I'm treating them to a five-course meal at my three-Michelin-star restaurant on the top floor of the Nightfall Tower. (Yes, there *is* a tower in the hotel, but my office is closer to the middle, so the Rapunzel comparison is still asinine.)

Being social isn't my strong suit. There are two things I

know how to do well: serve my people as their king and make a shit ton of money with investments, real estate, casinos, and more.

The irony of these business dinners, though, is that no one wants to talk about business, which is why Tiernan and Finnian always attend with me. Tier works his magic and charms anyone I put in front of him with jokes and flattery while Finn is great with the obligatory male sports talk and discussing current events.

It allows me to add cursory statements now and again without having to put too much effort into the conversation.

Tonight, however, I could've told my brothers to stay home, and it wouldn't have made a damn bit of difference, because they're not the ones stealing the show.

It's Bryn.

From the moment we arrived in the restaurant, she had all five New Yorkers eating out of the palm of her hand, drawing everyone's attention with ease and schmoozing like she was getting paid for it.

I guess she used to be. She said she was in public relations back home but was between jobs right now, and I can't help but wonder why that is. Had to be her doing because with the expert way she's working the room, a company would have to be stupid to get rid of her.

Our group of twelve is seated at a large round table, and despite the distance it creates, Bryn—who is seated to my left—has made sure to engage each of them in individual conversations as well as getting the whole group to talk and laugh about everything from the funniest Super Bowl commercials to arguing over whose state has the harshest winters.

Everyone is so wrapped up in having a good time with Bryn that they haven't noticed my silence or that I can't seem to take my eyes off her.

It's been almost a week since the night I fucked her in my bedroom, and we haven't been together like that since. We've shared a couple of meals, and she even convinced me to watch some silly reality TV show with her, Conall, and Connor.

But between my usual business dealings and responsibilities as king, I've had the extra stressors of preparing for the upcoming Fall Equinox meeting with Talek Edevane, the Day Court king, whom I'll be meeting for the first time, and following different leads that might point us in the direction of how to break this curse, or at least undo the marriage to sever the bond.

Needless to say, I haven't had a lot of extracurricular time.

Thankfully, Bryn has been keeping busy as well, working on the rebranding and marketing plan for the Tallons and their jewelry and crystal shop.

Something that has endeared her to me more than I'd like, but I'm doing my best not to overanalyze anything right now.

We have no idea how long we're going to be in this position, and there's no way I'll be able to hold out against this pull indefinitely—whether it's imagined, manufactured, or real. So, for now, I choose to take a page out of Tier's book and just "go with the flow."

Charles Anderson, the CEO of a major hotel chain based on the East Coast, laughs uproariously at something Bryn said that I missed while lost in my thoughts. "Verran," he says, trying to catch his breath, "where in the hell did you find this woman? She's an absolute delight."

Bryn turns to me, a megawatt smile lighting up her beautiful face.

Holding her gaze, I answer Anderson truthfully, as only I can. "She caught my eye one day, and I haven't let her out of my sight since."

"Well, I don't blame you for that. What did you say she does for you again?"

I answer before Bryn can respond. "She's my PR specialist for a new division at Nightfall Corp."

Her eyes widen on me, and I think I'm almost as shocked as she is. But now that I've said it out loud, I realize that it's the truth because I want it to be. I, of course, have a public relations team, but no one with the kind of natural charisma Bryn has.

And I know she has a passion for the work based on the way she's worked tirelessly on the rebranding campaign for the Tallons since offering to help them.

At her questioning gaze, I raise my brows in challenge and lower my voice for only her to hear. "You did say you were between jobs, and seeing as you'll be sticking around for a while…" I shrug, throwing the ball in her court.

"And will this be similar to my last term of employment with you?"

That makes me laugh. She's referring to her precious few hours as my assistant at the ToR before I "fired" her. She made a shit assistant anyway; she was so engrossed in observing every meeting I had that night that she didn't even pretend to write a single thing down.

"No, this is an honest offer for as long as you're in Vegas, Bryn. I don't need to see your résumé to know you're damn good at what you do. Watching you tonight would've been enough, but I've also seen the exceptional work you've done for the Tallons.

"There are others in my court who could use someone like you to help bring their small businesses into the twenty-first century. I'll pay you double whatever you made back home, and we can convert one of the guest rooms at the manor into an office space."

Moisture glistens in her hazel eyes, but she quickly blinks it back. "You're serious."

"I am." I'm learning that Bryn thrives on having a purpose

and helping others. This allows me to give her both under the guise of looking after my people.

And if I'm being completely honest, the idea of her immersing herself into my world satiates the primal part of me that wants to tie her to me in every way possible. So that when we figure out a way to set her free, she might find it too hard to leave.

Because I'm a selfish fucking bastard who wants to keep what he's not supposed to have.

Giving me her brilliant smile, she holds out her right hand beneath the table so no one can see. "I accept your offer, Mr. Verran, and look forward to working for your court."

Instead of shaking on it, I slip my left hand into her right and intertwine our fingers before bringing them both to rest in my lap. Frissons of our combined energy ripple up my arm and warm my chest. I've grown so used to the feeling that it doesn't even surprise me anymore.

I simply revel in it.

But Bryn's brow furrows as her gaze snaps down to where our hands are joined, and when she lifts her eyes back up to meet mine, there's a hint of wonder.

Is the bond finally starting to affect her?

A small thrill runs down my spine at that thought, even as my brain is warning me that a human feeling fae things can only mean our situation is getting more complicated, not less.

Before I have the chance to ask her about it, Anderson bellows to me from across the table.

"Better continue to keep an eye on her, Verran." He laughs, his ruddy cheeks practically hiding his eyes with his mirth. "I might just try to steal her away from you and take her back to New York with me."

Red tries to eclipse my vision, but I push it back and force a smile onto my face that feels more predatory than convivial. "Over my dead body, Charles."

Tiernan chokes on his water to my right, and Finni glares a hole in the side of my head (he doesn't find the humor in my situation and hates it when Tier makes jokes about it). Seamus doesn't seem to be amused, either, but Dougal, the senior manager of Nightfall Vegas, and Sean, our manager for the one we're building in Manhattan, laugh along with the rest of the table, oblivious to the fact that my statement wasn't made in jest but in truth.

"Lady and gentlemen, the dessert course has arrived." Three members of the waitstaff begin distributing large plates holding what look like tiny sculptures in shades of brown and cream as the head server, Quinn, announces what it is. "Tonight we have the chef's famous Michelin-starred whiskey-and-chocolate cremeaux with whiskey ice cream, coffee, and caramel."

As expected, my guests express their elation and a few even take out their phones for the obligatory pictures to post on social media or send to others for bragging rights. But my attention is on the head server, who's placing a different dessert in front of Bryn. "And for the special lady this evening, the chef has prepared a brand-new creation: a deconstructed hot toddy."

"Oh, wow," she says, her eyes big as she takes in the mini work of art. "He made this just for me?"

"He did. He's thinking of adding it to the menu and wanted to know your opinion. As the special guest of our"—Quinn's eyes flick up to mine. I raise a brow in a silent reminder that we're in mixed company—"esteemed employer, Chef would love to know whether it's worthy of Nightfall's reputation."

"Well, this is exciting." Picking up her fork, she takes a small bite as everyone looks on. She makes a surprised sound behind closed lips, then brings her fingers in front of her mouth before speaking. "Does this have lemon in it?"

"Yes, miss, it does. The main components are a lemon and

honey cake, lemon confit, ginger ice cream, and a whiskey gel."

Well, now I know why no one else in my party was offered to try the hot toddy dessert. Lemons don't agree with fae. When I pick up on a change in Bryn's energy, I home in on her. "What is it, Bryn?"

"Oh, it's nothing," she says, waving away my concern. "I've just never been a huge fan of lemon, that's all."

"Quinn, take it away."

"No!" Bryn puts her hands up to stop Quinn as he reaches for her plate. "Honestly, it's okay. It's not that strong, and I don't want to insult the chef." I open my mouth to argue with her, but she gives me a quelling look, asking me to drop it, so I do. Turning back to Quinn, she says, "Thank you so much. Please tell him it's delicious and would make a wonderful addition to the menu."

Quinn beams, obviously thrilled he doesn't have to deliver bad news. "I will, miss, thank you. Enjoy your desserts, everyone."

And with that, we're left to drift back into inane dinner conversations while eating the final course of the three-hour dining experience. Bryn hops back in, injecting her two cents and challenging the New York partners with thought-provoking questions. Foregoing my own dessert, I choose to sip my drink and keep my eye on her.

Tiernan leans in from my other side. "Brother, if you don't blink soon, our guests will start to wonder if you've turned into a statue."

Bryn sets her fork down, half her dessert gone now, and clears her throat before drinking some water, then trying to clear her throat again.

"Something feels off," I tell Tiernan quietly.

His tone turns serious. "Off like how?"

I shake my head subtly. "I don't know. Her energy, it's just...off." I'm not sure how to explain it except that after almost three weeks of feeling and learning our mate bond, I can tell that something isn't right. Turning my head toward my brother, I say, "I'm going to take her home. Can you and Finn finish up here with them?"

Tier gives me a confident nod. "Of course, go take care of your—"

Even before I see Tier's eyes widen on a spot past my shoulder, I *feel* her panic.

Whipping back around, my heart seizes in my chest at the terror written on Bryn's face as she gasps for breath. Her hands fist on the sleeves of my suit as she falls out of her chair.

"Bryn!" I lower her gently to the floor, kneeling at her side and scanning her for any clues. Seamus barks out for Sean to call 911, but with how fast her lips are turning blue, we won't need an ambulance in another few minutes.

Everyone around us stands up like a change in their positions will allow my mate's lungs to accept air, and their helplessness and mine only serves to enrage me.

"What the fuck is going on? What's happening to her?"

One of the partners speaks up. "Is she allergic to nuts or anything she may have eaten?"

My first thought snags on the dessert with lemon in it, but I quickly dismiss it. If she were fae, it would've mattered, but she's not. It has to be something else.

"Check her purse for an EpiPen."

Damn it, she doesn't have a purse with her. I look up and shout into the crowded restaurant. "Does anyone have an EpiPen?"

A woman from the other side of the room jumps up. "I have one!"

"So do I!"

I don't even wait to see who the other person is or which one will get to me fastest. All my focus is redirected at the woman I'm cradling in my arms on the floor of my restaurant, wishing I'd sent my brothers in my stead so we could stay back at the manor together.

"Hold on, Beauty, I'm gonna fix you, just hold the fuck on." I caress her face and brush away the tears streaming from the corners of her beautiful green-and-gold eyes.

As soon as the first syringe is shoved in my line of sight, I pull the cap off with my teeth and plunge the pen into her thigh and depress the medicine. Dropping it to the floor, I hold her face and will her lungs to open up. "Come on, baby, breathe for me. *Breathe, goddamn you.*"

Finally, she's able to suck a thin stream of air into her chest. And then another.

"That's it, Beauty, good girl. Nice and easy now."

"Caid..."

"Shh, no talking. Only breathing, understand?" Bryn nods weakly, her breaths still so labored, it sounds like she's sucking them through a cocktail straw. "Where the hell is that ambulance?"

Still on the phone with the 911 dispatcher, Sean says, "ETA three minutes, sir."

I decide right here and now that I'm never going anywhere without a fae healer in my entourage. Not that they can heal humans, but maybe there'd be a chance that our bond would allow fae magic to work on her, at least enough to give us time to get her to the hospital.

Somewhere behind me, I hear Finn say in a low voice, "That could've been bad, Tier. If she dies—"

A growl rumbles from my chest.

"Finnian," Tier barks quietly. "Now is not the fucking time."

I hear Finn start to argue back and Seamus putting a stop to it before he can get more than three words out when another spike of anxiety pierces my chest as if it were my own. "Bryn?"

Her airway is blocked again, and I can only look on as she silently pleads with me to help her.

"Give me that other EpiPen!" I plunge this one into her other thigh and pray to Rhiannon it will work, that she won't be taken from me right as I've found her. But my prayers go unanswered, because it's not fucking helping at all this time.

Pain and desperation rip me to shreds as her eyes—her beautiful, soulful eyes—roll back into her head, and she goes limp in my arms.

"Bryn!"

CHAPTER EIGHTEEN

BRYN

I'm not sure how long I've been floating in this endless space of nothingness or why I'm here at all, but I want out. Though there's nothing here that's frightening or threatening, there's a sense of needing to escape scratching at my subconscious, like something—or someone—is waiting for me to emerge.

And yet, no matter how much I want to get myself out, I can't. I can't walk, crawl, claw, or fight my way to the surface, if there even is one.

All I can do is merely *exist*.

Suddenly, a pinprick of light appears in the distance, no bigger than a star winking in the night sky, but I might as well be standing next to the sun for the intense relief washing over me.

Now that I have a direction and a destination, I'm able to will myself closer, drifting through the void as the pinprick grows to the size of a flashlight that grows to the size of a spotlight, and finally, the light eclipses the darkness...and my eyelids flutter open.

It takes me several minutes to get my bearings. Soft hums of machinery mingle with muffled conversations from the other side of a large door with a small rectangular window. The room is a bland tapestry of creams and beiges, the walls featuring diagrams of the body, a sign with a range of frowning to smiling emojis on it, and a whiteboard filled out with information I can't hope to understand right now.

Confirming my suspicion, I glance down at the thin white blanket covering my body as I lie in a slightly reclined position with metal bars on either side of my single bed. I'm obviously in a hospital, though how or why, I have no idea.

A quick wiggle of my appendages tells me nothing's broken, but my head feels clouded and heavy, and a tiny fire erupts in my throat every time I swallow.

What the hell happened to me?

Fear of the unknown threatens to make my blood pressure skyrocket. Then I see him.

Caiden.

He's over in the corner of the room, dozing in an ugly tan armchair that looks stiff and uncomfortable. Legs parted, he's sitting straight up with the exception of his head resting in the palm of his left hand. I don't know how long he's been here, but based on his rumpled appearance, it's been more than a few hours.

While my brain slowly comes back online, I take advantage of the opportunity to study him. He's always so put together, it's interesting to see him in a state of disarray.

His black suit jacket and tie are draped haphazardly over a thigh, and the top buttons of his royal-blue dress shirt are undone with the sleeves rolled up to his elbows. The dark stubble of his beard is longer than usual, and his styled hair has fallen into tousled pieces that hang over his forehead.

It's official: even disheveled and asleep, the man is just as strikingly handsome as when he's awake.

He's also just as intense.

Brows drawn together, jaw tense, and mouth set in a scowl.

As king of his people, Caiden carries the weight of the world on his shoulders, and it saddens me to think he's unable to lay down that burden even when asleep.

The door to the room opens, and a woman in lavender scrubs enters. Her blond pixie cut does nothing to hide the pointed tips of her ears, and her golden eyes shine bright as she does a quick scan of the room before quietly approaching my bed so as to not disturb Caiden.

She lays a comforting hand on my arm and speaks softly.

"Hi, Bryn, I'm your nurse, Marcie. I'm so glad to see you're finally awake." She offers me a full-fanged smile, then starts checking my vitals while she talks. "I wasn't on shift when they brought you in last night, but I hear it was touch-and-go for a while there. You're a very lucky woman."

Thinking of Mandy on my first day in Vegas, I whisper, "So I've been told." I cringe at the burn in my throat and the hoarseness of my voice.

Marcie winces sympathetically, then pours some water into a plastic cup and pops a straw into the lid before handing it to me. I drink it eagerly, the cold liquid soothing the rawness.

"Sorry, I should've warned you," she says. "It's natural to have a sore throat for a day or two after being intubated."

My eyes snap over to hers. I'd rather not talk, but I want answers more than I want to avoid a little pain. "What happened? Why am I here?"

"You went into anaphylactic shock last night."

At the deep rumble of Caiden's voice, Marcie stops what she's doing and bows her head. "I'm sorry, Your Majesty, I didn't mean to wake you."

"No need to be sorry. Will you please tell the doctor that Miss Meara's awake, and I'd like her discharged into my care?"

"Right away, Your Majesty." She gives me a parting smile and comforting squeeze on my arm, then turns to leave.

"Oh, and Marcie," Caiden says, "thank you for everything

you've done today. I'll be sending a note to Dr. O'Shea about your compassion and the excellent care you provided."

I don't think Marcie would've looked happier if she'd won all the money in Vegas.

Placing her hands over her heart, she performs a shallow bow. "It was an honor to do what I could for Miss Meara and you, sire."

Though he doesn't smile, his expression softens as he dismisses the nurse with a nod. When the door closes behind her, I ask, "Is this a fae hospital?"

"No, but a lot of the staff here are fae. She didn't bother using a glamour with you because you're part of the inner circle, as it were."

I nod, then absently sip on my water as I try to remember what Caiden was referring to about why I'm here. When all that's left are ice chips, I set the cup on the table Marcie had wheeled over earlier. "Caiden," I rasp, "what happened last night?"

Rising, he drops his jacket and tie on the chair and crosses the small distance to stand by my hip. "Do you remember the dinner we had with the New York partners at Nightfall?"

My brow furrows in concentration. It only takes a second for the memory to register. "I remember being in the restaurant and having dinner, but I don't remember leaving or going back to the manor."

"That's because we never made it past the dessert course. Something you ate triggered an allergic reaction. It took two doses of epinephrine to keep your airway barely open long enough to get you intubated at the hospital." He curses under his breath and grips the metal bar of the bed guard so hard, his knuckles blanch. "Damn it, Bryn, you almost fucking died. Why didn't you tell me you had a food allergy?"

For a split second, my heart swells at the devastation in his voice from the prospect of my death. Until I remember what he told me that night at the Temple of Rhiannon. That if I die, there's a good chance that he will, too.

Trying not to show my disappointment, I redirect my attention to his question. "I didn't tell you because I don't have one. Not that I know of, anyway, and I have a very eclectic palette, so I can't imagine I had something last night that I've never had before."

"What about lemon? You said you've never liked lemons."

"Yeah," I say, scrunching up my face in confusion. "I said I don't *like* them. Their flavor is overpowering and sour. There's a big difference between gross and deadly, Caiden."

He drags a hand over the scruff of his jaw and releases a heavy breath. Lines of tension bracket his eyes.

I frown. "What is it? You're not telling me something."

He stares at me for several seconds, then holds his hand out, palm up. "Put your hand in mine."

I hesitate, a sense that whatever happens next will be a pivotal moment for both of us, though I don't know if it will be good or bad, and there's a part of me that's scared to find out.

But I've always met the unknown head-on and at full speed, so there's no reason to stop myself now.

I lift my hand and place it into his.

The moment we touch, a warm vibration zings up the length of my arm. It starts out strong but gradually lessens as it travels to the rest of my body and finally fades away.

"Whoa," I breathe out. He releases my hand, and I try not to mourn the loss of his touch. "What was that?"

"Our energies flowing through each other. When fae are bonded, they become clairsentient, able to feel their mate's energy, even read it from a distance like a remote emotion detector."

My eyes lift to meet his. "I'm not fae, though."

"I know. But there's something else." Dread settles like bricks in my stomach. "Lemons are poisonous to fae, Bryn."

I lick my lips and think hard, looking for any shred of evidence to refute what he's implying. "You said the epinephrine eventually worked. It wouldn't have worked for something poisonous. I must have acquired an allergy for something, that's all."

"I said it worked *enough* to get you to the hospital where they administered a whole host of things to try and keep you alive." He pauses, his expression solemn. "Including the antidote for when a fae accidentally ingests something with lemon."

A shiver trips down my spine, and the tiny hairs on the back of my neck stand on end. "What the hell is going on, Caiden? Why is any of this happening?"

The muscles jump in his jaw as he shakes his head. "I wish I fucking knew. Maybe the longer we're bonded, the more fae qualities you'll take on, but I have no idea what that means for you or if it's even true. I'm just as in the dark as you are right now."

I close my eyes and let my head drop back on the pillow as I try to contain the dozens of questions swarming my mind. It won't do me any good to pelt Caiden with them when he's admitted to not knowing any of the answers, and I'm suddenly too tired to think anyway.

"I think I have a lead on someone who might be able to help," he says, and I perk up at that and open my eyes. "An elder, the oldest living Dark Fae in this realm. He's a recluse who lives away from civilization in the desert. There's talk that he's a seer, a fae with the ability to read energies on a deeper level and receive information about their past, present, or future."

"Like a psychic?"

"Yes, but as far as I know, their powers only work on fae, so I'm not even sure how much he'll be able to help. But I'm not leaving any stone unturned. One way or another, I'm going to figure out a way to sever this bond. Then the curse will be nullified and you can go back home where you belong."

I swallow thickly, the lump of emotion in my throat making the damage from the intubation even more painful. *Then you can go back home where you belong.*

Why does that sentiment hurt so much?

I knew this wasn't real, not for either of us, and three weeks ago, all I wanted was to go home to Wisconsin. But now I'm not sure where home is, and I sure as hell don't know where I belong.

Mustering a wan smile, I say, "Looking forward to it," and thank God for small favors that I haven't yet lost the ability to lie.

The door to the room opens and Tiernan and Finnian enter. Having all three Verran brothers in the small room makes it feel like it shrunk down to the size of a shoebox.

"Hey, there she is," Tiernan says with his megawatt smile. "Glad to see you're still in the land of the living, Brynnie-Bear. You gave us quite the scare last night."

Despite the melancholy still sitting on my chest, I give him a genuine smile. I can't not be happy to see Tiernan; he's the most easygoing of the three, and aside from locking me in my room that first day, he's always really sweet to me. "Sorry about that. Next time, I'll let you in on my plans for melodramatic dinner theater."

"I'd appreciate that." He ruffles my hair like I'm his kid sister, earning him a weak attempt to smack his hand away and a glare that only makes him laugh. Then he looks pointedly at the youngest Verran. "Finnian, don't you have something to say to Bryn?"

Finn stares at me, his huge heart in his golden eyes broadcasting his feelings for the world to see. Since Caiden and I were married, Finn has had a hard time separating who I am as a person from the fact that I'm a potential walking, talking death sentence for his oldest brother. I don't fault him for it. I only wish I could make it so that he didn't have to worry about Caiden.

Since that's not an option, I try not to push my presence on him, and I don't initiate interactions like I normally would. The best I can do is give him space.

Clearing his throat, he finally says, "I'm glad you're okay, Bryn."

Translation: *I'm glad you didn't kill my brother.*

"Thanks, Finn."

Caiden steps over to retrieve his jacket and tie. "I'm going to grab some coffee and get the discharge paperwork so we can leave. Do you need anything?"

I shake my head. "Just getting out of here will be good."

He holds my gaze for a bit, and I wish I could read his energy from a distance like he can probably read mine. At last, he gives me a clipped nod. "I'll be back. Finn, you can come with me."

When the heavy door closes, Tiernan lets out a soft whistle, then chuckles. "Damn, I did *not* see that coming."

"See what?"

"Big bro falling for his bride. I'm not sure whether to congratulate you or feel sorry for you."

Scoffing, I turn my head to peer out the window. "Very funny, Tiernan. The only thing your brother wants is to get rid of me as quickly as possible."

"Is that what he said?"

"What?"

"Did he *say* that he wants to get rid of you or anything even similar to that? Because I'm betting he didn't. You have to pay attention to a fae's words, Brynnie. We use them very deliberately. We can't outright lie, so we're either telling you the truth or talking our way around it to make you hear what we want you to hear. What did Caiden say to make you think he wants you gone? Come on, work with me, I'm trying to help you out here."

I sigh. "He said, 'One way or another, I'm going to figure out a way to sever this bond. Then…the curse will be nullified and you can go back home where you belong.' See? He wants me gone."

"Nowhere in either of those statements does he say he *wants* you gone. Does he need to sever the bond because it's dangerous for a king to be mated? Yes. But do I think he *wants* to sever it? No, I don't. For all his gruff aloofness, I think deep down, Caiden has always been a romantic." I arch a dubious brow at that. "Okay, maybe 'romantic' isn't the right word, but I think he's always wanted a relationship—a real one with real feelings, not the transactional kind that a king has with his consort. And I think he's found that with you."

I pick at a piece of lint on the blanket over my lap. "That's just the bond. It's affecting both of us in strange ways."

"Possibly. But do you want to know what my theory is about the bond?" He waits for me to look up at him, then says, "I think the bond can't create something out of nothing. I think it strengthens what's already there."

Before I have a chance to let that soak in, Fiona enters. "Girl, you're so lucky you're not dead, or I'd have to bring you back to life just to kick your a— *Oh*." She stops when she realizes we're not alone, her eyes wide. "Ti— Uh, Your Highness, I apologize. I didn't realize you were in here."

A sly grin slides onto Tiernan's face. "Fiona, what a nice surprise. Here to spring our Brynnie and get her back to the manor?"

"Yes, Your Highness, that's the plan. King Caiden is speaking with the doctor now. We should be able to leave soon."

"Excellent. Bryn, I'm sure you'll be back on your feet in no time with Fiona looking after you." He looks at Fiona and their gazes hold. "She's very good at taking care of others' needs."

Her brows raise in challenge. "If my services are held in such high esteem, perhaps I should be angling for a raise."

Tiernan traps his lower lip with his teeth, seemingly trying to bite back a grin. "You make a fair point, Miss Jewel. I'm sure an appropriate compensation can be arranged." My eyes are bouncing back and forth like a spectator at a tennis match. "Right, then," he says, snapping them out of their little tête-à-tête. "I'll leave you ladies to it."

As soon as he's gone, I pounce. "What was that?"

She busies herself taking clothes out of a duffel she brought in. "What was what?"

"Don't play coy with me, missy. There were so many heavy innuendos being thrown around this room, I'm shocked I wasn't hit with one and knocked back unconscious."

Fiona snorts and lowers the bed rails. "They must have you on the good drugs, because you're seeing things, girlie. Now, are you going to keep arguing with me about Prince Tiernan or are you going to let me get you dressed and out of here? One of those gets you recovering in the sun by the pool, the other gets you left here in this beige hell."

"Well, if you're going to get all huffy about it," I mumble. "All right, let's get me out of here. And when we're back, I could use something for my throat, like hot tea."

"You got it. Any particular flavor?"

"Anything except lemon."

CHAPTER NINETEEN

CAIDEN

Fear is not something I'm familiar with.

Even when faced with formidable conditions like watching my father take his last breath and having to push the pain aside because there was no time to mourn when you were suddenly the youngest king in fae history.

I had a court to rule, whether I was ready or not.

I don't know that either of my brothers could have done the same. But it's not in my nature to let my emotions overrule logic or my ability to tackle things from a place of intellect and strategy.

But when Bryn stopped breathing and fell limp in my arms, I became intimately acquainted with sheer fucking *terror*.

Not because I knew if she died, I would soon follow as the curse ran its course. That thought never even entered my mind.

It terrified me to think of losing her.

Somewhere along the line, Bryn has become essential to me. She continues to embed herself into my soul more each day, and I've finally stopped fighting it tooth and nail and accepted what I think I've known all along.

Bryn and I were inevitable.

I believe no matter the paths we chose in life, we were always destined to end up here, together.

And now someone is trying to take her away from me.

After I left in the ambulance with Bryn last night, Seamus interviewed the kitchen staff. He learned the chef had received a note on what appeared to be official Night Court stationary. But when Seamus held it up to the light, the embedded watermark of the Verran crest was missing.

The instructions were scrawled in a decent imitation of my handwriting and requested that the chef prepare a special lemon-flavored dessert for my female guest that evening.

Which means someone is aware of our bond and that it's changing Bryn on a physiological level.

Whoever it is either knew or at least hoped that she would be affected by the lemon as fae are. And when I find out who's behind her near-death, I will eviscerate them and feed their entrails to the buzzards.

For tonight, though, I'm setting all that aside so I can focus on caring for Bryn.

I was too shaken up at the hospital today and did a shit job of it. I never even offered to refill her water.

As soon as I left the room with Finnian in tow, I realized my bedside manner had been abominable and vowed to make it up to her after she'd had some decent rest in her own bed.

According to Fiona, Bryn has been awake for more than an hour and complaining about the doctor's orders to stay in bed and rest at least until tomorrow. So I thought a little field trip might be in order.

I rap a few times on her bedroom door before walking in. She's in bed with a travel mug of tea in one hand and her e-reader in the other. Looking up at me, she takes a sip of her tea. "You know the polite thing is to wait to be invited in after you knock, right?"

"Do you want to get out of here or not?"

Her hazel eyes widen, and her face alights with hope. "Definitely. Just let me throw some clothes on quick…" She sets her mug on the table and scrambles out of the bed, looking adorably rumpled in sleep shorts and a baggy T-shirt.

"That won't be necessary," I say and scoop her up into my arms.

She squeals in surprise but wraps her arms around my neck as I head back into the hallway and make my way to the opposite side of the manor.

"Caiden, what are you doing? I can walk fine, you know. I have a sore throat, not broken—"

I drop my voice a register. "Beauty." She bites her lip and stares up at me with willing obedience that pleases me greatly. "It's not a question of whether you *can* walk, it's whether I want you to or not."

Her fingers toy with the hair at my nape, causing ripples of pleasure down my spine. I carry her into my bedroom, then into my bathroom that's bigger than a two-car garage with various sectioned areas. We pass between the double floating vanities into the room with my bathtub.

Since building the manor after becoming king, I've never once used the bathtub. If I want to soak in hot water, I use the hot tub out by the pool. The designer insisted I add it for later resale value. I didn't bother telling him I doubted it would matter in a couple hundred years.

Before I went to get Bryn, I had Fiona bring me every candle she could find in the house. I set them out in clusters of two and three around the room and dimmed the overhead lights to their lowest setting, allowing the flames to do most of the work. I also started filling the tub so it would be about ready by the time I came back with her. Admittedly, I forgot how impressive it looks when the water is streaming down from the ceiling tub fillers on either side of the skylight.

"Caiden." There's a hint of awe in her voice that makes

this worth the effort, small as it may be. "You did this for me?"

Lowering her gently to her feet, I grab the hem of her shirt and lift it up and off. "I thought it might be nice to soak and relax together."

Doing my damnedest not to ogle her breasts, I hook my thumbs in her shorts and panties and drag them down her legs for her to step out of them. Rising again without detouring to where I know she'll be wet for me takes more control than I thought possible.

As I make quick work of getting out of my clothes, she runs her hands in a slow trek down her belly.

"I hope 'soak and relax' is code for something less relaxing."

Kicking our stuff to the side, I grab her hands before she makes it to her sweet pussy. "No, it's not," I say firmly. "You're still recovering. Nothing will be happening until you've had more rest and I'm certain you can handle *less relaxing* things."

Full lips turn into a pout. "Shouldn't I be the one to decide when I'm able to handle—" Her voice cracks at the end from raising it, cutting her off. She winces and places a hand on her throat, then resumes pouting.

My brow arches. "Yes, clearly you know what's best for you," I say wryly. "Come on, I have more tea for you once you're in the tub."

I hit the button to turn the fillers off, then help her into the stainless-steel basin. It sounds uncomfortable, but the sides are sloped in with the bottom rising up in a long curve that creates the perfect lounging position. She sighs audibly as her body lowers into the hot water. I tell her to scoot up a bit and slide in behind her, then pull her to lay on me with her back on my chest.

I hand her the fresh travel mug of hot tea Fiona prepared and wait for her to take a few tentative sips before setting it back on the ledge for her.

"Thank you," she says, letting her head rest on my shoulder.

"You're welcome." Grabbing the netted loofah, I begin to lather it with a moisturizing lavender soap.

When I set the bar down, she goes to grab the loofah, but I lightly smack her hand away.

She tilts her head up to look at me, her brows knitted together in confusion. "I'm perfectly capable of washing myself, Caiden."

Peering down into her hazel eyes, I wonder how long it's been since she hasn't had to do everything herself. At least three years would be my starting guess, since that's when she tragically lost both her parents. But I'd bet it was a good deal before then.

She told me she's lived alone since leaving home at eighteen, and Bryn is the kind of woman who would rather do things herself than depend on anyone else. She's strong-willed and resilient in times of adversity. I admire those qualities in her.

Good qualities for a queen.

Shaking that errant thought away of what can never be, I gently press my lips to hers. I don't seek entrance into her mouth because if I taste her, I'll have to have her. I only want her to lower that defensive guard she keeps in place.

When I feel her relax enough that her body melts against mine, I force myself to break the kiss, then stroke her cheek with my thumb as I speak.

"Listen to me, Beauty. Letting someone else take care of you for a change doesn't make you any less competent or independent of a woman. It simply makes you a woman who's cared for. All right?"

Moisture swims in her eyes before she blinks it away, as is her habit. Then, trapping her lower lip between her teeth, she nods. "All right."

Using the lathered loofah, I start with her arms and drag it softly over her skin in long strokes. Her breaths become deeper, her body heavier as she gives in to the pull of relaxing more and more.

I find myself doing the same. I've never been with a female like this before. I don't do intimacy. I can't afford it, nor have I ever wanted it.

However, with Bryn, intimacy is all I want lately.

Oh, the desire to fuck her within an inch of her life while torturing her in the most sensually wicked ways I can think of is still there. But now it's accompanied by the urge to do things like sit on the balcony with her between my legs while we take in the view and talk all night. Then, when the sun comes up, we'd move to my bed where I can wrap her up in my arms as we sleep the day away. Another thing I've never wanted to do, being the workaholic that I am.

But in another life, if our circumstances were different, Bryn would be a woman worth slowing down for.

Having finished washing her and narrowly succeeding in the herculean effort of keeping it nonsexual, I simply hold her, my cheek resting on the top of her head as I sift through my thoughts.

"Caiden," she whispers into the silence.

"Hmm?"

"Is this your way of apologizing for not being warm and fuzzy in the hospital today?"

Unbelievable.

Never has anyone seen through me so easily. I do my best not to grin, but I'm sure she can feel the twist of my mouth. "Yes," I say simply.

And now I can feel her smiling where her cheek is pressed over the place where my heart hides. "Accepted."

"Thank you, Beauty," I say in a low voice. Then I press a kiss to her forehead and hold her until the water grows cold and that shadowy place inside my chest becomes a little less so.

CHAPTER TWENTY

CAIDEN

Sitting in my home office with Bryn across from me, I'm grateful she's unable to read my energy. I'm sure the day is coming, though, and with how much I'm constantly on edge due to my current clusterfuck of a situation, I don't relish her gaining that particular ability.

I asked her to meet with me to go over some of the projects she's acquired in the last week for her new PR position for my court, and while I'm genuinely interested in what she's working on and will want regular updates about her business with my people, that's not the real reason I asked her in here today.

Soon, Seamus will be escorting the elder, Barwyn, to my office. He's the seer who lives as a recluse in the desert, and I'm hoping he can get a read on Bryn to finally give me some real goddamn answers.

The main question plaguing me now is why someone would want to poison Bryn. I've spent the last seven days thinking of little else with nothing to show for it.

It can't be a jealous lover hoping to become consort someday. For one, I rarely ever indulge that appetite. And two, every fae alive knows of the curse, so killing Bryn only ensures that I follow, which wouldn't get them a position as consort if that's what they were after.

The only thing that makes even remote sense is some kind of coup, that someone is using Bryn as a way of getting me out of the way to take over the throne.

But who?

Talek, the Day Court king, is ruled out automatically because of the treaty between our courts. It states that neither of the kings can kill the other without killing themselves, and the treaty is bound by magic; there's no way around that.

So does that mean I have someone in my own court rising up against me?

They'd need a large group of supporters to usurp the throne and all my assets to keep my brothers from retaining our right as the royal line of the Dark Fae. And while it stings my pride to even consider a betrayal as great as that, I can't rule it out, which is why Seamus is overseeing an intelligence team of trusted fae to try and suss out any information about possible revolutionary groups.

So far, they've come up with nothing, making my black mood worse by the day.

My only saving grace has been the time I've spent between Bryn's thighs. Since almost losing her, as soon as she was fully recovered, I've tried showing her how I feel the only way I know how: by fucking her within an inch of her life while introducing her to the kink world a little more each time.

I don't know how I ever thought Bryn would tuck tail and run at the first sign of my sexual tastes. I doubt she's ever run from anything, and when it comes to what I do to her body at night, I'm the one trying to pace us so I don't overwhelm her.

If we did it her way, I'd give her everything she begs for and more.

"Caiden, did you hear me?"

A crooked grin twists my lips. "Not a word. Sorry."

She lifts a dubious brow. "Are you, though?"

"You know I can't lie."

"Hmm," she muses, then gets up to round my desk as she talks. "You're sorry, but I know it's not about your poor listening skills."

I push back from the desk and welcome her into my lap. She winds her arms around my neck and our energies collide in delicious warmth through both of us. Bryn's no longer shocked at the sensation but revels in it as I do.

Staring down into my eyes, she gives me that coy little smile that acts like a starting gun for my dick. "So, what is it you're sorry for, my king?"

A low growl rumbles in my chest. She used the two words she knows will get her pinned to my desk with her legs kicked out. "I'm sorry you're not fucking naked and riding my cock."

Whispering, she says, "Then make it so."

Shooting to my feet, I plant her ass on my desk to do just that when a knock sounds on my office door. Cursing, I lower my forehead to hers.

"Tell them to go away," she says, moving to pepper my neck with kisses.

"I can't. I need to take this meeting." Pulling back, I frame her face with my hands. "And for that, Beauty, I *am* sorry. We'll continue this later."

She smiles, not a hint of disappointment in her hazel eyes. "I can't wait."

I allow myself to taste her lips for a heady moment before helping her off the desk.

Guilt weighs on me for keeping her in the dark about what this meeting truly is and the brief role she'll play, but I don't want her involved in any of this unless she needs to be.

Crossing to the door, I open it and allow Seamus to enter with Barwyn.

If the rumors are true, Barwyn is 572 years old. He prefers

to live far away from civilization and is obviously doing well on his own.

His snow-white hair is pulled into a braid that reaches his waist and his beard is almost equally as long. He's close to Bryn's height with a slight roundness to his shoulders from age. His body appears frail, but for anyone, human or fae, to survive in the desert alone, he's likely stronger and more hale than he looks.

"Barwyn, thank you for coming on such short notice."

He bows his head. "It is my honor to be received by my king, Your Majesty."

"Barwyn, this is Bryn Meara, my new PR specialist helping various members of the Dark Fae with their businesses."

"Hello, Barwyn. It's a pleasure to meet you."

Seamus informed Barwyn when he arrived that I'd like him to furtively read what he can from Bryn, which is why he gives her a kindly smile and takes her offered hand between both of his. "The pleasure is mine, my dear. What is it a PR specialist does? I'm afraid I'm a bit behind the times on such things."

"Oh, well..."

As Bryn launches into her passionate explanation, I watch Barwyn intently for any signs. Of what, I have no clue.

Considering seers are as scarce as conjuring fae, I've never witnessed one at work before. But nothing changes about him to indicate he's doing anything other than listening to Bryn with polite interest while holding her hand in a grandfatherly manner.

When she finishes, he smiles wider and pats the top of her hand. "You are a rare beauty, my dear. Thank you for indulging me. I wish you all the best in the future."

"Thank you, Barwyn, that's so sweet of you. I guess I'll leave you two alone now. I have lots of work to do myself." When she turns to me, she can't hide the heat in her gaze.

"Looking forward to continuing our discussion later, Your Majesty."

"As am I, Bryn."

I force myself to walk back to my desk instead of watching her ass as she leaves with Seamus. Drawing a cleansing breath to release the sexual tension vibrating through me, I gesture for Barwyn to take a seat and then do the same.

"I apologize for cutting straight to the chase, Barwyn, but I'm afraid this is too important to cover with niceties. Did you get anything?"

"Yes and no, sire. There are things working against me, preventing me from seeing too deeply."

Trepidation bands around my chest and starts to squeeze like a vise. "What does that mean?"

"I can only see what is on the surface, things about her life you could discover by simply asking her or investigating her with the thing on those computers you use."

"The internet," I clarify.

He nods. "But when I tried to go deeper, it was as though I hit a wall, thick and impenetrable."

I clench my teeth, making the muscles in my jaw jump in irritation. I know he's not trying to draw this out on purpose, but this is starting to feel like pulling teeth.

Summoning what's left of my patience, I prod him to elaborate. "Why would she have a wall, Barwyn, and who do you think put it there?"

"The wall is to hide the secrets she does not want revealed. As for its creator, I do not know; however, it was someone with great power."

I curse under my breath and rake my fingers through my hair. No answers, only more questions.

What the hell could Bryn be hiding and why? This shit is enough to drive me mad.

Stroking his long beard, he studies me carefully. "You are

bonded with the female, are you not, sire?"

That gives me pause, but of course he would know. He could probably see our bond as soon as he entered the room.

"Yes, we are bonded, though I have no idea how. She's human."

Barwyn shakes his head thoughtfully. "I do not believe she is human, Your Majesty."

Time stops. "She's fae?"

Again, he shakes his head. "She does not read as any fae I have met, but she is...*other*."

"Other?"

"Something other than human is the best way I can describe it. I am sorry I cannot give you more than that."

I wave away his concern, consumed with my own racing thoughts. "Don't be sorry, Barwyn, you've helped me a great deal." I suppose her being something preternatural, even if it isn't fae, might allow her to create a fae-like bond with the marriage rite.

It certainly makes more sense that it happening with a human.

"May I ask how you met her, Your Majesty? Perhaps that would help."

"Yes, of course." So I tell him. About our eyes catching in the lobby, then me seeking her out in the casino, the different way I felt around her, acted around her. Everything as far as I could remember of that night and then about waking up in her room with a ring on my finger and a video of the marriage rite on my phone.

"Forgive me, Your Majesty, but it sounds to me as though she spelled you."

"What do you mean?"

"That you were acting so far out of character indicates some type of coercion spell."

My fists clench so hard, I'm in danger of drawing blood

from my palms. "Are you telling me Bryn is a witch?"

"I do not think so. Or, if she is, her powers have been bound, because she has no power at her disposal. However, she may have used something that was spelled to affect you specifically, to make you feel things you normally would not. It would likely have been something small enough to hide on her person or something innocuous in appearance, like a watch or piece of jewelry."

"And if this something could be found, how would you know whether it had been spelled or if it was a regular common object?"

"Spells leaves marks. Somewhere on the object would be a kind of brand or scar not naturally found otherwise. Different spells leave different marks, but you'll recognize it when you see it."

The steel band presses in, my lungs losing their capacity for air. I stand and walk around the desk to help the elder to his feet. "Thank you, Barwyn, you've been extremely helpful. If ever there's something you need from the crown, you only need ask."

He takes my outstretched hand between his like he did Bryn's earlier and peers into my eyes. "I was fond of your father, you know. King Braden was a great ruler, and he brought peace to our people. If he were here now, his pride for you would be boundless."

Swallowing past the fist in my throat, I give him a solemn nod. "Thank you." I open the door and signal to Madoc, who's posted up in the hall. "Madoc will see that you get home safely."

Barwyn nods his gratitude and shuffles his way through the door, then turns back. "Your Majesty, one more thing. If you should need it, I believe there might be a way to get more distance from your mate, but it would require procuring her essence."

"Her essence. You mean her blood?"

"It is a blood curse, Your Majesty. Carry it with you and it should mimic her presence for a time. Test the boundaries slowly to make sure you don't fall ill."

Rubbing two fingers over my lips in thought, I wonder how long something like that might last if it works.

"I would not trust it for more than a few hours, sire."

I arch a brow at Barwyn. He returns it with a grin and a wink, then continues his slow trek down the hall. Holding Madoc back briefly, I ask, "Where's Bryn?"

"By the pool, sire."

"See to him, please, and make sure no one is following you. If you think you have a tail, lose them before taking him home. I don't want him caught up in whatever the fuck this is."

"Yes, Your Majesty."

Taking a different route, I head straight for Bryn's room. Once there, I shove the guilt down for what I'm about to do and then go through her things. Every drawer, every article of clothing, everything in the bathroom, even her purse, but I don't come up with anything.

I'm about to leave when my eyes snag on her suitcase tucked into the closet. Quickly, I search through every pocket and compartment, and when I get to the smallest one, my hand comes away with what I'd hoped I wouldn't find.

The teardrop-shaped obsidian necklace Bryn wore that first night we met.

It looks the same—flawless black stone surrounded by tiny, encrusted diamonds and a delicate silver chain.

Holding my breath, I turn it over in my palm…and almost double over from the pain. There, on the silver setting, is a black scorch mark too precise and large to be a flaw for such an expensive piece.

Bryn's necklace was spelled to coerce me, to make me act differently and imagine feelings that weren't there.

None of this is real. Everything I feel for her has been a lie.

Betrayal is an iron broadsword in Bryn's hand that cleaves me in two so she can watch me bleed out before her.

For weeks, all I've wanted was the truth to be brought to light. And now I'd give anything to climb back into the safety of the shadows.

My phone rings in my pocket, interrupting the maelstrom of emotions crashing through me. Operating on autopilot, I thumb the button to answer Seamus's call and bring the phone to my ear.

"Caiden, I have news."

I can tell by his tone I'm not going to like it. "Tell me."

"It's Gilda, the high priestess who married you and Bryn," he says. "Her body was found picked apart by scavengers in the desert, but it wasn't an accident. Her throat was cut with an iron blade, unable to heal. Someone didn't want her talking."

CHAPTER TWENTY-ONE

BRYN

Caiden's running cold again. Or maybe not cold, exactly, but definitely not warm.

The last time we were together was three days ago in his office before he met with the elder fae. We were supposed to continue what we started later that night, but he had to beg off for official royal business of some kind, and it's kept him busy the past few days.

So I was excited when he stopped by my makeshift office and picked me up for a quick escape. I've missed him, and with not seeing him at all after a whole week of nightly sex, my body is starved for his touch.

"What's this?" I ask as he punches in a key code to a door I've never seen before.

"You've done well with the intermediate level of kink. This is where we hold the advanced class."

He smiles down at me as he pushes the door open, but it doesn't quite reach his golden eyes.

I ignore whatever's on the other side of the threshold and lift a hand to caress the side of his face. His eyes drift closed, and he releases a quiet exhale. "What's wrong, Caiden?"

"I have a lot on my mind."

When they open again, I lock my eyes with his. "You know you can talk to me, right?"

My fingers move to tuck an errant piece of his hair behind the point of his ear—I've learned they're extremely sensitive and he enjoys my touch or my kisses there—but he captures my wrist and holds it away. "Believe me, I intend to do just that, Beauty. Now come inside."

He walks into the room and waits for me to follow before closing the door.

Though I've never been in anything like it before, I recognize it instantly for what it is: a sex dungeon.

The entire space is set up for a variety of different activities, most of which I couldn't swear that I'd guess right. The only piece of furniture that I recognize is the massive four-poster bed. Everything else is oddly shaped or at strange angles, and along the walls and on various tables around the room are dozens upon dozens of toys and tools, like he called up a sex shop and asked for one of everything.

Since starting our marriage-with-benefits arrangement, Caiden has introduced me to a lot of new experiences. There's been more impact play using different paddles, a leather belt, and a riding crop. Various toys, including a vibrating anal plug, anal beads, Hitachi wand, and a remote-controlled panty vibrator that he made me wear for an entire day when we were in the Nightfall offices and out shopping.

Exciting as all of that was, it wasn't anything like what's in here.

"This is definitely the advanced level," I say, my eyes wide as I continue to take everything in.

"Tell me your safe word."

The gruff command from behind me creates an immediate response. Warmth floods my body and my blood rushes to my nipples and between my legs. "Roulette," I say breathlessly.

"Strip. Then stand in front of the St. Andrew's Cross over there, the black X."

I follow his instructions quickly, taking care to fold my clothes and place them off to the side in a neat pile before making my way to huge X in the center of the left wall.

The lights in the room dim as I study the intimidating contraption. There are leather cuffs attached at heights obviously meant for someone's wrists and ankles, that much is obvious. But what happens after that, I can only imagine.

Turning around, I watch as Caiden moves silently about the room. He gathers certain tools and toys and places them on a table off to the side, but the lighting is too low for me to make out what they are. On either side of the cross are pillars with clusters of various-size candles on them, and he takes the time to light each wick, one by one.

Being naked and made to wait while he prepares everything is its own kind of domination. By now my mind has learned to slip into subspace with a mere tone change in Caiden's voice or his demand to know my safe word.

My submission wraps around me like a warm blanket as I wait impatiently, eager to obey him.

He begins to unbutton his black shirt as he holds my gaze, slowly revealing the hard body I've become intimately familiar with. Once he's freed himself of his shirt and tosses it onto the bed, he's left wearing only a pair of black leather pants, his ever-present wrist cuff, and the silver chain holding his wedding band.

Seeing it resting between his pecs always makes butterflies erupt in my belly. I've asked him on multiple occasions to tell me why he wears it, but every time he distracts me with orgasms or playfully changes the topic.

This session doesn't have the same feel to it that our other did, though. I'm not sure if it's the setting or something about his demeanor, but I don't dare ask him about the necklace now.

Caiden picks up a pair of black latex gloves and pulls them on as he approaches me. I frown, unsure of why he'd need them. Until he starts buckling me into the cuffs and I'm unable to read his energy.

No skin to skin contact.

My ability to read him relies on physical touch, and admittedly I've grown used to having it. Now, I've lost the advantage.

A sliver of worry slips through my warm-and-fuzzy feeling, but I brush it away.

We've played with blindfolds before, and it made for a very fun time. This will be similar; it's just a different form of sensory deprivation.

Grabbing something small from the table, he hides whatever it is inside his clenched fist as he steps in so close, the heat from his body kisses my bare skin. His intense amber gaze follows his free hand as it roams every naked inch like he's cataloging his possession.

"My nickname for you wasn't a flip choice or false compliment, you know. You're truly an exquisite creature, Beauty." The low timbre of his voice vibrates over my skin and causes a rush of arousal between my legs. "Deep down, I think I always knew you had to be something other than what you appeared to be. But I chose to ignore the signs because it allowed me to pretend I had nothing to be concerned about."

My brows draw together. What is he talking about? "Caiden, I—" A gloved hand claps over my mouth, and he shakes his head.

"No talking unless I ask you a direct question or you decide to safe out. You *always* have that option, no matter how much it might seem like you don't. Remember that."

Okay, now I'm starting to worry.

The flickering of candlelight makes shadows dance across his handsome face, accentuating the shadows in his amber eyes. Something is eating at him; I don't need to be able to read his energy to know that. But instead of asking him as I want, I simply nod, reassuring him that I remember I have the option to use my safe word.

Satisfied, he removes his hand and opens his other one, revealing three small items. They look like fancy hairpins with black rubber tips and three graduated beads dangling from the bottoms.

When he sticks a gloved finger in my mouth, I dutifully close my lips to make it wet as I know he wants. Then he withdraws it and paints my left nipple with my saliva, rubbing it and pinching it, making it erect and sensitive.

"These are adjustable weighted clamps. I can change the tension from pleasurable to extremely painful, depending on a female's tolerance," he says, placing the rubber tips of one at the base of my distended nipple.

Then he pushes the metal ring around the bottom and up the arms of the clamp. The higher it goes, the tighter it gets. When it's tight enough that the bite causes me to draw in a sharp breath, he stops. "We'll start there, then."

I think I'm already used to the sensation, but when he lets go, a whole new one happens because the beads aren't just beads. They're tiny weights, and with every move I make, they tug on my nipple. I roll my lips between my teeth to prevent any words from slipping out, but it doesn't do anything to stop the soft moan.

"I'm glad you like them," he says, repeating everything on the other side. "I've been eager to see you wearing these. They look lovely on you." When I glance down at the last one in his hand, he holds it up. "This one? This one is going somewhere different."

His free hand drops to my exposed pussy that's already soaking wet for him. Using my arousal, he strums my clit as he watches the pleasure play out over my face.

My breaths grow shallow, and the rise and fall of my chest causes the weights on the clamps to swing and stimulate my nipples without him having to do any of the work.

When he has my clit sensitive and swollen, he attaches the clamp to it in the same manner as he did with my nipples, sliding the lock up until the rubber tips are snug enough that the tiny toy will stay in place. Once he releases it, he gently flicks the weighted balls, sending vibrations through all eight thousand of my nerve endings to create a fresh wave of arousal to flood my sex.

Already an orgasm is sneaking up on me, but I know it's too soon. He's building up to something much bigger, and I want to give him that, no matter how badly I need the release to take the edge off. So instead of asking him for permission to come, I bear down and beat it back as though he already denied me.

Caiden thrusts two fingers deep inside, testing both my readiness and my resolve. When I don't break down and beg for what we both know I want, he rewards me with the barest hint of a grin and the two words that hold more power over me than most any others. "Good girl."

I melt, mentally and physically, sagging in my restraints like I always do when he says that simple phrase. He could be in the middle of spanking my ass bright red and feel like my skin is on fire, and as soon as I hear him praise me, all the tension leaks out of my body and I turn into a human puddle of contentedness.

Usually, he has a distinct reaction when he says it, too.

Not the same as mine, obviously, but the pride in my obedience and submission is always very evident in his tone.

This time was missing that, though. Instead of pride, there's a strong sense of frustration and uncertainty coming off him, like he isn't expecting to enjoy any of this for some reason.

And that's when I realize that I'm reading Caiden's energy without the benefit of physical contact. Even now, when he's not touching me at all, I sense his emotions clearly.

I'm torn between feeling aroused and worrying about him. I don't know what this is all about, but one thing is for sure: I'm going to do everything I can to fix whatever's bothering him.

"I have an intense session planned for us this evening," he says, his golden eyes staring into mine. "Ready, Beauty?"

"Yes, my king," I respond honestly. "I'm ready."

CHAPTER TWENTY-TWO

CAIDEN

For the past few days, I haven't been able to think of anything except my conversation with Barwyn and the necklace I found in Bryn's room that's burning a metaphorical hole in my pocket right now.

As much as I wanted to confront her right away, I forced myself to take the time to calm down and get my mind right first.

I wouldn't say it's exactly *right,* but it's as good as I'm going to get it until I find answers to my questions.

A good Dom never scenes when he's angry or in a volatile mood—it places the sub at risk– but I'm self-aware enough to know whether I'd be a danger to Bryn, and the answer to *that* question is unequivocally *no.*

There's nothing on this plane of existence or any other that could cause me to become unhinged enough that I would ever harm her or cause her pain that wasn't strictly meant for her ultimate pleasure.

Which is why I decided to have this conversation this way. I don't want her in a headspace where she has the ability to scheme or overthink her responses. I want them automatic, without any room for manipulation.

I want the fucking truth.

Using a thigh cuff, I secure a Hitachi wand along her inner thigh so that the top of the large head is just barely kissing her labia, which will send indirect vibrations to her hypersensitive clit that's being squeezed between the rubber tips of the weighted clamp.

I'm aware of her watching me intently and can feel her holding back her questions as well as her first orgasm without having to be told. A fact that both surprised me and made me proud of her, though I'm sure I did a shit job of showing it.

"I'm going to ask you a series of questions. If I'm satisfied with your answers, I'll allow you to come, but you're not to do so unless given permission. Understood?"

"I understand, my king."

"What's your safe word?"

"Roulette."

"Good. Then let's begin."

I switch the wand on at the low setting, then grab a flogger. Since this is her first time receiving a flogging, I chose one with falls—or strips—made of elk skin. The falls are soft like suede and provide more of a thuddy feeling with very little sting.

Bryn likes a bit of a bite with her pleasure, but she's not what's called a pain slut in the kink community, so my intention is merely stimulation through impact.

Using skills I've honed for more than a century, I begin wielding the flogger, expertly aiming the falls to land on her belly to warm her up and get the endorphins flowing.

"Why did you come to Vegas?"

She licks her lips and visibly tries to focus on answering the question despite her brain being consumed with what's happening to her body. "I thought a weekend trip would be a good way to destress after losing my job."

"Are you independently wealthy?"

She frowns. "Not even close."

I move the target of the flogger to her upper thighs. "Do you have a lot of money in savings?"

"N-No," she says, stuttering when I give her a light taste of how it feels when the falls land on her pussy.

"Then if you'd just lost your job with no prospects to replace it, why would you spend the money on a frivolous trip to the one place people come to *lose* their money?"

"Because the trip was free!"

Free? She's never mentioned anything about that before. Nightfall never offers free stays except to our high rollers.

I flick the falls of the flogger over my shoulder and let it rest there as I approach her.

Standing close but not close enough for our bodies to touch, I flick each of her clamps and watch her react from the way the swinging weights tug on her overly sensitive nipples and clit. "What do you mean it was free? Did someone purchase the trip for you?"

Bryn shakes her head. "I got a letter in the mail; it was a promotional offer for a free weekend stay at Nightfall, so I figured there was no reason not to take advantage of it."

I drag a hand over my jaw and step back. Since opening its doors, Nightfall has never run any kind of promotional offers, and certainly not to random humans who have never stepped foot in a casino before.

If she's telling the truth, then someone lured her for a specific purpose to Vegas: me.

Grabbing the handle of the flogger, I pull it down from my shoulder and begin a steady pattern of concentrated strokes on her pussy. "What did you do with the letter?"

Her hands close into fists and her whole body tenses with the overwhelming sensations hitting her from different places. "I brought it with me. In case I needed it. When I registered at the hotel."

"Where is it now?"

"I folded it up and tucked it into my w-wallet."

Stopping again, I give her a reprieve and ask, "Why?"

She takes several seconds to steady her breathing enough to answer. "To remember the night we spent together. Like a souvenir, in case you made me give the ring back."

I expected her to tell me she threw it out after settling in her room. That's what most people would have done. It's what *I* would have done.

But not my Bryn. She was sentimental about what we shared even when she couldn't remember more than half of it.

Gods but this woman turns me inside out.

If any of what she's telling me turns out to be a lie—if I find out she's in on whatever plan this is to take me down—it might very well destroy me.

Pretending that I'm simply returning the flogger to the nearby table of toys and tools, I slip my phone from my back pocket and shoot a text to Connor, asking him to check for the letter in her wallet. Then I turn back to her, needing to get the rest of this interrogation over with and learn the truth of who and what she is, once and for all.

By now, the clamps and vibrator are making her visibly shake as she struggles to keep her orgasm at bay.

"P-Please, my king, may I come?"

"No."

A whimper escapes, but she bears down like a good girl and obeys me.

"I'm sorry for hurting you."

I freeze, almost not sure I heard her right or that maybe my brain is projecting so hard that I'm imagining things. But the unshed apologies in her hazel eyes arrest the air in my lungs. "Are you finally admitting fault? To knowingly playing a part in this grand scheme against me?"

She shakes her head. "No, never. It's not for anything

intentional, but I can feel your pain. It's raw, like a fresh wound, and it's aimed at me. So if I've done something to hurt you—however unintentional it may be—I'm sorry."

Fuck me.

Bryn's fae qualities have leveled up again. She's reading me without the benefit of skin-to-skin contact. Making these godsforsaken gloves unnecessary.

Glad of that fact for more than one reason, I strip them off my hands and toss them on the table. It's time I move on to the second half of my questioning and take things to the next level, anyway. It won't matter if she can read me or not, because I plan on making her so mindless with orgasms, she won't be able to focus on anything but what I allow her to.

I switch the wand to high, delivering a much more intense vibration but not nearly as intense as it could be with it still barely touching her. And yet she moans and squirms, trying to simultaneously escape and gain more pressure for relief. It's a delicious dichotomy of sensations that scrambles one's thoughts and magnifies physical awareness beyond imagination until it's experienced firsthand.

I actually resent my decision to question her this way because I can't fully immerse myself in the moment and watch her reach these new heights I'm taking her to. Yet another reason to find out who's behind all this and make them suffer. And so I shall.

"I have a secret, Beauty. The elder Barwyn is a seer, and he had some very interesting things to say about you. The first being that you are not human as you claim to be, at least not only human. He says you're definitely *other*, though what kind exactly he was unable to determine. So why don't you end the suspense and tell me."

Her brows pinch together and she shakes her head hard, causing her cascade of blond hair to swing behind her. "I'm not, I swear. I'm just a regular Midwestern girl. There's nothing special about me."

No longer concerned about keeping my distance, I step in until her clamped nipples are grazing my chest. Reaching around her side, I grab a fistful of her hair and yank down, forcing her to look up and meet my steely gaze. "Now that, my pretty little slut, is an outright lie. Whether you're other or human, I don't ever want to hear you refer to yourself as nothing special. Tell me you understand."

"I understand."

"Do you want to come, slut?"

"God, yes, I do."

"Beg your king."

"Please, my king," she says so sweetly with her expressive hazel eyes. "Please may I come?"

"No, you do not have permission."

Her whimper turns into more of a keening cry, but I see her truth. Being denied only turns her on even more.

I adjust the wand to sit higher on her inner thigh so that it's pressed more firmly against her but still nowhere near her clit. It's now directly at her entrance with her slick labia trapped between the buzzing head and her drenched hole.

Finally, I pull the necklace out of my pocket and let it dangle in front of her face. "Why did you wear this the night we met?"

"I liked th-that one the best of all the ones I was offered."

"What do you mean? Be more specific, Beauty, or this will take all night, and I don't think you want to know what it's like to be edged that long."

Her eyes flare wide, then she explains on halted breaths. "Reservation mix-up...free VIP suite with...*necklace*." The last word is more of a groan as she fights harder to hold her orgasm back.

Eventually, she gets out all the pertinent details. How an assistant manager upgraded her to the VIP suite and offered her all the perks that went with it, including letting her choose one of five black obsidian necklaces to wear on loan.

Everything she's saying makes it sound like she's an innocent party in all this. Then again, maybe it's her cover story. If she's *other* as Barwyn claims and she knows how to mask her energy or emotions, I wouldn't be able to tell if she was lying or not. But agreeing to a plan that hinges on her being taken out for someone else to be able to usurp my throne doesn't seem like a very sensible thing to do. Maybe whoever it was told her she'd just have to go back home.

Fuck, none of this makes any goddamned sense.

Switching tactics, I remove the clamp on her clit, allowing the blood to once again flow to the swollen nub. Her back arches as she cries out, then tries to breathe through the need to come. She's about to wish she was still being denied.

Unstrapping the wand, I keep it on the high setting and hold it at the ready.

"From now on, you no longer need permission to come. You're to do it every time an orgasm hits."

She sags in relief. "Thank you, my king."

I give her a devilish grin, flashing my fangs. "Don't thank me yet."

Then I press the head of the wand hard against her overly sensitive clit and watch with satisfaction as she arches away from the cross and screams through her first of many explosions.

After about a minute of riding out the aftershocks, she starts to come back to herself, but I don't remove the wand. It's staying right where it's at, and every time she twists her hips to try and escape it, I follow her movements so that she can't.

Already I can see the next climax building. Forced orgasms are intense and each is more intense than the one before it.

"Let's assume for the moment that you're telling the truth, and you're completely innocent. This little bauble you wore was spelled to coerce me."

Bryn comes again, helpless to stop it. Beads of sweat pop out on her skin and dampen the tiny wisps of hair around her face.

So damned stunning. As soon as she's calm enough to hear me speak, I continue.

"Like a fucking love charm, your necklace turned me into a romantic fool who wanted nothing more than to sweep you off your feet and make you mine. And it fucking worked. Do you understand what that means?"

Again, she comes. Again, I watch, my dick so hard in my pants, I swear I'm going to come just from bearing witness to her ecstasy. And again, I continue.

"From the moment I laid eyes on you, everything I've felt has all been manufactured. Nothing more than a pretty fucking lie."

Bryn shakes her head violently. "No, that's not true," she says between panting breaths. "We have a connection."

"Wrong," I growl. "We have a bond that's feeding off the feelings we had at the time we were mated. *False* feelings. None of this is real; it never has been."

"No, I don't belie— *Ah fuuuuuuuck!*"

"Believe it or don't. It doesn't change that it's the truth." I'm not sure if she's even hearing me right now as her latest orgasm burns through her. Her entire body is trembling and her pleas for me to give her a reprieve are more incoherent babbles than actual words. But I understand them because I'm as fluent in this as anything else.

"Please don't make me come again, I can't do it, it's too much, pleeeeease…"

"I don't fucking think so." Purposely creating confusion, I turn the wand off and toss it on the table along with the necklace I'd like to smash into pieces for the lies it represents but also create a religion around it for being what ultimately bonded her to me.

Then I return to her and remove one of the nipple clamps as I drive three fingers into her greedy cunt. She comes instantly, screaming to the heavens as her inner walls, already so tight from multiple orgasms, squeeze my fingers like a fucking vise.

"That's it," I croon in a wicked tone. "You're going to come for me until there's not a drop of moisture left in your body. *Again.*"

I begin fucking her with my fingers, curling them to hit her G-spot and moving my hand in fast back-and-forth motions that make her so wet, it drips into my palm and makes the most delicious squelching sounds.

As her next orgasm builds and twists inside her, tears overflow and cause her mascara to run. I use the fingers of my free hand and smear the black drops into messy streaks down her face, then I grip the front of her throat and apply pressure on either side. Lips and nipples both swollen and red, cheeks painted in black tears…

It's the most beautiful she's ever looked.

It's in this purest of moments that I know without a doubt it won't matter if I discover Bryn did play a part in all of this, and it doesn't matter if what I feel comes from a spell. I don't care because I'm incapable of letting her go. I'm incapable of ever living without her.

More tears track down her cheeks and I lick them away, reveling in their salty essence, then I flay myself open and speak my truth against the shell of her ear. "Even if you are the cause of my ultimate demise, I will never release you. The night we bonded, you became mine, and that is what you shall remain. Now and always."

Feeling her climax overtake her, I release her throat and then quickly remove the other nipple clamp, giving her the rush of fresh oxygen and circulation that floods her system like getting a mainline of pure endorphins. Her body seizes up and shakes. Her mouth drops open, but no sound comes out, the silent scream signaling her ultimate pleasure and offering her throat to me like a gift.

And so I accept.

I sink my fangs into the side of her neck, causing aftershocks so powerful that it makes my gums tingle with pleasure. I only take a single sip, the euphoric experience already tainted with my guilt for the invasion…and the violation of trust I'm about to commit.

I pull back and stroke the hair out of her face, telling her what a good girl she is as she continues to float in subspace. With my other hand, I retrieve a tiny vial from my pocket and hold it against her skin just beneath where one of my fangs punctured to capture the small amount of blood that escapes before she heals.

Then I slip it back into my pocket and push everything aside to focus on caring for Bryn.

Grabbing the blanket that I laid out earlier, I carefully support her while I undo her cuffs. Then I wrap her up and carry her over to a chair where I sit with her cuddled in my lap. I offer her a bottle of water and insist she drinks at least half of it before letting her just snuggle against me as I rub her arms and back through the soft blanket as she comes down from subspace.

"Caiden," she says sleepily against my chest.

Resting my cheek atop her head, I speak in a low voice. "What is it, Beauty?"

"I wish you believed me."

"I do believe you, sweetheart."

I place a gentle kiss on her forehead and realize it's the truth, regardless of how naive it makes me.

"I'm glad." She sighs contentedly and snuggles in closer. "And if you ever use a scene to manipulate me again, I'll put my castration knowledge to good use."

Pride in hearing her stand up for herself helps to neutralize the acidic burn of my guilt. "Noted and justified."

Her satisfaction with my answer flows to me through our bond, and she finally succumbs to sleep. Soon after, my phone vibrates in my back pocket, and I take it out to find a text from Connor. It's a picture of the letter from Bryn's wallet, proving I'm not naive after all.

My gaze drifts to where I left that damnable necklace, and my heart sinks.

Because whether or not Bryn is innocent doesn't change that what we feel for each other is all still a lie.

And I think that might hurt worse than if she'd intentionally betrayed me.

CHAPTER TWENTY-THREE

BRYN

"Fiona!"

As I march through the halls of Midnight Manor on a Saturday evening, I can't get over just how eerily quiet it is.

I spent all day working in my temporary makeshift office and only realized how late it was when my stomach protested loud enough to echo in the room.

Since I take my food seriously, it wasn't until I was almost finished with the dinner plate the cook left for me in the warmer that I noticed how quiet the house is. And so began my epic quest of trekking through the twelve-thousand-square-foot maze to find my fae sidekick and ask her what the hell is going on.

"Fiona? Where are you?" Lowering my voice, I mutter, "Where is *any*one?"

I pop my head into the home gym and come up empty, releasing a small growl of frustration.

Then I remember I have a cell phone. Caiden gave mine back to me after the interrogation session a few nights ago. He finally trusts me.

I should be happy about that, and I am, mostly. Except

that ironically, we had a better relationship *before* he trusted
me. He's back to working all the time and making excuses
for why he can't see me. All because he thinks that whatever
we feel for each other is only because of that damn necklace.

Personally, I think it's bullshit.

I don't know anything about spells, but I like Tiernan's
theory about the bond, so I've chosen to apply it to spells, too.
They can't make something out of nothing. They can only
strengthen what was already there.

Even though Caiden and I had only met that night, I
believe there was a powerful instant attraction for the spell to
work from. The proof is what happened in the lobby between
us, which was hours before I ever had the necklace.

I'm trying to be patient—to let him work through his issues
on his own—but it's not an easy thing for me to do.

Hence why I've been burying myself in work.

At least now we know we have *one* thing in common.

Pulling my phone from my back pocket, I bring up Caiden's
number and shoot off a quick text as I continue making my
way through the lower level.

Hey, handsome, where u at?

When I don't see the three wavy dots right away, I force
myself to lock the screen and keep going. I will *not* stare at
my phone waiting for a response like a lovesick puppy.

After searching the game room and lower bar area, I climb
the stairs back up to the main floor. "Oh, I didn't check the
theater room. Maybe she's Netflix-and-actually-chilling."

Crossing through the massive great room, my phone
vibrates in my hand. I stop and pull up his response.

At a Night Court thing. Be back late. Don't wait up.

I furrow my brow and chew on my lip. Admittedly, his
vague statement stings a little. I thought we'd gotten past him
being secretive about fae business with me, but apparently not.

"Okay, don't jump to conclusions, Bryn. It's probably super-secret, high-level king stuff. Just because you're married to the guy doesn't mean you're entitled to be a part of everything."

K but u might find me in ur bed when u get home ;)

A thumbs-up bubble appears on my text. *He fucking thumbs-upped me?*

I continue to stare at my screen for several seconds before I realize I'm waiting for him to add an actual response. "Nope," I say to myself, kicking back into motion. "Not doing that. I can't expect him to be a chatty Cathy if he's in a meeting. It's fine, everything's fine. Fionaaaa!"

If I don't find her in the next five minutes, I'll be forced to seek out whatever Night Watch guys are on the property, but other than the Woulfe brothers, who will be wherever Caiden is, they all treat me similar to Finn—like an inconvenient ticking time bomb—so they're a last resort.

I reach out for the door of the theater room, but it's yanked open before I get there. Fiona jumps into the hall and slams the door shut behind her, greeting me with a too-wide smile.

"Hey, girl! I was just finishing up a movie. Super intense, major plot twist, you know how it is."

I blink a few times, not sure where to begin. The fact that she looks guilty as sin about something or that she was supposedly watching a movie while wearing a black satin sheath gown with a slit clear up to her hip.

I open my mouth to comment, but the door to the theater opens again. Only this time, it's Tiernan stepping into the hall, distractedly tucking his tux shirt into his waistband.

"Fuck, Fi, you almost took me out trying to get out—Oh, hey, Brynnie-Bear, how's it going?"

My eyes bounce back and forth between Fiona and Tier several times, the conspiratorial grin on my face getting bigger and bigger. "Super intense, major plot twist, huh? I'll say." A bubble of laughter escapes me, making her huff dramatically.

"This isn't what it looks like."

As Tier finishes putting himself to rights, he helpfully adds, "Unless, of course, it looks like I was banging Fiona in the theater. Then it's exactly what it looks like."

She spins to glare at him with fists planted on slim hips, her long red hair whipping around to fall in front of a bare shoulder. Tier gives her the classic *what'd I say?* look, and I laugh even harder. "Oh my God, this is fantastic. I knew something was going on between you two. Fiona, you little tart, how could you not tell me?"

At this, Tiernan raises his brows at her. "You're not bragging about me to your friends? Honestly, Fi, that hurts my feelings."

Fiona rolls her eyes. "Those aren't your feelings, it's your fragile ego. Get over yourself already." Turning back to me, she frowns. "Why aren't you ready?"

"Ready for what?"

"The Early Equinox Ball," she says, like I should know what she's talking about. When it's clear that I don't, she explains. "Every year on the night of the Fall Equinox, the Dark Fae have a grand ball to celebrate the coming of shorter days and longer nights. The only exception is on every tenth year, when the kings of the Day and Night Court meet in the desert at Joshua Tree on the Fall Equinox as a day that has the exact same hours of night and day. And on those years—which happens to be this one—we have the ball one week early and call it the Early Equinox Ball, or EEB."

"Or the Double-E for those of us who appreciate large breasts."

Fiona swings her hand back to smack him in the chest, but he catches her wrist with a sly grin, only releasing it when she gives her another eye roll.

The way they interact with each other is so fun, I could watch them all day. Where's a bucket of popcorn when you need one? In the theater, probably.

"Okay, so there's a ball tonight, and you're both going. Was that your point?"

"No, my point is that there's a ball tonight and *everyone* is going, so why aren't you dressed?"

My stomach drops as I finally catch on. "That's what Caiden's 'Night Court thing' is?"

Fiona's face falls as she realizes I was left behind on purpose, and Tiernan curses under the hand rasping over his stubbled jaw.

Turning away from their piteous expressions, I walk back over to the great room and plop down on one of the couches while I try to sort through a myriad of thoughts spinning in my head.

Fact: someone set things in motion to lure me to Vegas in order to get Caiden to marry me in a Dark Fae marriage rite for reasons unknown. Also unknown is why I was chosen specifically.

Unsettling to say the least, but as far as arranged marriages go, I think I hit the jackpot of grooms, so I'm good with the end result.

Fact: the bond has started changing me on a physiological level, giving me both strengths and weaknesses common for fae, which is both cool and scary. I try not to think about either very often.

Fact: Caiden believes that neither of our feelings for each other are real and is trying to push me away as a result.

Fact: Caiden is a dumbass.

Fiona takes a seat next to me and puts her hand on mine. "Bryn, I'm sorry. Let me go change out of this and we can hang out, have a girls' night in."

"Absolutely not," I say, my feathers more than a little ruffled now. "I'm hoping you have another gown somewhere because I'm going to that ball, even if I have to go in jeans and a T-shirt."

Her amber eyes light up, then dim when she frowns. "Damn it, I don't have anything like this here. I have a couple of cocktail dresses, but that's the best I can do."

"I can do much better than that." We both turn around to look up at where Tiernan is standing behind us.

Fiona narrows her eyes. "If you offer her some rando's dress that was left here after one of your many *interludes*, I will junk-punch you."

Shaking his head, he *tsk*s. "I'm offended you think me such an amateur, Fi. I always make sure my randos take all their clothes with them. Now, both of you, follow me."

I chuckle at the way my friend shoots fire at his back for all of five seconds before she's ogling his ass as we follow him up to the second floor.

"Take a picture, it lasts longer," I whisper.

She leans her head in and whispers back. "If you think I don't already have a whole collection in a hidden album on my phone, you have much to learn."

I roll my lips in to prevent an all-out laugh but forget my humor when Tiernan leads us into Caiden's bedroom. "Tiernan," I say, stopping dead at the threshold. "Wearing a dress from one of your past interludes would've been bad enough, but I don't even want to see one from Caiden's past."

He pauses at the door of the huge walk-in closet, his expression earnest. "Brynnie, give me a little credit. I would never suggest that. I'm getting *your* dress."

Before I can ask what he means, he disappears into the closet and emerges a few seconds later with the most beautiful black gown I've ever seen.

Fiona gasps next to me, then grabs my arm and drags me over to where Tiernan is holding it up from the hanger.

"Caiden *was* planning on taking you to the ball, Bryn," Tiernan says. "He had this custom ordered for you about two weeks ago. I don't know why he changed his mind."

I look him dead in the eye. "Because your brother is a dumbass."

He gives me a crooked grin. "No argument there. Here, put it on. Let's see if he got your measurements right."

Fiona grabs the dress from him and shoos me into the closet to help me into it, along with the matching heels we found. Then we stare at my reflection in the large three-way mirror standing in the corner of the closet.

"Gods, Bryn, it's perfect."

"It kind of is," I say reverently.

My eyes start to water knowing Caiden chose this dress for me, while also knowing he chose not to see me in it tonight, but I quickly blink them away and focus on committing every detail to memory.

Floor-length A-frame made entirely of tulle with a hidden slit on the left. The top is sheer nude mesh that gives the illusion of being naked except for the handsewn black flower appliqués that travel up from the waist to form the front of the bodice that covers my breasts and splits into a deep V past my navel. Black lace in the shape of thin vines with some leaves give the appearance of straps that stop at the top of my shoulders, leaving my entire back open with the illusion netting.

"Let's quickly do your hair and makeup and get you to the ball, Cinder—"

I hold my hand up. "Stop. Don't finish that sentence. I can only handle being in one fictional world at a time, thank you very much."

We both laugh, drawing the attention of our waiting prince. "Sounds like it's safe to come in. Whoa," he says, eyes wide as he takes me in. "My brother might be a dumbass, but he's a dumbass with taste. He's going to fall all over himself when he sees you."

Squaring my shoulders, I mentally prepare for battle.

"He'd fucking better."

Less than thirty minutes later, I have a Hollywood-worthy smoky-eye look, and my hair is curled and pinned into a pile on my head with loose tendrils framing my face. My phone and ID are in my wristlet, and I'm good to go.

Fiona and I meet Tiernan downstairs, then head for the garage where his midnight-blue BMW 8-series sedan is parked.

He opens the back door for me, but I stop when I notice a decal next to the left taillight that says, *I drive like a Cullen.* When I give him a look that says *seriously?* he's quick to defend himself. "What? It's funny." I laugh as I slide into the back seat. "It's also true, so buckle up."

He gets behind the wheel with Fiona in shotgun, then hits the button for the garage door and waits for it to raise.

"Do we need to tell security that I'm leaving?"

Tiernan meets my gaze in the rearview mirror. "Not if you want to surprise the king."

And with that, he proves just how accurate that damn decal is.

We arrive at Nightfall in what has to be a world-record time.

As we approach the entry to the event space, my nerves finally make an appearance in the form of angry butterflies in my stomach. Fiona glances over at me and must see it written on my face.

"Take some deep breaths, Bryn. Once the initial shock of you being here wears off, he's going to be too tongue-tied and horny to care."

Her attempt at levity works, and our quick laugh together takes the edge off. I should probably find the nearest server with alcohol to help with the rest, though.

There's a handful of fae guests milling around the outside of the ballroom, and Fiona grabs my hand excitedly as she points to one specifically. "That's my mom. I can't wait for you to meet her; she's the absolute best." Waving her down, she calls out, "Mom, over here!"

A beautiful strawberry-blonde in a strapless mermaid dress excuses herself from her small group and holds her arms out to envelop Fiona in a tight hug. "What took you so long? King Caiden is due to give his speech and blessing soon."

"I know, I'm sorry, but I was helping my friend get ready. Bryn, this is my mom, Erin Jewel. Mom, this is Bryn, the woman I was telling you about who's been staying at the manor."

Erin turns her smile on me, about to greet her daughter's friend, when she suddenly freezes and holds it so long, I wonder if somehow time is standing still.

The smile is still on her face, but it no longer reaches her warm eyes. In fact, she almost looks...scared?

My PR persona kicks in and I pretend that nothing is out of the ordinary. Holding my hand out, I say, "Hello, Erin, it's such a pleasure to meet you. Fiona speaks so highly of you, and I can't tell you how much I adore your daughter. She's been a godsend to me over the past month. You did an excellent job raising her."

Erin snaps out of her frozen state, but now her eyes are welling up with moisture she's trying desperately to blink back.

"Mom? What's wrong?"

"Nothing, sweetheart, I think it's just dust or something." She uses the back of a finger to help stem the water before it can spill over, then takes a deep breath and composes herself. "There, see? All better. Bryn," she says at last, taking my hand between hers, "it's so nice to finally meet you. I've been waiting for what seems like forever."

Fiona makes some comment about her mom exaggerating what was only a few weeks, but I'm not really listening. I'm lost in the way her soft hands feel cradling mine. A comforting motherly touch, one my own mother used to give me, and it causes an ache in my chest I haven't had in a while.

But the more I stare at her, the more something else starts to tug in my brain.

"I feel as if I've seen you before," I say, my brows knitted together in concentration.

Fiona chuckles. "Not unless you've been to Vegas before. My mom hates traveling, isn't that right?"

Erin offers me a tight smile. "It's true. I do hate to travel. Well, if you girls will excuse me, I was on my way to the restroom when I was stopped. Perhaps I'll see you inside."

"Okay, Mom," Fiona says, kissing her mother's cheek.

As soon as Erin is out of sight, Fiona takes my hand and gives me an excited smile. "Showtime. Let's go show that king of yours what he's missing."

The doors to the ballroom are opened for us by Nightfall employees, and when we cross the threshold, I feel like Dorothy crossing over into the Land of Oz. Picture the most extravagant celebrity wedding reception you've ever seen on TV and then triple the lavishness of the decor and guests.

At least a hundred crystal chandeliers hang at different lengths from the ceiling, except in the center where a section the size of a billboard is retracted to frame the moon hanging in the night sky. Beneath all of that is a midnight sea of mingling, dancing fae, all dressed in black and each more seemingly beautiful than the last.

And straight ahead, on the opposite shore, is a set of black marble stairs leading up to a wide dais where the royal family can watch over their guests. A massive steel-and-black-velvet throne stands proudly in the center with two chairs in a similar style sitting on each side. Seamus is in the chair to the far left. Next to him is Tiernan, and on the other side of the empty throne is Finnian, who's chatting to an older female in the last seat with dark brown hair and familiar eyes.

Though her posture is stiff—shoulders square, hands

folded in her lap, and ankles crossed—her expression is soft and doting as she listens to Finn with unmistakable adoration.

"Is that..."

Fiona leans in. "Morgan Scanell, the Royal Mother. Isn't she beautiful?"

"She is," I say, suddenly more nervous.

I never considered the prospect of meeting Caiden's mother tonight. I'm not sure I ever considered him even *having* a mother. If anyone seems like they appeared on this earth as the strong and dominant male he already is, it's Caiden Verran. I can't picture him as a troublemaking boy or a teen struggling through his hormonal ugly-phase. It doesn't seem possible for him to be anyone other than who I know him as.

But I'd like to know of those other parts of who he was, and talking to his mother would be the perfect way of doing that.

Will she like me? Or is she the overprotective type who feels no one is good enough for her son? Or maybe she'll disapprove because I'm human—or mostly human...I have no idea anymore, but not fae, at least—and formally snub me in front of the entire court.

Then again, it shouldn't matter if she doesn't like me, because Caiden has no intentions of keeping me around longer than necessary. Maybe that's why he didn't invite me tonight. Maybe he wanted to avoid a pointless introduction to his mother.

"Fi, I'm starting to think this was a bad idea." My hands press against my lower abdomen in an attempt to calm the butterflies that have gone from fluttering to straight-up moshing.

She grips my hand. "What? No way. You're already here, and you look freaking amazing in that gown. If he doesn't want to spend time with you tonight, let him watch all the males trip over themselves to get your attention. That'll teach him to leave you behind."

I'm about to argue when I see Caiden. He's flanked by Connor and Conall, meandering through the crowd and pausing briefly to speak to fae who stop him along the way. When he reaches the dais, the brothers post up on either side of the stairs as he ascends and takes a seat on his throne.

Staring at him from across the room, I'm mesmerized. I've seen him in three-piece suits, jeans and casual tops, sweaty workout gear, leather pants and shirtless, and completely naked.

But I've never seen him like this.

As usual, he's dressed all in black but with a royal flair. Over his dress shirt is a fitted, double-breasted vest with wide lapels and a silver brocade pattern. The coat is similar in style, showing off his broad shoulders and chest while nipping in at his trim waist, then splitting into tails that reach the backs of his knees.

But the most striking item of all is his crown. There are no embedded jewels or elegant designs; it's not made of anything shiny like gold or silver. It's not a symbol of his wealth or a peacock piece to make his subjects stare in awe. It's utterly plain and made of a dark, heavy-looking metal. The bottom is shaped by symmetrical shallow points, and three-dimensional triangles rise up in flared angles at different heights to form the top of the crown that sits on his head.

I'm used to his overwhelming beauty and sex appeal being a lot to handle, but the kingly version of Caiden Verran is likely to break my lady bits if I stare at him too long.

Look away, Bryn. You'll need those ovaries someday.

I'm about to listen to myself for once when it becomes too late. Caiden's golden eyes suddenly swing to mine as though he locked in on my presence, and any thoughts I had a second ago have been short-circuited all to hell.

"Finally," Fiona says. "Come on, it's time to formally make your arrival known."

She starts pulling me in the direction of the dais, and I can only hope she's leading me down a clear path because it's not possible for me to break his eye contact. "I don't know how to do this," I hiss under my breath.

"Don't worry. I'll tell you exactly what to do."

CHAPTER TWENTY-FOUR

CAIDEN

I've never seen a more magnificent female in all my long life. The moment I felt her presence, my gaze was like a homing beacon to find her in the crowd. Instantly, she stole my breath as her own, for I saw her lips part on a gasp.

Seeing her in the gown I chose for her fills me with pride. I want to spoil her with gifts, clothes, and jewelry. I want to take her out and show her off, knowing that everyone will want her, but I'm the one who has her. I want to put a leather collar around her throat at night and give her a symbolic one in the form of a necklace during the day, so that every time she touches it, she's reminded of who she belongs to.

I want all that and more with Bryn Meara.

But I know now that none of it is real, and I don't know how to handle the fact that I don't fucking care.

"Oh hey, big bro," Tiernan says on my right. "I forgot to mention I brought Brynnie. I'm sure it just slipped your mind to give your mate the dress you bought her and bring her to the most important event of the year. You're welcome."

Unable to look away from her as she slowly walks toward the dais, I speak to my asshole brother with a death wish under my breath. "I had my reasons for not bringing her, not the least of which was for her own safety. The lemon incident was no accident."

"What are you talking about?"

"Ask Seamus."

In my peripheral, I see Tiernan lean to the other side for a few seconds. Then he straightens and mutters, "Well fuck. You should've told Finn and me. We can't watch your six if we don't know what the hell is going on."

"Noted. We'll discuss this later."

As she and Fiona stop in front of the dais, I push to my feet, ready to meet her at the bottom of the stairs and escort her back out of the hall so Connor and Conall can take her back to the manor. But then she drops down into a low curtsy, holding my gaze until the very last second when her head finally bows in deference.

I'm momentarily stunned by the sublime elegance of her submissive pose that I don't realize I've made her hold it for longer than is necessary—or probably easy.

Descending the stairs, I stand before her and hold my hand out in her field of vision. She takes it and rises gracefully.

When her eyes meet mine again, they're full of fire, and not the pleasurable kind. By now we've caused quite the stir and have become the focus of everyone's curiosity.

"Bryn," I say before bending to place a kiss on her knuckles. "Tonight more than ever you embody the name Beauty, for yours is unparalleled in this realm and the next."

Her smile could pass for real to anyone else, but I know it for the fake it is. "Such sweet words from someone who left me behind like yesterday's trash."

I pop my jaw in aggravation, then lower my voice. "I didn't leave you behind."

She takes a step closer, the large skirt of her gown swinging from side to side with the simple movement. Sensing we need the privacy, the Woulfe brothers signal to two other Night Watchers and all four move into position around us.

"I see," she says in a clipped tone. "You merely forgot all about me, then. That's so much better."

A growl rumbles in my chest. "Bryn."

"Don't you use that voice on me right now, Caiden Verran," she hisses. "I'm pissed at you, and I *get* to be pissed at you. I don't care what your reason was for not bringing me, the *least* you could've done was say it to my face instead of ducking out of the manor like a fucking coward."

Conall has a brief coughing fit that sounds a lot like laughing. If I had heat vision, there'd be a melted hole from the back of his skull right now.

"Caiden, dear, I do hope you don't plan on monopolizing all of your guest's time without introducing her first."

Fuck. I'm not looking forward to the fallout that will come from this encounter.

Glancing over my shoulder to where she's standing at the top of the stairs, I say, "Of course not, Mother."

"Shit, I shouldn't have come. She's going to hate me."

Turning back to Bryn, I'm surprised to see the worry etched on her delicate features. I gather both of her hands in mine and squeeze. "She couldn't possibly hate you, Bryn. You've charmed everyone in my life, and she'll be no different."

Bryn's eyes cast over my shoulder and to the side. "Not Finnian."

For probably the first time in my baby brother's life, I have a strong desire to punch him when I hear the dejection in her voice.

Connecting with others is an important part of who she is, and the fact that Finn holds her at a distance weighs on her. I don't have to feel her energy to know that. Hating her abrupt turn in mood, I offer to let her kill two birds with one stone.

"Would it make you feel better if I let you kick him in his

royal jewels the next time he visits the manor?"

Her lips twitch only the slightest bit, but her mirth reaches her eyes this time. "Although I would never do such a thing, your offer does make me feel moderately better. Thank you."

"My pleasure. Now come," I say, offering her my arm to slip her hand through. "We best not keep the Royal Mother waiting any longer, or I'll get an unpleasant lecture later."

"Hmm. That holds merit, too, though."

"I'll just bet it does." The Night Watchers disband to let us through and take up their original posts. As we begin our ascent, I say quietly, "That was an impressive curtsy for a woman who I assume has never had to perform one before."

"I've seen *Bridgerton* six times."

I cut a quick glance down at her. "You really watch entirely too much television."

"Watched," she says, correcting me. "Now I spend my time— and your money—reading at least five books a week. I'd say that's an improvement, wouldn't you?"

One corner of my mouth curves up. "I suppose it is."

When we reach the landing, I disengage her hand from my arm so she's free to move as she pleases, then make the introductions. "Mother, I'd like you to meet my guest for the evening, Bryn Meara. Bryn, this is Morgan Scannell, the Royal Mother of the Night Court of Faerie."

"He forgot my most important title: *his* mother."

Bryn smiles with a mischievous twinkle in her eyes, and I immediately know her brat is about to make an appearance. "You sure you want to claim that last one? In my experience, he can be kind of a pain in the you-know-what."

Mother laughs, taken aback and delighted all at once. "Indeed, my dear, he *can*. I'm not sure anyone other than his father and myself has ever had the gall to tell him, so he's hard-pressed to believe it. I can see you've no such trouble, though."

"None at all."

"Well, I hope I'll have a chance to get to know you better on a less-formal occasion, but it's almost time for Caiden to give the annual equinox blessing." She leans around me and calls out to her second child. "Tiernan, be a dear and give your seat to your brother's guest."

Always the first to volunteer to get out of any official royal business, Tier practically jumps out of his chair. "It would be my honor, Mother. Here you are, Brynnie," he says, gesturing to the spot he's happily vacated.

Bryn doesn't move. Instead, she peers up at me and waits for my direction. I can still sense her anger, yet she continues to look for my guidance. Her trust and obedience is a gift I don't deserve but one I will always selfishly accept.

I want to lean over and whisper "Good girl" in her ear and feel the shudder of excitement tremble through her. Unfortunately, all I can do is nod my permission.

To my mother, she says, "It was an honor to meet you, and I hope we get that chance to talk someday soon."

"As do I, dear." Mother's warm smile remains in place while Bryn walks over by Tier and takes his seat. "And you," she says to me in a tone she used when Tier and I were young troublemakers. "I need to speak with you."

She walks toward the far side of the dais, not bothering to see whether I follow. I might be the king, but she'll be my mother no matter how important and rich I become.

I'm lucky she's allowing me to follow instead of dragging me along by the ear.

When she spins around to address me, gone is the congenial Royal Mother, and in her place is the strong, take-no-bullshit female who raised three hellions.

"You're mated." It's not a statement of observation. It's an accusation, one that stings like the crack of a single-tail whip. "Please tell me I'm mistaken. That my ability to recognize my eldest son's energy is failing me in my old age."

"Mother, you're barely four centuries and still as sharp and beautiful as if you were two."

"Distracting with flattery is Tiernan's method of weaseling his way out of trouble, not yours. You've always acted with a king's integrity, long before you ever were one. Tell me how it is you could be so foolish as to take a mate at all, much less one who is..."

"Human?"

She gives me a quizzical look. "Maybe I'm not the one whose senses are failing. She's no more human than you are, Caiden. Though I'm uncertain as to what she is; she doesn't quite read as fae, does she?"

Despite hearing it from Barwyn, I'm surprised my mother is able to sense it as well. Bryn still reads human to me, even with the fae qualities she's gained. But the truth of the matter is that something I've done is affecting her on a physiological level, and there's no way of knowing whether it will become irreversible at some point. Or gods forbid, already has.

I glance back to check on her and see the Tallons and a few others she met at the ToR all standing at the edge of the dais chatting enthusiastically with her.

"She seems to have made quite the impression," my mother says, pulling my attention back to her.

"Everyone loves her. Everyone except Finni," I amend.

"I imagine it would be hard for your brother, who thinks you hung Rhiannon's moon, to accept a female who holds your life in her hands. Now, son, tell me. How did this happen?"

I try to draw in a deep breath, but my ribs struggle to expand beneath the crushing weight of the truth. Dragging a course hand over my mouth and jaw, I give up trying to put this conversation off any longer.

"The night we met, she was given a spelled necklace to wear that bewitched me, for lack of a more creative term. Neither of us remembers more than the first few hours together, but we woke up the next morning married and mated. At first, I thought she had something to do with it. Then someone tried to poison her, and they nearly succeeded."

My mother's eyes fly wide as she grips my arm with both hands. "Caiden."

I place a reassuring hand atop hers. "I know, and I'm sorry. I didn't want to worry you before I have all the facts, which is why I tried leaving her at the manor tonight."

Slender brows knit together above the bridge of her nose. "But the curse…"

Discreetly, I reach into my coat's inside pocket and show her the small vial of Bryn's blood, then tuck it back into place. "An elder seer told me it would give me a few hours of mimicking her presence. Considering I don't know how to explain who or what she is to our people, I thought it best I came alone."

"My son, you're the king. You don't have to explain yourself to anyone. Except your mother," she adds with a pointed narrowing of her eyes.

I let my affection for her shine through. "Your admonishment has been noted, Mother."

She gives me a demure grin of appeasement, then I shatter the brief levity to return to the more serious topic.

"But a king does have an obligation to explain himself when he's done something that affects his subjects, which is now the case. Being mated to Bryn has activated the curse, and now someone is using her and our bond to get to me. If Bryn has a target on her back, then so do I."

Her tone turns ominous with her whisper. "The Day King."

I shake my head. "It can't be Talek. Neither one of us has the power to kill the other without causing our own deaths— it's in the treaty."

"The treaty specifically states that a king cannot be killed by the other's hand or by their order. It says nothing of manipulating the king into the fatal role of widower by using the blood curse against him."

Ice freezes in my veins. "No, that can't be right. Father never mentioned any specifics, and neither has Seamus. You must be mistaken."

Clutching her belly like she might be sick, she explains. "Seamus wasn't at the signing of the first treaty. I was, and I acted as your father's witness. Your father resented the need for a treaty—he believed a fae's enemy should never be another fae—so it doesn't surprise me he ignored his responsibility to teach you the finer details. The fool."

She mutters that last part under her breath, but it's hard not to hear the undertone of lasting affection for the man who refused to love her.

"If Talek is behind this, you need to get her back to the manor. It's too risky for either of you to be here. I'll give the blessing, and your brothers and I will take over hosting duties for the night."

"I appreciate that, Mother, but I'll give the blessing. I don't want to start rumors that my affiliation with Bryn is preventing me from performing my duties as king. After that, we'll go."

She nods, but her eyes that match mine are swimming with concern. "As you wish."

I bend down and kiss her cheek, then leave her and cross to Bryn's side.

She looks up at me and smiles—and thank Rhiannon, this one is genuine—then turns her attention back to the crowd. "This is amazing, Caiden. I've never seen anything like it."

Seeing everything through her eyes brings a fresh perspective to the elegance and grandeur of the ball. It's not that the shine has worn off, but when you've done something more than a hundred times, you forget that the shine is even there.

"Do you have the retractable roof so you can pay homage

to Rhiannon at your events?"

I give her an indulgent grin. "Yes, we do."

She returns my grin. "I thought so. But what is he up there for?"

"Who?"

Bryn turns her face up to the ceiling and points. "Him."

I follow her gaze and see a cloaked figure standing at the edge of the skylight. At first I assume Connor and Conall must have posted a Night Watcher up on the roof.

But then he raises his arms from inside his cloak and aims a bow and arrow straight at Bryn.

CHAPTER TWENTY-FIVE

BRYN

"*A*rcher on the roof!*"*

At Caiden's bellowed warning, the world around me detonates.

The sea of fae explodes into screams of confusion as they scatter for safety, running into one another like bumper cars in a fit of hysterics. Night Watchers appear out of nowhere to follow Connor's and Conall's barked commands. Some whisk the royals away from harm and some mobilize to attack the threat. Caiden grabs me by the arm to pull me out of the path of the arrow slicing through space and time straight toward my heart.

He yanks me to him in the nick of time...and also a millisecond too late.

I scream as fire erupts in my right shoulder, the arrowhead tearing through flesh, ligaments, and muscle tissue. My legs give out just as the archer, seeing they failed to hit their mark, runs away to make their escape.

Holding me close and taking my weight, Caiden calls to his personal guards and best friends. "Hunt that archer down, but I want them alive. *Go!*"

The brothers—gentle giants as I've come to think of them—release inhuman growls and leap into the air, magically transforming into massive wolves that take off running the second their plate-size paws touch the ground.

Sheer awe momentarily distracts me from all the pain and chaos. I've seen them in wolf form before but never witnessed them turn. I expected a grotesque display of bones cracking and reshaping, not the effortless transformation of being fae one second and wolves the next.

"Shapeshifters have it way better than werewolves," I bite out.

"You would be thinking about something like that with an arrow jutting from your body."

I'm about to comment on shock being a wonderful thing when Caiden gingerly scoops me up and the fire reignites to incendiary levels.

"Fuck, hold on, Beauty. I have to get you out of here before I take care of that."

Madoc and several other Watchers protect us until we reach a hidden door that blends into the wall on the far side of the ballroom. He tells the guards not to follow us but to stay behind and ensure his subjects' safety. We must be entering a secure section of the hotel or I doubt they would've so readily left us.

As Caiden carries me down a hall, the edges of my vision start to blur. I can feel that we take a few turns, but I'd be hard-pressed to retrace our steps if I had to find my way back to the ballroom.

Consciousness is a fickle thing, winking in and out, by the time I'm laid on my side on a soft mattress.

"I have to get the arrow out, Bryn. I'll need to break the shaft as close to your shoulder as possible, then pull it through from the back."

I think I answer, but I don't hear myself speak, so maybe I

don't manage it. Sweat coats my skin, and I'm starting to shiver.

"Hold still, baby. I'll be quick."

He snaps the wooden dowel in half, causing it to jerk in the wound. I cry out, unable to hold my scream back like I wanted. Caiden murmurs words of praise and sweet promises of bloody revenge as he pulls the arrow from my body.

As soon as it's out, I collapse back onto the mattress, my eyes closed and breaths labored. I sense Caiden leave my side and return moments later with a warm, damp cloth to wipe my forehead as he puts pressure on my wound with towels.

Several minutes later, I notice a significant change in how I feel. I open my eyes and stare up into his amber pools of concern. "Am I delirious or am I already starting to heal?"

He pulls the towel away from my shoulder and relief blankets his features. "Thank gods. It's already knitting itself back together. It'll take a bit longer, but you'll be okay." He blows out a heavy breath and replaces the towel, then sheds his blood-stained formal coat and tosses it on a nearby chair. "Fuck, that could've been so much worse. I never thought I'd be grateful for the bond giving you fae qualities."

My own gratitude dies on my tongue, coating it like ash.

By escaping death once again, Caiden has done the same thing.

I keep forgetting that his life is dependent on mine. And while it would only be natural for anyone in his situation to be grateful that I'll survive, I can't help but resent him for it the tiniest bit.

Does it make me selfish that I want him to be relieved I'm okay for no other reason than he cares about me? Probably, but it doesn't change how I feel.

"Now that I know you're healing, I need to go back and check on things. And when the assassin is caught and brought back, I'll question them and get the answers we've been looking for."

"You sound so sure that they'll be caught."

His voice drops low. "The Woulfe brothers are the greatest trackers this side of the veil, and they know I want that coward's head. They won't return until they're caught." A shiver rolls through me at his ominous tone. I'd hate to be on the other end of his wrath. "Stay here and get some rest. This is a private-quarters section of the hotel. No one can get in without a security code. I'll be back when I can."

Without so much as a hand squeeze of reassurance, Caiden stalks to the door and leaves me alone in the room. The adrenaline is wearing off and everything about my situation is coming into focus.

I've been nothing but a burden on Caiden and his family since arriving in this city, but it's not like any of this was something I planned or wanted, either. And now that he thinks any feelings we have for each other are manufactured by that ridiculous spelled necklace, he's been holding me at arm's length like it's his third fucking job.

And frankly, I'm sick of it.

Testing my strength, I rise from the bed. Surprisingly, I don't feel too bad. Kind of like the day after being laid up with a stomach bug—a bit achy and not quite operating at a hundred percent, but definitely better than someone should be after getting an arrow removed from their shoulder ten minutes ago.

I go into the bathroom and check the wound, front and back, and it's almost completely closed. "Whoa. Eat your heart out, Wolverine. Wait till Connor and Conall get a load of this."

Then it hits me.

No one is guarding me. The door isn't locked from the outside. I'm on the Vegas Strip where taxis abound. And I have my phone in the wristlet with my ID and credit cards programmed into it.

I can go home.

And why shouldn't I?

Caiden doesn't want me to be a part of his world. He hates that the bond is giving me fae qualities and spends more time avoiding me than he does anything else these days. It would be better for both of us if I was back in Wisconsin. I won't be in the line of fire there, and then he can focus on figuring out how to break the bond instead of worrying that one of these times I won't be so lucky and it'll be lights out for both of us.

Yeah. It's definitely time for this trip to end.

I only wish it didn't make me so fucking sad.

CHAPTER TWENTY-SIX

CAIDEN

I make my way back through the halls of the secured section of Nightfall, lethal determination in every step. When my cell vibrates in my pocket, I dig it out and answer without checking the caller ID or breaking my stride. "Tell me what I want to hear."

"We got him," Conall says. "We're waiting in the security wing for you."

"Good. Don't start without me."

Pocketing my phone, I approach the end of the corridor that will lead me back into the ballroom. Night Watchers will be armed and stationed at every entrance and exit, but knowing the threat was specifically for Bryn, the guests have been ordered to leave and, to be on the safe side, seek sanctuary in their own homes for the evening. My brothers, Seamus, and Mother will all be holed up with their personal guards in the other rooms back in the secure section where I left Bryn.

No civilian fae should still be on the premises, which is why I curse in surprise when a female practically jumps out at me as soon as I reenter the ballroom.

She quickly bows her head of strawberry-blond hair as she speaks urgently. "Your Majesty, forgive me, but I must speak with you. It's of the utmost importance."

"Were you harmed? I can have one of the Watchers take you to the medical bay."

Rising to meet my gaze, she has a grief-stricken expression on her face, surprising me. "No, sire, I'm fine. Please, I need a few minutes of your time."

I place a comforting hand on her shoulder. "I apologize, but I don't have any minutes to spare right now. But if you attend the next court session at the ToR, I promise to listen fully and help you however I can."

I'm not more than five strides away when she calls out, "It's about Bryn, Your Majesty."

Like yanking on the emergency brake around a turn, I stop my forward motion and do a one-eighty to march back to her. Narrowing my eyes at the female, I scrutinize every detail, trying to find clues about whether she can be trusted. "What do you know about Bryn?"

"I know everything about her, sire." She pauses, swallowing hard as she wrings her hands together. "She's a fae who was hidden in the human world twenty-six years ago."

My eyes fly wide at the wild implication of what she's claiming.

She opens her mouth to speak, but I hold my finger up to my lips, not wanting her to say anything until we're somewhere secure. Glancing around to ensure no one heard her, I indicate for her to follow me.

We leave the ballroom, and I lead her through the hotel lobby using a glamour to mask my presence; the last thing I need right now is a bunch of drunken guests mobbing me for selfies and sperm.

I enter a code at an Employees Only door near the front desk, which leads to the corridor where my security team is located.

In addition to their base of operations where they monitor the activity throughout the hotel and casino, we have five rooms used for holding and questioning. Anyone we catch counting cards or running other games at the tables, pickpockets preying on the guests, or anyone drunk and belligerent enough to start shit with the other guests or my staff, this is where we bring them until the authorities arrive. All of the larger Vegas establishments have them, but ours are also soundproof.

Because when you're running two empires in a place nicknamed Sin City, you're bound to make a few enemies along the way. And in those situations, sometimes it's not enough to simply hold and question. Sometimes it's needed to torture and interrogate.

Like tonight.

Sensing which room they're holding the archer in, I take one of the others and usher her through the door. It looks like any interrogation room you'd find at a police precinct—four walls and a metal table between metal chairs. Once we're inside, I gesture for her to take a seat. Then I turn off the video and recording equipment with a push of a button and sit across from her.

"All right, it's safe to talk now," I say. "Please tell me who you are and why you think Bryn is a changeling of all things."

"My name is Erin Jewel, sire. I'm Fiona's mother."

I nod for her to continue, too anxious to hear the rest to go through the normal pleasantries of meeting an employee's family member.

"I know she's a changeling because I'm the one who made her so."

A thousand questions crash through my mind, but I pull out the important ones and focus on getting those answered for now. "She's your daughter? Are you telling me Bryn and Fiona are sisters?"

She shakes her head. "She's my niece, my sister's child. I

made a promise to her that I would ensure her baby's safety. I found Jack and Emily Meara, a Midwestern couple who had tried conceiving without luck for years but desperately wanted a baby. So I left my infant niece with them, knowing they would give her a good home and keep her safe."

Sitting forward, I brace my elbows on my legs and ask the question I sense will be the final piece of this godsforsaken puzzle. "Why would she need to be hidden in the human world to begin with?"

"Because Bryn is the first and only of her kind. She is both Light and Dark fae, and there was one who vowed to hunt her down—Talek Edevane."

I hiss in a breath. "The fucking Day King."

"Yes, but he wasn't king then; he was captain of the Light Guard and also cousin to Uther Anwyl, Bryn's father. One night, Uther made a grave mistake. He confided in his friend and cousin that he'd fallen in love with a female of the Night Court—my sister, Kiera—and that they had been blessed, for Kiera was due with his child in two months' time.

"Talek feigned happiness for his cousin, then had him watched so he would know when Uther left the Day Court border. A week later, I went with Kiera to meet with Uther at Joshua Tree. They planned to run away together and live far away from both courts, where their child would either be in danger because of or sought out for any rare abilities her lineage caused.

"But Bryn was eager to enter the world, and Kiera went into labor before they could leave. I had just delivered my niece when we heard the trucks in the distance coming from the direction of the Day Court. We would have fled right then, but Kiera had internal damage and couldn't be moved without screaming from excruciating pain. Uther was from a long line of Light healers, but nothing he did helped."

"Unstable magic." I don't realize I spoke my musing aloud

until Erin nods sadly. "Queen Aine warned that if a child was ever born of both courts, they would have unstable magic."

"Yes, I think carrying Bryn all those months took its toll on her body and the birth put her over the edge."

"What happened when Talek arrived?"

"Uther and Keira made me swear an oath to keep her existence a secret and find a place where she would be safe. So I said goodbye to my sister, took her baby, and hid behind an outcropping of rocks just before the trucks carrying Talek and a dozen of his Light warriors reached us. Talek tortured them for information on where the baby was, but neither broke, making him furious. He vowed to them both that he would never stop searching for their child...then he slaughtered them."

I drag both hands down my face and push to my feet, needing to move. I pace the short length of the room as my mind reels. Her story has too many details and the pain in her eyes is too raw for her to be manipulating words into an elaborate fae truth—which would be an amazing feat—and yet so much doesn't make sense.

"How did you avoid detection? Talek would've searched the area," I say, thinking about what I would do if I were an insufferable psychopath. When Erin doesn't immediately answer, I stop and look over at her.

The burden of keeping a secret for a lifetime is etched on her fair features, and that's when everything falls into place.

"You're a conjuring fae."

Swallowing thickly, she nods. "Yes, Your Majesty. I am."

"Did you spell her? Is that why Bryn reads as human?"

Again, she nods. "When spells are used to create an illusion or cause reactions that normally would not be, the magic needs to be recharged over time. But spells to block or mute something can be made permanent. I spelled Bryn to block her fae essence, and because she was only hours old at the time, it dampened all her qualities. Her ears rounded out, her eye color dulled, and when her teeth finally came in, though her canines had slight points to them, they never elongated into fangs. I checked on her regularly until she was thirteen to ensure the block held and no one had grown suspicious. Then I finally let her go."

"Her eyes are hazel, a mix of green and gold." While Dark Fae have golden eyes, the Light Fae are inherently vivid green. "Gods, how did I not see it before?"

"Because you weren't meant to. No one was, Your Majesty. She's the first and only of her kind. Even if the block wasn't still mostly in place, she doesn't read as Light *or* Dark; she reads as an amalgamation of the two, something none of us has ever encountered before."

"Mostly in place?"

"I didn't know she was in Vegas until she showed up with Fiona tonight. Once I got over the shock of seeing her, I could sense the fractures in my spell. They're small, but they'll continue to grow the longer you're bonded." I arch a brow at her. "Yes, I can sense that, too. Apologies, sire."

"Honestly, Erin, that's the least of my concerns at present." I pinch the bridge of my nose, trying to stave off the mother of all migraines. And fae don't even get headaches. Thinking of how Bryn and I somehow ended up mated our first night together, I say, "One last question. Aine said that part of a hybrid's abilities would be to bend the fae of our courts to their will with a single thought. Does Bryn have that ability?"

"If she does, it's still being repressed by the spell. I didn't sense any powers of persuasion coming from her."

"What if it had been amplified using a spelled necklace made of obsidian?"

Erin's eyes grow round. "Obsidian is known to be a truth-seeking stone. Aided by a spell, it may have strengthened the truth of who she is enough to at least give her mild suggestive powers."

Exhaling heavily, I shake my head in disbelief. "That explains how we ended up mated and believing we have feelings for each other this whole godsdamned time." Cursing, I rake a hand through my hair and pull at the strands.

"Forgive me, sire, but if Bryn wore a spelled necklace when you met, it wouldn't have affected you past that first night."

I frown. "What makes you say that?"

"As I said, spells that create—such as intense attraction, for example—are merely temporary. Obsidian or not, something as small as a pendant wouldn't have held a spell for very long. I would guess maybe five or six hours at most."

"I see. Everything after that has been influenced by the bond, then. I suppose that makes more sense, especially since she hasn't worn the necklace since that first night."

She shakes her head. "No, Your Majesty. A bond cannot be manifested from nothing, just like a flower cannot appear if there is no seed. If Talek orchestrated this, he was fortunate that it worked in his favor. Had you and Bryn not felt a natural attraction to each other and forged a connection all on your own, his plan would have failed."

A hint of a smile lifts the corners of her mouth.

"Everything you and my niece feel for each other is genuine. You are bonded because you are true mates."

I'm familiar with the phrase of feeling like the rug has been ripped out from under you, but I've never experienced it personally. Until now.

I have to find my footing, though, because I don't have the time to savor this revelation properly. Later, when I'm back at home with Bryn, I can unpack this entire conversation and what it all means.

Gripping the back of the chair to steady myself, I force words past the sudden lump in my throat. "Erin, I appreciate how difficult it must have been for you to see Bryn this evening and tell me her story. You have my most heartfelt condolences on the loss of your sister and Uther, not to mention your niece, as you were forced to give her up as well."

Her eyes well with unshed tears. "Thank you, Your Majesty."

"I'd like to extend an invitation for you to visit Fiona at Midnight Manor. They've grown quite close, and it will allow you to spend time with Bryn and get to know her. For now, though, I ask that you not mention any of this to her. In five days' time, I have the Meeting of Kings with Edevane. Once I've dealt with him and I know she's no longer in danger, we can discuss the best way of telling her."

"Of course, sire," she says, bowing her head before rising from the chair. "Please let me know if there's anything else I can do, for you or for Bryn."

I offer her a smile I hope doesn't look as tight as it feels. "I'm sure that time will come sooner rather than later."

Like when I ask you to find a way to sever our bond, strengthen Bryn's block, then take her back home before removing her memories of ever having visited Vegas.

As a conjurer, Erin has the best chance of anyone at discovering a solution to this situation. Then Bryn would be free to live the rest of her days as the human she believes herself to be. "You have my sincerest gratitude, and I apologize for the abrupt end to our conversation, but there's something I need to attend to."

Escorting her out of the security wing and through the main entrance of the hotel, I ensure she makes it safely into a cab and pay the driver to take her home.

As I resume my original mission, guilt eats at me. I should have already asked for Erin's help with severing the bond. The faster we manage that, the faster Bryn will be safe back in her world and my people will no longer be saddled with a cursed king.

But of all the revelations I learned tonight, one in particular holds me back.

Everything you and my niece feel for each other is genuine. You are bonded because you are true mates.

Since I was old enough to understand, I knew I wasn't destined to have a mate or any kind of romantic relationship. A part of me resented that because of my ancestor's mistakes, I'd never know what it was like to love or be loved in return. But whether it's due to fate or the evil machinations of a power-hungry rival, I've been given a chance at something real with Bryn.

I'm not ready to kill it before I even have the chance to sit with the knowledge.

Keying my way into the security wing again, I start locking away all my emotions for what I learned about Bryn in preparation for what I'm going to do. The door slams shut behind me and echoes in the corridor. Three steps in, a shooting pain pierces through the center of my chest.

My steps falter, and I have to brace a hand on the wall to keep myself upright. I take a second to catch my breath as the sensation of an iron skewer presses in behind my sternum.

As painful as that is, the reason for it hurts a thousand times worse.

Bryn is gone.

I know it as surely as I know my own name.

And since I can't detect even a hint of her fear through our bond, it means she left Nightfall of her own volition and is getting farther away by the second. And I left my coat with the vial of her blood in the room with her. It probably wouldn't last much longer anyway.

Fuck...now what?

An hour ago, I might have ordered her to be tracked down and brought back. Then, when I got back to the manor, I could punish her in ways that would send her soaring so high, she'd never want to leave my bed, much less my city.

But after learning how much was taken from her when she was only hours old, that's not something I'm willing to do. If letting her go means my end, so be it. Seamus will be here to help my brothers take over.

I can't bring myself to rip her world away from her again.

It doesn't matter that *this* is her rightful world; it's not the one she grew up knowing. From the moment she stepped foot in Vegas, she's been a pawn in the revival of a centuries-old war, and her only crime is that her parents were never supposed to fall in love.

Neither were we...

Fishing the necklace out from beneath my shirt, I give it a quick tug, then drop the broken chain to the floor. With shaking hands, I slide the wedding band onto my finger for the first time since removing it.

Miraculously, my heart has finally emerged from the cold shadows to bask in the warmth of my feelings for Bryn. I hope it makes the best of it with the time it has left. Because regardless of any curse, I refuse to sacrifice Bryn's safety and well-being for my own.

Rolling toward the wall, I rest my forehead on the cool surface and squeeze my eyes shut. The effect from the curse is progressing faster this time. If I want to be the one to get the answers from the dead-man-walking down the hall, I need to put my best game face on and get going before I'm too weak to do shit.

I take a deep breath and draw on the last reserve of my strength to make it down the hall and enter the right holding room. The archer looks a little worse for wear...

But he's about to look a lot fucking worse.

He's tied to a chair with duct tape over his mouth that I'll rip off when I'm ready to hear him beg for mercy. Connor and

Conall are standing behind him on the back wall, their golden eyes glinting with eager violence that match mine. The table to my left has a variety of shining tools laid out on a black towel.

"Do you know the real reason I'm called the Dark King?"

His answer is to glare at me with seething hatred. My mouth twists into a devilish grin as I unbutton my cuffs and start rolling my sleeves up.

"That's okay. You're about to learn firsthand."

• • •

It only took a half hour to break the archer.

Granted, I was on a tight schedule—before the effects of Bryn being gone caught up to me—so I didn't bother easing into anything. My methods even raised the occasional eyebrow from my best friends, but they kept their opinions to themselves and let me do what I do.

The important thing is that we got all the information we needed.

Talek honored his vow to never stop searching for the hybrid child he knew existed.

The archer didn't know how he found her, only that he'd done so several years ago.

In fact, Talek was the one who orchestrated her adoptive parents' accident, knowing that anyone isolated is more vulnerable than if they have a support system. Then he got her fired and sent her the bogus promo offer for the free trip.

After that, it was a simple matter of threatening an assistant manager—who has since disappeared and likely suffered the same tragic fate as the High Priestess—to move us around like pieces on a chessboard.

All three Woulfes are with me in one of the other holding rooms as we discuss everything we've learned tonight. A lot of what the archer said didn't make sense to Connor and Conall until I filled them and Seamus in on what Erin told me.

Every once in a while, one of them will get a look of awe on their face as they shake their head and mutter "hybrid" in disbelief.

Fortunately, they're so focused on that our seemingly human Bryn is actually a fae anomaly with repressed magic of unknown power to notice that I'm in excruciating pain. I just need to hold it together long enough to give her time to get on a plane. There won't be any reason to bring her back once the curse claims me.

My body is covered in a cold sweat, and there's no way I could push to a stand right now.

Breathing feels like I'm inviting shards of glass to shred my lungs with every inhale, and my throat is drier than the desert under the midday sun. I start coughing and can't stop. That's when whatever acting skills I possess go to hell and the others finally realize I probably look like death warmed over.

Connor stops me from falling off my chair when I list to the side. "Dude, what the hell is wrong with you?"

"Don't know what you're talking about," I grate out between clenched teeth. "Never been better."

Seamus curses at the same time that Conall checks his phone. "Bryn is on Paradise Road and moving south. She's on her way to the airport."

"Goddamn you, boy, what have you done?" Seamus has never sounded more like my father. Anger and disappointment lace his rhetorical question that's more accusation than anything.

Unable to hold my eyes open anymore, I let them close and concentrate on not falling over or passing out. "Won't put her in danger anymore. If I'm gone…she's safe."

I sense Seamus leaning in for emphasis. "The unacceptable part of that plan is that *you* will be *gone*. You are the *king*,

Caiden. You cannot afford to be noble if it puts you at risk!"

Prying my eyelids open enough to meet my uncle's gaze, I say, "It's okay… One will step up and…you'll help him."

Connor shoves to his feet with an animalistic roar and punches the wall. It buckles beneath the force of his fist, bits of plaster exploding from the indentation and dust pluming.

Seamus gives his son a withering look that stops him from causing any more damage. Then he turns back to me with an apologetic frown. "I'm sorry, my boy, but I wouldn't be doing my job if I let this happen."

Those were the last words I heard before passing out.

CHAPTER TWENTY-SEVEN

BRYN

There's a persistent ache causing me to absently rub the site it's emanating from, but it isn't my shoulder. That feels miraculously fine. No, the pain is more centrally located, beneath my sternum where my heart still beats despite the hairline fracture created when I walked out of Nightfall and slid into a cab.

I made a pit stop to buy more travel-friendly attire, then came straight to the airport. The faster I'm on a plane back home, the better I'll feel, I'm sure of it. I probably have Stockholm syndrome or something, that's all. Once I'm back in my own place and surrounded by my own things, I'll find comfort in the simple familiarity of it all.

I'm standing in line at the ticket counter, and after ten minutes, I'm still five winding rows back. I didn't expect the airport to be this busy late on a Saturday night. Then again, for a city that thrives at night and sleeps during the day, I suppose it makes sense.

"Hello, Bryn."

Spinning around, I gape at the giant sporting a man bun and a glare that could kill and probably has. "Connor? How did you…"

"Come with me." His massive paw locks around my forearm, and he's dragged me all the way back through the line before I regain my wits and shake loose.

"No, Connor, stop. I'm going home, damn it."

If it wouldn't cause a scene, and likely his arrest, I think he'd throw me over his shoulder and haul me out kicking and screaming. Instead, he growls in frustration and scans the area quickly until he finds whatever he's looking for. "I need to talk to you somewhere we can't be overheard. Follow me."

Since he isn't manhandling me this time, and up until an hour ago, I considered this wolfish male a friend, I follow him over to an alcove for an Employees Only door.

"Look, Connor," I start, trying to get my point across before he has the chance to rip it away with whatever he wants to say. "If you think about it, me going home really is what's best for everyone. Caiden doesn't want me around anymore, and by staying here with a target on my back, I'm only putting his life at risk. Not to mention mine. Which, I have to say, surviving two assassination attempts in as many weeks is not something I was hoping to put on my résumé."

"Bryn, if you don't come back with me right now, Caiden will die."

"No, if *I* die, Caiden will die. He told me so himself, and as you know, he can't lie."

"Neither can I, and I'm telling you he's dying."

My blood freezes in my veins. "What do you mean, he's dying? Didn't you catch the archer? Did someone else attack him?"

"No one attacked him. He's dying because you're more than a hundred yards from him."

"Well, now I know you're lying because he was a lot farther than that from me when he left my ass back at the manor to go to his party."

I turn to walk away, but Connor grabs me by the arm. "He had a vial of your blood on him that tricked the curse for a few hours, but that's it. So if I don't get you back to the manor, and fucking fast, I don't know how much longer he has."

Pushing the question aside about how or when he would've gotten a vial of my blood, I focus on the direr topic. I hug my arms around my middle and shake my head. "No. This has to be one of those fae truths somehow. You're speaking metaphorically or something."

He curses and takes out his phone. It rings once before I hear Conall's barked, "You find her?"

"Yeah. Show me Caiden."

Connor faces his screen to me, and I get a brief view of his brother's face before he angles his phone to show me Caiden slumped in the back seat of the Range Rover. My hands fly to my mouth on a sharp gasp. He's so pale, his veins look like a neon-blue road map beneath his clammy skin. There are bruises under his eyes and his breaths are visibly shallow.

But the most frightening thing I notice is a web of thin black lines snaking up from where his shirt collar has been opened up his neck and threading their way through the scruff on his jaw.

"Caiden?" My voice breaks on his name along with my heart.

His eyes crack open enough to notice the phone being held in front of his face. His expression morphs from one of pain to anger as his gaze focuses past the phone, presumably on his friend holding it. "Told you…don't want…" He has to pause to get through a coughing fit that makes me clutch at my own throat as if it'll help him take a full breath. "…her here."

My stomach twists. He can't tell a lie.

Conall's voice comes through. "Too fucking bad, bro."

Caiden calls on whatever reserve of strength he has left and swipes out at the phone, knocking it out of Conall's hand hard enough to lose the call.

I look up at Connor, worry gripping me in a deathly clutch. "The line went dead."

He pockets his own cell. "That's what Caiden will be if you don't get back to the manor."

Nodding, I say, "Yes, take me back. Please."

Connor leads me to where he double-parked the Maserati, and my door is barely closed before he takes off and expertly winds through the slow airport traffic. Once we're on the highway, he opens it up and still it doesn't feel fast enough.

Now that I have nothing to do but sit and wait until we arrive, Caiden's words echo back in my mind. *Told you…don't want…her here.*

I stem the hot tears stinging the backs of my eyes. I thought my heart hurt before, but that was a pinprick compared to the evisceration I'm feeling now. Whether it's a sense of betrayal because I left or one of inevitability because chances of us ever breaking the bond are almost nonexistent, Caiden doesn't want me to come back.

Not even when the result would be fatal.

There are bad breakups, and then there's your mate deciding he'd rather die than take you back.

Fucking ouch.

When Connor turns into the driveway and follows it around to pull up in front of the door, I try to hop out, but my door is locked and I can't find the damn button fast enough. By the time I do, Connor is already at my door and closes it behind me. We enter the house and dash up the stairs. I start to go right toward Caiden's room, but he turns left.

"This way," he says. I make the correction and realize he's headed to my room. My heart, fractured as it is, does a little leap in my chest. Caiden's in my room; maybe he changed his mind or wanted to be near my things and my scent.

Connor opens the door for me, and I barge in. "Caiden,

I'm here." I stop cold in my tracks, because I might be here, but Caiden is not. "Where is he?"

"In his room, where he'll be recovering now that you're back." I step toward the hallway, but he blocks my path. "You, however, will be staying in here."

"What are you talking about? Connor, let me out—I need to see him."

He narrows golden eyes at me. "You don't, actually. As head of security for the Night Court king, I'm revoking your house privileges. Get comfortable, Bryn, because this room is your new cell." Stepping back, he pulls the door shut, and I hear the dead bolt slide into place.

"Noooooo!" I lunge at the door and pound my fists on it. "Connor! Don't do this. You have to let me see him. I can help him!"

His reply is muffled through the barrier, but the raw animosity in his voice comes through clear as a bell. "You've done enough."

The sound of his boots echoing down the hall is the breeze that finally topples my composure like a house of cards. A guttural sob rips from my chest as I collapse onto the bed and allow myself to openly weep for the first time since being locked in this room five long weeks ago.

CHAPTER TWENTY-EIGHT

CAIDEN

Sitting behind the desk of my home office, I stare into the flames dancing in the fireplace and polish off my glass of Devil's Keep. I've lost count of what number I'm on, but if I have any more, I'll be closing in on blackout drunk.

If it will numb me from feeling anything, I'll welcome it this time.

Once Connor brought Bryn back to the manor, I healed faster than the first time. But I also declined at a more rapid pace, leading me to believe that the stronger the bond gets, the stronger the reaction to the curse.

As soon as I was recovered, I called a meeting with my brothers and the three Woulfes. I chose not to hold their actions against them. Not only are they duty-bound to ensure my safety and my rule, they're my family and they'd happily sacrifice themselves for me.

I knew they wouldn't go along with my decision, which is why I tried to deceive them. I failed, and they acted accordingly.

What's done is done, and now I need to figure out where we go from here.

We filled my brothers in on everything that happened,

leaving out the part about my plan to let the curse run its course—they spared me that backlash, at least. Then we discussed options on how to handle Talek at the Meeting of the Kings.

Bryn and I won't be leaving the property before then, preventing the opportunity for another attack. I ordered Connor and Conall to take the archer's body out into the desert and make it look like they simply ripped him to shreds in their wolf forms instead of capturing and torturing him for information.

If it works, Talek will think we're still clueless about who's behind the attacks. Then we'll have the element of surprise at the meeting.

I glance at the clock on the wall. Nearly five o'clock in the morning.

That means I've been sitting here feeling sorry for myself for almost an hour. I don't know how my life got so fucking tangled.

A month and a half ago, my days were structured and blessedly predictable. During the day I went to work at Nightfall as king of this city, and at night I carried out my legacy as the Dark King.

I had the world by the balls, and no one dared threaten my rule of either empire.

Then Bryn showed up at my hotel, and it was all shot to hell in a single evening. Married, mated, and bonded, that's how I awoke the following morning. Not to mention cursed.

Since then, it's been nothing but near-death experiences and the most transcendent sex of my fucking life. There's nothing structured or predictable about my days now. And I've never been more content or felt so...*right*.

But that was before I went and fucked everything up beyond repair.

Right when I began thinking that regardless of how I got it,

I finally had something that was real and could enjoy it without guilt because I didn't intentionally choose a female over my responsibilities as king, I discovered the necklace among Bryn's things. Without any further investigation, I assumed the spell had been long-lasting and wholly responsible for any feelings Bryn and I shared for each other. And it shattered a part of me I didn't know could break.

Pulling away from her wasn't easy—if given the choice, I'd rather live in the fantasy world and pretend what we have is real than go back to my bleak existence before she came along—but it was necessary.

It still is.

I understand now why my father insisted on keeping my mother at a distance. Affection leads to passion, which leads to love. And when fae love, nothing is more sacred than becoming bonded as mates; anything less would feel unacceptable and lacking. So as king, allowing yourself to love another means putting yourself above the security of your people.

Where my heart and Bryn's best interests are concerned, choosing death over keeping her hostage for the rest of her days was the right thing to do.

But it wasn't in the best interest of my people, and I was wrong for that.

It doesn't matter that I have two brothers who could take my place as ruler. Neither has been groomed for the position as I have, and there's never been a case in any of the courts of Faerie where the eldest of a royal line doesn't remain king until his dying breath.

To upset millennia of tradition would put a stain on my family's legacy. I can't do that.

Not even for Bryn.

I still can't believe she's a fae hybrid. I should tell her about who—and what—she is; she has a right to know. But what good would it really do for her if Erin figures out how to break the bond or reverse the curse sometime soon?

Erin said that Bryn is blocking herself from embracing her true nature. Without the bond's influence or memories of her time here, she'll most likely repress her fae qualities again and continue on as a human back in Wisconsin, where she has a good life with cherished memories of her adoptive parents.

If I tell her the truth, I'll have disrupted her entire world a second time. Twenty-six years ago, Erin hid Bryn in the human world so she'd have a chance at a safe and happy life. Talek took that away from her by using her to get to me; now I have to do the right thing—for her and my people—and let her go as soon as I'm able.

Bryn...

The image of her in that gown, glowing with ethereal beauty, is branded into my memories. As is the image of that arrow piercing her shoulder and her screaming out in pain.

A violent storm of emotions churns inside me, and I have to force myself to set the empty glass on my desk before I give in to the desire to hurl it across the room for the satisfaction of seeing something other than myself shattered beyond repair.

She's in her room right now. She'll be sleeping at this hour. So close, so accessible.

And so fucking off-limits.

But I could check on her. Just to make sure she's all right, to see that she's safe with my own eyes. There'd be no harm in that.

Before I can think better of it, I find myself in front of her door. I silently turn the dead bolt and enter her room, closing it behind me. I don't make a sound as I approach the bed. She's curled in on herself and hugging a pillow to her chest like it's her only lifeline. The areas under her eyes are puffy and her cherry red lips are swollen as though she cried so long that even sleep isn't helping.

She's no less beautiful, though. Quite the opposite, for

even steeped in tragedy, my Bryn shines brighter than every female in my past put together.

Suddenly she wakes, as though pulled from her dreams almost violently. Her gaze automatically seeks me out as she pushes herself up to a sitting position. "Caiden," she whispers. "Oh, thank God."

She flings herself at me, her arms wrapping so tightly around my neck that I realize the pillow was a substitute for me. Instinctively, I hold her to me and bury my face in her wild hair, drawing her sweet scent deep into my lungs and letting it permeate every cell in my body.

"I sensed you were here. God, I was so worried, and Connor wouldn't let me see you."

Hello, crushing reality, so nice of you to join me.

Extracting myself from Bryn's arms, I step away from the bed and fix an emotionless expression on my face. "I was on my way to bed and wanted to make sure you were healed and settled in. Good night, Bryn."

I start to turn, but she clamors off the bed and stops me with a hand on my arm. "I get that you're upset with me for leaving, but how was I supposed to know that you would wither away and die? You never told me about that part of the curse, Caiden."

My top lip twists into a sneer. "Would it have really made any difference? I let my guard down. Literally. You saw your opportunity, and you took it."

Her mouth drops open in shock, but as always, she recovers quickly and matches me, ire for ire. "You haven't been straight with me since this whole thing began. You cherry-pick what information to give me and what I'm allowed to be a part of, instead of giving me the benefit of the doubt and dealing me in. We *should* be on the same team, but the great and powerful Dark King doesn't *do* teams, does he? No, he'd rather be a fucking island unto himself, regardless of the cost."

Her eyes land on the ring still on my finger. Without comment, I slide my hands into my pockets.

She scoffs, her disgust plain. "It's no wonder you like BDSM so much. If you control everything, you can keep your distance. Can't let anyone get too close, right? God forbid they actually start to care for you. Oh, and by the way, the next time you want a vial of my blood so you can escape my presence, you'd damn well better ask for it first."

"Noted." I fix her with a droll look. "You finished?"

"With you? Abso-fucking-lutely. This cell is only built for one." She crosses her arms over her chest, then jerks her chin at the door. "Get out."

"Gladly."

I fight my instinct to take her in my arms again and kiss her until she's forgiven me for all my transgressions, past and future, and leave her room as she demands.

When I flip the lock from the outside, I wait for her rage to boil over, for her to throw something at the door and curse my name. But it never comes, and it's then I realize that I can't feel her energy anymore, either.

Whether intentionally or subconsciously, Bryn has cut me off.

And that's the very least of what I deserve.

CHAPTER TWENTY-NINE

BRYN

"Why are we hiding behind this rock formation instead of going with everyone else to the Meeting of the Kings?" Glaring at Finnian, I don't bother hiding my irritation, just as he doesn't bother hiding his annoyance at my incessant questions.

Since returning to the manor with Connor, I've been kept locked up like a treasonous prisoner, only allowed out of my room for a couple of hours each day to stretch my legs or go for a swim. Always accompanied by a Night Watcher with Caiden nowhere to be found. They treat me more like an outsider now than when I arrived six weeks ago, so *irritation* is just the tip of my current emotional iceberg.

Today is September 22, and at exactly 8:03 p.m., it will be the fall equinox, which is when Caiden will meet with the Day Court king to discuss any business and re-sign the Treaty of Two Courts, reinforcing peace between the Light and Dark Fae.

Not that I'll get to witness any of it.

After I refused Caiden's—*extremely ballsy*—request for more of my blood, he was forced to bring me along to Joshua

Tree, but he has me stationed with Finnian and Madoc at the farthest location our bond will allow, once again shutting me out of fae business. I thought we'd gotten past all that, especially with the fae qualities I've taken on because of our bond.

But that's what I get for thinking it, because none of my questions have been answered.

The only things I know are the direction in which it's happening, because I watched Caiden walk off with the Woulfe brothers and a small cadre of Watchers, and that the next in line to the throne and the senior adviser—Tiernan and Seamus—stay behind in the event of foul play.

Which I can only assume to be a pre-exile tradition, since the blood curse would void the need for a contingency plan.

Finn glances over at Madoc, who's pretending not to listen from several yards away, then answers me in a low voice. "I already told you why."

"No, you said that Caiden told us to stay here," I argue, crossing my arms in defiance. "That's repeating a directive, not explaining the reason for which it was given."

With the small amount of light provided by the lantern on the ground between us, I can see the hard set of his scruffy jaw as his annoyance grows. "The Night King gave us an order, therefore we obey it. The reason behind said order is inconsequential."

I scoff. "Maybe to you, but I'm not much for not-questioning obedience. Especially from *him*."

Finn arches a dark brow. "You sure about that?"

My cheeks flood with heat at the possibility of Finn knowing intimate details of what I've done with Caiden. Although I know he's not the type to kink-and-tell, I'm sure his brothers are highly aware of his sexual proclivities. They might even share them.

Either way, it wouldn't be a huge leap for Finn to assume

I'm submissive to Caiden behind closed doors. And while I'm certainly not embarrassed about it, I'm in a pissy enough mood to retaliate just a little.

"I'm sure that you make a really nice puppet, *Finni*."

Madoc coughs into his fist to try to cover up his chuckle, earning me a death glare from Finn. He only tolerates the childhood nickname from two people, and I'm not either of them.

Stepping in close, Finn towers over me and leans down to get in my face. The unmistakable glint of dominance flashes in his golden eyes and his lips peel back to bare his deadly fangs. "That's enough sass out of you, Bryn. Either you sit your ass down and stop asking questions, or I'll bind and gag you myself."

Whoa. Guess there's an alpha in Baby Verran after all.

"Fine," I mutter.

Releasing a frustrated huff, I plop onto a craggy boulder still warm from the desert sun and waft the front of my shirt a few times. If I'm hot in a thin tee, jean shorts, and running shoes, I can't imagine how the rest of our party must feel. Caiden, Finnian, and all the Watchers came decked out in traditional Dark Fae warrior garb, made entirely of thick black leather.

Though it must suck to wear in these temps, I'm certainly not complaining from a viewer's standpoint. Sleeveless, fitted tunics with a mock collar that's open at the neck and crisscrossed with laces and lace-up leather pants to match. When I questioned the traditional accuracy of their footwear, Madoc told me that switching out the less-practical, flat-soled knee-high boots for the more rugged motorcycle boots was one of two changes they made once they were exiled to "the Devil's asshole," as he put it. The other change was getting rid of the long-sleeve shirts they used to wear under the tunics.

Personally, I approve of that last one. It puts all those

glorious shoulder and arm muscles on display. If I wasn't so pissed at Caiden, my tongue would've rolled out of my head when I saw him earlier. If I'd known he owned something as hot as his warrior outfit, I would've begged him to wear it for a session in the dungeon. He could've slipped floggers into the hip belt and— *Stop lusting after the sexy jerk, Bryn!*

My tendency to still lust after the male causing the cacophony of turbulent emotions surrounding me the past five days is infuriating. In the course of a day, I run the whole gamut of rage, sadness, frustration, denial, aggravation, and everything in between. Now, as I sit here on this boulder in the middle of Bumfuck, Nowhere, in the company of two surly and noncommunicative guards, I can't decide which of those feelings to settle on.

The sun set a couple of hours ago, and the moon is the barest sliver in the dark sky. The only light we have are a couple of low-level white LED lanterns that look like flashlights if the plastic casings lit up instead of just the ends. In the distance, the howling cry of a coyote echoes.

"If we're going to be here a while, can we at least build a fire or something? It's creepy out here."

"No fire. It's our job to keep you safe, and we will," Finn says stonily. "Unless you keep talking. Then I'll have Madoc use his coyote telepathy to tell them we brought dinner."

My wide eyes snap over to Madoc, who lets a hint of a smirk twist his lips. "I'm not a shifter, Bryn. He's fucking with you."

I look back, expecting to see Finnian chuckling or at least smiling like I've seen him do with so many others, but his expression is as serious and uninviting as it always is with me.

He wants me gone so badly, he probably *wishes* he could feed me to the coyotes.

I would've earned major brownie points in his eyes when I tried to fly home. You know, if it hadn't been for that whole almost-killing-his-brother part of the equation. I need to find a way to break through his hard candy shell and get to the melty chocolate underneath. Maybe Fiona will have some ideas.

"Careful, Finn, you're dangerously close to making a joke. And you know who people joke around with? That's right," I say as if he'd answered me. "Their friends. And once we're friends, there's no going back to Mr. Not Nice Guy."

"Noted."

Noted. Ugh, he sounds just like his brother. With a single word, they effectively end any conversation like they're cutting it off at the knees.

I pretend not to be irritated, and both males return to their earlier stoicism, focusing on our surroundings. Madoc stands with his arms crossed while Finn loosely grips the sword hilts at his hips. Yes, *swords.* Apparently traditional garb includes carrying various types of ye olde weapons on your person—long swords, short swords, daggers, and other sharp and pointy things.

I noticed some Watchers prefer to stick with the same kind and some like to mix and match. Some use scabbards belted around their hips like Finn and some use the kind that form an X on their backs like Madoc.

And all of this for a supposedly *peaceful*, routine meeting.

Part of me says it's no different than the Marines carrying swords with their dress blues—a symbolic display of their roots and traditions. But the other part of me says that if that were the case, they wouldn't each be armed to the fangs.

Giving in to my insatiable curiosity, I decide to risk being turned into a coyote kebab. "I have a question..."

Finnian growls my name in warning. "Bryn..."

"I know, I know, no talking. But why—" I gasp as two figures materialize out of thin air behind Madoc. Dressed in white versions of the leather gear, their pointed ears, fangs,

and bright green eyes give them away as fae warriors of the
Day Court.

My shocked reaction is enough to put my bodyguards on
alert, but I don't find my voice in time to warn Madoc before
a blade callously slices through the front of his neck. Golden
eyes widen as his body drops to the ground. Arterial blood
sprays in an arc, painting my clothes and skin in specks of a
life ended, a soul dimmed.

My vocal chords finally open and a scream escapes.

Spinning to place himself in front of me, Finnian draws
his swords and sinks into a battle stance, his muscles bunching
and vibrating with adrenaline.

Madoc's murderer raises his fist in the air. "Death to the
queen brings death to the king!"

The strange battle cry is like a starting gun going off, and
all three lunge at one another with weapons raised. Opposing
swords clang and spark, crashing against one another as Finn
works to fight off both assailants, while I remain frozen in
place like a macabre tableau of shock and horror.

I should be helping him. I need to help him!

Why didn't I ask to learn how to fight?

My brain doesn't care that there was no reason for me
to believe I'd be in this situation. It only wants to admonish
my lack of foresight. The more Madoc's blood spills from
his body to seep into the desert floor, the more my guilt
consumes me.

Finn kicks the stockier fae in the chest so hard, it sends
him flying backward until he hits the trunk of one of those
Dr. Seuss–looking trees, then uses the reprieve to focus his
strikes on the other guy. "Bryn, get out of here and hide."

That snaps me out of my shock. "What? No, I'm not
leaving you!"

Slamming his fist into Fae Number Two's face hard enough
to knock him on his ass, Finn spares a glance back at me. I

cringe to see the tip of his ear cut and bleeding and one of his cheeks split open with a huge gash.

"They don't want me, Bryn; they're after *you*," he says through labored breaths. "That's why we're out here. Talek is trying to use you to take Caiden out."

Oh, Jesus. My mind reels as all the pieces fall into place. Or maybe they were always there, trying to give me the whole picture, but I kept looking at it upside down, not wanting to see what was right in front of me. That I've been a pawn in a much larger game. One where the objective is to take out the Dark King, the king I fell *in love* with.

The night I married him, I transformed from a mere pawn into a queen, making me the key to his downfall. To his *death*.

All Talek has to do is kill me or keep me away from Caiden far enough and long enough, and it's checkmate. Game over.

"Bryn!" Finnian's shout brings me back to the present.

The guy he knocked down is already shaking it off and getting to his feet, and the other one is racing toward us again. Finn grabs me by the shoulders and pulls me off to the side. "You need to hide. When I'm done here, I'll come find you."

"How will you know where— *Fuck!*" I look down at where my upper arm is now bleeding slightly from his dagger, which he places firmly in my hand.

"You're bonded to my brother," he says. "I'll recognize the scent of your blood. Now go!"

He barely has time to turn around and stop the swinging arc of a sword that was aimed at his neck. Everything in me balks at leaving him like this, but Finnian is a trained warrior and can take care of himself. The best thing I can do is get somewhere safe so I can't be used against Caiden.

With that, I take off running in the direction of the meeting so I don't accidentally get out of range and inadvertently weaken Caiden. Adrenaline and fear pump through my veins and fuel my muscles as I dodge the large tufts of desert grass and try not to twist my ankles on the uneven terrain.

My lungs feel like they're on fire, and I start to give up on ever finding anything more than a few trees huddled together when I finally see another outcropping of rocks in the distance. It could be a mirage, but it's enough to give me hope and a shot of extra energy to keep me going.

But the closer I get, the more it sounds like what I just left times a thousand. Grunts and shouts and the clanging of metal on metal...

Then I reach the crest of a small hill and peer down into a valley of utter chaos.

The rock formation I was running toward is massive, at least a hundred feet high and just as wide with a vertical crevice from top to bottom wide enough for three people to enter side by side. In front of that, though, is a battle.

Day versus Night, Light versus Dark.

I scan the area, searching for somewhere else I can run to, but there's nothing near that I wouldn't collapse trying to get to. Feeling a thrum in my veins, I turn back to see Caiden on the other side of the long passageway through the rock face. It looks like there's a clearing in the middle. That must be where he's meeting with the Day Court king.

Caiden's back is to the opening. It doesn't seem like he's even aware of the fighting happening. What are they talking about in there? Is Caiden confronting Talek about using me as an unwitting accomplice in his plans for regicide?

Anger burns through me like the flame on a trail of gun-powder, gaining in strength and speed. My hand grips the hilt of the dagger so hard, it feels like a part of me, and I want nothing more in this moment than to watch its blade sink into Caiden's enemy and free him from the danger my existence now poses.

The Dark King might not be able to kill the Light King...

but *I can*.

I'm running down the hill before I'm even aware of my decision, but I don't stop. My actions are driven by the single-minded focus of getting to that meeting and plunging the dagger into the fae asshole who set all of this into motion six weeks ago.

I zig and zag my way through the melee, the warriors from both sides too busy attacking and defending to notice me darting around them. Finally, I reach the mouth of the passage. As soon as I'm inside, the world becomes silent. I grind to a halt and spin around to make sure I didn't enter some kind of time portal.

"Wow," I mumble in awe as I stare at the battle still happening like it's a silent film. I look up at the expanse of the opening but don't see anything. The cavern must be spelled to keep the kings' meeting private, in turn keeping them from knowing if a battle royale breaks out in the valley.

Hearing the deep timbre of Caiden's voice sparks me back into motion, running through the darkened passage to get to him and my target. Anger turns into rage and rage turns into fury so that by the time I reach the end and see who I can only assume to be Talek walking casually in the opposite direction, giving me his back as though it were gift wrapped.

Releasing a battle cry of my own, I raise my arm and fly past Caiden, eager to put an end to this nightmare.

"Bryn, *no*!"

Just before I reach Talek, Caiden tackles me, turning in midair to take the brunt of the impact as we hit the ground. "What are you doing? I almost had him," I shout, scrambling to my feet.

"You're my mate, Bryn. To the blood curse, you killing him is the same as if I did it myself. Our bond makes us virtually indistinguishable."

I gape at him. "You've got to be fucking kidding me."

Talek chuckles, his patronizing amusement so palpable, I practically choke on it. "It's a tricky curse Aine placed on us, to be sure, but I have to admit I love the challenge of it all. Your bond must be why you were able to get through the protective barrier. It was a spell put in place by a conjurer at the time of the original signing of the Treaty of Two Courts," he states conversationally, as though we're in an academic discussion about fae history. "Only those with royal blood may pass through. But seeing as you're the first royal mate since our mutual exile, the exact rules where you're concerned are as of yet unknown. Thank you for continuing to be so accommodating, Miss Meara. I couldn't have planned this better if I'd tried."

The sound of metal scraping echoes in the cavern as Talek draws his sword, followed immediately by Caiden doing the same thing as he places his much larger frame in front of mine. "Bryn, go back through the passage to Connor and Conall."

"About that," I say, scanning my surroundings in a desperate attempt to find some way of getting us out of this alive. "Talek's forces must have been ordered to attack, because I had to get through the Second Fae War just to get here."

Caiden snaps his head to the side to see for himself—an involuntary reaction due to the shock and outrage I can read coming off him in pulsing waves—giving Talek the advantage.

"Caiden!" I push him out of the way of the sword arcing down, realizing too late that of course he isn't aiming for Caiden. He's aiming for me.

My legs are swept out from under me by Caiden's foot at the last second, causing me to crash to the ground and the sword tip to miss me by mere inches.

Faster than I can blink, Caiden lunges at Talek and there's a brief scuffle on the ground before they both roll to standing positions and start circling each other with swords at the ready.

Talek rakes a gloved hand through his long blond hair to get it out of his green eyes that shine like twin emeralds. If I'd met him on the street, I would've pegged him for a Hollywood actor or model. He's gorgeous in the way all fae are, but there's a cruelty lurking behind his classically handsome features that makes him absolutely hideous.

"I can't tell you how satisfying it is to finally be in this moment after twenty-six years," he says with a sickening grin, displaying fangs longer than I've seen on fae before. The sight makes me shudder. "It took me twenty-one just to find her, then two years of careful planning before I killed her adoptive parents, just like I killed her real ones the night of her birth."

"Shut the fuck up, Edevane," Caiden growls. "You've done enough damage. Leave her out of this. None of it has anything to do with her!"

Talek laughs, malice pouring from between his lips. "You fucking imbecile, it has *everything* to do with her. I knew before she was even born that she would be the key to my gaining control over both our courts. And once I have your crown, Verran, I'm going after the others in Faerie. And finally, I'll invade the One True Queen's court and rip everything away from Aine, just as she did to us. Only I won't banish her. I'm going to keep her chained and tortured and revel in her begging me for mercy until the end of days."

Talek strikes with the quickness of a snake, but Caiden deflects it with lightning-fast reflexes. Head reeling and nerves shot, I jump at the sound of their swords glancing off each other. Then I gather my wits enough to speak.

"You killed my parents?" I ask incredulously. My voice rises as my panic increases. "Are you telling me that I'm adopted, and you not only caused the crash that killed my mom and dad who raised me, but you also killed my biological parents?"

At another circling standstill, Talek shrugs like he's admitting to eating the last of the Oreos in the pantry. "I'd say it wasn't personal, but considering your father was my cousin, that would be a lie. And as I'm sure you know by now, that's not a talent we fae possess."

My stomach lurches, and I turn just in time to throw up behind a nearby boulder as my skin breaks out in a sweat.

"You fucking bastard. I don't care what the consequences are, I'm going to kill you for hurting her like that."

Caiden lets out the most animalistic growl I've ever heard right before the sound of swords clashing start back up with a vengeance.

His vow penetrates the thick fog of pain and sucks it all into a box to sort through later. After I make sure my husband and mate doesn't kill himself with a pointless vendetta. Nothing he does can change the past or bring back any of my parents. All he'll succeed in doing is breaking my heart and ripping out my soul if he ends up dead.

Think, Bryn, think!

Looking around, I find a rock the size of a large melon. Small enough for me to pick up with two hands, big enough to knock an evil king unconscious. If we can apprehend him and lock him away for the rest of his life, maybe his plans for Faerie world domination will end with him and our problems will be solved.

It's a start, anyway.

Picking it up causes the cut on my left arm to twinge, but I quickly forget about it as I cradle the rock against my stomach. I need to maneuver into a position where I can wield it effectively. I'll only get one chance. If I miss, I lose the element of surprise, and Caiden could lose his life.

I do my best not to flinch every time their swords clash,

but it's not easy when the most violent thing I've witnessed in my life is road rage during rush hour on the beltline. Each of them is getting his shot in, taking turns hitting the marks and opening up fresh wounds.

I can feel Caiden getting weaker the more blood he loses, almost as though I'm weakening in the process. If I wait much longer, I might not have the strength to raise the rock high enough to do any good.

At last, I see my opening as their fighting places Talek not far with his back to me. He performs a roundhouse kick to Caiden's solar plexus, knocking him backward enough that it pauses the fight. Hoisting the rock as high as I can, I'm about to drop it on his head when he surprises me by spinning on his heel to face me, a wicked glint in his eyes like he'd known my plan all along and I fell into his trap.

Time slows down to a crawl as I realize he's holding an ancient-looking dagger as he thrusts his arm forward, putting the blade on a straight path to my heart. There's no time for me to move. I've failed, and now Caiden and I will both die because of it.

I have the briefest moment to be thankful that at least I won't be left behind before accepting our fate with tears streaming down my face.

Suddenly I lose sight of Talek as my field of vision is eclipsed by the back of a black leather tunic. It jerks on a pained grunt. And that's when I realize that the blade meant for me is now plunged into the chest of the one who stepped in as my personal shield. My eyes widen in horror as his massive frame crumples to the ground.

"Oh my God, no. *Finn!*" His golden eyes stare up at me with a mix of anguish and satisfaction. Caiden shouts his name and scrambles over to us. Finn coughs, blood dripping from the corner of his mouth.

Motion in my peripheral gets my attention. Talek is

backing up toward the passageway. "Not the one I was going for, but any dead Verran is a good one. Until next time." Then he spins on his heel and darts off toward freedom.

"Fuck!" I wince at the torment on Caiden's face.

Letting the Light King go means both our lives are still in danger, but there's nothing in the world that could get Caiden to leave his baby brother's side. And I love him all the more for it. "Hold on, Finni," he says, his words thick with emotion. "I need to get this out of you."

Caiden grips the handle of the blade but yanks his hand back on a hiss. He tries again, this time gritting his teeth as he pulls, never stopping—not when smoke seeps from between his fingers and not when Finnian screams like he's being burned alive.

As soon as the blade is out, Caiden tosses it aside. Then he takes one of his own knives and cuts Finn's tunic down the middle, peeling the sides apart to reveal the wound—angry and red and bleeding like the dagger nicked an artery.

"Why isn't he healing?" I ask weakly, already knowing the answer.

Finn coughs up more blood and his breaths sound thin and reedy. Caiden's voice is barely above a rasp, his eyes full of unshed tears as he stares helplessly at his youngest sibling. "It's an iron blade. His body can't heal from it."

"It can with a healer's help." Our gazes snap up to find Fiona's mother, Erin, rushing in and joining us on the ground around Finn's prone body. "Bryn, you have the power to heal him. You just need to focus and believe in yourself."

I frown and shake my head. "I don't understand why you would think that. I have some fae qualities because of the bond, but nothing like that."

Erin's amber eyes widen with some kind of realization, then she looks to Caiden. "Your Majesty?"

Something I can't quite read flashes across his face, but

he doesn't hesitate to nod.

Erin turns back to me and gathers my hands in hers. "Listen to me carefully, child, because Prince Finnian doesn't have a lot of time. I can explain everything later, but right now I need you to hear this."

My heart begins to race and an overwhelming sensation comes over me that my life is about to irrevocably change forever.

Swallowing hard, I say, "I'm listening."

"You are the daughter of my sister, Kiera, and her mate, Uther. As Uther was Light Fae, their bond was forbidden and you, a miracle. Uther was a powerful healer, and his blood flows in your veins, as does my sister's, who comes from a long line of conjurers. *You* can heal the prince, but you have to stop believing that you're human. That's what's blocking you from your potential. The bond to King Caiden isn't giving you fae qualities, Bryn. You *are* fae, both Light and Dark, the only one of your kind. You just have to believe it."

There are no words in the English language or any other, for that matter, for what I'm feeling right now.

It would be a natural reaction to deny what she's saying. Logical, even. But something deep inside me is rejecting logic in favor of something I've never had before—*instinct*.

Instinct is telling me to believe her, to understand that the reason I've always felt as though I never belonged is because I didn't. Not before. But now I do. The sentimentality I've felt since the moment I stepped into this world is because *I belong here.*

I'm not just "other." I'm fae.

And if I'm willing to believe that part of what Erin is telling me, then there's no reason not to believe that I can heal Finnian. Remembering Madoc, my heart squeezes painfully. I've already been the cause of one death tonight. I won't survive another.

Finn—giant, sweet, loyal Finnian—stepped in front of a blade for me. Whether it was to save me or ultimately spare his brother doesn't matter.

I know that even if there was no bond and no blood curse, Finn would've sacrificed himself to save me regardless. That's just the type of male he is. He's the quintessential knight in leather armor, and I'll be damned if I'm going to stand by and watch him die if I have the power to stop it.

Meeting my aunt's gaze, I pull my shoulders back and nod. "Tell me what to do."

CHAPTER THIRTY

CAIDEN

Erin guides Bryn's hands over Finnian's chest until they hover on the garish wound left by Talek's iron dagger. If I wasn't so tortured by watching my baby brother slip away in front of my eyes, I'd be hunting Talek down to the ends of the earth and beyond.

For now, I'm thankful that his cowardice caused him to flee, signaling to the spelled barrier that the meeting is over and allowing Erin inside. I can plot my vengeance later, after Bryn saves Finn from certain death.

Please, goddess, let her save him.

"Close your eyes and search inside yourself," Erin says, her voice gentle and confident. "Find the connection with your parents, Kiera and Uther. Their power flows through your veins and exists in each of your cells. Picture the wound in your mind. See it mending, the bleeding slowing and eventually stopping. See the torn muscles and flesh stitching back together as though they were never torn."

Bryn's eyebrows pinch together, her expression one of concentration. I check the wound. Nothing is happening.

Panic rises like a fist in my throat, threatening to cut off my air. I peer up at Erin. She still appears calm, but when she speaks again, her tone is more firm and earnest.

"Bryn, you *must* shed your human mindset telling you this is impossible. It's not. Think of everything you've witnessed, everything you've experienced since learning that fae exist. We are a people of magic and power beyond that of human capabilities. *You* are a part of that. *You* can heal him. The magic and power is already inside you. Believe in yourself."

Energy begins to crackle in the air around Bryn. It builds and builds until her silky blond hair starts to lift as though an updraft is causing it to dance around her head, revealing the tops of her ears as they become pointed. When her lips part on a heady sigh, I glimpse the tips of her fangs elongating in her mouth. Her skin takes on an ethereal radiance like she's being lit from within.

I don't know what I expected it to look like when Bryn finally learned she was fae, but it certainly wasn't this.

"That's it, Bryn, *yes*," Erin says, drawing my attention to my brother's wound, which is healing like it would as a normal injury. "Keep going, almost there."

The huge gash continues to become less severe as Bryn uses her powers. Finn's breathing grows stronger, then normalizes, his chest rising and falling with ease. And as soon as the skin completely closes, I feel as though I can breathe again for the first time, too.

A puckered red scar about four inches in length mars Finn's left pectoral, most likely due to the weapon being made of iron, and has nothing to do with Bryn's abilities.

"My gods, she did it," I rasp.

Finn groans and rubs at the spot like it's sore. I help him sit up, then clasp the back of his neck and press my forehead to his. I'm so overcome with joy and gratitude, I'm in danger of bleeding out emotionally and ruining my reputation as a stoic, unfeeling asshole.

"That's enough, Bryn, you did it. You can pull away from that connection now."

The concern in Erin's voice is more than alarming, especially when I see the energy literally sparking around Bryn like it's about to catch on fire. Finn gives me a look that asks what the hell he missed, but I wave him off to say *not now*, then start to edge closer to Bryn. I drop my voice an octave, hoping it'll trigger her submission and get her to listen before she escalates any more.

"Bryn, I need you to do as Erin says and pull back from your powers. Can you do that for me, Beauty?"

As soon as I use her nickname, everything intensifies and her eyes snap open.

I hear Finn curse and Erin draw in a quiet gasp. Her soft hazel irises are now a glowing amalgamation of both her Light and Dark heritages—green in the center that mixes into the surrounding bright gold. They're beautiful and somewhat terrifying, because while she's staring right at me, it also looks like she's staring right *through* me.

In all my years, I've never been in the presence of so much power. She's like Jean Gray in her Phoenix form, and if we can't find a way to contain her, the unstable magic of a hybrid fae that Aine warned of will be the last thing any of us sees right before we turn to ash.

Erin closes her eyes and lays a hand on Bryn's shoulder as she whispers an incantation I can't hear and probably wouldn't understand even if I did.

In a matter of seconds, everything Bryn was emitting appears to be drawn back inside. She sags against Erin briefly before sitting back up and looking as though she experienced nothing more than a fainting episode.

Blinking a few times, she reaches up and presses her fingers into her temples. "Thank you," she says to Erin. "I wasn't able to pull back."

Erin nods. "It's okay, child. I suspected you wouldn't be able to. As a hybrid, your magic is unstable. I might be able to teach you how to control it, but time will tell. Until then, I've put a sort of containment spell on your powers. It's not quite the same as the one I used to block your fae qualities when you were a baby. There's no reason for that anymore. Now it's time to learn about who you are and embrace your place in our world."

"I can't tell you how much I'm looking forward to that," she says, her emotions playing in her eyes that are now a softer version of the green-and-gold combination.

Then she turns to me, and all the softness dissolves from her features. "You knew," she says accusingly. "You knew who and what I am, and you didn't tell me."

"No," I admit. "I didn't. Bryn, I'm s—"

"I can't tell you how uninterested I am in hearing anything more."

Getting to her feet, she brushes the dirt off her shorts and knees, then directs her attention to my brother, who's still sitting next to me, his tunic splayed open. Her eyes land on his scar. "I'm sorry I couldn't fix you all the way. But if it's any consolation, there's a saying in the human world: chicks dig scars."

"Thank you, Bryn," he says solemnly. "I owe you my life."

"No, you don't. We're even. Now, if you'll excuse me, I need to be…anywhere else, honestly."

Then she walks away from me with determined steps. And I hope like hell it's not a sign of something more permanent.

CHAPTER THIRTY-ONE

BRYN

"Come on, Bryn, you've only got thirty seconds left. Don't quit on me now."

Sweat pours down my face as I hold a sitting position against the wall with a giant weighted ball hugged to my chest. Glaring at Finnian, I grunt out, "I'm seriously starting to regret saving your life."

For the last week, I've been spending a lot of time with Fiona and Erin. Erin's been telling me all about my birth parents, Kiera and Uther Anwyl. They sound like they were amazing people, and their love story—how they fell in love against all the odds—is the most beautiful thing I've ever heard.

Erin's also been giving me a crash course in All Things Fae 101, and she said she'll start teaching me how to control my powers soon, which I'm equally excited and freaked out about.

But when I'm not getting to know my aunt and cousin better, I've been training with Finn.

I asked him to teach me how to fight so I can defend myself, since I know he's proficient in multiple fighting styles. He agreed on the condition I paired it with daily torture sessions (he calls it "strength training") in the manor's home gym. An agreement I now realize I made too hastily. I've always been more of a cardio girl and even that wasn't regularly.

"You say that every session." Finn lifts his gaze from the stopwatch in his hand and grins, flashing his fangs and those killer dimples hiding in his facial scruff. "It's how I know when to push you even harder." My legs start to shake from muscle fatigue, but I refuse to let them give out on me as I growl through the last few seconds. "Time. Take five for a water break."

With the last drop of my reserved strength, I push to a stand and chest-pass the medicine ball with extra oomph in retaliation. It rockets through the air like a cannonball with nearly the same force. Finn catches it easily, but if he were human, I would've put him in the hospital.

"Oops," I say with a grimace. "Didn't mean to throw it that hard."

He chuckles and tosses the ball one-handed off to the side. "Still getting used to things, huh?"

I grab my water bottle and drain half of it before coming up for air, wiping the sweat from my forehead with the back of my hand. "Uh, yeah. When you live your entire life as human and then suddenly become She-Hulk, it's an adjustment. Especially since nothing is consistent."

Until I can learn to control them, the containment spell Erin cast on me at Joshua Tree allows me access to a very limited amount of my powers, but it's not perfect. Well, I'm sure the spell is—Erin's an extremely powerful conjurer—but because my magic is unstable, I have unpredictable surges that get through it.

So far, they've been harmless and Erin says I don't have to worry, but I'm waiting for the day I accidentally blow something up.

And having powers isn't the only thing I'm adjusting to.

I keep shocking the hell out of myself every time I catch my reflection in a mirror. I still look like me...but not. Where I've always objectively known I was blessed in the physical-appearance department, save the gap in my teeth that I don't so much mind anymore, with the arrival of my fae attributes, everything has been kicked up a notch. Like Emeril Lagasse got a hold of my DNA and went, *Bam!*

My skin looks like it's been airbrushed, my hair flows around my shoulders like a Pantene commercial on a loop, my green-and-gold eyes have an ethereal brightness to them, and the pointed tips of my ears are kind of sexy in a Tolkien sort of way.

But it's my fangs that have taken the most getting used to. I nicked my tongue on multiple occasions, and my usually sweet smile now has a feral edge to it simply because my pointy canines grew twice as long.

"How much longer are you going to be staring at yourself in the mirrors, Bryn? I have things to do after this."

Snapping back into the present, I meet his gaze through the mirror and glare at the boyish smirk that lets him get away with murder, I'm sure of it. I actually love seeing it. I love that Finn no longer avoids me or feels conflicted about my presence now that the immediate threat from Talek is over, or at least on a hiatus.

He starts to bring his gallon jug of ice-cold water to his lips. Focusing all my concentration, I try the tiniest bit of magical manipulation.

Pour the whole jug of water over your head.

I watch in amazement as he bypasses his mouth and turns it upside down above his head.

He gasps as the frigid temp first hits him and his body tenses as he dutifully waits for the entire contents to glug through the opening until it's empty. I cover my mouth with my hands and try to stifle my giggle, but as soon as he turns to me and stares out from the parted sections of wet hair, I lose it.

"Oh my God, I didn't think it would work, but I'm so glad it did." My giggle turns into total uproarious laughter as he shakes himself like a wet dog, spraying water everywhere.

Finn pushes his hair back and grabs his second jug of water over by his gym bag. Dude takes his hydration seriously. "I can't wait to hear how Caiden punishes you the first time you try that with him."

"Alas, it doesn't work on him." I wrinkle my nose in disappointment. "Erin thinks the bond prevents it."

He frowns. "How do you know it doesn't work on him?"

"I may have tried to make him slap himself in the face," I deadpan. "Several times."

He rubs one huge hand over his mouth to wipe away his amusement. "I'll pay you a hundred dollars to do that to Tier. But I have to be present to witness the look on his face when he hauls off and smacks himself for no damn reason."

I laugh again and take advantage of this rare occasion where he's not barking another impossible exercise at me to sit on the floor and rest my back against the mirrored wall. "Fiona's going to want to see that, too. Hell, if I took an ad out in the Vegas paper, I bet at least half the female population in Vegas would pay me to see that spectacle."

"It'd definitely be a good side hustle," he says, tossing a bunch of towels over the puddle on the floor. Then he takes a seat on the weight bench across from me and his expression grows somber. "How much longer are you going to freeze Caiden out, Bryn?"

Dropping my gaze to my lap, I pick at the hem of my tank top. "Is indefinitely too long?"

"Come on, you don't want to do that. I know my brother can be a hardheaded asshole, and keeping information about who you are was the last straw for you that day. But he never meant to hurt you. He's just clueless, that's all."

I snort. "Your brother is the *least* clueless person I've ever met."

"I don't mean in general." Bracing his elbows on his knees, he asks, "How many romantic relationships have you had?"

My eyebrows draw together. "Several short-term ones that lasted a few months each and three long-term."

"Exactly. Caiden's had none. Zero, Bryn. So while you've had multiple experiences to learn how best to communicate with partners and things you should or shouldn't do, Caiden hasn't. He knows exactly what to do for a kink scene—how to make his partner feel comfortable and safe even while doling out pain and fear—and how to take care of her afterward as she comes out of subspace. But anything beyond that and he's so far out of his depth, he might as well be where you were with your very first boyfriend.

"Now add to that trying to navigate an unplanned marriage to a virtual stranger who has the potential to kill him, still trying to run two kingdoms, plus discover who was behind his new mate's attempted assassinations, and all of that is happening as he's feelings things for a female he's never felt before. Can you maybe see why he took a few wrong turns along the way?"

I chew on my lip as I take in his point. I never looked at it that way.

Caiden is so confident in everything he does that I never stopped to think he might be floundering when it came to me or the mysteries surrounding me since my arrival.

Hello, Perspective.

And if I'm being honest with myself, I'm already on the verge of breaking down and talking to him. I miss him so fucking much.

That doesn't mean that he didn't still hurt me. But it does mean that he probably deserves the benefit of the doubt and at least be given the chance to speak his piece before I condemn us both to a miserable existence of avoiding each other while forced to be within a hundred yards of each other for possibly the rest of our existence.

"I'll hear him out. But I can't make any promises that what he has to say to me will fix anything."

Finnian nods. "I'm good with that. Just give him a chance—that's all I'm asking."

"I will, I promise."

Pushing to his feet, he holds a hand out to me. "Let's seal the deal with some push-ups."

"I hate you."

He grins wolfishly. "I know."

CHAPTER THIRTY-TWO

CAIDEN

I've never felt at such a fucking loss on how to fix something before.

And as soon as I complete the thought, I berate myself for my own audacity at oversimplifying the situation.

You didn't break a vase, you insensitive prick. You broke her. *The woman who's more precious to you than the life-giving air you breathe.*

I drop my head between my shoulders and curl my hands into fists where they're braced against the stone wall of my shower room. More than fifty jets aimed and pelting me with hot water and my muscles refuse to give up their vise grip on my tired bones.

I don't care, though. I welcome the pain, for it's nothing less than I deserve.

Clenching my hands tighter, my nails sharpen with the turbulence of my emotions and slice into my palms. I hiss on an exhale and watch as the blood mixes with water and runs down the stones to the floor and snakes between my feet to rush toward the drain. Feeling pain on the outside to match my inside is cathartic somehow. But the wounds on my hands are superficial and will heal as soon as I relax my grip. The damage to my heart, however, has the potential to be irreparable if I can't find a way to convince Bryn to listen to me.

She's ignored me at every turn, and I can't even blame her.

I withheld vital information about who she is as a way of keeping her close. I wasn't yet ready to deal with the repercussions of her knowing the secrets that were rightfully hers to know. And in the end, it's cost me everything.

It's cost me *her*.

Any other time with any other female, I would've asserted my dominance by now. Carted her off to my bedroom or maybe even the play room, restrained her, and forced her to listen to what I have to say. But I held Bryn against her will one way or another from the moment she came to Vegas nearly two months ago—am holding her *still* because of my blood curse.

I refuse to force my will on her in any other capacity, no matter how desperate I am for her to listen to me.

I'm so lost in my own misery, I almost miss the thrum in my veins that signals my mate is near. It's like she's a tuning fork struck against my bones, creating the perfect frequency of vibrations that set my blood on fire and light up every cell in my body.

Except I don't trust that she's actually near enough for me to see her. Since she embraced her identity as a hybrid fae at Joshua Tree and transformed into her true self, our bond has strengthened to the point where she can be several rooms away and feel as though she's right next to me.

It took me days to stop turning around, expecting her to be standing there. Being so in tune to her presence while respecting her wish for me to keep my distance feels like a fresh new hell every day.

But then I hear the door to the shower room open, and the air in my lungs gets trapped in my chest as I dare to raise my head and glance over my shoulder.

Bryn...

She's really here. Standing inside the shower but just outside of the direct spray of water.

She's wearing a cotton sleep outfit I've seen her in before: a small pair of hot-pink shorts and matching spaghetti strap crop top with the word "Princess" across the chest. An inaccurate title for a female who is every bit a queen in more ways than one.

Her long blond hair is unbound and draped in front of one shoulder, and even through the thick steam in the room, I can smell the vanilla scent of her skin that still clings to my pillows and haunts me as I sleep.

I tell my cock to stand down, but he doesn't operate on emotions and couldn't give a shit that this isn't the time for him to rise to the occasion, so I'm half hard when I drop my arms and turn to face her. To her credit, she doesn't even give him a cursory glance, which helps keep him mostly in line.

For now.

Curling my hands back into fists, I use the pain to ground myself as I find my voice. "Why are you here, Bryn?"

Her only answer is to cross her arms under her breasts and lean back against the wall. Her bright eyes are more golden amber right now, but hints of her Light heritage are still there in green flecks that make the most stunning combination I've ever seen. The sensitive tip of her exposed ear is calling for me to trace it with my tongue, and though her lips are closed, just the thought of her fangs is making it difficult to hold myself in check.

I didn't think it was possible for Bryn to be more beautiful when she was masked as human. But now that she's fully fae? I'd bet both my kingdoms there isn't a more beautiful creature in existence—human, fae, or god.

"I have so much I've wanted to say to you..." I don't realize I've said the words out loud until she arches a delicate brow.

And that's when I understand what she's doing here.

She's finally giving me a chance. A chance to apologize, to tell her how I feel. To grovel at her feet.

So that's exactly what I do.

Relief and gratitude carry me across the expanse of the shower, walking through numerous jets of water that cause my hair to fall forward again, but I barely notice. I stop in front of her and take a few precious moments to drink in every detail. Her hair growing damp from the fine mist still managing to reach her from the nearest sprays, the drops of water clinging to her sable lashes, her flawless skin dewy and slightly flushed from the steam...

But what guts me like an iron blade is seeing the unscalable wall protecting her heart.

Each brick laid by my own hands with my betrayals, its strength fortified by the pain *I* caused her. And that's when I do the one thing I've never done for another living soul: I kneel.

Slowly, I sink to the floor, welcoming the bite on my knees from the unforgiving stone tile. The act of prostration is new to me, and yet, in this moment and for this woman, it feels right.

It doesn't matter that I'm her king. When it comes to Bryn, ultimately I'll always be the one at *her* mercy, even when I'm the one wielding the whip. If she ever allows me to so much as touch her again.

Just the thought has me reaching out and gently gripping her hips as I rest my forehead against the soft skin of her belly. A shudder of pained joy rolls through me. It's the first physical contact I've had with her in two weeks, since the night of the Equinox Ball.

A veritable eternity.

I lean back and hold her gaze.

"Bryn," I begin, my voice thick with emotion. "I've played out this conversation in my mind at least a hundred times, but I'm afraid that nothing I say can repair the damage I've caused."

I pause, wondering if she'll say something, give me a jumping-off point that will clue me in on the direction I should take. But she offers me nothing, and I can't blame her. Sighing, I close my eyes and let my battered heart lead the charge for the first time and hope like hell it's up for the challenge.

"I've always been confident in my ability to excel at everything I do. From being the youngest king to ever rule a fae court, to growing the Vegas empire through new business, to creating a balance of pleasure and pain tailored to fit any sub's needs.

"But when it came to doing the right thing by you...I didn't."

Without breaking contact, I shake my head at my own foolishness and grip her hips tighter.

"I should have let you in from the very beginning instead of always holding you at a distance or pushing you away. I told myself it was for the good of my people, that I had to protect our secrets. I told myself it was better for you to have minimal memories that would need erasing when I thought you were human. But they were nothing more than excuses, logical reasonings I wrapped myself in so I wouldn't have to acknowledge the truth or the unfamiliar fear that came with it."

Delicate fingers slide into my hair, her short nails causing shivers along my scalp in their wake before she tugs down so that my face lifts and I can meet her golden-green gaze. "What truth, Caiden? What fear?"

I swallow thickly, trying unsuccessfully to dislodge the fist in my throat. Her image blurs and ripples before me from the hot prick of tears welling up in my eyes. They're the liquid manifestation of my admission, and after so many weeks of holding everything inside, I finally open up and let her see all of me, including my weaknesses.

"The truth is, Beauty, that I've loved you from the very

first. Before the bond, before any spell. It was when I saw you in my lobby. Something inside me shifted, changing me irrevocably and tying my soul to you in a way I couldn't possibly understand in that moment, but with each passing day—each passing *minute*—my love for you only continued to grow until I felt consumed by you and never felt happier."

Her features soften as she stares down at me. It's enough to give me the barest spark of hope and the courage to keep going. "My fear…"

I pause to draw in a shaky breath and release it.

Even now, allowing the thought near the front of my mind is enough to shake me to my core. "My fear was that you would be taken from me—whether you did the smart thing and left on your own or an assassination attempt succeeded—taking with you my will to live, with or without a blood curse."

She frowns, her brows knitting together. Is that a look of doubt? Unhappiness?

I have no idea. She's still blocking me from sensing her true energy, so I'm totally clueless. Suddenly I empathize with every human in existence who's ever been hopelessly in love.

"When you left, I told Connor not to go after you because I hated the idea of holding you against your will. I wanted you to go home where you'd be happy and safe, away from the danger and my inability to love you the way you deserved. But when he brought you back, I let you assume the worst about my reasons. I never felt more monstrous than the night I stood in your room and acted as though you were nothing more than a means to an end, and I'm—"

The fucking fist in my throat flexes, cutting my words off with the torrent of emotions crashing through me. I inhale a shaky breath and release it slowly, finally dislodging the wall of moisture from my eyes to stream down my face along with the droplets of water.

Bryn's endless compassion shines down on me from her

golden-green depths, giving me the strength to continue.

"I'm so fucking sorry, Beauty, for everything. I lost count of the number of mistakes I made with you, but all of them stemmed from me pushing you away or keeping you in the dark about things you had a right to know. I don't blame you for not giving me the time of day these past weeks. I wouldn't even blame you if you hated me, but I pray to Rhiannon that isn't the case.

"You've given me so many chances, and I know I don't deserve another one, but I'm asking for it anyway. I'm willing to beg on my knees every day for the rest of my life if that's what it takes. Just one more chance, and I swear you won't regret it. Please, Bryn, let me prove to you that I can be the mate you need, the one you *deserve*."

Time stands still for an eternity. The only sounds in the world are the splashing of water on stone tile, the pounding of my galloping heart, my breaths sawing in and out of my chest, and the roar of blood rushing through my ears. Instinct to dominate the situation and coax an answer from those full lips by any means necessary is riding me hard, but I push back even harder.

I will not force or coerce her into saying something she doesn't mean by using her body's desires against her.

There's nothing for me to do but wait, whether it's a minute, a year, or a lifetime. I will wait.

What if she doesn't feel the same way but doesn't know how to tell you?

Goddamn this energy block all to hell.

Trying not to show the doubt or frustration on my face—not that it matters because I don't have her blocked from reading my energy—I feel compelled to offer her an out. "If you don't want to or can't bring yourself to give me that chance, I understand, and I promise to find some way to break the bond or the curse so you can return home."

Bryn sighs and shakes her head as though disappointed. "That's where you kept going wrong, Caiden. Always assuming I wanted to get away from you when all I ever wanted was to be closer."

I can't say anything in defense of that because she's right. I did always assume she wanted to leave. She proved otherwise by showing interest in what I do, by asking to be included, and by offering to help my people, and still I didn't listen.

"I believe that you love me, Caiden. But love isn't enough to sustain a relationship on its own," she says, sadness etched in her features that I know must mirror my own. "You always choose to see everything in black and white. It either is or it isn't, and you've lived your entire life knowing you have a responsibility to make the best decisions possible for the sake of those in your care.

"But you can't do that in a romantic relationship—at least not the kind I'm interested in. In the proverbial bedroom, there's nothing I love more than letting you control the situation and make the decisions. But outside of those parameters, I need a *partner*. I need to be an equal with someone who will always be open and honest with me about everything, even the unpleasant things."

Cupping my face in her hands, her thumbs stroke the stubble of my beard that's grown longer for lack of caring about much of anything lately. "For you, Bryn, I will learn to see things in every shade of gray there is, and I'll share them all with you. I promise."

She holds my gaze for one beat, then two, before finally putting me out of my misery. "Every relationship has learning curves, and while you did a spectacular job of messing things up, you've done an even better job at apologizing for it. As long as you promise to treat me as your equal, there's nowhere I'd rather be than standing at your side or kneeling at your feet. I love you, Caiden."

More tears spring to life, but this time I'm able to blink them back so nothing obstructs my view of her. "I promise, Beauty. Fuck, I love you so much."

Bryn lets her mouth curve up in the most beautiful smile I've ever seen, complete with a new set of fangs that have my dick twitching to life again. "Then show me," she says, using a finger to brush a wet curl away from my eyes. "Make me yours. Claim me as only my king can."

Suddenly the block cutting me off from her dissipates and the strongest energy I've ever felt crashes over me in a tidal wave of love and desire. My cock swells and my fangs ache, both parts of my anatomy pulsing with the need to penetrate her flesh and mark her as ours for eternity.

I almost surge to my feet to impart my dominance and take her in a frenzy of fevered actions that will blur together until we blow and collapse in sweaty, panting heaps.

But I stop myself.

That's not what I want to do with Bryn right now. That can be later—because thank fuck there will be an eternity of laters—but in this moment, I need to savor every inch and every second.

Reaching up, I pull the spaghetti straps down her shoulders, pulling the top along for the ride and baring her breasts. I continue my trek south, snagging the waistband of her shorts on the way until she's able to step out of both articles of clothing, leaving her gloriously naked.

I close my eyes and reverently place open-mouthed kisses over the soft skin of her stomach where I'd rested my head as I groveled and begged for forgiveness. I don't deserve her, not as the male I am now, but I won't squander this chance she's given me to become everything she deserves and more.

Moving lower, I find the center of her with my mouth.

Her gasp turns into a moan as I suck on her clit and run circles around it with my tongue. I lift one of her legs and hook it over my shoulder, allowing me to feast between her thighs. Hands fly to my head and fist my hair as she stares down her body at me.

My gaze locks onto hers, pride swelling inside me at the ecstasy written on her face. Cheeks flushed, jaw slack, lids at half-mast, and pupils blown. I want this look on her every fucking day—the look that says I've pleasured my mate beyond her ability to speak without prompts.

The look that says she loves me.

"Oh fuck...*Caiden*..."

I had no idea how satisfying it would be to hear her use my name instead of the submissive responses I relegated her to in the past. I don't think *anyone* has used my name during sex, and the fact that she's the first and only is not only right but fucking perfect.

There will be times when I want to dominate her and hear her use the proper protocol as my sub. But there will also be plenty of time likes this. Times where it's just me and my mate, the love of my very long life, losing ourselves in each other's bodies and strengthening the bond of our souls.

Bryn begins rocking her hips and riding my face as I spear my tongue into her hot cunt the way my cock is aching to do. It has to wait its turn, though, because I need her to come like this first. I need her to flood my mouth with her honey-sweet nectar and feel the pulsing of her channel on my lips as I drink every last drop of her down.

Growling against her sensitive flesh, I bring a hand up to rub her clit with my thumb, relentless in my mission.

"OhmyGod, yes, yes, yesyesyes, right there, don't stop!"

I make a mental note that she has a strike one for even implying I might be a quitter, then double my efforts, eating her with voracious abandon until finally she breaks apart on a strangled scream that echoes in the shower for a full minute, and in my mind for eternity.

Ignoring the pain for having knelt on the stone for so long, I push to a stand and pick her up in one fluid movement, placing her back against the wall. She wraps her legs around my waist, then looks around for something. "Where do you want my hands?"

"On me, Beauty," I rasp. "I want them on me."

With love shining in her eyes, she frames my face with her hands and squeezes me with her thighs. "Take me, Caiden. I'm yours. For now and always."

"For now and always," I repeat.

Then I line myself up and thrust home, taking her in multiple positions and locations before finally ending up boneless in my bed.

CHAPTER THIRTY-THREE

BRYN

Holding me close, Caiden lightly strokes his fingertips up and down the curve of my spine. "How are you doing with this new version of yourself? I've been worried it might be a difficult adjustment."

"You were?"

He grunts in confirmation. "I hated that my actions prevented me from being there for you. I can't tell you how much it gutted me to know that I failed my mate so miserably." He tips my chin up to meet his gaze. "I meant what I said before, Beauty. You won't have to know what that's like ever again. From this moment on, I live to serve you above all else."

"You can't say that, Caiden. You're the king; you have a duty to your people above all else, even me."

"*Our* people, Bryn. You are both Dark Fae and my queen, which makes them doubly yours as well."

His words permeate my soul and wrap around my heart like a warm blanket.

As happy as I was growing up and as much as I loved my parents, I never quite felt like I fit in with my classmates or coworkers. There was always a sense that I was missing some

322 the dark king

fundamental part that allowed me to connect with my peers on a deeper level. Now that I know why and have finally found where I *do* fit in, I have this overwhelming feeling of belonging that sometimes is hard to contain. I've had more than a few private moments this last week where it comes out in the form of happy tears.

"I know," I say with a soft smile. "I'm still getting used to the idea of including myself in your world." He arches a brow. "*Our* world."

"Better." Lifting my hand from his chest, he places a kiss into my palm before holding it against the place where his heart is beating strongly. "And to address your concern about me putting you above all else, the way I see it is that anything that does not serve you will not serve them. I believe the saying is, *Happy True Mate, Happy Dark Fae.*"

I smile so big, my cheeks hurt. "That's not a thing."

"Oh, that's right. It's *Happy Queen, Happy Peen.*"

Bursting into laughter, my heart soars to see this side of him for the first time since the night we were accidentally married. "While incredibly accurate, that doesn't have anything to do with the rest of *our* people."

The arched brow reappears. "It does so. If the king is cranky, it doesn't bode well for anyone. Therefore, I need to make sure you're happy so that you in turn make me happy and then I don't get murdery."

"You mean so you can help make everyone else happy."

"That's what I said. No murdering," he deadpans.

I lightly smack his chest. "You're so full of it. You're not as scary as you think, you know."

His chin dips down to shoot me an incredulous look. "You're aware of my reputation as the Dark King, yes? That's the very definition of scary."

"No, it's literally the definition of your title because you're king of the Dark Fae. Everyone just lets you think it's for other more nefarious reasons to stroke your ego."

"I'll give you something to stroke, you brat," he says, flipping me onto my back and pinning me down. I squeal with surprise and utter happiness as I squirm under his fingers dancing up my sides. Thankfully, he only tortures me for a few seconds before switching to cradling my face in his strong hands. Peering down at me, his golden eyes bounce between mine as though searching for problems to fix.

My expression softens, and I reach up to brush an errant curl off his forehead. "I'm fine, Caiden."

"I know you are, my love." His thumbs caress my cheekbones. "But I'll always worry about you because it's my nature. However, that doesn't mean you're not the strongest woman I've ever known."

My lips twist into a wry grin. "Aren't you supposed to call me a female now?"

He gives a slight shake of his head. "Fae or human, I'll forever think of you as the woman who coaxed my heart from the shadows. The woman who captured my soul before we were ever bonded. I needed to hear you say that you're mine. But the truth is that I am wholly yours, Beauty. I have been from the moment I saw you in my lobby, and I'll be yours until I see my last moonrise. If you'll still have me, that is."

"Oh, Caiden," I whisper. I don't even bother trying to stem the moisture pooling and let the tears escape from the corners of my eyes. "You're the most stubborn and infuriating male I've ever known. But you're also a loyal friend, generous lover, and a fierce protector, and those are just a few of my favorite qualities of yours.

"I feel as though I started loving you the moment I took my first breath, and I'll love you more each night until I take my last. You are forever my king, in this life and the next."

"Fuck, I love you," he rasps, his amber eyes glistening suspiciously.

Smiling up at him, I answer, "I love you, too."

He crushes his mouth to mine and our tongues tangle in heated abandon, pouring every drop of emotion into each other until our hearts are drowning in our love.

Feeling a surge of strength flood me, I turn the tables and push him onto his back and sit astride him with his wrists pinned near his head. The shock on his face is priceless. If there were security cameras in here, I'd have the frame frozen and blown up to poster size to hang in the living room over the fireplace.

"I see your training sessions with Finn are paying off."

"They are," I say with a smile. "Don't tell him, though. I like annoying him by bitching the whole time."

"Wouldn't dream of ruining your fun, love." In some tactical move, Caiden twists out of my grip and grabs onto my wrists before holding them behind my back. "But the day you can best me is the day you can put me on the Cross and have your way with me."

I light up like he just offered me a fae's lifetime of chocolate truffles. He curses, realizing his mistake. "Challenge accepted."

"It was a flip remark, Bryn. I'm not subbing for you."

I actually have no desire to top him, but I like making him squirm. Laughing, I say, "Too late. No take-backsies. I'mma make you my bitch, Verran."

Tightening his delicious abs, he crunches up into a sitting position and releases my wrists in favor of banding his arms around my waist. He starts pressing kisses along my neck as he talks. "I was thinking…"

"Uh-oh," I say breathily. "Does Seamus know you've been thinking without his guidance?"

That gets me a swift crack on my ass, which is more likely to encourage than deter me, but he knows this. He lifts his head and tries to give me a stern look. He's not very successful. "Cage the brat for a second—I'm trying to be serious."

"Okay, but she's feeling feisty. You've got five minutes before she breaks free, tops."

"Noted." I grin like a loon. Such a Caiden thing to say. "Can I continue now?"

"Please do."

"I thought maybe we could get married again, to have a wedding that we both remember. You can decide if you want the true Vegas experience with just us in a chapel on the Strip and an Elvis officiant or hundreds of guests at an extravagant event fit for a queen. What do you think?"

I've never been in love before. I didn't know I'd be able to fall deeper in love with him from one second to the next. "I think…"

I'm not sure why I hesitate or why there's a tiny part of me that's worried this still isn't real. That maybe he'll change his mind and push me away again. But I shake the fear off and tell it to get lost. Because everything I see in his eyes right now says I couldn't get rid of him if I tried.

"I think that Elvis is more my style," I say with a smile.

He grins wide. "Yeah?"

"Yeah." I bite my lip, then think of something. "Would I leave the chapel as Bryn Meara or Verran?"

He kisses me sweetly on the forehead and makes me melt. "I would love for you to have my name, Beauty, but that's up to you. I'd understand if you want to keep your name to honor your parents. I know how much you love and miss them."

He's right. I do and I always will. But I don't want to honor only my past without also honoring my future. "Bryn Meara-Verran. I want them both."

"And so you shall have them both, along with anything else your heart desires, my queen."

"Mmm, I like the sound of that."

He chuckles and lays back, pulling me down until I'm draped on top of him. I sigh contentedly and press my face against the scruff of his neck.

"Now all we have to do is get rid of Talek the Terrible and life will be perfect."

I feel him tense beneath me. I could kick myself for ruining the moment, but it won't do us any good to pretend the threat against my and Caiden's crown is gone.

Talek Edevane isn't the type to take defeat lightly. He's only gone as long as it takes him to lick his wounds, regroup, and form another plan of attack.

"About that," he says. "I think I have an idea of how to keep you safe from future threats." I lift my head to meet his gaze, but he's quick to hold up a hand. "I don't want to tell you what it is yet. I need to discuss it with Seamus first."

"That sounds a lot like keeping me in the dark instead of treating me like your partner, Caiden."

"That's not it, Bryn." He holds my face and stares into my eyes. "If Seamus agrees that it's a viable plan, I'll fill you in on all the details, I swear. I just don't want to get your hopes up unnecessarily."

"Okay," I say reluctantly. "I suppose I could be convinced not to make a stink about it."

His luscious lips twist up in one corner. "What's it going to cost me?"

"Since you asked, I'd like a library. I'm talking a *Beauty and the Beast* grand gesture kind of library, with the rolling ladders and window seats and lots of cozy spots to curl up next to gas fireplaces."

Black brows shoot up under the curls hanging over his forehead. "Is that all?"

"That's all."

"And what else?"

"Nothing," I say innocently. "That's it."

He narrows his eyes at me. "I know how you make deals, love. Just come out and tell me the rest so we can get to the part where we seal the deal."

"I also want a cat."

"A cat?"

"Okay, *two* cats, but that's only so they aren't lonely and have someone to play with when we're not home. But that's it. Scout's honor."

He rolls me to my back and braces himself up on his elbow. "You drive a hard bargain, Beauty, but I think that can all be arranged."

"Really?" My face almost breaks, my smile is so big, and I laugh. "I didn't expect you to say yes."

"I think you'll find I'm extremely accommodating when my queen wants something, as long as she's every bit as accommodating when her king wants things from her. Do we have a deal, Beauty?"

Winding my arms around his neck, I pull him down until my lips graze his as I answer him with my favorite response. "Yes, my king."

And then we spend the rest of the night sealing the deal, again and again. And again.

CHAPTER THIRTY-FOUR

TIERNAN

"Ow, there's a shelf corner in my ass."

"Sorry, hold on." I grab Fiona's ass with both hands and do a quarter turn so her back is pressed against the door of the storage closet. "Better?"

"Much, thanks," she says, attacking my belt buckle. "We have to hurry or we'll miss your brother's big announcement."

Rucking up the floor-length skirt of her dress, I scowl. "I'll thank you to not mention my brother as you're—*ah, fuck*—pulling my dick out."

She gives me a few skilled strokes as she stares up at me. "Aw, what's the matter? Does Prince Tiernan have a complex about how his dick measures up to his big brother the king's royal staff?"

Fiona laughs, and as always, it hits me deep in a spot somewhere behind my sternum.

And, as always, I ignore the sensation in favor of focusing on the sensations she's creating in my balls.

"You'll pay for that one. I don't know how or when, but it'll be when you least expect it."

Part of me wishes I was referring to the kind of punishment

I'd given her twenty years ago, but I locked that part of myself away more than a decade ago. Besides that, what Fiona and I have isn't anything serious. We have a great time hooking up in random, semi-public places—like this utility closet inside Nightfall around the corner from the ballroom entrance—and pranking each other during my frequent visits to Midnight Manor where she works for Caiden.

Casual, mutual fun, that's what Fi and I have, and we're both completely content with it.

Okay, I'm *mostly* completely content with it.

But the part that isn't is so small, it's barely worth mentioning.

So I won't.

"You haven't rattled me yet, Tier, but give it your best shot."

I know she's referring to our pranks, but my cock has a brain of its own right now, and it takes her words as a personal challenge. Spinning her around, I press her front to the door, hold her dress up with one hand, and pull her hips out to give me access to her already slick pussy.

"Fuck, Fi. I love it when you skip the panties."

"I got tired of you tearing them off. This is easier."

Fisting my cock, I rub the head up and down her crease, teasing her as I lean in and speak next to her ear through the curtain of her glossy red hair. "I think it's more than that. I think you like being ready for me, Little Red. I think it turns you on to know that at any time, I can reach between your legs and sink my fingers deep inside you."

With her cheek pressed to the cool metal, she looks at me from the corner of her eye and smirks. "Whatever fantasy helps you perform, Your Highness."

"Such sass." I *tsk*, feigning disappointment.

In reality, I love her sharp fucking tongue. It goads my darker half into reaching through the bars of its cage, letting just enough of my deviance through to make things interesting without inviting danger.

"I'm going to fuck that sass right out of you," I say.

"Promises, prom—"

A sharp inhale cuts her off when I drive my hips forward and slam myself home into her hot, tight sheath. I bite back my own hiss of pleasure as Fiona punishes her lower lip with her teeth. I don't know why, but we both fight making our pleasure known during these interludes.

It's like a competition we have, to not let the other know how much we're enjoying ourselves, all while screwing like we're racing against the clock of a ticking bomb.

I don't know what Fiona's sexual history is or whether her current sex life includes others besides me—I don't allow myself to speculate because I lose my good nature real goddamn fast when I do—but I've made an art form out of quickies. I'd love nothing more than to take my time with a female—or woman, I don't have rules against fucking humans like Caiden did after becoming king—but if I'm not in and out before my brain has a chance to catch up, I start to want things I shouldn't.

Things like restraints, ropes...and whips.

When the memory tries burrowing out from the depths of my mind, I set a punishing pace to smother it with white-hot pleasure.

I stare down and drink in the view of my cock disappearing between her thighs, her perfect pussy lips swallowing me whole. Pistoning my hips harder and faster, the only sounds the wet smacking of our bodies meeting violently again and again as we chase the high in strained silence.

My free hand grips the round globe of her ass cheek. The beast inside me craves to do so much more. To mark and claim. To see my handprint blooming in shades of pink and red on her pretty skin.

He might be caged, but the motherfucker still has a voice,

and his taunts are echoing in the halls of my mind.

Mark her... Claim her...

Fuck off.

Instead of releasing her to answer the temptation of letting my hand fall, I flex my fingers and dig them into her flesh like I'm holding on to my sanity for dear life.

Then I change my angle slightly and hear her soft mewl that signifies my victory. She broke first and now I don't have to hold back anymore. Growling, I increase my efforts to drive us those last few inches over the finish line. Her walls clench around my thick shaft in tight pulses as she comes and drags my own climax from me, along with every drop of my seed.

There's no post-coital afterglow, no taking the time to come down together wrapped up in each other's arms. That's not what this has ever been between us, and that's how I want it, despite the incessant dreams I have that say otherwise.

Within minutes, we've cleaned ourselves up and righted our clothes. I must have a smug look on my face, because she arches a brow as she smooths her hands down her dress and asks, "Pretty pleased with yourself, Your Highness?"

My mouth twists up on one side to give her my panty-melting half grin. "Not at all. I was just thinking for the millionth time that I'm glad I'm not Caiden."

She laughs. "What's so wrong with your brother that would make you grateful to not be him that many times?"

"It's not him; it's his job. When we were kids, he was always so accepting of his role as future king—eager even. I, on the other hand, saw the pressure our father put on him and all the things he had to learn, the responsibilities of it all. I never wanted that.

"I like the freedom of just being me and doing whatever I want on a whim. Like this, for example. If I were king, I wouldn't be having a closet quickie in the middle of the Ivy Moon Celebration Ball. I'd be up on that dais and bored as fuck, while watching everyone else have fun."

"So the moral of the story is: being great king bad, being rebel prince good."

"Being rebel prince *very* good," I say, snaking an arm around her waist to pull her in for a brief kiss hot enough to reignite the desire in my balls. "We'd better get out there or we'll miss whatever big announcement Caiden has."

"Don't you already know what it is?"

I open the door, check for anyone who might be lurking around with a camera phone, then let us out when the coast is clear. "See, I should know—there was a meeting about it this afternoon—but it conflicted with my weekly four o'clock, so I skipped it. There's no reason I can't find out at the same time as the rest of our people, right?"

"Whatever," she says as we round the corner and approach the closed doors of the ballroom. "I'm just here for the free food."

I snort. "You're here for the free fuck."

"Definitely the food. The fuck was just a bonus."

I laugh, loving her snark and the way she enjoys putting me in my place. Fiona is a lot of fun to be around, and we get along well. I haven't been seeing any of my other regular hookups lately, making more time for her because I flat-out enjoy her company more.

Yeah, sure, that's *why.*

Shut up, you sarcastic fuck.

When we get to the large double doors, I can hear Caiden already speaking. I mumble a curse, knowing my mom is going to ream me good for this one.

"Okay, game plan," I say quietly. "We're going to sneak in and stick to the walls as we slowly make our way up to the front."

Tonight's configuration will be different from that of the EEB. As king and queen—gods, it's so bizarre to think we have a queen—Caiden and Bryn will be the only ones on the dais. Finni, Mother, Seamus, and I will all have seats off to the side facing the guests, and the Midnight Manor staff along with any Night Watchers not posted elsewhere for security will all be standing behind us.

She gives me a dubious look. "Maybe we should just hang out in the back until he's done talking."

"Everyone's eyes and ears will be glued to my brother, so just don't trip or sneeze and we should be fine. Now, close those luscious lips of yours and follow your rebel prince's lead."

She rolls her eyes but doesn't hesitate to do exactly that as I open one of the doors enough for us to slip through. Easing it shut behind us, I resist the temptation to grab her hand as we make our way along the back wall slowly enough not to draw any attention. Meanwhile, I tune in to Caiden.

"During this past Meeting of the Kings, the treaty between the Night and Day Courts was broken by the Light King, Talek Edevane."

Whispers and murmurs ripple through the crowd, but Caiden holds his hands up, and they instantly settle down.

"I understand this is upsetting, and while it's definitely a cause for concern, I want to assure you that so far, it seems as though Edevane is acting without the support or knowledge of his subjects. We are not going to war with the Day Court."

The relief flowing through the room is palpable. Those who were around during the war have no wish to live through it again, and those too young have no desire to know what the elders went through.

"At the Equinox meeting, Edevane revealed his intentions to take me out by using the blood curse. By now, you all know that he manipulated Bryn and me into a fae marriage ceremony so that if he eliminated her, I would perish by default. Then he planned to overthrow my administration and seize control of the Night Court to reign over both Light and Dark Fae factions."

As we reach the corner, I look back at Fiona and she gives me a small smile and nod that she's good, so I keep going, taking us along the side wall that will bring us out right by where we're supposed to be. Another sixty seconds and we'll be home free.

"It's no secret that if I should fall, our court will be vulnerable from the vacuum of power created by my death. In addition to that, unless we can find a way to break the royal line's blood curse, my mate—whom I love more than my own life—will always have a target on her back, and I can't stand by and do nothing about that."

Caiden pauses to look down at his gorgeous wife standing at his side as he lifts her hand to place a kiss on her knuckles. Brynnie smiles up at him with her brilliant green-and-gold eyes shining like gems illuminated by sunlight. It warms my heart to see them both finally truly happy and free to love each other.

Although I don't envy the hardships they're about to face as the first royal pairing since our exile. Yet another reason I'm glad as hell to not be the king.

"I discussed possible solutions at length with my senior adviser, Seamus Woulfe. In the end, we both feel there is only one viable action I can take that will ensure the safety of both my mate and the fae under my protection as king. As my father's best friend and adviser, Seamus has dutifully served this court for centuries. He expertly guided my father during his reign and has done the same for me these past seventeen years, just as he will do for the king who takes my place."

Absently, I wonder what sort of youth potion Caiden thinks Seamus is taking in order to be around long enough to advise Caiden's future heir, but then my attention is drawn to finishing the last leg of this plan. Fiona and I have finally reached the front of the room. Quietly, we start crossing the dozen or so feet to where her group is standing behind the four chairs with three people in them. I won't be able to sit down without making a scene, so I'll stand with Fiona and the Night Watchers like I've been there all along. Easy peasy.

"As long as this court has a king with an activated blood curse, we will be constantly vulnerable. That is why, as of this night, I will be abdicating my throne." The room draws in a collective gasp as Fiona and I stop dead in our tracks, frozen in shock with only a few feet left to go. "The one to replace me will be the next Verran in line for the crown, Prince Tiernan."

Hundreds of golden gazes swing in my direction and land on me with the crushing weight of a freight train. Under her breath, Fiona whispers, "What was that you were saying, *Your Majesty*?"

"Fuck my life."

THE END

ACKNOWLEDGMENTS

Thank you to my work wifeys and soul sisters, Cindi Madsen and Rebecca Yarros, for everything and anything: plotting, reading, sprinting, blurb-shaping, whip-cracking, encouraging, supporting, laughing, and a thousand other things I could never list even if I tried. My life is immeasurably better with you in it, and I seriously don't know what I'd do without our daily conversations and weekly video chats. As a tearful Jerry Maguire once said, you complete me. #UnholyTrinity

To my incredible agent, Nicole Resciniti of the Seymour Agency, for her never-ending advice and support. To Liz Pelletier for believing in me and my ability to bring this series to life. I'm so thrilled to be working as a team again. To Jessica Turner, Stacy Abrams, Heather Riccio, Riki Cleveland, and everyone else at Entangled who had a hand in getting this book baby out into the world, thank you so much for all your hard work. To Elizabeth Turner Stokes, who created this gorgeous cover, I can't wait to see how phenomenal it's going to look on store shelves.

To Erin McRae, my bestie and number one cheerleader. I never want to write a book without you in my corner. To Miranda Grissom, without whom I couldn't function as an author. To Kristy Jewel, aka Caffeinated Fae in the book blogging world, whose vast knowledge about faeries was key to me creating this world and keeping Caiden honest (damn fae rules). To Leah Em for making me laugh during a hectic deadline. To Kaitlyn, whose excited mini-reviews of my sex scenes in other books gave me the motivation to finish the sex scenes in *this* book.

To Ella Sheridan, Ruthie Knox, and Mary Ann Hudson, some of my oldest author friends and CPs who immediately and faithfully answer the bat signal whenever I send it up. I'm so freaking grateful I have you spectacular ladies in my life.

To everyone in the Maxwell Mob: Thank you for sticking with me all these years and getting excited about my new projects in my ever-shifting publishing schedule. Your constant support, enthusiasm, and posts about Jason Momoa are what keep me going. Every. Single. Day.

A very special thank-you to all the bloggers, bookstagrammers, and booktokers who work tirelessly and *for free* to shout out about my books, make graphics, invite me for takeovers, offer advice, take time to read and review my ARCs, and are just in general super-amazing people whose passion is to lift up authors and their stories. You are the foundation of this book community we all love, and we couldn't reach nearly as many readers without you. I'm forever grateful for your help and humbled by your generous spirits.

As always, a thousand thanks to you, the reader, for giving my book a spot on your shelf and a place in your heart.

With literary love & kitten kisses... ~ G ~

The Dark King is a sexy fantasy romance with a happy ending. However, the story includes elements that might not be suitable for some readers. Mentions of kidnapping, murder of a loved one, torture off-page, and unknown parentage/adoption are included in the novel. Additionally, there are scenes discussing sexual assault off-page, scenes depicting excessive alcohol use leading to a blackout, and dominance/submissive scenes including consensual acts of asphyxiation, anal play, and immobility. Readers who may be sensitive to these, please take note.

Cinderella has a darkside in this sexy new series from #1 New York Times *bestselling author Helen Hardt*

FOLLOW ME
DARKLY

She's a take-charge woman. But he's a master of control.

Skye Manning knows what she wants. Her job as assistant and photographer for a major social media influencer isn't perfect, but it's a rung on the ladder to bigger and better things. She's confident she'll one day take feature photos for National Geographic.

Self-made billionaire Braden Black didn't get where he is by taking no for an answer. When a chance encounter with the refreshingly innocent and beautiful Skye piques his interest in more ways than one, he's determined to make her submit.

Dating a billionaire soon has Skye in the middle of a Cinderella story...until the clock strikes midnight and Braden reveals his dark side. Heat sizzles between them, and Skye finds herself falling hard.

But Braden Black is no Prince Charming, and his dark desires are far from his only secret.

Twelve erotic fantasies...
one made just for you.

aphrodite
in bloom

**Don't miss this extraordinary collection of twelve inventive and
sophisticated stories guaranteed to awaken the forbidden desires
of a new generation. From the sweetly romantic to the sublimely
taboo, each provocative novella offers an opportunity to explore
your most secret fantasies.**

A virgin receives an especially satisfying gift at a masked ball...

A duke offers to settle a man's debt for one night with his wife...

As an introduction to a secret club, a viscount's heir is made over
into a woman—and discovers her true self...

Plus nine more sensual stories of libidinous lust, catering to the
tastes of varying sexual appetites. Whatever your fancy, *Aphrodite
in Bloom* is ready and willing to serve...

AMARA
an imprint of Entangled Publishing LLC